The Wines of th

FABER BOOKS ON WINE
General Editor: Julian Jeffs

Bordeaux by David Peppercorn
Burgundy by Anthony Hanson
Italian Wines by Philip Dallas
Port by George Robertson
Sherry by Julian Jeffs
Spirits and Liqueurs by Peter Hallgarten
Vineyards in England and Wales by George Ordish
Wines of Germany by Frank Schoonmaker (rev. Peter Sichel)
Wines of Portugal by Jan Read
Wines of Spain by Jan Read

The Wines of
THE RHÔNE

John Livingstone-Learmonth
and
Melvyn C. H. Master

faber and faber

First published in 1978
by Faber and Faber Limited
3 Queen Square London WC1N 3AU
This new and revised edition 1983
First published as a Faber Paperback 1983
Filmset by Latimer Trend & Company Ltd, Plymouth
Printed in Great Britain by
Redwood Burn Ltd
Trowbridge Wiltshire

© *John Livingstone-Learmonth and*
Melvyn C. H. Master, 1978, 1983

Library of Congress Cataloging in Publication Data

Livingstone-Learmonth, John
The wines of the Rhône

Includes index
1. Wine and wine making—France—Côtes du Rhône (Region)
I. Master, Melvyn C. H.   II. Title
TP553.L55   1983   641.2'2'094458   82–24207
ISBN 0–571–18075–2
ISBN 0–571–13055–0 (pbk)

British Library Cataloguing in Publication Data

Livingstone-Learmonth, John
Wines of the Rhône.—2nd ed.
1. Wine and wine making—Rhône Valley (France)
I. Title   II. Master, Melvyn C. H.
641.2'2'094458   TP553

ISBN 0–571–18075–2
ISBN 0–571–13055–0 Pbk

To
David Edgerton, Timothy Johnston,
our mutual friend Dinsdale
and, of course, to K. G. and Janie
Sans erreur, sans progrès!

Contents

Maps

Preface to the Second Edition

Several years have passed since I first met John in Aix-en-Provence and we decided to collaborate on a book on the wines of the Rhône. Research for the book took considerable time, many miles of travel and, of course, hundreds of samples. In the end *The Wines of the Rhône* was the most thorough study of the subject available.

Since the publication of that first edition many changes have taken place in the area, and substantial updating was essential. I would like to take this opportunity to point out that the tremendous amount of work and research for this second edition was undertaken entirely by John, since I now live in the USA. Although the text published in 1978 was a joint venture, the credit for this fine new edition is his alone; to me has fallen the pleasurable task of reading it.

Bien fait, mouette!

Bethlehem, Connecticut   Melvyn C. H. Master
January 1983

9

Foreword

This second edition of *The Wines of the Rhône*, half as long again as the first, has grown for several reasons. First, there is the question of the research and information gleaned between 1975 and 1983, which has enabled me to draw comparisons of a grower's work over an extended period and, I hope, to offer a fuller, livelier portrait of the growers whom I now know that much better. Second, there has been an enormous increase in the number of vineyards bottling at source—this is particularly evident in the Côtes du Rhône sector. The finished wine and those who make it can therefore be discussed to the advantage of the person who may find a bottle in a store or in a restaurant. Third, I have tried to sharpen up my vinous history of the Rhône Valley, using sources in both France and England. Finally, my enthusiasm for the wines of the Rhône Valley has grown still more, which may explain the book's extra length.

There is a quirk in the measurements used throughout the book, and that is that while I can accept the publishers' desire to go metric, I cannot believe that as a unit of area the hectare has the slightest meaning for those used to Imperial or American measures. The acre is therefore retained, while measures of volume have been converted into litres and hectolitres. As a bottle of wine is three-quarters of a litre, that is at least something to which we can all happily relate.

London
January 1983

John Livingstone-Learmonth

10

Acknowledgements

FIRST EDITION

During the research and writing of this book the authors realized that they had fortunately chosen to chronicle one of France's most warm-hearted and welcoming wine regions. Throughout the two years of this project, we were both consistently well received by the Rhône growers; discussions and tastings would be held in the intimate Rhône cellars at hours when many self-respecting merchants from other parts of the country would have locked their cellar doors and gone home. In particular we would like to thank the following growers for their kind help and co-operation: Etienne and Marcel Guigal, Max Chapoutier, the Jaboulet family, Thomas Morel, Gérard Chave, Auguste Clape, Louis Reynaud and Pierre Lançon. At the same time invaluable general advice and information was given by M. Pierre Ligier of the Comité Interprofessionel des Vins des Côtes du Rhône in Avignon.

Great thanks must also go to Martha Bounoure and Judy Herren, who bore with the vagaries of life in Aix-en-Provence to type as polished a manuscript as any publisher could wish for. Bob Baker, too, helped to further ample discussion and tasting of the Rhône wines. Perhaps we shall all meet at the Bourse again one day.

Meanwhile we would also like to extend grateful thanks to Captain Hugh Dalrymple-Smith who produced the captioned tailpiece sketches included in the book; to Hal Jurgensen for encouraging a love of, and interest in the wines of the Rhône Valley; and last but not least to Tim Johnston whose constant patrolling of the Rhône Valley ensured that the authors were never less than well informed.

J. L.-L.

M. C. H. M.

SECOND EDITION

With a lapse of eight years between the first and second editions, it was absorbing to observe just how much had changed in the Rhône Valley with regard to many aspects of wine-making. Hospitality and co-operation remained just as wholehearted, however, and I would like to thank all the growers who have been visited on and off during these years for their readiness to help in the formulation of as extensive a manuscript as could be expected.

In reiterating my special thanks to the growers who particularly helped on the first edition, I would like also to thank Georges Vernay, Jean-Louis Grippat, Robert Jasmin, Georges Bernard and Baron Le Roy, all of whom have given extra information and advice for this edition.

The publishers received another almost impeccable manuscript, and for this I am extremely grateful to Amanda Reeve, Karin Stretford-Grainger and Georgiana Franklin, all of whom came to my rescue at one time or another.

Extra help came from M. Michel Durand-Roger of the Comité Interprofessionel des Vins des Côtes du Rhône in Avignon and from Claude Rougerie, their industrious press officer, while the more cerebral side of matters was expertly covered by my mole resident in the British Library, Timothy Burnett.

M. Robert Bailly, although I have never met him, has proved to be eminently knowledgeable about the Rhône and its environs; his book *Histoire de la vigne et des Grands Vins des Côtes du Rhône* has helped to illuminate the normally somewhat obscure history of this region.

At extremely short notice Mary Treherne conjured up some striking likenesses of the growers and of one or two Côtes du Rhône landmarks; her work will certainly alleviate the text, and I cannot thank her enough for working so hard to have the drawings ready in time.

Mark Williamson and Timothy Johnston made a good pair of

ACKNOWLEDGEMENTS

likely lads capable of charming even the most obdurate of country growers during their patrolling runs down the Rhône, and their help with tastings organized in Aix-en-Provence and at Willi's Wine Bar in Paris was greatly appreciated. Their comments, destructive and constructive, also helped me out of a few tight corners on the manuscript, and I would particularly praise Tim for his news bulletins and extraordinary help throughout the hectic six months of revision.

Thanks should also go to Robin and Judith Yapp in England for keeping me posted about the development of the better wines; their hospitality has been gratefully received.

Finally, I feel sure that Julian Jeffs had a major say in prompting the publishers to consider a second edition of this book, and I remain very indebted to him for his support and encouragement.

J. L.-L.

INTRODUCTION

The Rhône

The Rhône Valley possesses some of France's most remarkable and distinguished wines, and its vineyards are probably the oldest in France. It is therefore quite amazing that even today it should still be a comparatively unexplored, little noticed wine region. Magnificent wines like Côte-Rôtie and Hermitage have been made for over 2,000 years but have strangely never become widely known as two of their country's best red wines. Wines like St-Joseph and Cornas, only marginally lesser, have themselves existed for over 1,000 years, and are practically unheard of outside the immediate Rhône Valley area. These are by no means the only really good wines of the region: there are the exceptional white wines of Château-Grillet and Condrieu, made from the rare, highly perfumed Viognier grape. There is the sturdy, strongly flavoured red wine of Châteauneuf-du-Pape, which, when genuine, is almost certainly the best red wine from the South of France. And there is of course the rosé of Tavel, generally recognized as the leading rosé in France, and most probably the world.

Quite apart from the extremely high standards of these wines— and there can be little doubt that *marques* such as Côte-Rôtie's La Mouline and Hermitage's La Chapelle are some of the best red wines in the world—there exists enormous variety in the Rhône Valley. Reds, whites and rosés of many different styles are made near the river between Vienne and Avignon, and there are even additional local specialities such as the excellent Muscat de Beaumes-de-Venise.

Despite all this, much of the Rhône Valley wine region remains an unknown quantity. 'Côtes du Rhône' implies to most people a medium-quality, low-priced and highly alcoholic red wine. Traditionally, wine merchants have never looked to the Rhône as a

15

source of their finest wines and have preferred to turn to Bordeaux and Burgundy. The euphoric wine-buying days of the 1970s changed this, however. Bordeaux and Burgundy reached such unattainable price levels that interest naturally started to focus more intently on the Rhône. The northern part of the Valley, containing the finest wines, was by and large unappealing due to its limited production, but the southern part suited the market admirably. The mixture of panic buying and natural greed that followed, however, thrust wines like Châteauneuf-du-Pape and Gigondas firmly into the limelight, and the old disease of high prices struck yet again. As a result, Châteauneuf-du-Pape and Gigondas became two of the least sought-after wines from the Rhône. To illustrate: on 31 August 1972 stocks of wine held at the property in Châteauneuf-du-Pape amounted to 58,910 hecto-litres. On 31 August 1974 the figure had risen to 112,505 hectolitres. At Gigondas the respective holdings were 17,440 hectolitres in 1972 and 33,903 hectolitres in 1974. The growers could see their cellars practically overflowing with wine and in 1975 very slowly started to realize the error of their ways. A fall in price was the only solution to their problem.

This is an important story because it shows that many merchants' first experience of the Rhône was an unhappy one. The more adventurous who persevered with their search, however, were amply rewarded. Underneath all the full *Appellation* wines—there are fourteen of them—is a series of very good, little explored wines from all over the southern part of the Valley. For instance, there are seventeen Côtes du Rhône Villages, communities making good, and sometimes very good, wines: leading names here are Cairanne, Chusclan, Laudun and Vacqueyras. Then there is the less strictly regulated Côtes du Rhône *générique* wine, the main reason for the area's fame and its prosperity. Even in this category there are some agreeable finds to be made, generally in the small barrel-lined cellar of a private grower. Some of the Co-opératives also make good wine and, as wine-making techniques become more professional, the standard can only rise.

The above words were written in 1975, and in the seven years since some changes have obviously occurred in an area that, although old by origin, is young and relatively unsophisticated in practice. Many *Appellations* are now better-known; several are at a crossroads in their development; and some are teetering on the edge of a sorry decline. New influences, particularly on cellar work and vinification, have filtered into the more avant-garde *domaines*, and attitudes towards wine-making have certainly become less parochial.

Many of the progressive influences have reached the open-minded growers through visits to California rather than through encouragement from within France. In the northern Rhône the best *vignerons*, such as Guigal and Chave, are also the ones who show most interest in seeing how other people make their wine. Not that they will necessarily change their technique—Chave is the most thoroughly old-fashioned and competent grower in the Valley—but they are better able to evaluate the worth of their equipment, their methods of vinification and the manner of their wines when they have seen parallel cases a long way from home. Marcel Guigal keeps some of Joseph Phelps's Syrah wine in his cellar at Ampuis to remind himself how the cuttings taken from the vines at Côte-Rôtie and transplanted to California are performing.

In the south of the Valley Châteauneuf-du-Pape is where the most exciting things are happening. Growers such as Henri Brunier at Domaine du Vieux Télégraphe, MM. Abeille and Fabre at Domaine de Mont-Redon and M. Boisson at Père Caboche have set up very sophisticated and well thought out installations, where a premium is put on logic, cleanliness and efficiency. Their wine is not made in a clinical, off-hand manner, as this might imply; it just means that they are reducing the various elements that can make up into a failed vat and indifferent wine.

Contrast their enthusiasm, their search to make their red wine more elegant and less clumsy than some of the old Châteauneufs, and to make a refreshing, well balanced white Châteauneuf as well, with the state of affairs in one of the most famous *Appellations*, Côte-Rôtie. Here the good name is being upheld by no more than four or five growers; the vineyards are being inexorably expanded, off the slopes and up on to the mediocre soil of the ill-exposed plateau above them. The maximum permitted yield per hectare has been increased from 35 to 40 hectolitres, while the growers seem to be as becalmed as the Ancient Mariner's boat on its painted ocean: very few have modernized any of their cellar equipment but feel the need, derived partly from fashion and partly from economic necessity, to make a lighter wine. The result is evident in some *cuvées* of Côte-Rôtie that are disgracefully pale and wishy-washy. There is no zest in the *Appellation*, no firm leadership, and the resulting inertia is a bitter pill to swallow for those such as the authors who are confirmed addicts of good Syrah wines. May the growers of Côte Rôtie remember that quality will always sell, that their wine is undoubtedly better-known today than it was ten years ago and that they are in danger of slipping out of the top bracket.

This view about Côte Rôtie is reinforced when one sees the depth of good quality wines that exists at Hermitage, for instance. There the name of the wine is not founded on just one or two outstanding *cuvées*; several growers are making quite exceptional wine without any recourse to lowering their standards or to enlarging the vineyard.

Elsewhere in the Rhône there are areas of hope and pockets of gloom. Hope at Crozes-Hermitage, where the number of private domaines bottling their own wine has risen substantially; the general quality of their wine is not yet irreproachable, but standards are rising and the future looks good. Hope, too, in the Gard *département*, where there has been a massive increase in the amount of *domaines* undertaking their own wine-making, bottling and selling of ordinary Côtes du Rhône; their wines are admirable, concentrating on fruitiness and drinkability without necessarily sacrificing the depth and backbone whose absence would render them much less interesting.

Some gloom exists, however. Growers at St-Péray and Cornas are depressed about the future of their vineyards, as few young men are showing an interest in looking after these steep hillside vines. At 35, Robert Michel is the youngest *vigneron* at Cornas, and there are no enthusiastic teenagers in sight—they have all gone to seek work in the neighbouring towns.

Then there are problems that have arisen from the authorities' tampering with the laws, with the result that growers are forgoing the chance of making superior Côtes du Rhône Villages wine and electing to make more simple Côtes du Rhône *générique*, which is already a very crowded category. This means that villages like Cairanne are unlikely to progress to full individual *Appellation* status, as did Gigondas in 1971, if their leading growers are all settling to make ordinary Côtes du Rhône—hardly the best-quality advertising for the community, which will remain stuck in its Côtes du Rhône groove.

Overall a tendency has arisen to try to make lighter wines that carry less overriding tannin; in some ways this strips the area of one of its main characteristics, but in others it is a positive development—especially for wines that previously suffered from over-extensive ageing. Often those growers who use casks for really prolonged periods of ageing seem unsure about just why it is wood that should be ageing their wine. They fall into the trap of acting on blind instinct, on customs handed down from father to son, and fail to realize that casks need just as much treatment, just as much maintenance and cleanliness, as do concrete or stainless steel vats. The contradiction is that while many growers in the New World are turning to the use of wood, but ensuring that their casks are replaced with great regularity, some growers in the Rhône are tending to move away from it, without grasping that well cared for casks can make a valuable contribution to a wine's development.

Lighter wines are also resulting from the move away from crushing and destalking the grapes prior to fermentation. The *raisin entier* technique leaves the grapes to macerate and subsequently commence fermentation mostly within their skins. The process extracts the fruitiness from the grapes without all the accompanying tannins and is proving very beneficial when well applied. It does not involve the use of carbonic gas and should not be confused with the *macération carbonique* process, which strips many wines of their intrinsic character.

In the vineyards the march of the Syrah continues. Its plantation in the southern Rhône has increased extensively, but the most widely planted vine of all is still the Grenache, which like the rest of the Rhône Valley 'regulars' is relatively unknown outside its region. A vine of Spanish origin that may have originally entered the Roussillon area of France, it gives wines characterized by their red ruby colour and by their high alcohol degree; they have a marked tendency to fade after about eight years, however, which is one of the reasons why the Grenache-based Châteauneuf-du-Pape cannot be considered a really long-lived wine.

Important white grape vines include the Viognier and the Roussanne. The Viognier is extremely rare, and its cultivation in

19

France is limited mainly to Condrieu and Château-Grillet in the northern Rhône, although lately one or two experimental plantings have been undertaken in the southern Rhône. A tender plant, its grapes are small even when fully ripe, so that its yield per acre is never large. Its wines are generally excellent and are marked by their very strongly scented bouquets. The origin of the Viognier is disputed, although some of the Rhône growers believe that it came from Dalmatia, now Yugoslavia, around the third century AD.

The Roussanne is the other good white-wine grape in the Côtes du Rhône, but grafting of its root stock over the years has changed the characteristics of its wines, so that they now do not work well on their own. Like the Viognier, it is not a hardy vine, being susceptible to oïdium in particular, and needs frequent sulphur treatments. Jean-François Chaboud of St-Péray has experimented with the making of *cuvées* of Roussanne on their own but is happy with the wine only when it is blended with that of the Marsanne grape, for instance. Otherwise the Roussanne wine is too delicate and starts to decline and to lose its length of finish after as little as a year. The Marsanne is a higher-yielding vine that is also more resistant to the diseases of the vineyard and is therefore more widely favoured by the white wine-makers of Hermitage, St-Joseph, Crozes-Hermitage and St-Péray.

In the southern part of the Rhône Valley other important red-wine grapes are the Mourvèdre and the Cinsault. The Mourvèdre, which has always enjoyed a certain fame as the grape that makes the south-coast wines from Bandol, ripens late due to its having a large second growth around the month of July. In Provençal it is known as the 'strangle-a-dog' grape, a rather harsh assessment based on its hardness of style. With its dark colour and its backward style of wine, it is often useful as a prop to the weaker Grenache.

The Cinsault is a grape that does not always enlist great support from the growers. Although its colour can be an attractive, even red, it is a little thin on both bouquet and palate and has a tendency to fade very quickly within three or four years. Of course, no pure Cinsault wine is ever made, and it acts in a constructive way to soften the sturdier Mourvèdre and Syrah, as well as being a crucial element in the southern Rhône rosés.

Finally, the Syrah vine is the one that gives the Rhône's best red wines and which holds the key to the region's viticultural history. Syrah wines are always well coloured, rich in tannin and flavour and very long-lived. The only red-wine grape included in the red wines of the northern Rhône, it has recently become extremely popular in the southern Côtes du Rhône, where it is regarded as capable of bringing extra finesse to the slightly coarser, more alcoholic wines made from the Grenache. Its nature was altered during the 1970s by what is known as 'clonal selection'; this refers to the attempt to purify the strain by selecting for the vines better root stock and shoots. These derive from studies of the soil and climate, with the result that a more unmixed strain of Syrah has been developed, one that better resists the disease of *coulure*, or the dropping off the vine of its fruit in the early stages of its ripening.

The represents an advance for some growers, who are happy with their increased yields, but doubt persists in the minds of several traditional growers. They point to this new Syrah vine's propensity to produce larger and more numerous grapes, which dilute the plant's fruit. Nor need the new Syrah be trained in the old Guyot manner, the three-stemmed Gobelet training sufficing. A lower degree and less colour result in the wine from such grapes, and the cloning is evidently not to everyone's satisfaction.

Meanwhile the origin of the Syrah merits close inspection, for it provides possible evidence that the Côtes du Rhône is by a long way France's oldest wine-producing region. Some people believe that the Syrah originates from Syracuse, the connection being founded on the linking of names, but the authors do not subscribe to this. They believe that the Syrah came originally from around Shiraz, which is today the capital of the state of Fars in Iran. About 850 kilometres from Tehran, and 50 from the ruins of Persepolis, Shiraz was, until recent Islamic developments, the wine-growing centre of Iran. At Persepolis, founded in c. 518 BC, stone tablets have been found bearing inscriptions that mention wine and vintners. Such evidence would seem to suggest that the wine of Shiraz was already quite famous around that time.[1] Furthermore, the likeness between the words Syrah and Shiraz is

[1] William Culican, *The Medes and Persians* (London: Thames & Hudson, 1965), p. 115.

evident, and M. Paul Gauthier of Hermitage, a leading *négociant*, once found in a book published in 1860 six different spellings of the word Syrah: Syra, Sirrah, Syras, Chira, Sirac and Syrac. Their common denominator would appear to be the word Shiraz.

An obvious question arises, however. How did the Syrah vine arrive in the Rhône Valley, which is more than 5,000 kilometres from Iran? The answer could be that it was the Greeks of Phocaea, the founders of Marseille, who brought it with them. Phocaea used to be on the west coast of Asia Minor, about 50 kilometres south of the Aegean island of Lesbos. According to Herodotus, the Phocaeans were the first Greek tribe to undertake distant sea journeys and, around 600 BC, opened up the coasts of the Adriatic, France and Spain: Marseille was founded by them in 600 BC under the name of Massilia.

No connection between Phocaea and Shiraz can be established until the middle of the sixth century BC, so it seems that it was not the actual founders of Marseille who introduced the Syrah vine into France but some later Phocaean generation. The reasons for this supposition are as follows: in 546 BC the Persian King Cyrus I roundly defeated the Lydian Croesus, and the western capital of the Persian Empire became established at Sardes, only 120 kilometres south-east of Phocaea. The Lydian Empire, which bordered on Phocaea, was, incidentally, a rich vine-growing country.

The defeat of the Lydians by Cyrus opened up the western seaboard for Persia, and Phocaea continued thereafter under Persian rule. Then, some time after 546 BC, a large group of Phocaeans reportedly tried to escape by sailing west towards the Mediterranean and their own city of Massilia. Many are known to have turned back after reaching Chios, but a few boats continued on to Marseille. With their country then under Persian rule, it is therefore not improbable that it was these Phocaean voyagers who brought the Syrah vine to France, and not those who founded Marseille around 600 BC.

As Persian domination continued in Phocaea, links between Marseille and its mother country naturally receded, and trade had to be sought within France itself. The natural route towards the interior was the Rhône Valley, and Massilian coins, dating from 500–450 BC, have been found along it as far as the Alps, near the river's source in Switzerland. At that time wine was a fairly major element of trade, and old Greek amphorae have been found in both Marseille and Tain-l'Hermitage, about 240 kilometres farther north. This could indicate that it was at Hermitage that the Syrah was first planted: no similarly ancient amphorae have been found around the other northern Rhône vineyards. As if to support this contention, it is also interesting to note the naming of the Syrah vine in Australia today; there it passes under one of two names, either 'Shiraz' or 'Hermitage'.

The Roman invasion of Gaul naturally secured the continued cultivation of the hillside vineyards in the northern Rhône, and the area around the important Roman town of Vienne—today the Côte-Rôtie—became particularly famous for its *vinum picatum*, or resinated wine. Terraces were carefully structured into the hillside slopes and their basic form remains the same today as it was 2,000 years ago.

The Roman era was in many ways the Golden Age of the Rhône Valley south of Lyon, and its legacy has been both striking and long-lived. Vienne is distinguished by its splendid Temple of Augustus and Livy, similar in style to the famous Maison Carrée in Nîmes, its theatre, not excavated until the 1930s, and its Pyramide, once the finishing post for chariot races and now the name of one of France's most eminent restaurants. The Roman influence continues all the way down the Valley, most notably at Orange, where there is an antique theatre with a marvellously preserved front wall ('The finest wall in my Kingdom', according to Louis XIV), and a fine Arc de Triomphe that makes the Paris version look very junior indeed.

The Romans' departure from Gaul was accompanied by a decline in wine-making. The peasant farmers and small Gallic communities had not the resources to maintain extensive vineyards, and wine therefore lost much of its utility value. As a means for barter or exchange it became more localized, and most cultivators were content to make just enough for their own consumption.

Then, around the ninth century AD, the Church emerged as the most prolific owner of vineyards. Well disciplined and well organized, its members possessed the resources to produce wine on a scale not seen since the expulsion of the Romans. Wine had always been needed for their religious services and it slowly evolved as a useful source of income. Complex deals were often drawn up with the region's nobility and cultivation became more widespread. Its scale was probably very limited by comparison with today's, however, as can be judged from local documents found at Cornas, Rasteau and other places. All vineyards were strictly defined according to their size and were generally mentioned by a specific name—the Coteau St-Martin at Rasteau, for instance.

As wine became more accepted as an everyday drink, so more was made. In the fourteenth century the country surrounding Avignon seems to have been quite widely planted with vines—encouraged, no doubt, by the imposing needs of the Papal Palace. Demand remained largely localized at this time, although visiting monarchs or royal emissaries would take back their favourite discoveries to the Court of France; there was then just as much pleasure to be derived from finding a 'new wine' as there is today. Favour could also be curried by introducing the king to a fine country wine, and aristocratic families were not slow to realize this. The Grignan family at Chusclan were a case in point.

Slowly, individual wines started to be known and recognized in their own right, and enterprising owners would put out legendary stories concerning their wine's life-giving properties, general excellence and so on. All this helped to raise the price, and little by little export came to be considered a worthwhile undertaking. The *vinum picatum* of Vienne had been the very first wine export from the Côtes du Rhône region, being regularly sent to Rome in the first century AD.

Until the eighteenth century the wines from near the Rhône bore a mixture of different names, based on the name of the vineyard owner, or of the vineyard, or of the nearest village or town. Respective examples of this were the *vin de Mure* from Crozes-Hermitage, the *vin de la Nerte* from Châteauneuf-du-Pape, and the *vin d'Avignon*—also probably Châteauneuf-du-Pape—that was bought by the Earl of Bristol in 1704, according to P. Morton Shand in his *Book of French Wines*.

In 1731 the first official grouping of wine villages was made in the Gard *département*, and the title chosen for the group was 'La Côte du Rhône'. This represented the wine from many small communities on the west banks of the Rhône opposite Avignon; the most important villages were Orsan, Chusclan, Codolet, St-Victor and Tavel. In 1737 it was decided to mark the letters 'CdR', along with the vintage, on all barrels coming from member communities, and this agreement lasted into the early twentieth century.

The Gard *département* grouping marked a significant advance in relations between the various Rhône Valley wine villages, since earlier local decrees are all full of protectionist laws and regulations. Many villages, notably Tavel, had previously completely forbidden the entry of any 'foreign' wine or grapes within their community boundaries. The purpose was probably twofold: to ensure that all the village wine was drunk, and the vineyards therefore well kept up; and to eliminate the possibility of blending with any inferior local wines.

The need for strict, well-defined laws in order to preserve standards of quality emerged very strongly in the twentieth century, by when the world market for wine was growing very quickly. The *vignerons* of Châteauneuf-du-Pape, led by the Baron Le Roy, therefore instituted a series of quality controls over themselves, so that only sound, honest wine be made there. Unfortunately, they did not, and could not, legislate for what happened to the wine once it had left its place of origin. This is still a pressing problem today.

The Châteauneuf-du-Pape rules were drawn up in 1923, the first of their kind in the world, and by 1936 the French had made them broadly applicable to the whole country. High-grade wines were obviously the most restricted, with regulations governing which grapes could be used, how much wine per acre could be made, and so on, and it was decided that these were to possess their own *Appellation d'Origine Contrôlée*. Beneath them, the lesser wines were subject to less rigid stipulations.

The first *Appellations* in the Côtes du Rhône were divided into three groups. There was a northern group, consisting of Côte-Rôtie, Château-Grillet and Condrieu; a middle group, consisting of Cornas, St-Péray, Hermitage and Crozes-Hermitage; and finally a southern group, made up of Tavel and Châteauneuf-du-Pape. The additions to this list, now generally regarded as being split on a purely north–south basis, have been Lirac, Muscat de Beaumes-de-Venise and Rasteau *vin doux naturel* in 1945, St-Joseph in 1956 and Gigondas in 1971.

On the periphery of the Côtes du Rhône region there are some other local country wines—Coteaux du Tricastin, Côtes du Ventoux, Châtillon-en-Diois, Côtes du Vivarais and Clairette de Die. The first four make red, rosé and white wines of no great pretension and have for a long time been barely known beyond their immediate area of production. Suddenly, however, the French National Institute of Appellations of Origin has promoted the first three to full *Appellation Contrôlée* status—a move that seems to set a dangerous precedent.

Certainly the respective areas are now growing better-quality vines, but, with the exception of Tricastin, the wines have barely advanced their quality so as to merit the highest accolade in French viticulture. It is not easy, but it is possible, to alter growers' attitudes towards the way they look after and run their vineyards; it is much less easy to change the casual, haphazard mentality that many possess when it comes actually to making their wine. The authors' experiences with some of these wines (excepting also the good sparkling Clairette de Die) have strongly suggested that full *Appellation Contrôlée* status is today being won too easily; it is no use having a hierarchy if everyone is at the top of it, and such a situation is also downright misleading for the average consumer.

The importance of the central *Appellation Contrôlée* policy is emphasized by the increasing role played by the Côtes du Rhône in the French wine export field. It is a story of constant development. In 1965 Rhône exports, in bottle and cask, came to 122,278 hectolitres; in 1970, 191,416 hectolitres; in 1975, 418,025 hectolitres, in 1980, 516,282 hectolitres, and in 1981, 602,182 hectolitres. The Rhône is now exporting more wine than Burgundy, having overtaken that area for the first time in 1979, and more than Beaujolais, which it overtook in 1976. It is now second only to Bordeaux in volume of exports, and while the world feels the effects of a steady, uncompromising recession, that is a fortunate position to be in.

Apart from its wine, the Rhône Valley is an important industrial and commercial artery for the rest of France. The River Rhône runs for 808 kilometres altogether, from its torrential source in the east of the Swiss canton of the Valais all the way down to the Mediterranean, west of Marseille. South of Lyon it extends for 370 kilometres and is joined by several fair-sized rivers, all of which help to boost its imposing flow. These rivers include the Isère, the Drôme, the Ardèche, the Aigues, the Ouvèze and the Durance.

The area is therefore naturally suitable for hydro-electric

projects, which have brought an influx of both money and skilled labour into the surrounding countryside. Important schemes exist at Pierre-Bénite near Lyon, at Donzère and at Valence, for instance. Along the river other heavy industries have sprung up during the last fifty years, including large cement works near Montélimar and some of the country's leading metallurgical industries at Givors, near Vienne, and at Ardoise, near Roquemaure. In the south, at Pierrelatte and Marcoule, the French atomic system has its centre.

In some cases, notably in the northern part of the Valley, these factories have brought problems for the owners of vineyards. Young men derive considerably greater financial benefit from entering their local industry than from continuing to work the land. Where all vineyard cultivation must by necessity be manual, the fall in the total size of the vineyards has been most marked: this is the case with the lesser-known *Appellations* that lie between Vienne and Valence—Cornas and St-Péray.

The Rhône Valley is extremely fertile, however, and its agriculture, although diminished, has broadly remained on a sound level. North of Montélimar the main fruits are peaches, pears, apricots and cherries; to the south there are pears, apples, cherries, plums, melons and peaches. The main vegetables are artichokes, asparagus, cabbages, lettuce and tomatoes. All are grown on an extensive scale and are sold both inside and outside France, with a particularly large proportion going to Paris.

In addition to these staple fruits and vegetables, the surrounds of the Rhône produce other fine local specialities. The *département* of the Isère is rich in walnuts, while the *département* of the Ardèche grows plentiful raspberries, bilberries, blackcurrants and chestnuts. On either side of the river between Lyon and Montélimar a variety of local goat and cow cheeses are made—notably the Rigottes of Condrieu and the St-Marcellin of the Isère. In the north of the Vaucluse *département*, around Valréas, there are widespread lavender plantations, as well as a steady production of olive oil, especially around Nyons and Beaumes-de-Venise. South of Montélimar, in the Tricastin country, high-grade black truffles are another important local speciality.

The countryside around the river is also rich in poultry and game, and the regional cooking is shaped accordingly. Favourite dishes are the *poulet aux écrevisses* (chicken cooked in a crayfish sauce), *quenelles de brochet* (a sort of pike soufflé), *agneau grillé aux herbes* (lamb roasted in herbs), *perdrix aux choux* (partridge cooked in cabbage) and *charcuterie*, or selected pork meats. The *gratin dauphinoise* (potato gratin) and the *lièvre en poivrade* (hare cooked in pepper sauce) are other favourites. To finish any meal there is the celebrated nougat of Montélimar.

This is the context in which the wines of the Côtes du Rhône are made and drunk, and the combination of wine and food can be well appreciated in the best restaurants of the Rhône Valley. These include the impeccable Restaurant Pic at Valence, where the cuisine has reached ever greater heights of refinement in recent years; the restaurant Beau Rivage at Condrieu, with its outstanding *quenelles de brochet*; the very famous Pyramide restaurant in Vienne, which, although not as good as it was, is still the possessor of an extensive wine list; the attractive Restaurant Bouvarel at St-Hilaire-du-Rosier, with its impressive local *raviole* dish, and its *poulet aux écrevisses*; the restaurant Hiély at Avignon, with its *mousseline de brochet aux morilles* (pike mousse cooked with wild mushrooms). Other very fine establishments near the Côtes du Rhône are the Hostellerie Renaissance at Rive-de-Gier, with a very inventive cuisine, the Hostellerie du Château at Châteaubourg, whose Mme Reynaud is one of the best wine tasters in the Rhône, and La Table du Comtat at Séguret, which enjoys one of the best views of the southern Rhône vineyards obtainable anywhere and has excellent food to match.

Very personal favourites of the authors are a little less grand but supply excellent food, wine and a friendly attention at prices that will not make the bank manager tremble. These are the Restaurant Roger Lanaz at Granges-les-Beaumont near Tain-l'Hermitage, with splendid cooking at splendid prices; the Bellevue at Les Roches-de-Condrieu, where the fish is prepared to perfection to accompany the local Viognier wines; Le Pistou at Châteauneuf-du-Pape—excellent value and a good selection of wines; the Hostellerie du Seigneur at Tavel, where good food and accommodation are provided by the affable M. et Mme Ange Bodo; and La Fourchette in Avignon, where the cooking is very good and the prices reasonable.

Finally, to match the finest examples of gastronomy that can be found around the Côtes du Rhône, the authors have drawn up a personal list of those wines that they consider to be the very finest in the Côtes du Rhône and, by logical extension, among the greatest in France.

CÔTE-RÔTIE	La Mouline and La Landonne, E. Guigal
CHÂTEAU-GRILLET	Neyret-Gachet
HERMITAGE	La Chapelle, P. Jaboulet Ainé
HERMITAGE	J.-L. Chave
CORNAS	A. Clape
TAVEL	Domaine de la Genestière, G. Bernard

At the end of each chapter there is also a further guide to each *Appellation*'s finest wines with the leading growers—up to five or six—listed in order of personal preference, based on tasting and experience of the wines, and the remaining growers listed in alphabetical order. At Châteauneuf-du-Pape a subjective ranking has been established for the first time, with the better properties divided into three categories.

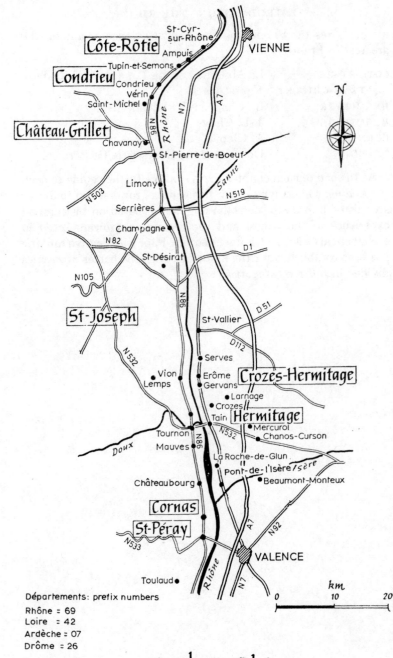

Côte-Rôtie

St-Cyr-
sur-Rhône

VIENNE

Ampuis

Tupin-et-Semons

Condrieu

Condrieu

Vérin

Saint-Michel

Château-Grillet

Chavanay

St-Pierre-de-Boeuf

Limony

Sanne

N519

Serrières

Champagne

N82

St-Désirat

D1

N105

St-Joseph

St-Vallier

D51

D112

N532

Serves

Crozes-Hermitage

Vion

Erôme

Lemps

Gervans

Larnage

Crozes

Hermitage

Tain

Mercurol

Tournon

N532

Chanos-Curson

Mauves

La Roche-de-Glun

Doux

Pont-de-l'Isère/*Isère*

Châteaubourg

Beaumont-Monteux

Cornas

St-Péray

N533

N92

VALENCE

Toulaud

km

Départements: prefix numbers

Rhône = 69
Loire = 42
Ardèche = 07
Drôme = 26

0   10   20

Northern Rhône

1

Côte-Rôtie

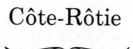

Côte-Rôtie, one of the world's foremost red wines, bears a splendidly evocative title. The 'Roasted Slope', the 'Burnt Hillside': both call to mind very precisely the dark fieriness of this majestic wine. As the northernmost vineyard in the Côtes du Rhône, Côte-Rôtie accomplishes the awkward transition between Burgundy and the 'hot' South with ease and modesty. The very best wines undoubtedly merit the word 'great'.

But comparatively few people have ever heard of this startling red wine. Côte-Rôtie is a small, 252-acre *Appellation* just south of the old Roman town of Vienne and its vineyards are lodged over five inconspicuous communities on the west side of the River Rhône. The centre is the village of Ampuis, a plain-looking place on the road from Lyon to Nîmes. Precious little activity is ever observable even around the sombre car park that serves as the village square, and the back streets appear to be dominated by ferociously barking dogs that howl at the occasional passer-by. Around Ampuis the hamlets of Verenay, Tupin, Semons and St-Cyr-sur-Rhône complete the picture of smallness and anonymity.

Côte-Rôtie is a wine that dates back to Roman times, and its cultivation still takes place mainly on the original steeply graded Roman terraces that overlook the Rhône. There are some researchers who nevertheless believe it to be an even older wine. For instance, Professor Claudius Roux, the author of a detailed monograph on Ampuis and Côte-Rôtie, has stated that the vineyard probably dates from the sixth century BC, the time of the Phocaean Greeks' arrival in southern France.

This view has been disputed by local growers with an interest in ancient Greek history. They say, on the contrary, that the Phocaeans were a predominantly seafaring race who liked to establish and restrict their colonies to the edge of the ocean. If the vine shoots were brought up the Rhône Valley at such an early date, it was more probably traffickers or pirates who took them.

By the early years after Christ, Vienne and its wine had risen to exalted eminence within the Roman Empire. Vienne was then the thriving capital of mid-Gaul and its local wine, the *vinum picatum*, had become famous as the first Gallic wine to reach Rome. According to the writings of Roman authors of the time, such as Lucius Columella in his *De re rustica* (c. AD 60), the *picatum* seems to have been a deeply coloured wine with a certain 'pitchy' taste— hence the description *picatum*.

Both Pliny the Elder, who was born in AD 23 and died in the destruction caused by the eruption of Vesuvius in AD 79, and Martial (AD 40–105) had encountered the *picatum*, which was apparently quite a snob wine in their day. In his *Epigrams*,[1] Martial boasted to his doubting friends that he had been sent the wine from the vine-growing area of Vienne by a friend of his called Romulus. Martial appears to have visited Vienne and seen the vineyards himself, since he had a circle of friends living there.

Pliny discussed the wine with more reverence,[2] as befits probably the world's first wine chronicler. In the thirty-seven books that comprise his *Natural History*, he refers to more than forty different wines with an expertise undoubtedly acquired from frequent tasting. Pliny was drawn by the very 'pitchiness', or coarseness, of the wine from Vienne and found it to be a good example of a country wine—one that was better appreciated in its native place than overseas. Pliny solemnly concluded that one could not know what real *picatum* was like unless it had been drunk in Vienne itself: a handy let-out for a host in Rome if his *picatum* was found to be disappointing!

Vienne started to decline in importance around the second century AD, when the Emperor Marcus Aurelius (AD 121–80) conferred his favours on his preferred Gallic town of Lyon. At the same time the Viennois wine disappears from all chroniclers' records and does not re-emerge until the mid-nineteenth century, when the French authors Jules Janin and Cochard praised it under the name of Côte-Rôtie.

The scourge, phylloxera, hit Côte-Rôtie around 1880 and most

[1] *Epigrams*, XIII, 107.
[2] *Natural History*, XIV, 26 and 57.

of the vineyard was destroyed within two years. By 1893 it had been built up again, but not on the same scale. Many farmers had turned swiftly to fruit-growing as a more immediate means of remuneration. They could not afford to wait the four years before the Syrah vines gave their first worthwhile fruit. Another blow was dealt the vineyard by the First World War, for the loss of young men needed to tend the slopes meant that some growers gave up their plots for want of labour. Meagre prices during the Depression further compounded Côte-Rôtie's difficulties, and during the Second World War the wine was sold mainly as *vin ordinaire*. By 1949 Côte-Rôtie was fetching only about one franc a litre—a ridiculous price in view of the work involved and the quality of the wine.

Côte-Rôtie is now slowly regaining its lost eminence, and its true merit, as well as its true value, is well recognized by some discerning buyers and connoisseurs. The vineyard's fundamental problems remain, however, and it is just as difficult as ever to find the labour required for the upkeep of those vines planted on the precipitous slopes. Local industry in Vienne and Lyon is a big, well paid counter-attraction, while the current vogue for developing rural land for building represents a growing menace to the hillsides' continued cultivation.

The hillside vineyards themselves are some of the steepest in France, and in places their incline is as much as 55°. There are European vineyards—notably along the River Mosel—that may possess a more startling abruptness, but few can lay claim to such ancient traditions as well. The packed stone walls that form the terraces have not changed substantially since the days of the Romans and are still generally held together without the aid of cement. Under the joint attack of wind and rain, these walls need annual maintenance; they are often higher than a man, and only skilled hands can perform the delicate task of repairing them.

Along the narrow escarpments are planted two different vines, the red grape Syrah and the white grape Viognier. Although it is a tenacious plant that thrives in modest conditions, the Syrah has to be specially trained at Côte-Rôtie by the Guyot method in order for it to produce well: four support sticks of different lengths are hammered into the ground around the foot of the plant, and the vine shoots are then led outward along the sticks so as to achieve the greatest possible exposure. The job of hammering these sticks

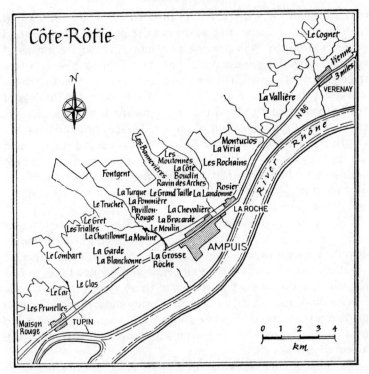

into the rocky ground is arduous indeed and is repeated every year when the growers plant their young vines. The hammer and the pickaxe used to be the only tools for this operation, but now some *vignerons* blast holes in the ground with agricultural explosives. This is not always as time-saving as it should be since the blast often affects the terrace walls as well. When this happens, passers-by on the main road below can encounter some rude shocks from falling debris!

Since the late 1960s the general nature of the vineyards has altered a little as the area under vines has been extended by the principal method of planting on untilled ground on the plateau above the slopes. By 1983 there were probably 80 acres out of the *Appellation*'s total of just over 250 acres planted in this way. These younger vines are not yet capable of yielding concentrated fruit; it also appears that the plateau is by no means the best place for growing vines at Côte-Rôtie, especially if former high stan-

34

dards are to be maintained. Already one can detect this in tasting the less well-known growers' wines, which are often very pale in colour and so light as to be unworthy of Côte-Rôtie's deservedly famous name. These plateau vines are planted 2·5 metres apart for tractor working, while in the steep slopes there is only half the distance between the vines, space being so precious. But on the slopes the granite soil, the high mean temperature and the vines' admirable exposure combine to provide an intense grape juice that is the true characteristic of good Côte-Rôtie.

The Syrah forms nearly 95 per cent of the total plantation. The growers refer to it as the 'Serine', an entirely local name that means nothing to a *vigneron* at Hermitage, for example. Although a Côte-Rôtie can be made with up to 20 per cent Viognier in it, many *vignerons* have completely forsaken the white grape. It is a much less consistent producer than the Syrah and seems very particular about where it will grow. One of the best parts of the vineyard is the Côte-Brune, for instance, but the Viognier has never shown very well in its clayey soil, and Marius Gentaz is perhaps the only grower with any Viognier vines on his Côte-Brune holding. Being 60 years old, their grapes are few but generally well formed and go some way to matching the quality of grapes from the more commonly found Viognier vines that are grown extensively on the lighter, limestone-based ground of the Côte-Blonde next door.

The Côtes Brune and Blonde are two adjacent hillsides above Ampuis, and are Côte-Rôtie's most famous denominations. Indeed, in a 1909 showcard made for the Paris *Concours Agricole*, the Brune and the Blonde were stated to give 'the *premiers grands crus*', while 'the various other slopes give the *grands crus classés*, the *crus classés* and the *crus bourgeois*'—terminology which is very rarely used today, although Guigal's La Mouline calls itself a *Premier cru de la Côte-Blonde*.

Much Côte-Rôtie is subtitled 'Brune et Blonde', and a blend of the two slopes is said to provide the most attractively balanced wine of all the *Appellation*. Among the best vineyards figure La Mouline, La Chatillonne, La Viria, La Landonne, La Côte-Boudin and La Chevalière. The first two are on the Côte-Blonde, while the last three are on the Côte-Brune.

The 'Brune' and the 'Blonde' are the subject of Côte-Rôtie's most often repeated legend, which runs essentially as follows. In dusky, feudal days an all-powerful aristocrat named Maugiron is said to have inhabited the *château* of Ampuis. His two daughters were ravishing beauties, one possessing fair, golden hair, the other long, dark tresses. Whether out of simple kindness, or whether out of a desire to evade his tax commitments, Maugiron decided to bequeath the two slopes to his daughters; they in turn were christened according to the colour of the girls' hair.

Such are the bare bones of a story that appears in some form or other in most textbooks on wine. Sometimes it is the similarity between the girls' characters and the wines of the two slopes that is said to have prompted the choice of names: the Blonde being bright and lively when young, but fading quickly, the Brune starting off quiet and reserved, but growing into a splendid eminence. This would certainly correspond to the style of the two principal wines made by the House of Guigal, La Mouline and La Landonne. The Mouline wine is always extremely rich and well balanced but has an added delicacy that makes it a little less long-lived than usual; after about its tenth birthday a touch of the damp, almost herbaceous aromas of age have entered the bouquet, even though the fruit on the palate still seems compressed and very intense. Thereafter the purple colour starts to fade grace-fully, and the most powerful vintages of La Mouline, such as the 1969 and the 1978, should be drunk before they are 18 to 20 years old. The La Landonne wine, by contrast, starts life extremely backward, with a black-purple colour and a bouquet that for its first five years only reveals a small amount of raw fruit. Possessed of deep and tannic flavours, the wine has a slightly spicy finish that furnishes all the promise that it will develop into a glorious complex richness in later years. The Guigals only started to make La Landonne in the 1978 vintage, but give this first *cuvée* a life-span of up to thirty years.

The other growers who bottle specifically titled wines under Brune or Blonde are Marius Gentaz-Dervieux and Joseph Jamet with their Côte-Brune and René Rostaing, Vidal-Fleury, Chol et Fils and Gilles Barge who has taken over Joseph Duplessy's vineyard on the Côte-Blonde. The vast majority of Côte-Rôtie remains a blend of all the wines that come from the many little plots or *parcelles* that each grower has dotted about the *Appellation*.

The Syrah and Viognier grapes are invariably well ripened by the time of the *vendanges*, which commence around the end of

September or sometimes early in October. Thirty kilometres south of Lyon the climate has started to acquire a warmer tone, and the sun has an intensity that is not apparent farther north in Burgundy, for example. With the Côte-Rôtie hillsides perfectly angled towards the south-east, the vineyards receive the sun from dawn to dusk, and the grapes ripen well accordingly. Extra heat is also generated in the sloped vineyards through the enclosing effect of the terrace walls, and the grapes are often harvested by workers stripped to the waist or in shirt sleeves. Their toil is accentuated by the tiring steepness of the slopes, since the *vendange* of red and white grapes has to be brought down to the plain in bulky wooden holders known as *beneaux*. The *beneau* is carried on one shoulder, while a counter-weight such as a sandbag rests on the other. Carrying the full *beneaux* is exhausting work, and when the highest vines are being harvested human chains have to be formed down the hillside in order to pass them along.

The growers attempt to complete their harvesting as quickly as possible, since they do not want to take in grapes with widely differing levels of sugar and acidity that will complicate the task of vinification. Nor do they want to be caught out by sudden rainfalls that can come up the Rhône Valley driven by the south wind, the *vent du midi*. Thus a grower with around 7 acres of vines will finish in four or five days, with a team totalling about twenty-five pickers. Such stop-gap labour for the harvest is drawn mainly from Spanish and Portuguese women whose husbands work in local factories, with an irregular sprinkling of students. The students often disgrace themselves, however, by going to sleep among the vines after a winy lunch.

Once the *vendange* has reached the grower's cellar, the grapes receive only a light crushing, still mainly performed by treading down rather than by using modern presses, which are inevitably a little more severe on the grapes. The growers do not destalk their grapes and, after the trampling by foot, place them in time-honoured solid oak vats for an extended primary fermentation of up to two weeks. A few *vignerons*, such as Jasmin, Guigal and Gentaz-Dervieux, have switched to using concrete fermenting vats, but as they make top-class wine still, there seems no cause for complaint!

The solid oak vats are as high as a man and can be closed up with thick planks of wood once the grapes have been put in, so that the *chapeau*, or top of the fermenting grapes, can be kept from bubbling over. Such old-fashioned vats are obviously much more susceptible to outside temperature changes and bacterial problems than contemporary closed concrete or stainless steel vats, and so, should the October weather be particularly cold, for instance, fermentation will proceed very slowly.

Using a covered vat enables the winemaker to maintain a more regular speed of fermentation, as well as to maximize the wine's freshness. However, it is unlikely that most of the growers will change to the covered vats, since the French country *vigneron* in traditional areas such as the Rhône and Loire valleys is remarkably resistant to new ideas. He prefers to pin his trust, sometimes blindly, on the methods and utensils employed by preceding generations. Thus when it comes to pressing the pulp at the end of the primary fermentation, the Côte-Rôtie growers dust down their old vertical wooden presses and set to work. Bit by bit, the old presses are turned downwards, with the broad backs of the workers straining over them. Like carrying the harvest, this is an energy-sapping task—not a thing to volunteer for!

The young Côte-Rôtie is transferred to the cask for ageing towards the spring following the harvest, by which time the malolactic fermentation will have been completed. Views differ as to which size of cask or which combination of barrels should be used for this, and while growers such as Gentaz-Dervieux and Jasmin use the 225-litre *pièce* throughout, others such as Pierre Barge and de Vallouit prefer a mixture of sizes. Barge's wine spends the first two-thirds of its ageing process in casks of between 1,000 and 3,000 litres and the final third in his *pièces*. De Vallouit, whose light, feminine style of wine is similar to Pierre Barge's, puts his Côte-Rôtie for the first third of ageing in *foudres* of around 4,000 litres and, for the final two-thirds, in *demi muids* of around 650 litres.

The clearest exposition of the attitude towards ageing in cask is given by Marcel Guigal, who fully understands the importance of the role played by wood in the development of a wine. He does not, like many growers, hang on to his barrels for years on end, since he realizes that after a certain time their spotless cleanliness cannot be guaranteed. A fault that is not uncommon in the Rhône is to find a wine whose construction is sound but which has been invested with an overriding smell of dirty wood, something that helps to destroy the fruit that the wine may have possessed.

Guigal therefore has a steady turnover of *pièces*, many of which come from Burgundian barrel-makers. He explained how he used these: 'The *pièce* develops the wine's bouquet more than the *foudre* but ages the wine itself more quickly. What I like to do therefore is to put 35 per cent of my wine of any one vintage in the 225-litre *pièces* and the rest in *foudres* of around 5,000 litres before blending them together.' M. Guigal's two best wines, La Mouline and La Landonne, will always receive well over three years in cask before being bottled, but there are few growers who are able to remain so traditional in their approach. Increased demand for Côte-Rôtie during the 1970s has meant that a lot of the wine now rarely receives even two years' ageing before being released for sale. The style of the middle-quality growers has therefore become one of light wines that can be quaffed without too much ado when they are only three or four years old. This is a tremendous pity, since the character and complexity of Côte-Rôtie are what make it so memorable. There are enough light, fruity wines around as it is, without Côte-Rôtie joining the bandwagon.

When first put into cask, the young wine is thoroughly 'green', or coarse, and the lower the percentage of Viognier grapes that it contains, the greener it is. The best growers therefore set out to round the wine out, so that, despite the extra work involved, such tasks as racking and topping up the casks (*l'ouillage*) are undertaken as a matter of course. A wine aged for three years in wood, for instance, would have to be topped up on more than 150 occasions.

Once bottled, a Côte-Rôtie is not in possession of all its powers. Its grace or finesse, and notably its bouquet, will still be immature. In the stronger vintages, such as 1976, a bottle life of at least five years is desirable if the wine is to blossom fully, and in the most powerful years, such as 1978, it is better to wait up to eight years if the wine is to be given a chance to show its best harmony. By contrast, lighter vintages, like 1977 and 1979, which gave attractively scented, rather feminine wines, are excellent to drink before they are 5 or 6 years old.

Deep purple when young, a good Côte-Rôtie's colour only starts to fade after fifteen years, but its bouquet meanwhile attains a velvet-like perfection. The presence of the Viognier in a Côte-Rôtie acts without doubt to soften the wine—particularly as it has to be fermented with the Syrah rather than added in wine form afterwards—and helps to heighten its already flowery (some say 'violet-like') bouquet. It is a pity that the plantation of Viognier is decreasing at Côte-Rôtie, since it is precisely this young floweriness that the sturdy wines of Hermitage tend to lack and that prompts the suggestion that Côte-Rôtie is the Queen of the Rhône, Hermitage the King.

On the palate Côte-Rôtie is rich but elegant. Its full-blooded flavour makes the drinker think he is almost 'eating' his wine, but the long, supple aftertaste will persuade him to raise his glass again, and again ... Drinking Côte-Rôtie from *vignerons* such as Guigal, Jasmin and Gentaz-Dervieux is a vivid experience, which should instantly convert anyone to an unqualified enthusiasm for wine; Côte-Rôtie of this standard can certainly be rated as one of the world's most striking and totally enchanting red wines.

Côte-Rôtie does, of course, come from a very restricted vineyard, so it is all the more surprising to note that there are over eighty-five individual growers in and around Ampuis. No more than thirty make and sell their own wine, though; the rest harvest their grapes and sell them to the local *négociant* houses, such as Guigal and Vidal-Fleury in Ampuis and Chapoutier and Jaboulet in Tain l'Hermitage. These cultivators will sometimes own less than half an acre of vines and will also grow fruit and vegetables on the narrow stretch of flat land between the hillsides and the Rhône.

The oldest *maison du vin* in the northern Côtes du Rhône is the House of Vidal-Fleury, which dates back to 1781. From 1908 until his death in 1976 the *patron* of this business was the latterly stooped but none the less compelling figure of M. Joseph Vidal-Fleury. Now his daughter is the proprietor and is, coincidentally enough, married to a gentleman called Vidal, so at least half the family name has been retained.

An hour spent with Joseph Vidal-Fleury was a wonderful education, for he had a Pandora's box of knowledge and anecdotes that was hard to rival. He had seen a whole era of wine-making, and attitudes towards wine-making, evolve before his eyes; in his later years he saw in cellars around him metal vats, pneumatic presses, chestnut instead of oak casks and so on, but throughout it all his confidence in the old methods had remained unshaken. As he would frankly admit: 'It is difficult for me to talk about new things. I am a believer in ancient processes, which I esteem to be the best, the most honest and the most efficient. Wine just needs a lot of care, cleanliness, racking and a minimum of chemical products. Like that, one makes very good wine.

'The company has always been like a family and I have been repaid with a cohesion and team effort that would be difficult to match. I have 20 acres of well-sited vines on the Côtes Brune and Blonde, vineyards such as La Chatillonne and Le Clos on the Blonde and La Turque, La Pommière and Pavillon-Rouge on the Brune. Many of my staff have been with me for twenty-five years or more, which shows that we are above all a house of tradition.' Until the mid-1970s M. Vidal-Fleury's words were amply reflected in the style of the house wines, which were invariably strong-bodied and classically made, with a dependable consistency about them. In the latter part of the 1970s, however, this consistency has been lost, and the Côte-Rôtie and Hermitage, on which Vidal-Fleury most pride themselves, have tended to be unbalanced and disappointing. It is to be hoped that this is only a passing phase.

Ampuis's other main wine house is owned by an ex-pupil of M. Vidal-Fleury. In 1946 M. Etienne Guigal, who had been both cellar master and head *vigneron* at Vidal-Fleury, formed his own business. La Maison Guigal now makes the best, most fully characteristic wines of Côte-Rôtie.

A grey-haired, unpretentious man, M. Guigal flits around the family cellars in a most diffident way, and one obtains the impression that his real forte is caring for the vineyards. He has obviously passed on all his expertise to his son, Marcel, who runs the business with him, for Marcel is extremely articulate about what he is doing in his cellars and why. He is one of the new wave of Rhône growers who are not content with merely drawing ideas from the area round about and who will spend a summer holiday in California so that they can learn about other styles of making wine, other philosophies about vinification, harvesting and so on.

Marcel explained that the family owned 7·5 acres of vines on the Côtes Brune and Blonde but that they augmented their annual production by buying grapes from about fifty small cultivators. They make three qualities of Côte-Rôtie: a very good Brune and Blonde mixture that sells as Côte-Rôtie, a wine that comes entirely from the Côte-Blonde, which is sold under the name of La

M. Marcel Guigal

Mouline, and an entirely Côte-Brune wine called La Landonne. Marcel Guigal first made La Mouline in 1966, having bought an extensive plot of vines on the Côte-Blonde from Mme Dervieux, a famous wine name at Côte-Rôtie. He is justifiably proud of this wine, whose depth of flavour, complexity and stunning richness have made it the best of the *Appellation*, but in 1978, not content with having achieved such a pinnacle of excellence, he launched a wine to rival La Mouline.

'You can't imagine the trouble we went to in order to buy up the Landonne vineyard. It belonged to seventeen small holders, and I'm sure I shall never have to be so patient again when it comes to buying a vineyard. It took more than ten years, buying each plot individually, but I have no doubt that it will prove worth while.' Certainly La Landonne will be the most massive wine at Côte-Rôtie, able to live up to twenty-five or thirty years in the best vintages according to M. Guigal, and one that will justly bring worldwide fame to the *Appellation*, being the embodiment of a top-class red wine. It is shipped in wooden cases, with a label reproducing a Roman mosaic found near by that depicts the crushing of grapes at harvest time.

Apart from their excellent Côte-Rôties, the House of Guigal also sells a complete range of good southern Rhône wines and very distinguished red and white Hermitage and Condrieu, which are close to the top rank in their respective *Appellations*. These are fine examples of what *négociant* wines can be like if well looked after.

Around the corner from the Maison Guigal lives a family which makes a splendidly styled wine. The Jasmins have been at Côte-Rôtie since the time that M. Georges Jasmin's grandfather came down from Champagne to work as chef at the *château* of Ampuis. Developing an eager interest in the village's principal activity, he bought the vineyard that went with the *château*: this is well situated at one end of the Côte-Brune. The Jasmin family have continued from there, and now it is Georges's son Robert who mainly looks after their vineyards and intimate little cellar. Robert's son is just learning the family occupation, but his wife Josette still works in a local factory to supplement their income; otherwise, as Robert candidly admits, there would not be enough to live on for the two of them and their two children.

Georges Jasmin is now in his late seventies but looks nearly ten years younger. He has a fine twinkle in his eye, and his strong leathery face is always ready to crinkle into a smile or a chuckle. Robert is justifiably proud that he is able to say that he is still aided by his father, since Georges suffered from the debilitating illness of hepatitis when he was 76. 'He imposed a strict regime— no Côte-Rôtie, of course, for several months—and now cycles off up the hillside to do the pruning on even the coldest winter days. That takes some doing, and I can tell you that I am having to look to my laurels, so well recovered is he.'

M. Georges Jasmin

43

Robert, a jovial man in his early forties, who has a fine instinct for good food and wine, explained that their harvest was never very large, not only because they grow some Viognier—a small producer—but also because they have some Syrah vines that are more than 50 years old. These vines never yield much more than 15 hectolitres a hectare, well under half the quantity permitted, but their grapes carry a very concentrated juice, which helps greatly towards making a highly scented, complete and rich wine. Less long-lived than Guigal's wines, the Jasmin Côte-Rôtie invariably displays attractive fruit and flavour, with aromas reminiscent of vanilla and garden fruits. Its soft, rather approachable style dictates that it should ideally be drunk before it is 10 or 12 years old.

The Jasmins have some very fine barrels in their small, cobwebbed cellar, and Robert explained that they had recently been obliged to change their *tonnelier*, or barrelmaker, since their former supplier in Serrières, 25 kilometres south, had retired for lack of regular business. 'He lasted longer than any other local *tonneliers*,' said Robert, 'mainly because he used to make ladders and boxes for collecting fruit. Now we go to Pouilly-Fuissé, where we buy 5-year-old barrels that have previously contained the white wine. We are very pleased with them, especially as we receive them at half the new price.'

Each *Appellation* possesses its own Growers' Union, and the President of the Côte-Rôtie *Syndicat des Vignerons* since 1953 has been M. Albert Dervieux, a well-known and well-liked figure in the northern part of the Valley. Small and almost wiry, with glasses, M. Dervieux does not resemble a typical *vigneron*, and he does indeed find that much of his time is spent keeping abreast of government rulings on wine and local land deals, as well as looking after the interests of his fellow growers. In a year in which the crop has been extremely abundant, it is the *Syndicat* that tastes the wine and decides whether to apply to Paris for a *dérogation*; that is, the right to sell anything in excess of the statutory 40 hectolitres a hectare (about 2,150 bottles an acre) as genuine Côte-Rôtie. When this extra wine is not considered good enough to carry the *Appellation*'s name, it is sold as *vin ordinaire*—a pretty good one, no doubt!

M. Dervieux is, surprisingly, one of the only people at Côte-Rôtie to have an anciently stocked personal cellar. This goes back to 1929, the 'year of the century', and includes all the best vintages since—1945, 1947, 1955, 1961, 1969, 1971 and 1978. 'I drank one of my 1929s in 1969, and it was still in marvellous condition. The colour had turned almost brown, I grant you, but the wine still retained much of its strength and all its character. Normally I would say a Côte-Rôtie can live between twenty and thirty years, but they should be good to drink after ten or twelve years. As for my 1947s, they're still in perfect order, and I'm quite looking forward to drinking them,' he added drily.

French vineyards have over the years become very attractive propositions to foreign investors, and since 1971 a Franco-American group headed by the local Senator and Mayor of Ampuis has owned an ever-increasing portion of the Côte-Rôtie hillside, and particularly the plateau plantation. The Senator-Mayor, M. Alfred Gerin, related how the alliance came about in the first place: 'In 1961, confident about Côte-Rôtie's future and anxious to see more wine produced here, I approached a number of local friends with the idea of buying up untilled plots of land that could be transformed into vine-growing land. We started absolutely from scratch and regrouped many of the plots into better-sized, more workable units. Once we had begun producing and selling our wine in France and abroad, some Americans from New York expressed their desire to import more Côte-Rôtie than we were able to give them. We decided to go straight to the source of the problem and expand our holding. Some of them entered our concern in 1971, and we now own 25 acres of vines. I am still the only professional in the group and am responsible for both the vinification and the marketing of our wines. We've now got openings for it all over the United States, and are pleased with the way things have gone.'

The group has naturally caused some finger-wagging and café comment among the winemen of the area, especially as the quality of the Gerin wine has not always been startling. There are some who feel that French vineyards are a part of their national heritage and should be kept for the French, since foreign investment will herald the departure of most of their wine overseas. This is, in fact, the case more in Bordeaux than in the Rhône, for there the ownership of certain *châteaux* by large multinational firms does indeed mean that their wine is drawn into the complex marketing channels that they already possess—

principally in countries other than France. What should be remembered, though, is that without such funds the wine often would not be produced and that *vignerons* employed by such groups would not be as well off. Of course, wine-making is a very personal affair, and such group organization tends to go against the grain in a country of individualists like France.

One of the younger growers beginning to make a small name for himself is a man who only started to vinify and bottle a part of his wine in 1978. Edmond Duclaux, lank dark hair swept across his forehead, ruddy outdoor complexion prominent, talked about his vineyard with a slight stutter that one thought was reserved only for certain sections of the British theatrical class: 'My vineyard is called the Maison Rouge, at Tupin, and was bought by my grandfather in 1924. He immediately replanted it with new vines, but the Depression of the 1930s drove wine prices down, and my family planted a lot of peach trees instead. It wasn't until the 1950s that wine became worth while again. The whole property in effect covers 15 acres, but half of it is inaccessible, being in little wooded gulleys and short ravines, so I can't consider planting there. I work on my own, anyway, and wouldn't be able to cope with 15 acres. I'll just have to make sure that my two sons grow up big and strong!'

M. Duclaux's wine is intended, demand permitting, to spend eighteen months in cask. Already he finds that this is a difficult discipline to adhere to and is therefore facing the problem that seems to be affecting the general style of wine at Côte-Rôtie. Wine that he has aged for eighteen months is markedly superior, with deeper fruit and a subtle extended finish, than anything bottled earlier. There must be a cautionary note in this tale.

Côte-Rôtie Vintages

1955   An excellent vintage, with harmonious wines of long-lived charm.

1956   A mediocre year, with light wines.

1957   A very good year. The wines were sturdy, yet attractive. They are now in decline.

1958   A mediocre year, with acid wines that faded early.

1959   An excellent vintage of extremely high-class wines. Tannic when young, they were nevertheless very well balanced.

Well kept bottles could give fine results until the mid-1980s.

1960 A poor vintage. Wines of little distinction.

1961 A tip-top year. The wines were stronger than 1959, and perhaps lacked a little of that vintage's striking finesse. Nevertheless, they have mellowed superbly and should be drunk in the next five years or so before they start to fade away.

1962 A good year. The wines were soft and well structured. They have shown ample charm and length of finish with ageing, but decline is beginning to set in.

1963 Poor. Frost hit the harvest, and the wines were light and unmemorable.

1964 An excellent year. Well-coloured wines that combined strength and elegance. A little fuller than 1962, this is a vintage to drink soon for maximum enjoyment.

1965 A poor vintage. Light wines.

1966 A very good year. Dark-coloured wines of good balance that took some time to round out. They are now showing very well, and should be drunk before about 1986.

1967 A very good vintage, although lighter than 1966. The wines were a little deficient in colour, but more than compensated for this with a strong heady charm. They have now started to pass their best.

1968 A mediocre year, although there were some good bottles made by the best vinifiers.

1969 A truly memorable vintage. A tiny crop gave wines that were on a parallel with 1961, with perhaps even greater finesse. Very full-bodied, these wines still display vigour and richness of flavour and are delicious to drink now before the elements of old age creep in. An outstanding La Mouline wine.

1970 A very good year of well balanced wines that were notable for their flowery bouquet. They are not long stayers, and should be drunk before around 1987.

1971 An excellent vintage. Big, strong-bodied wines with a classic Rhône 'warmth' about them. Deeply coloured, they are now very elegant and will be good to drink until the late 1980s.

1972 A disappointing, mediocre vintage. The wines were high in acidity and lacked harmony. They have now faded.

1973   A good year. A huge crop yielded some well coloured wines of good balance. They are a little light, however, and are recommended for early drinking.

1974   A mediocre vintage. An abundant crop for the second consecutive year took its toll of the vines. The wines were light and lacking in colour and degree. They should already have been drunk.

1975   Again a generally mediocre vintage with even less character than the 1974. The crop was fairly small, but the wines have proved light and undistinguished. They have lost their colour and fruit by now.

1976   A very good vintage indeed. Although a little deficient in acidity, the wines are notable for their dark colour, their powerful bouquet and their general harmony. They are developing well and will show to great effect during the 1980s.

1977   An average year with wines that, despite their even colour, were rather acidic and astringent at first. As the acidity wears off some attractive bottles are emerging for early consumption.

1978   The vintage that has most excited the growers in the last ten years. Immense, almost black colour, a closed-up bouquet of infinite promise and a powerful surge of unrealized fruit and thick tannin on the palate make this a 19 points out of 20 vintage. A hot month of September helped the ripening and growers such as Guigal have made wines that will live for at least twenty years—thirty years in the case of La Landonne.

1979   Quite a good vintage where the style of the wines is light and attractive. They can be rather pale and lack tannin, and will prove to be good for drinking until about 1985, by which time decline will have set in.

1980   Another quite good vintage. The wines are darker than the 1979s and although they are short on tannin have an uncomplicated charm about them. They will be most successfully drunk before 1990.

1981   An average year. Some of the wines are an attractive bright red, but many show the results of the rain that fell during harvesting, being pale and unimpressive. A vintage that sorts out the good and bad vinifiers; a slow, extended fermentation was necessary and some successful *cuvées* will result. A vintage that will probably need to be drunk before it is seven to ten years old.

Earlier Exceptional Vintages   1953, 1952, 1949, 1947, 1945, 1929

Leading Growers at Côte-Rôtie

Guigal, E.	69420 Ampuis
Jasmin, Georges et Robert	69420 Ampuis
Gentaz-Dervieux, Marius	69420 Ampuis
Barge, Pierre	69420 Ampuis
Duclaux, Edmond	69420 Ampuis
Barge, Gilles	69420 Ampuis
Bernard, Guy	69420 Ampuis
Bonnefond, Claude	69420 Ampuis
Brugaud, Roger et Bernard	69420 Ampuis
Chambeyron, Marius	69420 Ampuis
Champet, Emile	69420 Ampuis
Chapoutier, M.	69420 Ampuis
Chol et Fils	42410 Chavanay
Clusel, Jean	69420 Ampuis
Clusel, René	69420 Ampuis
Delas, Frères	07300 Tournon
Dervieux, Albert	69420 Ampuis
Dervieux-Thaize	69420 Ampuis
De Vallouit, L.	26240 St-Vallier
Drevon, André	69420 Ampuis
Gérard, François	69420 Ampuis
Gerin, Alfred	69420 Ampuis
Jamet, Joseph	69420 Ampuis
Minot, Henri	69420 Ampuis
Remiller, Louis	69420 Ampuis
Rostaing, René	69420 Ampuis
Vernay, Georges	69420 Condrieu
Vidal-Fleury, SA	69420 Ampuis

2

Condrieu

Condrieu sees the Rhône at its most inviting. The village was
actually called *Coin du Ruisseau*, or 'Corner of the Stream', since
the river runs past it in a gently curling arc. Bounded by lush green
undergrowth, the swirling waters here appear to possess no
malice: there is no torrent, no crash of water on rock. Such
unaccustomed calmness is reflected on the riverside. The quiet air
is disturbed only occasionally—perhaps by a chugging barge, or
by a tethered dog, or even by a game of *pétanque*, with the 'clink-
clink' of the *boules* resonating in the unhurried stillness.

Above the river there is a more melancholy picture, however.
Large tracts of the gently inclined slopes are uncultivated and
overgrown, and the dim form of old, well ordered terracing arises
out of the patches of scrub and bramble to offer a ghostly reminder
of this community's heyday, some time before the First World
War. Now the abandonment of much of this land has left solitary
little clumps of vines that are barely discernible upon the pitifully
disordered slopes. Thirty-five acres—that is all there is of the
Condrieu *Appellation*, and the contrast with the precisely
delineated and well covered hillsides of Côte-Rôtie is immediately
striking.

The Viognier grape is the only one allowed in the making of
Condrieu, and indeed the wine is often referred to as 'Viognier'. It
is a vine of obscure origin, one that sets off instant and animated
discussion between fellow *vignerons*, all anxious to flaunt their own
theory of where it came from. Some say that it was brought up
from Marseille by the Phocaean Greeks around 600 BC. This is
dubious, for it is more generally assumed that the Phocaeans
carried with them only one grape variety, the Syrah. The other
leading theory relies heavily on legend and local history books

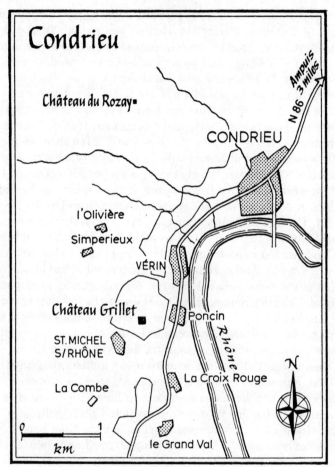

record it as hearsay. According to this, it was the Emperor Probus who imported the Viognier from Dalmatia in AD 281, after the total destruction of the Condrieu vineyards by his predecessor Vespasian. The latter seems to have been an austere figure, and it is suspected that he ordered the total clearance of the vines as retribution for a local uprising, fomented, it was claimed, by too much drinking of Condrieu's wine by the Gallic natives. Although this story is shrouded in parochial gossip, the most learned *vignerons* tend to plump for Dalmatia as the source of their vine.

Whatever the exact origin of the Viognier (and no precise

history of it has ever been put forward), it is certain that wine was made at Condrieu during the Roman occupation. In the third century the poet Martial sang the praises of the 'violet perfume of the wines of Vienne', and today's hillside terraces date back at least as long. Whether the wine was red or white, or whether it was similar to the *vinum picatum* of Côte-Rôtie, is not known.

The expulsion of the Romans from Gaul in the fifth century constituted a severe setback, and it is thought that the vineyards went uncultivated until the ninth century. Even then only very little wine was probably made, the local peasants being content to drink it all themselves. Slowly the wine's reputation grew, and by the fourteenth century it was being shipped down to the Papal Palace in Avignon from the ports of Condrieu and St-Pierre-de-Boeuf. The fact that more than one port of embarkation was used would indicate that the wine was perhaps ordered several times.

Condrieu was exported to England by 1714. P. Morton Shand relates that the Earl of Bristol then introduced it into his already well stocked home cellar. However, despite such early shipment abroad, Condrieu remains a rarity. It used to be well publicized by the late Fernand Point, one of France's most famous chefs of this century; he considered Condrieu to be one of his country's three best white wines, and his restaurant, the Pyramide at Vienne, has successfully introduced the wine to many a discerning drinker.

That represents a limited clientele, though, and one of the wine's main problems has always been how little there is to go round. The Viognier vine is now restricted principally to a 22-kilometre stretch above the western banks of the Rhône and as yet seems never to have successfully adapted itself anywhere else. It thus remains one of France's rarest vines, which Condrieu's largest grower, M. Georges Vernay, accounted for as follows: 'The Viognier is a difficult vine, full of caprice and never wholly predictable. Some years we will have a really successful flowering in June and expect a large crop as a result. The weather may remain healthy right up to the time of the *vendanges*, and yet for some unknown reason the grapes will still be shrivelled and undeveloped. You can't use fruit like that for your wine, and it's at times like that that I start thinking—well, only half-thinking— what on earth am I doing here at Condrieu making wine?'

In its defence, the Viognier vine does live a long time, from fifty to seventy years. Its best fruit is borne between the ages of 30 and

50, but never in great quantity: the average yield over the period 1962 to 1978 was approximately 17 hectolitres per hectare (690 litres per acre), just over half the total amount permitted.

The Condrieu *Appellation* extends in a very straggling way over four communities altogether: Condrieu, and to its south, Vérin, St-Michel-sur-Rhône and Limony. Apart from four vineyard owners—Vernay, Delas, Dézormeaux and Multier at the Château-du-Rozay—the plots are tiny, spread out and grow around and in the middle of lines of fruit trees that cast unwelcome shade over the vines and divert water from their roots. These smaller *viticulteurs* are delighted if they have an acre of Viognier to look after and come from families that have traditionally worked in mixed agriculture, with greatest emphasis being placed on the rearing of cherries, plums, apricots and apples. These have in the past provided a rapid and ready source of income, as the growers set their wives, nieces and nephews (the children being in the vineyard) to man the impromptu fruit stalls that they establish beside the main road in summer.

Now that Condrieu is fetching such high prices—over $11 a bottle in the grower's cellar in the early 1980s—the mixed *agriculteurs* are doing their sums and finding that it is worth their while to divert at least part of their fruit plantations back to the vine. This is good news, except that vinification techniques that are somewhat confused are combining with the effect of young vines to produce wines that are at present rather raw and acid, lacking in the finesse offered by those of the main growers.

The slopes at Condrieu tend to be less steep than those of Côte-Rôtie and, although rock-based, carry a very fine topsoil of decomposed mica. This very powdery substance, known locally as *arzelle*, is said to contribute much to the wine's flowery and refined bouquet. Such soft rock is highly vulnerable to heavy rains or extremes of temperature, however, and remounting the fallen soil is an annual task. M. André Dézormeaux of St-Michel recalled that in 1972 he had had to retrieve 100 cubic metres of soil from the bottom of his 3-acre vineyard: 'I had to carry it all up on my back, and it makes me wonder what I did wrong to deserve such a severe penance,' he remarked ruefully.

Being part of such a small *Appellation*, the growers naturally fear all adverse weather that may in any way restrict their total crop. Only 19 hectolitres of Condrieu were made in 1969 after a disastrous storm in July: even tiny Château-Grillet next door made more wine that year. It is when a quarter of an hour's hail can destroy a year's work that the *vigneron*'s heart is well and truly broken.

Almost all Condrieu is now a dry wine, but over the years it has also been made as a sweet and sometimes slightly sparkling wine. When M. Vernay first joined his father in the family vineyard in 1944 the prevailing taste was just changing from a sweet and sparkling wine to a drier version. Now he makes all his wine dry, and it is only the very small growers, such as Lucien Lagnier, Jean Pinchon and Pierre Corompt, who bother to make any of the sweet wine, which they call either *doux* or *demi-sec*. This they reserve for friends and neighbours, luckily.

Vinification of the two types of wine differs little. In both cases the grapes are pressed the moment they enter the cellar, nowadays on modern horizontal presses; after being left to settle for about a day, the juice is run into 225- or 650-litre oak casks to commence its fermentation. This process, known as the 'tumultuous fermentation' by the growers, can last for three to four weeks, depending on the atmospheric temperature.

One or two growers, notably Georges Vernay and Pierre Perret, have started to use stainless-steel tanks for the primary fermentation, but it is still very early days to judge this method. M. Vernay ferments no more than one-fifth of his wine in this way and seems loath to dispense with his oak casks, which have always invested his wine with a floweriness of flavour and fullness of bouquet at an early stage. The Perret family seek the obverse of this style in that they, too, aim for the traditional Condrieu fullness, but in a fresh, almost Loire Valley manner. Their wine possesses exuberant fruit backed by a young acidity that makes it a must for drinking in its first year.

If the malolactic fermentation follows on close behind the primary and is out of the way by early in the new year, then the growers are well satisfied and start to bottle part of the wine in the spring. The remainder of the wine is released for sale towards the end of the summer. The only exception to this is Georges Vernay's special *cuvée*, the Coteaux de Vernon, which is left an extra year in cask. Such ageing diminishes the racy fruit shown by young Viognier and imparts an added richness that makes this wine similar to a Château-Grillet. The quantities of Coteaux de Vernon are very limited, however, and even in the abundant year of 1980 M. Vernay made only four *pièces*, or about 1,300 bottles.

Vinification of the sweet wine diverges, in that its fermentation is prematurely halted while it still contains definite quantities of unfermented sugar. To do this, the *vigneron* pumps his fermenting wine into barrels that have had sulphur sticks burned in them beforehand. The sulphur fumes serve to kill all remaining yeast particles that are capable of reactivating fermentation. The wine is thus left with a natural sweetness.

The dry wine is superior by far, however. It possesses a wonderfully fine combination of powerful fullness and flowerlike delicacy. When young, the wine is a firm yellow, often with a hint of pale gold in it, and its intrinsic richness is but partly developed, manifesting itself more as a sort of spicy earthiness. The oft-quoted *goût de terroir* is perhaps the nearest French description: the wine has a basic profundity that underlies all the superficial fruit and aromas.

Condrieu's main difference in style from Château-Grillet is probably this overt and often remarkable fullness of fruit, which makes it a more immediately striking wine. Young Condrieu displays a compelling fruitiness on its bouquet, giving the impression of slightly underripe pears or of eating the fruit near the pear skin. It is singular, and therein lies much of its charm for the drinker. As the years advance, the golds become more prominent in the wine's *robe*, and the early soaring fruit settles down into a complexity of rounded flavours, among which the sensations of honey and apricots are sometimes mentioned by the growers. Condrieu is not a real staying wine, though, and after about eight to ten years its fruitiness and bouquet naturally start to fade.

'I myself like to drink my wine within two or three years,' says M. Georges Vernay, basing his opinion on the experience of more than forty years' wine-making. M. Vernay is a strong-voiced, big, ruddy man of around 55, who explains matters in deep stentorian tones while his bushy eyebrows zoom up and down like working pistons when he comes to the more contentious points. He has been working the vines since he was 15 and has large hands and broad shoulders to prove it. He is now the major vineyard owner at Condrieu, with 15 acres, and has fought hard to prevent the *Appellation* from slipping into obscurity by reclaiming abandoned terraces. M. Vernay learnt his art first-hand from his father and it is a sign of the times that his own son has instead acquired much of his skill at the Wine School of Beaune: few of M. Vernay's generation ever benefited from such opportunities.

As President of the *Syndicat du Vin*, M. Vernay is closely involved with Condrieu's well-being and future. He has already seen too much potential wine land go towards the building of weekend homes for residents of Lyon and is worried at the temptingly high prices offered to fellow *vignerons* to make them sell their land for development.

'It's impossible to use machinery in the vineyards,' said M. Vernay, 'which really makes it a young man's profession here. What I would like to see created is something like a Protected Wine Zone, given over to viticulture and nothing else. In this way the Wine Syndicate would rent vineyards from older growers and pay them extra according to the size of the crop, the state of the market and so on. It's been a little more encouraging lately to see that people like the *négociant* house of Delas have undertaken to increase their property under vine, so that their 5-acre Clos Bouché at Vérin is now the second largest holding here. What you have to remember, though, is just how much time (and, obviously, money) it takes to plant vines on these hillsides. For the small grower who works on his own it can mean employing someone to help, but the yield from the vines can be so small as to make this completely uneconomic. *Voilà notre problème!*'

M. Vernay dominates the *Appellation*, since the total size of his properties at Condrieu, Côte-Rôtie and St-Joseph is sufficient to justify his extending his cellars and buying modern equipment to make his wine. He therefore acts as something of a guru for those *viticulteurs* with tiny vineyards, giving advice, letting them use his Vaslin press and so on. Up to the late 1970s he also vinified all the wine from one larger estate, the Château-du-Rozay, owned by M. Paul Multier.

M. Multier is one of those *vignerons* who stand out by their zany enthusiasm for what they are doing. He strides around the *château* and its cellar, clad in a cloth cap and wearing large green wellington boots that give every impression of wanting to gobble up his small frame. Information tumbles out of him, be it on Rozay itself, on the wine or on Lyon and its traditions. Twinkling-eyed, he affirmed that in 1978 he had decided to strike out on his

M. Paul Multier

own, having finished his tutelage with M. Vernay, and that he was now increasing the size of his vineyard. This is mostly on the Coteau de Chéry, just south of Condrieu, and is bounded by an attractive low stone wall that ends in a little tool hut, a picture that is reminiscent of some of the famous *clos* in Burgundy.

M. Multier's family have been at Rozay since 1898. The *château* stands at about 300 metres at the start of the plateau right above Condrieu, and is painted pink, with three pointed turrets peeping out from it. One assumes that because it belongs to M. Multier, there is a good reason for there being three not four turrets, but he swiftly swoops away from the architecture and on to the family history: 'My family was Lyonnais and used Rozay as a secondary residence. My grandparents manufactured braided uniforms and gilded vestments for the military and the Church, and it wasn't until the 1940s that they started to concentrate on replanting the vineyard, which had become pretty abandoned. The vines on Chéry date from that time and, being 40 years old, are now giving excellent grapes.'

The concentrated juice obtained from these vines makes M. Multier's wine potentially the most impressive in the *Appellation*. It has an excitingly flowery bouquet, great depth and balanced richness and is splendid to drink between 2 and 4 years old. In early 1982 M. Multier drank a bottle of 1951 Condrieu that had lain unobserved in his cellar and pronounced it as being in correct shape; the commencement of oxidization had not yet overrun it. 'I would never set out to keep my wine that long,' he added, 'and would really counsel drinking it before it is about 6 years old.'

M. Multier is fortunate that his son Jean-Yves is interested in continuing Rozay's wine tradition and that the size of the vineyard can justify his full-time attention. Not as lucky was M. Pierre Dumazet, whose father Marc made a very good wine from just two-thirds of an acre on the most precipitous hillside imaginable near Limony. M. Dumazet senior was an inspiration to the young, for in his seventies he would still look after the vineyard, make the wine and sell it—all by himself. The Dumazets have been making wine at Limony for over 100 years, but the vineyard was not large enough to support Pierre full-time. He therefore left to work in Lyon, and when his father died in 1978 he was only lightly versed in the art of wine-making. His first vintages have been successful, however, and he is making a style of wine that should be drunk within three years of its harvest.

The Dumazets used to grow fruit as well as vines, and Pierre's grandfather would make spectacular journeys all the way to London in his 1930 truck to sell the fruit at the Covent Garden market. Now Pierre is a *vigneron* only at weekends, and the fruit trees have been sold off.

The family still like to hold a big reunion at the time of the *vendanges*, with all the grandchildren eagerly helping, and hindering, the collection of the grapes. Marc Dumazet always picked his grapes early in the morning, before the sun rose high, and Pierre has maintained this system. One of the dangers of harvesting high up on the slopes under a hot sun is that the grapes are liable to start slowly fermenting as they lie crammed together in their large baskets. When M. Dumazet's grapes go into the press, they are cold to the touch.

Near Château-Grillet at St-Michel-sur-Rhône lives M. André Dézormeaux, who has changed not only his style of wine but also his philosophy towards his vineyards since the early 1970s. In those days M. Dézormeaux was Condrieu's sweet-wine producer, and his vines would grow mixed up with peach trees, which meant that they always gave a tiny yield; in years such as the abundant 1973 M. Dézormeaux produced a mere 891 litres of wine. M. Vernay, whose vineyard was then four times the size, came up with over twelve times as much wine.

M. Dézormeaux seems to have realized now that his vineyards need better exposure and has taken out the offending peach trees. 'The vines are now giving much better grapes without those umbrellas over them,' he admits with a wry smile. A lean man with grey, short-cropped hair, he appears almost spectral when dressed in his blue working clothes. He comes from an old wine-producing family and has noticed how sharply tastes in wine have changed in recent years: 'Until 1970 I used to make nothing but a sweet wine, but demand for it fell off, and now the wine that I bottle is all dry.' This is undoubtedly an improvement, for the overriding sugariness of the sweet wine would overwhelm the Viognier's delicate scent and flavour.

Condrieu Vintages

Condrieu is not essentially a wine that repays long keeping. The *vignerons* believe it best drunk around 2 to 4 years old and would rarely advise drinking it at more than 7 years old. That is undoubtedly the *goût français*, and perhaps it would be fairer to say that outstanding vintages can live for ten to twelve years. Recent vintages have been as follows:

1959 Very good.
1960 Poor.
1961 Very good. Rich, attractive wines that with age developed tremendous bouquet.
1962 Mediocre.
1963 Mediocre.
1964 Excellent. Very complete wines.
1965 Mediocre.
1966 Very good. Full-bodied wines.
1967 Very good.
1968 Mediocre. Light, often acidic wines.
1969 Very good, although the tiny crop meant that few people ever saw the wine.
1970 Very good. Strongly perfumed wines that were rich and well balanced.
1971 Excellent. The wines were full and possessed a good colour and alcohol content. A vintage that has aged well, but one that should be drunk without delay.

1972 Good, although a few of the wines were disappointingly acidic.

1973 Good. A large crop, but one that produced wines of pleasant balance.

1974 Very good. Well balanced, agreeably perfumed wines.

1975 Very good. The wines came round to achieve a good balance after a difficult vinification when the malolactic fermentation was very slow to start. They should be drunk by around 1984.

1976 Good to very good. There was a lack of rain during the summer which left the wines short on acidity. They have developed quite rapidly, and *cuvées* such as Vernay's Coteaux de Vernon are now showing well.

1977 A light year, with the wines tending to be acidic. They should be drunk without delay.

1978 Excellent, very richly flavoured wines with a bouquet that has blossomed in fine style. They are so well structured that they will live as long as any Viognier vintage can reasonably hope—perhaps twelve years.

1979 Although rather a pale yellow, the wines have shrugged off their early acidity and are now showing a balanced richness and a pleasing long finish. A vintage that merits 'good', but which should be drunk for best results before 1984.

1980 A reasonable vintage. The quality was uneven from one grower to the next, as it seems to have been difficult to achieve a satisfactory balance between the fruit and acidity. The wines were only lightly scented, and will be best drunk within four or five years.

1981 A very good vintage, with plenty of robust elements to it. The wines are strongly perfumed, and have a high degree of alcohol and depth of flavour that make them certain to develop well over the next five years. They will live longer, however—perhaps until around 1990.

Earlier Exceptional Vintages   1949, 1947, 1929

Leading Growers at Condrieu

Multier, Paul
    Château-du-Rozay   69420 Condrieu

Vernay, Georges	69420 Condrieu
Dumazet, Pierre	07340 Limony
Cuilleron, Antoine	42410 Chavanay
Corompt, Pierre	69420 Condrieu
David, Emile	42410 Vérin
Delas Frères	07300 Tournon
Dézormeaux, André	42410 St-Michel-sur-Rhône
Jurie-des Camiers, Robert	69230 St-Genis-Laval
Lagnier, Georges	42410 Chavanay
Perret, Pierre	42410 Chavanay
Pinchon, Jean	69420 Condrieu

3

Château-Grillet

Château-Grillet has the distinction of being France's smallest single *Appellation*. From just under 7·5 acres of vines comes a white wine of long-commended eminence. The French gastronome Curnonsky, writing in *Lyon et le Lyonnais gastronomique* in the 1920s, was moved to rank Château-Grillet as one of France's three best white wines. Curnonsky possessed a sublime confidence in all things French, as he demonstrated when writing:

> But of all the white wines made from the Viognier around Condrieu, the palm must go to a very great, exceptional, marvellous and suave white wine: the most rare Château-Grillet, a golden and flamboyant wine cultivated in a vineyard of less than 5 acres, a wine above commercialization, just about untraceable and jealously guarded by its one owner ... This wine is quite simply the third (and rarest) of the five best white wines of France (and therefore the world). The wine of Château-Grillet is lively, violent, changeable like a pretty woman, with a flavour of the flowers of vines and almonds, with a stunning bouquet of wild flowers and violets, and reaching up to 15° alcohol. In short, a *très grand seigneur!*

Château-Grillet stands below the village of St-Michel-sur-Rhône, a little to the south of Condrieu. Backed against a sheltered hillside, it carries a curious mixture of architectural styles. The *château* records date back to the reign of Louis XIII (1610–43) and indicate that it was then a small lodge or dower house. In subsequent years successive owners built on as the fancy took them, their main criterion seemingly being size rather than charm.

The façade dates from the Renaissance, while in the cellar below there is a blocked-in window that the owner, M. Neyret-Gachet, believes to be even older. In places the outer walls suddenly become as much as a metre thick, and judging by such defences it is clear that possession of the property was hotly contested until 1820, when the Neyret-Gachet family moved in.

Thereafter the wine became well-known in select circles, particularly outside France. In the 1830s Château-Grillet was sent on several occasions to both Moscow and Odessa, the price of 4 francs a bottle being charged to the Russians, while the home French price was only 3 francs a bottle. And in 1829 the Court of St James's ordered two cases of seventy-two bottles each for King George IV; James Christie, the Lord Steward, wrote the following letter to the Wine House of Faure in St-Péray to secure the order:

> Gentlemen, I beg you will have the kindness to forward immediately the undermentioned wine for the use of His Majesty the King of England with directions to your agent at Bordeaux to ship it by the very first vessel for this Port, the Bill of Lading to be enclosed to me; the Invoice I request you will send to me and for the amount you may draw a Bill at thirty days Sight on the Lord Steward of His Majesty's Household, St. James's Palace. In selecting this wine I trust you will be careful that it is of the very first vintage and such as may be fit for immediate use.[1]

Certainly, two things have changed little in over 150 years: the method of arranging for an importation of wine and the thirst of people for Château-Grillet—hence the declaration that the wine was wanted 'for immediate use'. Who would blame King George for that?

Only 100 metres away from the *château* is the site of an ancient Roman community, traces of which were discovered at the turn of the century. One can only imagine that the Romans enjoyed a better view than that which now extends before the château, for across the river at St-Clair-du-Rhône is a large chemical plant built in 1971. Streams of smoke drift slowly south, aided by the light north wind. Below the *château* trains rumble past at regular intervals. From the shaded terrace of the old house all this makes an incongruous scene.

[1] R. Bailly, *Histoire de la Vigne et des Grands Vins des Côtes du Rhône* (Avignon: Imp. F. Orta, 1978).

As at Condrieu, the Viognier is the only grape permitted, and the irregular rows of vines crouch up above and all around the *château* in the form of an amphitheatre. It is a conveniently exposed amphitheatre, too, for the vines, facing full south, benefit from great sunshine and warmth and are perfectly protected from the *bise* wind by their encircling hillside, which mounts steeply to a height of 240 metres.

The vines are all tied in the Guyot way, and grow on surprisingly light and powdery soil that makes movement on the hillside a slippery operation. In bright sunshine tiny particles can be seen glinting here and there; these are little pieces of decomposed mica, also found in the Condrieu vineyards.

Since the 1960s M. Neyret-Gachet has gradually increased the size of his vineyard by restoring a series of little terraces adjoining the property; he does not like to talk about such unseemly subjects as expansion and pushing for a higher production, but the figures speak for themselves. The vineyard has been enlarged from 4·2 acres in 1971, to 5·7 acres in 1977, to 7·4 acres in 1982. The wine made from it, taken as an average for five-year periods, has risen from 4,455 litres per annum for 1966–70, to 5,663 litres for 1971–5, to 7,840 litres for 1976–80 (and the last figure is severely depressed by the tiny crop of only 2,900 litres for 1978, the smallest since the 2,600-litre harvest of 1969). There is no point in fantasizing over Château-Grillet—it is a down-to-earth commercial enterprise.

Harvesting does not take long in this minuscule vineyard. Three days in early October are sufficient to clear the rugged terraces of their fruit. A team of two dozen cutters and carriers demonstrate laudable agility in bringing down the harvest from the sometimes highly restricted ledges. There is only one narrow and awkward approach stairway from the vines to the cellars, and this presents one final challenge to the flagging *porteurs*.

Inside the small *cave*, the equipment is modern. M. Neyret-Gachet has taken deliberate steps to update his utensils to ensure that his wine is scrupulously cared for. A pneumatic press has replaced the *château*'s 1892 vertical wooden version, and well maintained enamel-lined vats now stand where once there were old concrete *cuves*. The basis of the vinification has not changed, however, and the pressed juice still remains with its lees until midwinter.

At that point the wine is racked into oak barrels, where it stays for about eighteen months, an unusually long time for a white Côtes du Rhône. Meanwhile, the warmth of spring encourages the development of the malolactic fermentation, and the following winter cold acts to clarify the wine into near whiteness. After bottling, the wine is left for several months before being released for sale. It should then be in a near-perfect state for drinking.

On a more mundane level than Curnonsky, it is true to say that one of Château-Grillet's main charms is its entrancing finesse. Setting aside the aura of its high price, its rarity and its simple, classical presentation, it is always evident that this is indeed a high-class white wine, one that seems curiously off-course when found tucked away south of Lyon. It is a dry wine but carries with it a rich fullness and undoubted depth of flavour, engendered in part by the prolonged ageing in wood. A fresh light gold in colour, it has a bouquet of varied aromas, some of which are occasionally described as apricot, truffle and honey. With age Château-Grillet becomes dark gold and its flavours blend into a lengthy amber-type smoothness that helps to accentuate its prolonged aftertaste.

Château-Grillet is now the only Côtes du Rhône *Appellation* to use distinguished dark yellow and brown Rhine bottles of 70-centilitre content (most wine is sold in 75-centilitre bottles). In days gone by the Viognier growers of Condrieu also used flute-shaped bottles, which were specially blown for them at a glass factory in St-Etienne. The custom in Condrieu may have died out, but Château-Grillet continues with its long-established domaine bottling tradition, started in 1830 by the Neyret-Gachet family. Before this date the wine had always left the property in cask.

Today M. André Neyret-Gachet is responsible for the running of the vineyard. He makes an impressive figure, standing with his walking stick, and would be many people's idea of the distinguished Gallic gentleman with his strong features and confident, almost stern pose. He is a rarity in the Côtes du Rhône, a gentleman farmer, since his main work is in business in Lyon, where he lives during the week. He says: 'I am of course very attached to Château-Grillet, but it is not a commercial enterprise in its own right. I would be very hard pressed to live solely off the proceeds of the vineyard, since the costs of its upkeep are very high. Take my three full-time employees, for instance: they all receive the same wage as the chemical workers across the river. I wouldn't be able to keep them if I paid them less.'

65

M. Neyret-Gachet considers that one of the outstanding joys of his wine is its ability to go well with almost any dish, be it meat, fish or vegetable. His preference is also to drink the wine young, generally before it is 5 years old, never after its eighth birthday.

At its best, Château-Grillet can be a marginally superior form of Condrieu, possessed of a delicate fineness not always apparent in the latter. In recent years, however, there appears to have been a very slight lowering of standards in Château-Grillet, as the aim seems to have been to make as much wine as possible at the highest possible price. Wine drinkers are no longer prepared to pay exorbitant prices for wines of good but not startling talent.

Among recent vintages 1981 and 1978 have been very good indeed, while 1979 produced a very attractive, elegant wine which was just a bit lighter. Only the most favoured can afford to pick and choose their year, however. In 1978 no more than 4,140 bottles of Château-Grillet were made, and in the largest vintage ever, that of 1980, the total was only just over 16,500 bottles. For this reason a visit to this unique *château*, giving advance notice, is a virtual obligation for any wine enthusiast who happens to be passing down the Rhône Valley.

Château-Grillet Vintages

1965   A medium vintage that has now started to dry out and pass its best. When young, the wine was light and quite fruity.

1966   A very good year. A richly scented wine of great style and finish. Inevitably it has started to decline, although well kept bottles could still prove to be interesting.

1967   A sound, heavy wine that possessed more body than finesse. It is now tasting old.

1968   A light-coloured year that needed time to develop its full bouquet. The wine became very agreeably fruity, but is now showing great age.

1969   An excellent year, one that blended remarkable fruitiness with sound body. The wine has great length of finish, but is now more than fully mature. Well conserved bottles could give delicious surprises.

1970   A good year, with the wine possessing much of the fruitiness of the 1969s. A little lacking in body and style, this vintage is now becoming *passé*.

1971 A light, fairly refined wine that took time to develop its full aromas. It should now be drunk up.

1972 Similar to 1969 in that a small vintage of some 3,680 bottles produced an excellent, highly concentrated wine. It has developed very well, but should be drunk soon.

1973 An extremely large crop resulted in a fine, rather light wine. It is now past its best.

1974 Another large crop, with nearly 11,500 bottles made. Despite such a large yield, the wine bore a good combination of fruit and body. It has started to wane, however.

1975 A small crop whose wine was unexceptional. Only lightly scented, it is thin on the palate and has begun to slip away.

1976 A wine of good bouquet, full of intense aromas that have developed well. It possesses good balance and now tastes very well, although it can be kept for a few years more.

1977 A limited crop gave a light but attractive wine. It has evolved rapidly, and is extremely good for drinking now. It can be kept for another two or three years.

1978 A tiny crop, but a successful wine. It possesses ample flavours and length of finish, and is still developing. It is obviously very difficult to encounter, but seize a bottle if you see one! It could live until the late 1980s.

1979 An even yellow colour, this wine displays richness but lacks a little verve through the absence of abundant fruit and freshness. It is coming along well, however, and will be an excellent partner for refined fish dishes for two or three years more.

1980 The largest harvest ever, amounting to 116 hectolitres. The wine was somewhat hard and slightly lacking in refined elegance. It will develop quickly and should not live much beyond the end of the decade.

1981 A very pleasing wine notable for its general warmth of flavour and classic Viognier bouquet. It will be very good indeed and shows signs of developing its balance and flavours very well by around 1986.

Grower at Château-Grillet

Neyret-Gachet
   Château-Grillet   42410 Vérin

4

Hermitage

The Hermitage hillside is a truly spectacular home for a vineyard. Curved to follow the course of the Rhône, the roughly hewn hill mounts forcefully towards the skyline. Its vines follow an irregular pattern, seeming to zig-zag across the hill's contours until reaching their summit near the tiny chapel of St Christopher.

In summer the hillside, resplendent in its green mantle, loses its customary severity. In winter, the dour granite colours and the long lines of oddly contorted vine plants lend an air of lunar austerity. It is then hard to imagine that here is the home of such a magnificently rich wine.

In the lee of the hill, wedged between it and the fast-flowing Rhône, is Tain-l'Hermitage, the uncrowned capital of the Rhône wine industry. A small, busy town, Tain shares with Tournon opposite the privilege of housing many of the Valley's larger *négociant* companies, which have traditions that date back to the early nineteenth century. It is a noisy place, lacking in charm, but this is more than compensated for by the glorious wine maturing slowly underneath its streets. As the local people are apt to say, there is only one reason to go to Tain, but that's a good one!

Tain went by the name of Tegna in Roman times, when it is known definitely to have been a wine-producing community. In their works, the *Natural History* and the *Epigrams*, both Pliny and Martial mentioned the wine of Tegna, which would suggest that it enjoyed a certain fame. Indeed, Hermitage is thought by some regional historians to be the oldest vineyard in the Rhône Valley and, therefore, in the whole of France. They are joined by local growers in believing that the famous hillside was first planted with vines around 600 BC—Syrah vines, that had come up the river from Marseille with the first band of invading Phocaean Greeks.

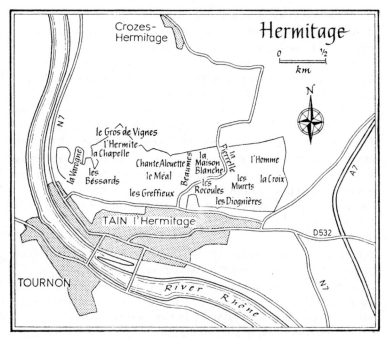

The accuracy of this view is difficult to assess, for the evidence (see Introduction) is obviously somewhat circumstantial: perhaps it is safer to say that a later band of Phocaean Greeks was responsible for bringing the vine to Hermitage—somewhere around 500 BC.

Tain still displays a relic from its Roman days—an ancient altar called a taurobole that was used for the sacrifice and offering of bulls to the god Mithras. It dates from about AD 180 and is the town's most jealously guarded possession, as the following story illustrates.

In 1724 a British traveller arrived in Tain expressly to buy the altar, claiming that its sale to England would help promote the *entente* that was noticeably lacking between the two countries. The town officials refused his request out of hand, however, and to make absolutely sure, took advantage of a dark night to carry off the taurobole and hide it in the cellars of the Town Hall. The next day the British visitor was informed by grief-stricken, angered officials that the taurobole had been scandalously stolen. The poor man took pains to console them and, as some sort of remedy,

69

bought a small barrel of their wine: to have kept the taurobole and to have exported some of their wine in the process proved an eminently satisfactory outcome for the locals!

Meanwhile varying legends have grown up over the years as to how the vine came to arrive at Tain and how the name, which used to be written 'Ermitage', originated. These legends tend to vie with one another in romanticism but are none the less worth recounting. One is the work of the modern Irish writer James Joyce, who claimed that it was St Patrick who planted the first vines on the slopes of Hermitage, taking a quick break there on his way to convert Ireland. This is beautiful storytelling and a fine piece of national trumpeting from a people known for their endearing art of exaggeration; there is absolutely no evidence to uphold Joyce's theory. In fact, one of the few written references to this tale does indeed come from another Irishman, Maurice Healy, in his *Stay Me with Flagons* (1940). Healy wrote, with broad Irish charm, as follows: 'Hermitage has an Irish link; there is a Clos Saint-Patrice there, which is supposed to be the site of a resting place of St Patrick on his way to Ireland . . . it is producing a red wine that would almost convert Hitler to Christianity.'

The Irish tale must in all honesty take second place to the much better-known, oft-quoted legend that concerns the holy knight Gaspard de Stérimberg. This gentleman's name now appears on the labels of the house of Jaboulet's white Hermitage. Returning wounded in 1224 from a crusade against the Albigensian heretics, Stérimberg was making his way home when he came upon the Hermitage hillside: he climbed it, found it quite enchanting and decided to stay—but, of course, had no roof over his head. As befits a knight, he dutifully applied to the then Queen of France, Blanche of Castille, for permission to build a retreat. This was granted, and he is said to have lived there for thirty years until his death. His chapel still stands in solitary splendour near the top of the Hermitage hill.

A final local legend, attributed to Brother Benedict—of whom nothing else is known—dates from the time of the Roman persecution of the Christians, when a hunted priest is said to have taken refuge on the Hermitage hill: his basic source of nourishment, bread and cheese, was brought by the wild animals all around him. Nothing could be found to drink, however, and the holy man was on the point of death when the timely intervention of the good Lord saved him. As is well-known, all *vignerons* eventually find their way into Paradise, and so there suddenly appeared a band of angelic growers ready with fruit-bearing vines which made wine overnight. The priest drank and was saved.

Between Roman times and the seventeenth century Hermitage surprisingly disappears from the history books, but in 1642 it acquired a royal connection that eventually spanned three centuries. In that year King Louis XIII was touring the Rhône Valley, which at Tain reaches one of its narrowest points. The king's travelling companions advised him to descend from his carriage and be carried over the most dangerous part of the river, a large protruding rock. Of course, Louis's itineraries always allowed for impromptu glasses of wine, so when a subject offered him some of the local wine, he was quite happy to accept it and appreciate it at his leisure. The rock where he was forced to descend is known as the King's Table, for it was there that Louis decided that in future he would serve the wine at the Court of France—a decision that did much to advance the fame of Hermitage.

The grandson of a former French President records that the Court of Russia was equally drawn to the wine. When his grandfather, M. Emile Loubet, visited Czar Nicholas in 1903, he was served red and white Hermitage at the imperial banquet. M. Loubet took this as a friendly sign of recognition that he came from Hermitage's Drôme *département*, but the Czar said, no, the wines of Hermitage had in fact been regular Romanov favourites since the time that Nicolas Boileau wrote his satire *Le Repas ridicule* in 1663. True to form, the cynic Boileau had commented not on the wine's worth but on its apparent falsification:

> *Un laquais effronté m'apporte un rouge bord*
> *D'un auvergnat fumeux, qui, mêlé de lignage,*
> *Se vendait, chez Crénet, pour vin de l'Hermitage.*[1]

Since Boileau's time, Hermitage has been a source of inspiration to a wide variety of writers. The Frenchman Jean-François Marmontel stopped in Tain in 1755 to buy half a dozen bottles of the white wine; they cost him only 50 sous each, but he was quite

---

[1] A cheeky flunkey brings me my red wine brimful
With a heady Auvergnat, which, mixed with dregs,
Was cold a Crénet's as wine from the Hermitage.

entranced by their 'nectar bouquet' (*Memoires d'un père*). The English novelist Henry Fielding (1707–54) obviously had a soft spot for the wine, for it crept into several of his works, *Tom Jones* included; while the Scottish author Walter Scott held no doubts about Hermitage's ability to charm: in *Charles the Bold* (1831), he wrote: 'I shall have a snack with you, and I shall satisfy you with a flask of old Ermitage.' Shortly afterwards, the famous French novelist Alexandre Dumas recorded his impressions of Hermitage. In 1834 he went on a trip around the Midi region of France with his friend Jadin and arrived one night at Tain-l'Hermitage.

> The next morning [he wrote] I was up first and went for a walk. On returning to the hotel, I took Jadin to the window and invited him to salute the hill that dominated the town. Jadin hailed it wholeheartedly, but when I told him that it was the hill of Hermitage, he immediately repeated his action quite of his own accord; . . . we both considered Hermitage to be one of the best wines of France.

Dumas's words are still largely true, but Hermitage has known its ups and downs since his day. During the nineteenth century, and up to phylloxera, the wine was used extensively as a strengthener for the finer wines of Bordeaux. H. Warner Allen, in his *History of Wine* (1961), quotes from *The Letter Books* of Nathaniel Johnston, written between 1799 and 1809, to his partner Guestier in Bordeaux. Johnston wrote thus of the 1803 vintage:

> I was averse to using Roussillon on our best wines, unless it be a gallon or two, and that if you could get a sufficient quantity of good Hermitage to put a couple of Cans of it, it would be better. The Lafitte 1795, which was made up with Hermitage was the best liked wine of any of that year.

Hermitage undoubtedly invested all the best *châteaux* with superior staying powers, and E. Penning-Rowsell, in his *Wines of Bordeaux* (1969), mentioned a Château-Ausone 1880 he had drunk, 'without much hope', in 1967:

> It was surprisingly good. The colour, though pale, was much truer than the previous bottle (of Ausone 1880), the nose was fruity, and the body had a fullness that did actually suggest a

St-Emilion. It had been *château*-bottled, and perhaps was *hermitagé*.

That year was certainly quite late for Hermitage still to be boosting the great *châteaux*, for the practice seems to have reached its peak around the 1860s when, according to M. Paul Gauthier of Tain-l'Hermitage, labels like Margaux would proclaim with some pride that they were 'Château-Margaux-Hermitage'.

After a series of bleak, profitless years during the early part of this century, Hermitage has inched its way back to popularity and renown, but it will never be very widely known because of its restricted production. The vineyards cover only 303 acres, and although their gradients are a little less steep than Côte-Rôtie's, they still require the same manual cultivation. Work on them must run from dawn to dusk, and under the early morning sunshine little bands of *vignoble* workers weave their way slowly up the hillside, where they spend the rest of the day. These specialized vineyard workers often belong to the large *négociant* companies like Chapoutier and Jaboulet, and traditionally pass down their expertise from father to son.

The soil that they must work on is granitic and, in places, quite unyielding. The rock base is sprinkled with a fine layer of decomposed flint and chalk, which after heavy rain escapes the bonds of the retaining walls and slides steadily down the hillside; carrying it back and tightly repacking the terrace walls is therefore a difficult but regular task.

The unusual fact that the Hermitage hill, on the east bank of the Rhône, should be granite is explained by a geological transformation which took place many thousands of years ago. Then the Rhône flowed past the other, more easterly, side of the hillside; Hermitage was consequently a part of the granitic Massif Central mountain range which lies behind Tournon. At some indeterminate date the river changed its course and burrowed out today's beautiful valley.

Hermitage red wine is made principally from the Syrah grape, although because most vineyards have been planted—normally with Syrah as well as Marsanne—in a rather unplanned way over the years, a maximum of 15 per cent white grapes are permitted to enter the fermenting vats with the Syrah. This is a decree designed to make the *vigneron*'s life easier—so that he can harvest a whole vineyard instead of having to return later to one or two *souches* of white grape vines—but as the Marsanne has quite a high glycerine content, it is thought that its presence can give the red wine a little extra richness and profundity. Apparently, few growers ever use much more than 5 per cent Marsanne in their red Hermitage, although they can be tempted to add more in years when the Syrah crop is small.

The exposed Hermitage hill is an ideal home for the Syrah, since sun and wind are abundant, while the granite acts as a useful heat retainer. Temperatures on the top of the hill on a sunny summer's day are surprisingly high, with so many terraced walls all around absorbing and radiating the sun's heat. It is similar down at the foot of the vineyards, for there a low stone wall provides shelter as it runs along the curve of the hillside and is broken only every 45 metres or so by iron gates that indicate the entrance to a new *clos*.

A meteorological study conducted at the end of the last century revealed an average temperature in the vineyards of 13·9 °C, a figure more normally associated with Mediterranean France. Under such conditions the Syrah produces well and consistently, and its regularity contrasts somewhat with its performance at Côte-Rôtie, where it is even pruned differently. At Hermitage the simple Gobelet method is employed; the shoots are trained upwards and outwards and are tied by straw to high wooden sticks in order to prevent damage from the strong *mistral* wind.

A little over a quarter of all the wine is white, and this is made from two grapes, the Marsanne and the Roussanne, which are generally planted across the hillside in small patches of clay-topped ground. The Marsanne is the more favoured, as it is considerably less prone to disease and therefore cheaper to look after. Hermitage is now one of the few places in the northern Rhône where the Roussanne is planted in any quantity, and it is likely to go on gradually disappearing from the region in the future.

Nowadays, the red and white wines are seldom sold with a specific vineyard name mentioned on the bottle. Most growers own plots dotted about the Hermitage hill and attempt to make one definable style of wine, whose content differs only according to when it has been bottled. The wine from any one harvest is bottled in two or three runs.

Consequently, the wines from the scattered vineyards are

blended together, but it is interesting to note just how diverse their characters are beforehand. In his 1866 edition of *Topographie de tous les vignobles connus*, A. Jullien listed three outstanding vineyards: Les Béssards, at the westernmost part of the hill, which produces a deep-coloured, sturdy wine; Le Méal, next to it, with very small stones, chalky soil and a fine, perfumed wine; Les Greffieux, below Le Méal, the producer of generous, supple wine. The ideal bottle of Hermitage is traditionally said to be a combination of these three growths, although the presence of wine from the Beaumes vineyard is almost obligatory, so well scented and full of fruit and finesse is it. Therein lies one of the great annual tasks facing the conscientious grower—to select in which proportion to blend his wines from different vineyards, since no harvest ever precisely resembles another.

The best-known red wine at Hermitage is the House of Jaboulet's La Chapelle, which is a registered title that they use for their most select wine. There is a vineyard called La Chapelle, near the top of the slopes, but it is the tiny chapel rather than the whole vineyard that belongs to Jaboulet. The most famous wine sold under its grower's name alone is undoubtedly that of M. Gérard Chave, whose red and white are both superb.

The most celebrated white wine growths are two that run across the upper half of the hillside—the pleasantly named Chante-Alouette and Les Murets—and Les Rocoules, whose wine invariably reveals the classic nuttiness or peach stone scent given by white Hermitage. Wine from Les Murets tends to be a little finer, although equally well balanced, while Chante Alouette is the most robust of the three.

From such innocuous-sounding vineyards comes the mighty wine of Hermitage, a wine that displays abundant strength and massive depth of flavour, be it red or white. Hermitage red is still one of the world's longest living wines, which in a fine vintage such as 1978 will last for a good forty years. When young, it is robust, rich in different flavours, alcohol and tannin. Its colour is a brilliant purple, with traces of jet black in it, while the bouquet is closed, difficult to draw out; the main sensation is that of underripe blackcurrants. Such a wine excites simply through the inordinate promise that all the diverse elements and aromas display, and for anyone seeking the best, most classic example of young Syrah to be found anywhere, he can do no worse than to

75

seek out a bottle of Chave or Sorrel, for these are wines in the grand old manner.

With all but the lightest vintages—years like 1975 and 1977—it is a crime even to consider touching a bottle of red Hermitage before its fifth birthday. The wine is uncomfortably backward and tannic on the palate and, as is characteristic of the Syrah grape, needs ample time to develop and unfold all its potential. With age, the wine acquires an uncommon balance and finesse, and its softness on the palate, and the long raspberry-like aftertaste, leave the drinker with the most vivid realization of the wine's all-round powers. Great Hermitage about 20 years old, when it is from the best vintages and the best makers, stands alongside the best wines of Bordeaux, or of anywhere on earth for that matter: try the La Chapelle 1961 and see.

One of the main reasons why Hermitage lives for so long is that it is still usually vinified by traditional methods. Few attempts are made to over-hasten the early development of the wine, and most of the cellar equipment remains old and wooden: concrete and covered metal fermenting vats are even less known at Hermitage than at Côte-Rôtie, for instance.

Harvest time is always one of excitement at Tain, for that is what the town lives for. Teams of pickers, between fifteen and thirty strong, are dispatched up the hillside, and their progress can be monitored from across the river in Tournon, so prominent is the Hermitage hillside and so colourful the harvesters' clothing. As in most of the northern Rhône vineyards, the work is exacting; heavy wooden containers are often used to bring the grapes to tracks running alongside the vineyards, where donkeys and carts are waiting to take them down to the cellars in the town.

After a light treading by foot, the grapes are loaded into thick wooden fermenting vats, which are generally open, and which give the wine-maker extra hard work when he wants to control the fermentation better. In such cases, a grower like Jean-Louis Grippat of Tournon will resort to his *pichet*, a short wooden stump on the end of a handle that resembles a croquet mallet, in order to immerse the *chapeau* and cool the vat off. This work of striking the *chapeau* down while leaning over the top of the vat is strenuous and takes at least twenty minutes for each vat. Once in the morning and once in the evening for up to a week means a lot of time spent on this one task, but it is an indication of the desire to seek what the grower regards as perfection.

Primary fermentation lasts for a good two weeks, sometimes longer, and the wine subsequently spends at least twelve months ageing in wooden casks, whose size ranges from the normal *pièce* of 225 litres up to a *foudre* of 3,000 or more litres. Slowly the early discordancy wears off, but a bottle life of at least another five years is desirable if the wine is to attain any sort of harmony. Then, during its advance to middle and old age, Hermitage is inclined to throw a substantial deposit. Decanting is therefore an advantage before drinking it.

White Hermitage is credited in many books with almost the same remarkable keeping qualities as the red wine, but this is an exaggeration. With one notable exception, Jaboulet's Chevalier de Stérimberg, the wine is made in the classical manner, with a fermentation away from the skins of about two weeks. Generally this is undertaken in wood, but in recent years Grippat and Chapoutier have used enamel-lined vats, while Jaboulet have used a combination of enamel-vats and stainless steel tanks, always at strictly controlled, low temperatures of around 14 °C. After the primary fermentation, the 'old-fashioned' wine of growers like Chapoutier, Chave and Sorrel will spend between one and a half and six months in *pièce*, prior to bottling, by which time it will always have completed its secondary, malolactic fermentation.

Here lies the great point of divergence between the white wine-making philosophy of the House of Jaboulet and that of most of the rest of the *Appellation*: does one allow the 'malo' (as it is called) to take place before bottling or not? In opting for a bottling in the spring following the harvest, having kept the wine at low temperatures for up to four weeks, Jaboulet are striving to make as fresh and fruity a wine as possible and to 'maintain its acidity and enhance its prospects of long life', according to M. Louis Jaboulet. He went on: 'The white wines here at Hermitage are lacking in acidity by nature and if you let the malolactic take place, the wines end up with even less acidity and a tendency towards flabbiness. Yes, I admit, we are trying to make a lighter style of white wine than we used to with Chevalier de Stérimberg.'

Quite apart from considerations of taste, there seem to be two points to be made against the new Jaboulet technique. One is that a wine normally comes into its own and shows its real character and depth of flavour once its secondary aromas have been allowed to develop, for these are the most profound and lingering flavours that a classically made wine possesses. One touches on a similar observation made at Côte-Rôtie—in this case that there are plenty of light, quaffable white wines from high acidity areas such as the Loire Valley without white Hermitage having to abandon its intrinsic style and join them. The other point to be made is about the cellar treatment of a wine bottled before its malolactic has taken place. Obviously, the grower cannot guarantee that all purchasers of his wine will store the wine in cool surroundings; if a bottle is left in a kitchen, for instance, it is highly likely that after a few days the heat will have set the malolactic in motion—unless the grower takes necessary precautions such as the judicious filtering of the wine, as well as the application of sulphur dioxide to kill bacteria in it. Such processes are commonplace before the bottling of wine, but when that wine has not completed its malolactic, not only is it in a fragile state but also a heavier filtration and a little more sulphur dioxide will probably have to be used than is normal . . . just in case.

The new-style Chevalier de Stérimberg is an interesting wine, for while it is well scented, with a hint of peach-like fruit on the bouquet, on the palate its flavour is indeed clean and fresh—this when the wine is not even eighteen months old, for instance. The old-style Stérimberg was a classic white Hermitage, generally backward and revealing only a faint nuttiness when under a year and a half old, and it was a wine that would grow into a splendid fullness after about eight years. It is obviously a matter for individual taste, but what is inescapable is that the new style of Chevalier de Stérimberg has less profundity and complexity than the old, and it is generally more satisfying to watch a wine develop over a few years than over a few months.

The best classically made white Hermitages start life a pale yellow, with sometimes a trace of a darker colour like straw present. They are always well scented ('peaches or apricots', say certain growers) and extremely rich and round on the palate. Some tasters detect a *goût de noisette* on the long aftertaste—a sort of nuttiness that lurks at the back of the throat. After around eight years the wine has taken on a firm golden colour, and its extraordinary richness is more than ever apparent. Some wines, however, have a tendency to pass through a 'dumb' phase at between about 3 and 6 years old; this sounds strange, but is also observable with certain traditionally made white wines at Châteauneuf-du-Pape. One finds the colour correct—showing rich yellows—but both the bouquet and the palate fail to reveal the full extent of the aromas and the flavours, almost as if they were being held back by a magic hand. Return to the same wine when it is 8 years old and one is often bowled over by its all-round appeal and by its complexity of taste, both elements acquired with age. Perhaps these wines do not like being middle-aged and would rather pass straight from being quite young to quite old!

By the age of 15 white Hermitage has nearly run its race, and only the very greatest vintages, if well kept, will live for much longer. Because of its happy balance of power and elegance, most white Hermitage is the ideal accompaniment for chicken, veal, wild mushroom dishes, fish with heavy sauces and, very particularly, poached Scotch salmon. And when around 8 years old, it is excellent to drink with game pâtés and terrine.

Until the turn of the century another white wine was regularly made at Hermitage, the *vin de paille*, which today is found in the Jura region of France, east of Burgundy, although the Hermitage growers still possess the right to make it. Indeed, one of them, M. Gérard Chave, actually satisfied his curiosity about this legendary wine in 1974 and now finds that he himself has a legendary wine on his hands. He is besieged by all France's best chefs to sell them just a little of this wine, but he resolutely refuses to do so, averring that he made the wine for his own amusement, once, and that is how matters will remain.

M. Chave tells the tale of his *vin de paille* very well, especially when all present are seated with a glass of this extraordinary wine in their hands. 'I had been thinking of trying this experiment for several years, and eventually selected the 1974 crop. I didn't leave the grapes on the vines particularly late, choosing to pick them at the end of normal harvesting. I then separated them one by one and laid them out individually on straw on the floor of the attic above the *cuverie*; I used the straw that ties up the vines against their support stakes in the vineyards.

'The grapes stayed in the attic for a month and a half, and I was careful not to let them dry out since this would have robbed them of their remaining concentrated juice. I remember that my parents always used to give us dried raisins on Christmas Day,

79

having let the grapes completely dry out. Anyway, I then pressed the grapes and started off the fermentation. Normally I estimate that to make a bottle of my white Hermitage I need to use a fraction under one kilogram of grapes; with the *vin de paille* I needed 4 kilograms for each bottle.

'The straw wine fermented in cask on and off for two years. I did no racking during this drawn out fermentation, mainly because the must was entirely clean—the grapes had been especially healthy at the time of pressing so that there seemed no need to disturb the wine. Once the malo had taken place, I bottled the wine, and here it is.'

The delivery is not quite deadpan, for there is a tiny wry smile right at the end, as is permitted with men who know that their experiment has been a glorious success. Chave's *vin de paille* has the writer scrambling for his *Thesaurus* as he seeks the correct array of adjectives that will put such a brilliant and probably unrepeatable wine into perspective. A bottle drunk in 1982 presented a lustrous dark gold *robe*, with a soaring bouquet of concentrated richness, the aromas being most reminiscent of flowers and honey. Then the surprise—the incredible richness continued right on to the palate and through on to the aftertaste, but left a crystal clear, bitingly clean finish. The flavours—similar to honey and fresh fruit jams, such was the concentration—ended with a winning dryness, and not once did one gain the impression that here was a wine of 14·5°.

Probably the oldest bottles of Hermitage still existing are of *vin de paille*. The well-known Chapoutier family of Tain have an 1848 *vin de paille*, decanted in 1910, 1948 and 1977, in their personal cellar, while M. Max Chapoutier, the head of the family firm, recalled that until only recently, they had had two even older bottles. Producing from the sideboard of the company's reception room a thickly blown old bottle with a faint, blurred label saying 'Hermitage 1760', he related the following story.

'This bottle of Hermitage *vin de paille* was drunk by my father in 1964. There were two other bottles of this wine, but in the late 1970s they were given back to the Cambourg family, who had originally made the wine, and have since been drunk. The bottles had certainly moved around, as we had earlier given them to the Sizeranne family after buying a leading Hermitage vineyard from them some years ago. When my father drank this particular bottle, the wine, whose degree was around 17, was in an impeccable state, showing plenty of full-bodied flavour, even though there was a little ullage.'

Chapoutier is the oldest and largest wine house in Tain, having been founded in 1808. It is a typical family affair, with the energetic and enterprising Max Chapoutier as its President and Director-General, a position he took over from his father Marc. Many of the employees, be they office or cellar staff, have worked with the company all their lives and would never dream of placing their allegiance elsewhere.

Max Chapoutier, who is just 50, entered the family business at 23, having only very briefly considered another profession— 'Perhaps I might have been a doctor or a lawyer, but those professions took a definite second place to wine'—and under his guidance the company has maintained the expansion started by his father. Max Chapoutier himself always tells the story that when he first decided to extend the company interests beyond merely the northern Côtes du Rhône, Grandfather Marius was seized with indignation. The proposal was to buy a vineyard at Châteauneuf-du-Pape, but Marius declared roundly that he would never stoop as far as selling simple *vin ordinaire*!

Marius did not have his way, and the 66-acre Domaine de la Bernardine at Châteauneuf-du-Pape is now one of the company's main possessions, second only to their holding of 77 acres of choicely sited vines on the Hermitage hill. In addition, Chapoutier own 15 acres at both St-Joseph (the select St-Joseph hillside vineyard included) and Crozes-Hermitage and 7·5 acres at Côte-Rôtie. Max Chapoutier it was who bought into the underrated vineyard of St-Joseph, and he has also actively promoted the southern rosé wine of Tavel.

Such an impressive array of vineyards was formerly the envy of rival wine houses and the pride of the House of Chapoutier. But the 1980s have ushered in some stern economic realities about vineyard ownership. Max Chapoutier explained: 'The hard truth is that slope vineyards are now becoming extremely costly to run, and most of the time are loss-making for a relatively large organization such as my own. At Côte-Rôtie and St-Joseph, for instance, we have lost money every year since 1973. At Côte-Rôtie we employ two full-time vineyard workers, and that is one of the problems. You see, we should either have them working with machines on flat-ground vineyards like Châteauneuf-du-Pape, where they could look after a much larger area each, or the slope vineyard must be much larger to justify the fixed costs. At Hermitage, with our income derived from 77 acres, our overheads are much more easily covered than we can ever hope for at Côte-Rôtie.'

Vinification and outlook at Chapoutier remain thoroughly traditional, and not an inch is conceded to techniques that may unduly hasten the development of a wine or are likely to alter its time-honoured style. The red grapes are fermented in giant 12,000-litre open oak vats, except for the Domaine de la Bernardine at Châteauneuf-du-Pape, where the Grenache grape is very liable to oxidize if exposed to air. The principal white wines, like the Hermitages Chante-Alouette and the Cuvée-des-Boys, always spend three months or more in wood in order to gain extra roundness. All the red wines age in the maze of cellars at Tain in long, neatly stacked rows of casks that sometimes rise right up to the ceiling. As he surveys the barrels with obvious pride, Max Chapoutier rocks back and forth on his heels, the always-buttoned jacket of his suit puffing out. He wants everyone to love his wines and is visibly disappointed when one has the ill grace to mention a small grower who perhaps is making better wine. Up he leaps from his seat—'Well, if you like small growers so much, what about me?'—and his diminutive frame darts around the side of his desk.

In 1965 Chapoutier stopped giving a part of their wines a vintage so that they would be allowed to blend selected *cuvées* from different years together. These are now called the Grande Cuvée wines and are most commonly found inside France. 'Our wish is to make wines of a continuing and recognizable consistency,' stated Max Chapoutier, 'and having the ôption of blending a single vineyard's wines from different years allows us to achieve this.' Chapoutier's wines, which are headed at Hermitage by the red La Sizeranne and the two whites Chante Alouette and Cuvée-des-Boys, reflect this point of view. They are old-fashioned, thickly constituted wines that always have much fullness and alcohol. They repay ageing in bottle, and so heady are the white Hermitages that they should never be drunk without food, preferably a heavy fish dish being chosen for accompaniment.

Close by Chapoutier is Tain's other large family business, the house of Paul Jaboulet Aîné. The senior generation of the brothers Louis and Jean, both in their late sixties, recently moved aside to let their sons climb the family ladder but find, according to the charming Louis, that they are working harder than ever.

Louis's sons Gérard and Jacques are now the President and Director-General and the Director of the Cellars respectively, while Jean's son, Philippe, the youngest of the three at 31, looks after the vineyards. The three sons, and particularly Gérard, are important ambassadors for the fine wines of the Rhône Valley, and their success in exporting to more than fifty overseas countries, the principal of which are Britain and the United States, derives from their lively attitude.

Founded in 1834, the company produces probably the most consistently high-class wines from the entire Côtes du Rhône. Their vineyard properties are restricted to Hermitage and Crozes-Hermitage, but they own 62 acres at Hermitage, including the tiny chapel of St-Christophe, near the top of the hill. Like some of the other leading companies, Jaboulet uses one or two of its long terrace walls for free publicity and paints on them 'Paul Jaboulet Aîné' in large letters.

Jaboulet also owns an 86-acre vineyard in and around the Domaine de Thalabert at Crozes-Hermitage, and the red wine given the title 'Thalabert' is the best at Crozes. Otherwise the wine is sold under the simple Crozes-Hermitage *Appellation* on its own. For the other main Rhône *Appellations* the firm buys young wines from carefully selected *vignerons*. These wines are matured in their cellars at Tain and all carry a brand name as well as a vintage; thus their Côte-Rôtie is called Les Jumelles, their Châteauneuf-du-Pape Les Cèdres and so on. Most attention is centred on their two Hermitage wines, however. The red La Chapelle is a consistently exceptional wine, always very much in demand from knowledgeable overseas buyers. Its best years, like 1972 and 1978, show Hermitage in an impressive light; very dark and intense, the wine bears a concentration of flavours that maintain their complexity as it ages. Such fruits as blackcurrants spring to mind when the wine is young, and when over 15 years old the balance on the bouquet and the palate give it an elegance that is only found in the very top Bordeaux *châteaux*. La Chapelle certainly repays keeping this long in all except the lightest vintages such as 1975 and 1977. By contrast, the white Chevalier de Stérimberg, already discussed at length, should be drunk before it is around 5 years old.

Jaboulet and Chapoutier are Hermitage's largest merchants; the other *négociant* companies tend to be quite a lot smaller. In Tain there is the house of Léon Revol, whose offices look out on the spacious Place du Taurobole. Revol owns no vineyards but instead buys its wine when young from all over the Côtes du Rhône. The company director is M. Paul Gauthier, who is a warm-hearted, earnest man, totally engrossed by the subject and aura of wine. Although he has been in the wine trade for over forty-five years, he retains a young man's enthusiasm for it, and much of his spare time is spent busily researching the history of wine and the vine, with particular reference to Hermitage and the Syrah.

The house of Revol was founded at the start of the twentieth century and now sells most of its wines, which are consistent without being spectacular, in France itself. M. Gauthier added that his profession was definitely a passion: 'I am in contact with life, with living beings and of course with wine, which is just as much a living thing. Take the vine plant, for instance: it is born, it lives and it dies, the same as man, and even succumbs to illnesses and diseases as well. Often it lives as long as a man, and during its life it will have demanded that much the same care and attention be paid to it.'

Across the Rhône near Tournon are the offices and head-quarters of a firm that until the late 1970s was a family enterprise, Delas Frères. Founded in 1835, they own a very small vineyard at Hermitage, as well as having vines at Cornas, Côte-Rôtie, Crozes-Hermitage, Condrieu and St-Joseph. While they have recently sold most of their old vineyard at Hermitage, they have been discreetly acquiring *parcelles* of vines at Condrieu, which is helping to stimulate interest in that *Appellation*. Delas is now owned by the Champagne house of Deutz, and the most prominent member of the family, Michel Delas, has become the Marketing Director. A bustling, big man in his late fifties, M. Delas has the reputation of being an expert taster. When asked if he could imagine himself in another profession, his answer is forthright but shows his passion for the world in which he was brought up: 'I would perhaps be exporting something else, anything else—but wine is the most interesting field of trade anywhere, that's for sure.'

The main Delas wines are their special Hermitage, Cuvée Marquise de la Tourette, their Cornas, Chante-Perdrix, and their Condrieu. They are all quite good and better than the firm's other wines, which are sometimes lacking in the wholehearted characteristics expected of their *Appellations*.

None of the big wine companies is able to match the incredible wine-growing tradition of one local family, however. M. Gérard Chave's family has owned vineyards in the area since the far-off time of 1481, which in all probability makes them the oldest wine family in the Côtes du Rhône. M. Chave is known far and wide in the surrounding country and has a confirmed band of followers outside France, particularly in Britain and the United States. This is not surprising, since his wines are made in a classic old-fashioned way, are thought out to the last detail and possess outstanding qualities.

'Thinking out' wines may not be a pastime commonly attributed to *vignerons*, but in M. Chave's case the phrase is relevant. Since the early 1970s it has been fascinating to observe the development of M. Chave's skills. Not only is he fully master of the necessities of his vineyards, but in his cellars he appears to practise a form of wizardry in the vinification and assembly of his wines. His famous *vin de paille* has already been mentioned, but there can be no more educative exercise than to accompany M. Chave in his intimate, intriguingly musty cellar and to taste the wines from his different plots on Hermitage hill. Then it becomes clear just how varied the styles can be, from the thick, almost hard Péléat to the finer and lightly scented Greffieux. To know how to bring these different styles together into a well-knit unity—that is the real art, one that is admitted by growers to be among their hardest tasks every year.

One of the clues to M. Chave's expertise is that he can make a good wine in a generally poor vintage. To do this, he must understand the state of the grapes and then adapt his cellar vinification accordingly. Of his neighbours, only Guigal at Côte-Rôtie and Clape at Cornas are consistently able to make good wine in poor vintages and excellent wine when the harvest has been good. Nicknamed the 'Trio' by the authors, they are the three men in the northern Rhône who come closest to a complete mastery of their art.

M. Chave lives with his wife, Monique, who runs the business

M. Gérard Chave

side of matters, and their two children in the little St-Joseph village of Mauves, 3 kilometres south of Tournon. A good-looking man, with a rather Pinocchio-styled nose and a splendidly rugged countenance, M. Chave vinifies all the grapes from his 25 acres of vineyards on the Hermitage hillside in his cellars at Mauves.

M. Chave's red and white Hermitages are among the longest-lived of the *Appellation*, the red sustaining its enormous depth of intricate flavour for a good thirty years and the white obtaining a really big apricot-inspired aftertaste after eight or ten years. M. Chave also amuses himself by making around 3,000 bottles of red St-Joseph from his 2·5-acre vineyard at the foot of the Tournon hill, and the wine is delicious, displaying ample fruit both on the bouquet and the palate.

As with all *vignerons* in the northern Côtes du Rhône, M. Chave encounters much difficulty in tending his vines: 'I can't use any machines, and generally rely on the *bigot*, or pronged hoe, for the everyday upkeep of my vineyards at Hermitage and St-Joseph. Our wines may have risen in price over the past few years, but so have all wines, and I feel it is more justified here precisely because of the really high cost of labour.' Meanwhile, M. Chave boasts a private cellar that bears ample testimony to his family's long involvement in wine, and he must be one of the few people anywhere to have some bottles of 1923 and 1929 Hermitage tantalizingly awaiting consumption. 'They are still very good,' said M. Chave, 'but I'm afraid I don't have many of them left.'

With the large companies dominating the vineyards, there are only very few private growers like M. Chave at Hermitage. One, M. Henri Sorrel, was the Notary at Tain for many years but confesses that he preferred being a *vigneron* all along. His son Jean-Michel is the Notary now, while M. Sorrel, a kindly man in his seventies, has retired from running his vineyard on his own and has handed it over to his third son, Marc, who is learning to be a wine-maker at the age of 34.

The Sorrels own a total of 8·5 acres at Hermitage, with their major holdings on Le Méal, Les Greffieux and Les Rocoules. On Rocoules they are among the only people to grow the Roussanne vine, which accounts for about 15 per cent of their plantation there.

Until the early 1970s, M. Sorrel sold his grapes to local *négociants*, but now takes evident satisfaction from completing the vinification himself and selling his excellent red and white wine, mainly inside France. His style of vinification is old-fashioned, with fermentation undertaken in open wood vats and both red and white receiving an ageing in cask, the red eighteen months and the white a month and a half. He likes to age his wine in a mixture of old and new wood and has recently been buying 2-year-old barrels from the Burgundian Domaine de la Romanée-Conti in order to renew his stocks of old casks.

Although M. Sorrel's white Hermitage is of a high standard, his best red, called Le Méal, can be exceptional, as it was in 1978 and 1979, for instance. A sleek black cherry colour, it is remarkable for its tremendous elegance; even when it is young, and the fruits and tannins have not properly rounded themselves together, the wine shows a striking balance and abundant promise, and would certainly live for thirty years.

Many of the smallholders on the Hermitage hill do not have the resources to start their own private cellars, so these *viticulteurs* subscribe to the Tain Cave Co-opérative, which serves all the surrounding area—Hermitage, Crozes-Hermitage, St-Joseph, Cornas and St-Péray. The Co-opérative was founded in 1933 by 150 wine-growers from all round Hermitage, but it now works on a much larger scale, with 550 members and a total annual production of all wines of 34,000 hectolitres. This is the only Cave Co-opérative in the Rhône Valley with a resident *tonnelier*, a

Martiniquais who gives virtuoso barrel-making displays to the public from time to time to demonstrate the skill behind this fading craft.

With its uniform, mass-produced wine, the Co-opérative cannot hope to compete with the more individual suppliers of Hermitage, and some of its wine is of fairly dubious quality. At the moment Cornas seems to be the best.

Another small grower who is not a member of the Co-opérative is an Irish gentleman, now in his eighties. Terence Gray owns an 8-acre vineyard at Hermitage, the Domaine de l'Hermite, which he purchased from the Delas family in 1934. An Egyptologist and founder of the Festival Theatre in Cambridge, Mr Gray has some interesting reminiscences of the wines and vines of Hermitage. For instance, he recalls offering six bottles of 1869 *vin de paille* from the cellars of M. de la Sizeranne on the Festival Theatre Restaurant wine list some time after 1926. Equally, he remembers the 1935 vintage with affection: 'Winemakers can receive some funny surprises from their wines, and my 1935 red Hermitage from the Mas du Péléat was a case in point. Early on, it seemed to all who tasted it to be a very poor wine and, as such, was used to refresh the postman when he called at the Domaine on his long rounds. A few years later this same wine became a marvel and was called *le vin du facteur* in memory of its ignoble younger days.'

The indefatigable Mr Gray still sells his wine to a variety of countries. It may not be quite as full-bodied as it was, but one can still savour the memory of Maurice Healy's description of it in *Stay Me With Flagons*: 'It is great, rich, glowing red wine, with a mouthful of bouquet to every sip, if you know what I mean.'

Hermitage Vintages

1955   A very good vintage. The whites lived for at least twenty years, while the reds, latterly very charming, are now fading gracefully.

1956   Mediocre. Many of the wines were disappointingly light.

1957   A very good year which produced full-bodied wines. A little 'harder' than 1955, they have begun to dry out.

1958   Mediocre. Variable wines that tended to be light in colour and body.

1959   A very good year, with some *cuvées* of excellent quality.

The wines attained great elegance and harmony with age; although they have lost some of their vigour, well kept bottles could still be very interesting.

1960   A generally mediocre year, with wines lacking in strength.

1961   An excellent vintage, which ranks with 1929 as being the best of the century. The wines were enormously full-bodied and ample in every respect—colour, bouquet, flavour and aftertaste. A memorable La Chapelle from Jaboulet, which is now showing a little age, but also a stunning complexity of flavour. The best reds can live for another ten years or so, while the well constructed whites have started to decline.

1962   Very good. Not surprisingly lighter than the 1961s, the wines were none the less quite full and very well balanced. They have passed their peak, but are still capable of showing the interesting aromas of well matured Syrah. The white wines are becoming oxidized.

1963   A poor year. Wishy-washy wines.

1964   An excellent vintage. The red wines were slow to shake off their tannin, but, always very well coloured, are now tasting well. They can be kept until the late 1980s. The white wines were very full, and the odd well looked after bottle could prove excellent drinking.

1965   Disappointing. Some good *cuvées* were made, but the wines were generally weak-bodied.

1966   A very good year. The strongly scented red wines possessed good balance, and were richly flavoured. They are still in good order. The whites were extremely full-bodied, but should now be drunk without delay before they become too dried-out.

1967   A very good vintage. The wines had good colour and richness of flavour. They have softened out, and are proving excellent for drinking now, while there is still some soft fruit present. The whites are golden and show some of the complex nutty flavours of old white Hermitage.

1968   A disaster. Very light wines, many of which were never bottled.

1969   Very good. The red wines were rich and well balanced. They have achieved great style with ageing, their bouquet being particularly striking, and will remain good for drinking for another ten years or so. The white wines have started to fade, but only slowly.

1970 Very good. The strongly coloured red wines were perhaps marginally superior to the 1969s, just a little more body to them. They are reaching a state of great equilibrium with the fruits and tannins well softened out, and should remain sound until the early 1990s. The whites were less full-bodied and should be drunk soon.

1971 A very good vintage. The red wines were harmonious and possessed attractive bouquet. They are now very charming—well rounded and supple—and will prove good to drink until around 1990. The white wines have aged very well and still show some of their early rich flavours.

1972 An excellent vintage for the best wine-makers. The crop was small and the quality of the wines correspondingly high. Initially very full in colour and flavour, the reds have advanced more quickly than expected and are already displaying the complex, almost herbaceous aromas of middle age. For best effect they should be drunk in the next eight years. The whites were fruity and fairly rich and are now tasting very well.

1973 Generally a very good year, even if parts of the vineyard were affected by hail. The reds, initially sturdy and quite tannic, have softened out to a large extent and look like keeping until around 1992. The whites were very well scented and have held together through their agreeable balance; they could still drink well around 1986.

1974 A fairly good vintage. The red wines were attractively coloured and quite full-bodied. They should be drunk without much delay. The light, fruity white wines are generally past their best.

1975 A small crop produced some light red wines. Deficient in colour and depth of flavour, their fruitiness has made them good to drink already. The whites, with an attractive colour and scent, are showing well now, but are likely to live for a few years more.

1976 A good to very good vintage that fell victim of the growers' early hue and cry that it was quite exceptional. The red wines have come along more rapidly than anticipated and their early purple colour is losing a little brilliance and profundity. On the palate some of the *cuvées* are showing a relative lack of balance, with the alcohol coming through as the fruit dries out. Wines from growers such as Jaboulet and Chave will live for fifteen to eighteen years. The white wines are beginning to unfold very well as they lose some of their initially high acidity and are marked by an impressive fruitiness and prolonged aftertaste. They have a good future in store.

1977   A light vintage where the reds lacked a little colour and tannin. They should be drunk in the next two or three years. The whites suffered from excessive acidity and were not very successful. They should be drunk soon.

1978   An excellent vintage, the best since 1961. A small harvest, very healthy grapes, and wines that are therefore notable for their richness and balance. The reds are very dark, with bouquets of great latent promise; still very backward, the wines have indications of strong fruit behind the tannin and look like making up into memorable bottles. The growers consider them capable of living for twenty-five to thirty years. The whites were very good, with a fullness of flavour that will ensure them an interesting development over the next five or six years. Note the red of Chave and La Chapelle from Jaboulet, although the latter's white Stérimberg was less impressive.

1979   Very good. The reds are strongly coloured and notable for an expansive, flowery bouquet. They hold a good acidity and tannin level that will ensure a very sound development for the next ten years. The whites are also striking for their rich bouquet and flavour and should be excellent to drink around 1986–9. Note the red of Sorrel and Chave and the white of Grippat.

1980   Generally a good vintage, although the harvest was interrupted by rain. The red wines are quite well coloured, but are most favoured by their agreeable harmony, which will ensure that they drink very well over the next ten years. The whites will not live very long, either, but show good fruit and length that will make them enjoyable well into the decade. Note Jaboulet's white Chevalier de Stérimberg and Chapoutier's white Cuvée-des-Boys.

1981   Quite a good vintage, better for the whites than the reds.

The latter are reasonably coloured, but do not possess a depth that indicates a life of much more than ten or twelve years. The whites are better balanced and will make some attractive bottles by around 1985–7.

Earlier Exceptional Vintages   1953, 1952, 1949, 1947, 1945, 1943, 1933, 1929. Any of these wines could be quite marvellous, but their well-being depends very much on where and how they have been kept. The 1953 red from Chapoutier, for example, is still in extremely good shape, while the 1952 has the 'coffee beans' flavour of old age and should be drunk before too long.

Leading Growers at Hermitage

Chave, Jean-Louis	07300 Mauves
Jaboulet Ainé, Paul	26600 Tain-l'Hermitage
Sorrel, Henri	26600 Tain-l'Hermitage
Grippat, Jean-Louis	07300 Tournon
Chapoutier, M.	26600 Tain-l'Hermitage
Cave Co-opérative de Vins Fins	26600 Tain-l'Hermitage
Delas Frères	07300 Tournon
Desmeure, Père et Fils	26600 Mercurol
De Vallouit, L.	26240 St-Vallier
Faurie, B.	07300 Tournon
Faurie, P., et Bouzige, J.	07300 Mauves
Fayolle, Jules et ses Fils	26600 Gervans
Ferraton, Jean et Michel	26600 Tain-l'Hermitage
Gray, Terence	26600 Tain-l'Hermitage

5

Crozes-Hermitage

In 1846 the tasting panel of the Lyon Wine Congress had this to say about the wines of Crozes-Hermitage and Hermitage: 'If they are not brothers, then they are certainly first cousins.' This is a slightly flattering over-all evaluation of the comparatively unknown wines of Crozes-Hermitage. When they are good, they begin to resemble their illustrious neighbours' undoubted style, but on the whole they lack the consistency, harmony and general 'touch of class' that any bottle of Hermitage can pretend to possess.

The *Appellation Contrôlée* area is made up of eleven villages around Tain-l'Hermitage and derives its name from one of them, a tiny community whose agreeable red wine was in the past referred to simply as 'Crozes'. Tain serves as the unofficial centre of the *Appellation* and is ringed by Crozes-Hermitage, Serves, Erôme, Gervans and Larnage to the north; by Mercurol and Chanos-Curson to the east; and by Beaumont-Monteux, Pont-de-l'Isère and Roche-de-Glun to the south.

The villages all lie within easy distance of the main Paris to Nice highways, the A7 and N7, but somehow contrive a strangely timeless existence. The central café is likely to have its shutters firmly closed; the main square looks almost derelict. Horse and cart go clopping serenely around narrow streets that end abruptly in uneven clumps of vines; old women in black watch with listless eyes from behind closed windows, their eternal vigil only rarely interrupted by the movement of a passing vehicle. There is no one in the streets, not even the traditionally observed group of old *pétanque* players. Away in the vines the heavy silence is fleetingly broken by guttural cries that urge a stubborn mule to greater endeavour. Here the land is man's master, and its

93

dominance is reflected in the lifeless, detached villages all round.

The Crozes-Hermitage *Appellation* is much larger than Hermitage and covers about 2,230 acres. It is an expanding area, too, for most of the vines are planted on gentle slopes and flat ground away from the east bank of the Rhône. As they are able to work nearly all their vines mechanically, *vignerons* are encouraged to extend their vineyards; due to the recent change in the delimitation of the St-Joseph *Appellation* area, these are now the only two places in the northern Rhône where this is so.

Historically, the wine of the region is obscure. Very little is recorded about it until the eighteenth century when, it appears, wine from the village of Larnage was sold on a fairly regular basis to England; this was called, not *vin de Larnage*, but *vin de Mure*, after Larnage's leading family, and it was always sent across to Bordeaux before being shipped north. This was not the first local wine to go abroad, however, for the white wine of nearby Mercurol was sent to England around 1309, according to village archives. To whom it went is not known.

Today the best red wines come from a small place called Les Chassis, which lies south of Tain on the way to Roche-de-Glun, and from Gervans; while the best white is undoubtedly from around Mercurol. It is no coincidence that the vineyards of Gervans are on steep, well exposed slopes overlooking the Rhône, and indeed the village possesses a situation nearly identical to that of Hermitage, with its southward-facing hillsides and granite topsoil. The vineyards at Les Chassis stand among dry stones and give a good, well-balanced wine that local *propriétaires* such as Jaboulet, Chapoutier and Tardy and Ange like to use as a principal constituent when they are making up their red wine *cuvées* from their holdings in different parts of the *Appellation*. Meanwhile at Mercurol the vineyards are mostly on hillsides, and the predominantly sandy soil seems ideally suited to the cultivation of the Marsanne and Roussanne grapes.

Red Crozes-Hermitage is usually made entirely from the Syrah grape, although the inclusion of up to 15 per cent of white grapes is permitted at the moment of fermentation. The Cave Co-opérative at Tain and one or two other growers would sometimes take advantage of this ruling but nowadays find it less necessary to do so because the white wine is selling well in its own right. Such is the ambiguity of some of the French wine laws that one is forced to wonder whether they are designed always to protect quality and not just the wine community's local interests.

Vinification of the red wine follows the same basic form as that used for Hermitage, although in a somewhat abbreviated form. Thus some growers still ferment in wooden vats, although most have taken to using closed concrete vats. The primary fermentation rarely lasts more than ten days, while views differ on the ageing process. One school of thought, represented by Marcel Collonge of the Domaine la Négociale at Mercurol, has opted away from ageing in wood except in the very strongest vintages such as 1978: he is seeking a lighter, more quickly accessible style of wine, and as yet his red Crozes is a little thin and atypical of the rich Syrah taste that is associated with the northern Rhône.

Then there are those *vignerons* who are pursuing a sensible course of equilibrating the nature of the local red wine with an ageing process that will help to display its flavours and its potential to the full. One has to face the fact that red Crozes-Hermitage is simply not as corpulent or tannic a wine by nature as is Hermitage, so that an ageing period of much over eighteen months in wood can seriously impair the wine's native fruit and harmony. Growers who are vinifying in this balanced way, using their casks for between six and fifteen months, include Jaboulet, with the *Appellation*'s best red wine, Domaine de Thalabert; Tardy and Ange at the GAEC de la Syrah; Alphonse Desmeure et Fils of Domaine des Remizières; M. Borja of Cave des Clairmonts; Robert Michelas of Domaine St-Jemms; and finally the Domaine de la Pradelle, although the last-named would like to age longer than eighteen months if demand permitted. One can only hope that demand keeps up, for the wine of the young Pradelle brothers, who only started to bottle in 1978, is potentially very good indeed—as long as it doesn't become *boisé* (woody) from too long in cask, as is observable with one or two of their *cuvées*.

Finally, one is confronted with some lamentable horror stories. How times change. In the early 1970s two of the very best growers at Crozes-Hermitage were Albert Bégot and Raymond Roure, from Serves-sur-Rhône and Gervans. M. Bégot was keen on making a completely natural wine, with no inorganic substances in it, and was making an excellent red, while M. Roure was cropping only a limited amount of grapes per acre so that his red wine, too, was full-bodied and thoroughly laudable.

95

Now both growers have fallen into the trap of too much ageing in cask. M. Bégot likes to leave his red wine two or three years in wood, and the originally excellent 1978 vintage was left four years altogether, until every last trace of fruit had fled before the assault of his old, untreated casks, a by-product of the decision to make an entirely 'natural' wine. Taste M. Roure's *vin de l'année* from the cask four months after the harvest, and its exuberant fruit explodes on to the palate; but the wine is never given a chance to show its true colours, for it is left for two years in wood and is bottled only when M. Roure can fit it in with his extensive fruit-growing interests. Open a bottle just over two years old, and the marvellous early fruit has slowly, inexorably been squeezed out of it, and all that remains is a disagreeable woody taste. Obviously, *vignerons* can make errors of judgement, but these are basic philosophical errors that cause one to shake one's head in disbelief.

Although red Crozes-Hermitage is lightly perfumed but vigorous, it has to be admitted that, with the exception of the Domaine de Thalabert, it is the least memorable of all the northern Syrah wines. However, it is very much an *Appellation* in transition, for in the last ten years there has been a considerable exodus from the Tain Cave Co-opérative as vineyard owners have wanted to strike out on their own, vinifying, bottling and selling their wine themselves. The number of subscribers to the Co-opérative fell from 710 to a startling 550 between 1974 and 1982, as growers with the better sloping vineyards and therefore the generally better-quality grapes tired of receiving exactly the same price for their fruit as those growers on run-of-the-mill plain vineyards. Coupled with the natural desire to progress, this has meant that the *Appellation* now has more private growers tentatively feeling their way in their first experiences of vinifying on their own. It bodes well long-term for the quality and reputation of Crozes Hermitage, but, recorded as this is in 1982, it is still early days.

When well vinified and cared for, red Crozes does indeed display considerable depth of character. V. Rendu, in his *Ampelographie française sur la Côte du Rhône* (1857), recalled that some years earlier Docteur Ramain had written glowingly that the Crozes reds 'have a beautiful flavour of raspberries and hawthorns'. The good doctor's enthusiasm was admittedly somewhat fanciful, but the red wines of Crozes-Hermitage can be said to possess in some measure this scent and flavour of raspberries.

Not all the red wine is now being made on these broadly traditional lines, for in recent years the Tain Cave Co-opérative has been vinifying some of its Crozes by the *macération carbonique* technique that is common to the Beaujolais and parts of south-west France and Provence. By leaving the grapes to ferment in carbonic gas-filled vats, the grower can make a Beaujolais-style wine that is light, fruity and quite unassuming—a *vin de tous les jours* almost. This method has already enjoyed agreeable success with some of the small country wines of the Mediterranean, but it seems a pity to try to change the style of a sturdy but basically sound wine such as Crozes-Hermitage. There is also debate as to whether the Syrah lends itself well to *macération carbonique*, for it is by nature a strongly fruity grape anyway. Perhaps *macération carbonique* is not the answer; instead, a foreshortened fermentation with a three-month stay in cask might give better results.

Only minor experimentation has been tried with the white wines, which are made in a way similar to the Hermitage whites. On average about one-tenth of the *Appellation*'s wine is white (about 3,375 hectolitres), and, following fermentation in enamel-lined vats, the wine is bottled, without being put into cask, anything from six months to two years after the harvest. Of course, the younger the wine is when it is bottled, the fresher it tastes. White Crozes does not draw near to the richness and intensity shown by Hermitage whites, and it therefore suffers from prolonged storage prior to bottling. One of the problems that the growers face is the malolactic fermentation, which they find can start abruptly and just as suddenly stop in a way unknown with the red wines. Jacques Pradelle explained it in the following way: 'The white wines here tend to be rather fat and lacking in acidity, so we try not to let the "malo" take place, in order to keep the acidity level higher and make the wine fresher. There would probably be around 3·5 grams of acidity left when the wine has done its "malo", but 4 or 5 when it hasn't. We therefore have to choose our moment for bottling carefully and always recommend that our white be drunk young.' This view is in keeping with the attitude of families such as the Fayolles of Gervans and the Jaboulets, whose white Crozes-Hermitage is called La Mule Blanche. Until the mid-1970s the Fayolles would always leave their white in cask for a year, but now they want to make a fresher wine with as much fruit as possible—and this they have success-fully achieved. Such wines, which still show a traditional Crozes nuttiness of scent and flavour, are excellent to drink before they are 3 years old.

Obtaining a similar freshness and attractive fruitiness with their white wine are Tardy and Ange, who sound like a music hall duo but who are very serious about their wine-making. Outside the *négociant* houses, they are the first people in the *Appellation* to perform a temperature-controlled fermentation on their white wine; they leave the juice on the lees for between twenty-four and thirty-six hours, rack it and then ferment it at between 16 °C and 18 °C for about two weeks. Depending on the acidity level in the wine, they will choose to bottle without the malolactic fermen-tation, as in 1980, or with it naturally out of the way, as with their 1981. Once the wine has been bottled, in the spring following the harvest, they believe that it should be drunk within two years. Pale yellow, with an interesting element of Chablis-style 'greens' in the colour, their white wine reveals good fruit and almost a honey type of flavour on the palate, which make it one of the best whites at Crozes.

The majority of Crozes-Hermitage is still made or sold by large local companies, including Jaboulet, Chapoutier, Revol, Delas and the Tain Cave Co-opérative, but it is also a wine that frequently appears on the lists of Burgundian and Bordelais merchants, often with apparently deceptive qualities. Those growers who make and sell their own wine number about twenty, several of whom have just emerged from the fold of the Cave Co-opérative at Tain.

Two such *émigrés* are Charles Tardy and Bernard Ange, who are both natives of Chanos-Curson. They started to bottle a part of their wine in 1980 and declare that their long-term objective is to bottle all the wine that they make from their 25 acres of Syrah and 6 acres of Marsanne and Roussanne vines. Their cellars are a little north-west of Chanos-Curson, and the building's dry-stone ex-terior is set off in summer by a dazzling blue wisteria that dominates the whole courtyard. They are brothers-in-law, Tardy being the senior member in his mid-forties and Ange, with his curly dark brown hair and pervasive enthusiasm, appearing younger than his thirty years.

'We combined our vineyards upon leaving the Cave Co-opérative', remarked Ange, 'and so half are at Beaumont-Monteux and half at Chanos. The Chanos vines are more on the slope, and we find that the Syrah there produces a tougher, more backward wine, rather in the style of Gervans, than it does from the more typically plain vineyards of Beaumont. But that's no problem, because we can blend the two styles with great success.

'You may wonder about the name of our domaine, but we both like the Syrah enough to call ourselves the GAEC de la Syrah. No, we're not in any Syrah Confréries or anything like that; we're just happy to make the wine—and drink it occasionally!' Their emphasis is on a soft, fruity type of wine which shows good harmony and a latent fullness that does not make it harsh to drink even when young. As a rule, they would say that their red Crozes should be drunk before it is seven years old.

Close neighbours of MM. Tardy and Ange are the Pradelle brothers, Jacques and Jean-Louis, whose father used to be in the Cave Co-opérative but who had latterly been selling his grapes to the Tain *négociant* house of Chapoutier. With both sons in their twenties and both eager to make wine themselves, the father agreed in 1978 that they would start to vinify and bottle all their own wine. They have 7 acres of predominantly Marsanne vines and 22 acres of Syrah, all at Mercurol, half of them on the zig-zag of short slopes and half on the plain, which in their *quartier* contains quite an element of smooth, rounded stones which are evidence of the Rhône's old route past the east side of today's hill of Hermitage.

A bouncy man with a woolly bobble hat perched on the top of his head, Jacques said that both he and his brother had studied at Wine School at Beaune, which had been an invaluable training. 'We now know more about things like when to age our wine in *foudre* and when to age it in a smaller *pièce*, and a lot of little details that add up to helping you make a better wine. Demand for our wine means that at the moment we are unable to age it much more than one year in cask, which is about half the time we should ideally like. The other great thing that bottling our wine has brought is the new friends and people we have met. We have a completely new horizon now, since we sell half our wine to Germany, Switzerland, the Netherlands and Denmark, and it's very interesting and educative to hear foreign people discussing our wine.' Dark-coloured and with an old-fashioned backward style, the Pradelle wine is already one of the leading reds at Crozes, and there is no doubt that as the modest brothers go on learning more about their *métier*, the wine will improve even more.

Many of today's *domaines* in the area closest to Tain have been making wine since the early part of the nineteenth century at least; the Domaine la Négociale records show wine being made on the property just after the Revolution, while the Michelas family have been wine-growers at Domaine St-Jemms near Mercurol since 1851. Both properties belonged originally to powerful local families, in the case of Domaine St-Jemms the powerful Counts of Revol back in the sixteenth century.

Robert Michelas is another ex-*Co-opérateur* who cultivates 5 acres of mainly Marsanne and 25 acres of Syrah at Mercurol and Pont-de-l'Isère, with some of his Syrah in the favoured Les Chassis *quartier* just south of his *domaine*. He is only bottling about one-quarter of his production, something like 18,000 bottles a year, but one day expects to be selling only a little wine in bulk. 'Maybe that day will come soon when my daughter passes her *sommelière* exams and starts telling lots of restaurants about my wine,' he adds, with obvious pride.

One of the families who have been bottling their wine longer than most are the Fayolles, who live down the hill from M. Roure at Gervans. To arrive at their farm it is necessary first to traverse the main Paris–Nice railway line, whose crossing near the centre of Gervans is always firmly placed in the down position. Shades of the France of old Jean Renoir films are recalled when a solemnly dressed and straightfaced *madame* emerges from a little house, waddles over with the utmost aplomb and slowly proceeds to wind the level-crossing gate up, no doubt swearing under her breath at the unwanted disturbance.

M. Fayolle, a lean man with startling black eyebrows that look as if they will only just stay on his face rather than suddenly taking off, has been making wine since he was a boy. He is now assisted by his two sons, Jean-Paul and Jean-Claude, who took up the family business at the tender age of 14. However, as Jean-Claude was quick to point out, 'It wasn't until we were a bit older that we were allowed *really* to get to know our wine!'

While their neighbour, Raymond Roure, has recently increased his vineyard to 25 acres and is now making much more wine per acre, the Fayolles have kept their vineyard at 18 acres, although they also part-own 3 acres on the Hermitage hill, at a *lieu-dit* called Les Dionnères. Their Crozes vines are mainly on half-slopes, which are simpler to upkeep and tend to encourage a larger crop than the full, steep slopes that run sharply down from M. Roure's domaine. They rarely have major worries about their grapes failing to ripen, since they are favoured by the same micro-climate as is enjoyed by Hermitage, with a mean temperature of about 13 °C; it is remarkable to observe the pansies and mimosa in full bloom on the Gervans hill in January, for instance.

Another private grower making sound wine with the help of his son is M. Alphonse Desmeure of the Domaine des Remizières at Mercurol. He has increased his plantation to just under 30 acres, with vineyards at Crozes-Hermitage, Mercurol and Larnage, and although only about one-third of his wine is white, it is on this that his name is founded. M. Desmeure is content to bottle his white wine over a year after the harvest but, surprisingly, feels that traditionally made white Crozes can live for longer than the red— up to twenty years, as opposed to the red's ten-year maximum.

Finally at Erôme, next to Gervans, lives M. Robert Rousset, who, in addition to his red and white Crozes Hermitage, also makes a sparkling white wine from a mixture of his local grapes. This *vin mousseux* does not possess *Appellation Contrôlée*.

Crozes-Hermitage Vintages

The best recent years have been 1981, 1979, 1978 and 1976. Before that, 1973, 1971, 1969, 1967, 1966, 1964, 1961 and 1959 were all good or very good. Disappointing for both the whites and the reds were 1975, 1977 and, to a lesser extent, 1980.

For details, see Hermitage. There is generally very little difference in any one year between the general style of the wines, red and white, from the two *Appellations*. A Crozes-Hermitage will usually live for under half the time of an Hermitage, however.

Leading Growers at Crozes-Hermitage

Jaboulet Ainé, Paul
   Domaine de Thalabert   26600 Tain-l'Hermitage
Tardy, Charles et Ange, Bernard
   GAEC de la Syrah   26600 Chanos-Curson

Pradelle, Jean-Louis
Domaine de la Pradelle   26600 Chanos-Curson
Borja
Domaine des Clairmonts   26600 Beaumont-Monteux
Desmeure, Père et Fils   26600 Mercurol

Bégot, Albert   26600 Serves-sur-Rhône
Bied, Bernard   26600 Mercurol
Cave Co-opérative de Vins Fins   26600 Tain-l'Hermitage
Chapoutier et Cie
Les Meysonniers   26600 Tain-l'Hermitage
Chave, Bernard   26600 Mercurol
Collonge, Marcel
Domaine la Négociale   26600 Mercurol
Delas Frères   07300 Tournon
De Vallouit, L.   26240 St-Vallier
Fayolle, Jules et ses Fils   26600 Gervans
Ferraton, Jean et Michel   26600 Tain-l'Hermitage
Margier, Charles   26600 Mercurol
Martin, Michel   26600 Crozes-Hermitage
Michelas, Robert
Domaine St-Jemms   26600 Mercurol
Peichon, Pierre   26600 Erôme
Roure, Raymond   26600 Gervans
Rousset, Robert   26600 Erôme

6

Saint-Joseph

St-Joseph is a young *Appellation*, which was created in June 1956. Its vineyards are centred mainly on Tournon, across the river from Hermitage, and take their name from a nearby hillside—not, as some fanciful *vignerons* would have you believe, from St-Joseph himself, who is supposed to be the patron of betrayed husbands.

Exactly how long wine has been made in this region is not known. All talk of the Syrah's early cultivation refers to the eastern banks of the Rhône round Hermitage and, strangely enough, Tournon is not mentioned as a wine-producing area until the reign of Louis XII (1498–1515). Then, according to Elie Brault, in his *Anne et son époque*, the monarchy would only allow its very own wines to be served at the Court of France. There were at the time three royal vineyards, those of Beaune and Chenove in Burgundy and the much-esteemed Clos de Tournon.

The wine of Tournon remained in royal circles for some years more, for it is recorded locally that King Henry II (1519–59) always kept a personal reserve of several barrels. The style of the wine he so liked can be judged from a quotation of 1560 by the first head of the College of Tournon, now one of France's oldest secondary schools, who praised the 'delicate and dainty' wine of Tournon and Mauves, which was sold as far away as Rome and which the Princes and King of France were prepared to acquire for themselves at no little cost.

Mauves is a little village just south of Tournon. Old history books have spoken of its wine as being the worthy rival of the mighty Hermitage—and not without reason, for it is today the home of all the leading wines of St-Joseph. The celebrated French writer Victor Hugo (1802–85) had evidently encountered, and enjoyed, the wine, for he mentioned it in *Les Misérables*.

103

Describing a social gathering, Hugo wrote that, in addition to the ordinary table wine, there was served a bottle of 'this good wine of Mauves'. Hugo hastened to add that no more than one bottle was brought out because it was 'an expensive wine'.

During the 1970s St-Joseph's delimitation changed very substantially, and while the best wine still comes from Tournon and Mauves, the area of land where vines can be grown within the *Appellation* has been expanded enormously. Whereas only seven communities composed the *Appellation* in the early 1970s, now over twenty-five account for the whole wine-making zone, which runs for 65 kilometres from top to bottom.

In the period 1972–6, the average crop of red and white wines was 3,447 hectolitres, while during the period 1977–81 the average rose to 7,345 hectolitres. Much of this extra wine is of a lighter style than the traditional St-Joseph, the best of which comes from the steep slopes of Mauves, Tournon and St-Jean-de-Muzols.

Consequently, local legislation is changing the nature of St-Joseph, and of all the new wine being made there are few successful examples. Guilherand is the southern outpost, with vines planted on flat, rather unpropitious ground, and after that St-Joseph can be made in a continuous line north from Châteaubourg as far as the old northern limit, Chavanay. There are some hillside vineyards in this new area, like M. Maurice Courbis's Les Royes at Châteaubourg, but not many, and the wine being made from the vineyards on the plain is unflattering to the good name of the *Appellation*. The best *cuvées* made by the Co-opérative at St-Désirat-Champagne are about the only exception to this.

The total area under vines at St-Joseph came to 605 acres in 1982, a sharp increase on the 240 acres of 1971. Indeed, in the pre-*Appellation* days of the early 1950s, the wine was sold mainly in bulk as *vin de table*, at a purely nominal price. The vineyards were therefore tiny, since many local farmers found it more profitable to concentrate on growing fruit. There is a thriving fruit Co-opérative at Mauves, for instance, which has always been well patronized by the big jam manufacturers of Lyon.

Gradually, St-Joseph started to become known as a wine under its own name, and the trend away from the vines was halted by increased demand for it and therefore rising prices. In some places anciently abandoned vineyards were brought back to life. The large *négociant* companies began to take an active interest in it,

104

especially as they found St-Joseph a conveniently cheap alternative to the more expensive Hermitage wines.

In general, the older vines are grown on slopes above the Rhône and have to be tended manually. The local word for the dried stone terraces is *chalais*, and these are worked with a combination of horses, pulleys and the reliable *bigot*. Both the horses and the pulleys are used for carrying, be it grapes at harvest time or fallen earth after storms.

The Syrah vine forms over 90 per cent of the total plantation and is generally used on its own to make the red wine. Since 1980 a maximum of 10 per cent of white grapes, the Marsanne and the Roussanne, can also be used in the making of the red, provided that they are all fermented together at the same time. Again, it is not quite clear why this change of ruling should have occurred; one suspects that it is a purely commercial decision, rather than one inspired by a desire to seek a better quality of wine. The red St-Joseph is much better-known and easier to sell than the white, so the inclusion of white grapes in it would mean that there was that much more to sell.

Although these 'west bank' vines around Tournon and Mauves are grown on granite-based ground similar to that of Hermitage, they do not yield wines to rival the depth and fullness of their neighbour across the river. Growers generally propose two reasons for this: first, the soil at St-Joseph is a little less granitic and has clay and sand mixed in it. This is thought to be a restricting factor but is never narrowly defined. Second, the St-Joseph vineyards do not benefit from quite the excellent exposure of the unshielded Hermitage hill, which is always open to sun and wind.

This is not to belittle the wine, however, for it is another fine example of the excellence of the Syrah. St-Joseph is the lightest and fruitiest of the northern Côtes du Rhône reds, yet it often succeeds in surprising the drinker with its dark purple to black colour and heady bouquet of blackcurrants and raspberries. Lacking the complexity of a Côte-Rôtie or an Hermitage, and the full-bloodedness of a Cornas, it is a thoroughly appealing wine, one for quiet enjoyment and regular drinking, that will prove to be a good friend rather than a respected acquaintance. Because of its easy, uncomplicated style, St-Joseph is not really a *vin de garde*. If well looked after, a top-class vintage can last for around twelve years: ideally, the wine should be drunk between 2 and 8 years old, depending on the chosen style of the vintner. Leading growers like Coursodon and Chave make an initially firm, tannic wine that requires three or four years to soften out, while Grippat and Marsanne seek a fruitier, more accessible style that can be drunk with great success when 2 or 3 years old. Whatever the style, St-Joseph is always a good partner for veal, pork and simple poultry such as roast chicken or quail.

Some of the very small farmers continue to vinify their wine in an entirely traditional way, with massed family gatherings preceding a concerted harvest and treading down of the grapes. In some regions of France vintage time seems to have lost its customary carefree, jolly aspect, but not in the northern Côtes du Rhône: the *vendange* brings together more of the family than does Christmas, and the fresh evening air of early autumn resounds to the clink of glasses and the merry hum of voices at the end of a long day's picking.

On average, about 9,250 hectolitres of wine are made every year, of which only 6 to 7 per cent are white. Both the red and the white are generally vinified in the same way as Hermitage, although the red has a shorter ageing, something like nine to twelve months in cask. The Cave Co-opérative at St-Désirat-Champagne and the House of Jaboulet have both made *cuvées* in the past by the *macération carbonique* method, and although their wines made in this way have been fruity, they have lacked the aromas and finer flavours of a classic St-Joseph.

The white wine is bottled around April following the harvest and, after another six to nine months, is ready for drinking. When soundly made it is a surprisingly good wine, undoubtedly one of the best white wines of the Côtes du Rhône. Although not as 'complete' as Hermitage, it none the less contains a lasting delicacy and an appealing peach-like bouquet: when drunk in winter, for example, a good white St-Joseph brings to mind luscious, balmy summer days. Such a wine will last for six to eight years, by which time it will have acquired great richness and fullness of flavour.

One of the few growers to make both the red and white wine is M. Gustave Coursodon. At 60 he claims that he is retired, but he does a very good job of concealing it, for he travels to all the regional wine fairs to show his wines, attends local *Syndicat des Vignerons* meetings and so on. He is helped by his good-looking son Pierre, who has attended wine school and whose interest in continuing the family wine-making tradition encouraged his father to more than double their vineyard to a little over 17 acres.

The Coursodons live on the main square in Mauves, and their vineyards are dotted about on the slopes above the village. Not since Pierre's grandfather's time had they cultivated parts of the vineyard, and the recent reclaiming of terraces that had been left abandoned for over twenty years necessitated the building of a road to gain access to the *parcelles*, quite apart from the arduous task of clearing and replanting. This vineyard had caused certain problems for his grandfather in his day, as Gustave explained. 'Since my father was both mayor of the village and owner of a fair-sized vineyard, the Germans had no hesitation in occupying our house early in November 1942. As we depended on our vines for our existence, like everyone else we had to carry on as usual in order to earn our living. The Germans certainly accounted for a lot of our wine, but over all I would say that the Occupation didn't directly hamper our daily working of the vines, except for the time when an aeroplane fell on them.'

Gustave Coursodon is very French-looking, with a beret permanently perched on the top of his head as he darts sidelong glances here and there that back up his wry sense of humour. His wines are fermented in open wood vats and the reds enjoy as long an ageing in wood—around one and a half years—as they have always had, despite the pressures of demand these days. The white is a full, rounded wine, good to drink before it is 4 or 5 years old, and the red is often thickly flavoured and quite tannic when young. Good vintages like the 1978 and the 1980 need at least three or four years before obtaining a smooth harmony; without doubt, they are among the best in the *Appellation*, red wines that show the classic wild fruit and body of the Syrah to great effect.

M. Coursodon recognizes that the granting of *Appellation Contrôlée* to his wine has been a great incentive, and the same feelings apply to all the St-Joseph *vignerons*. M. Raymond Trollat, who at 52 looks ten years younger and whose healthy outdoor complexion is a good advertisement for life on the top of a well exposed hillside, lives at St-Jean-de-Muzols. He outlined the main differences that *Appellation Contrôlée* had made to him. 'Well, of course, our wine sells for more than before, which is very welcome, and we also now bottle most of it. I must say, though, that I really

107

enjoy being out in the vines, and even vinifying the wine, but when it comes to bottling and sticking on labels one by one . . .' His Gallic shrug and sharp whistle of breath were sufficient to demonstrate his feelings about *that* particular aspect of progress!

The Trollat family make a very good red wine from their 7·5-acre vineyard at the top of a hill directly facing Hermitage. Again, traditional methods of vinification are used, and the red shows an impressive amount of fruit, with a backbone of tannin to support it. About 20 per cent of M. Trollat's wine is now white, since he has found a firm demand for it from the United States. This is good to drink young, when its peach-like flavours show to best effect.

In the early 1970s the Trollats lived in complete isolation at the top of a winding road that leads up the hillside from near the old railway station of St-Jean-de-Muzols. Vines and apricot trees surrounded their farm, and there was not another house in sight. Now there are eight or ten houses-cum-villas, and the road up to the top of the hill has become rather like one long driveway. In the past two years two *vignerons* from St-Jean have succumbed to offers to sell their vineyards for housing development. Both men, M. Paul Réat and M. Jean Minodier, are in their late sixties and, without sons to help continue looking after the vineyards and the cellar, have taken an obvious decision. The disturbing aspect is that it is the quality vineyards of St-Joseph—the terraced hillsides of St-Jean-de-Muzols, for instance—that are disappearing. They are being replaced by vineyards planted on the plain that runs alongside the Lyon-to-Nîmes railway line. The new communities allowed to make St-Joseph from these vineyards are simply not in a position to match the quality vineyards of St-Jean, and the over-all standard of wine at St-Joseph will inevitably fall. The exceptions to this will remain the communities of St-Jean itself, Mauves and Tournon, and it is to be hoped that they will be able to uphold the previously untarnished name of the *Appellation*.

M. Minodier had himself found that bottling his own wine was a worthwhile development. Not only did he and his wife meet a wide selection of French visitors, including film stars from Paris, but he was also determined not to yield to the financially tempting offers made for his wine by the big *négociant* houses of the region. As he said, 'I want to keep my identity as a true *vigneron*.' Now the dream is over, and as M. Minodier settles into retirement and the bulldozers move in to clear his vineyard, one is left with a lingering feeling of sadness.

With MM. Minodier and Réat retiring and M. Louis Berthoulat abandoning wine-making in favour of growing evergreen trees, St-Jean-de-Muzols is a sorrowful place. Luckily, Tournon and Mauves still possess thriving vineyards, and the leading grower at Tournon, Jean-Louis Grippat, is making eminent wines from his 8·5-acre vineyard. This is spread out, ranging from the Clos des Hospitaliers, rented from the Benevolent Hospital of Tournon on the Tournon hillside, to the St-Joseph vineyard itself, just north of Mauves, where he has 2·5 acres of Marsanne and 3 acres of Syrah planted.

M. Grippat is enthusiastic about his wine-making and takes the visitor through the finest points of it as he wanders through his cellar, extinguished cigarette end in his hand much of the time and piece of chalk at the ready. This last is whipped out of recessed pockets in his working trousers and serves to illustrate details by graphic design on his cellar floor. M. Grippat is also distinguished by what comparatively few Rhône growers possess—a finely angled nose that is a definite advantage for tasting. 'My family have always been wine-makers, as far as I know, and used to live in St-Péray. In 1884 a branch of them moved to Mauves, choosing their wine country well, and later my branch came from there to Tournon. What this means is that I have access to a good selection of Rhône wines, since Bernard Gripa here at St-Joseph and Pierre Darona at St-Péray are both cousins.'

M. Jean-Louis Grippat

In addition to his St-Joseph vineyards, M. Grippat also owns nearly 4 acres of vines at Hermitage, mainly on Les Murets, a well-known white wine *clos*. Both his white St-Joseph and his white Hermitage are very good wines; the St-Joseph is the paler yellow of the two and has a lighter fresh fruit bouquet when a year or two old. The Hermitage recalls the scent of apricots and is notable for an attractive balance and elegance—a wine to drink before it is about 5 years old.

M. Grippat's red wines are studiously made, the St-Joseph displaying a marginally lighter style than some of the Mauves reds but still retaining an agreeable combination of racy fruitiness and steady Syrah backbone.

While M. Grippat concentrates entirely on wine-making, two of his neighbours in Mauves work at mixed agriculture, which is not surprising in an area well-known for its apricots and cherries. The Marsanne family is composed of three brothers, Jean, André and René, who tend about 5 acres of vineyards divided between Mauves and Tournon and who also grow delicious apricots. The Marsanne wine is all red and is distinguished by the ample fruit that it invariably shows; it could be deemed to be in the lightest category of St-Joseph, wine that is very attractive without harbouring any great depths of tannin. It is very good to drink before it is 4 years old.

As befits someone who is a protégé of Gérard Chave, Jean Maisonneuve makes a full-bodied, traditionally styled, red St-Joseph from his 2·5-acre vineyard at Mauves. He laments the fact that most of his land is more suitable for fruit trees than for vines, for he would clearly rather be a *viticulteur* than a mixed *agriculteur*. He has been bottling his wine since 1977 and is pleased with the new range of people whom he has met through selling it from his home on the main square. Although his wine label is not very scenic, the wine inside the bottle is good and offers further testimony to the right of Mauves to be called the unofficial capital of the St-Joseph *Appellation*.

St-Joseph Vintages

1961   Excellent. The wines will now be fading.
1962   Very good.
1963   Poor.

1964 Very good.

1965 Poor.

1966 Very good.

1967 Excellent. The wines are now generally past their best.

1968 Poor.

1969 Very good. The red wines were robust and developed very well.

1970 Good. The large crop undermined the strength of the wines, but their over-all balance made them attractive drinking.

1971 Excellent. A strongly flavoured vintage that matured very well. The reds are now beginning to fade away, while the very good whites have lost their appealing freshness.

1972 Good, particularly for wines made in Mauves. They were not very full-bodied, however, and have passed their best. A good, fruity year for the whites, which are now over the top.

1973 Very good. Despite the very large crop, the red wines were dark and well scented; they are now rather old. The whites, attractively styled when young, are in decline.

1974 Mediocre. Better for the whites than the reds.

1975 A small crop of light wines similar to the 1974s. The fruity red wines were for early drinking, while the whites were acidic and unbalanced.

1976 Generally good. There was some rain just before the harvest, but growers managed to make a generally full red wine, with an attractive colour and bouquet. It has developed well and should be drunk before about 1985. The whites were rich and powerfully flavoured, and will live for almost as long.

1977 Disappointing. The summer was cold and rainy, and light, irregular red wines resulted. The white wines were also light, and neither should be kept.

1978 Very good. A healthy harvest that permitted the growers to make strongly coloured and well constructed red wines, which are notable for their good balance. The more traditional style of wine will live for at least twelve years. The whites were also very fine, and will drink well in the next three or four years.

1979 Quite good, although lacking the depth of the 1978s. The reds are likely to show up well to around 1987, but their emphasis is on fruit and quite early drinking. The whites are soundly put together and will be best drunk before they are 6 years old.

1980   Good. The wines held more balance than the 1979s and the reds in particular display a bold fruitiness that will prove very enjoyable until around 1986. The whites are richly flavoured, and should do well for a similar length of time.

1981   Rather an uneven vintage, affected by rain during the harvest. The reds can be well coloured, but lacking in the balance that will help them to improve. They should be viewed with caution. A small crop for the white wines, which are light as well.

Earlier Exceptional Vintages   1959, 1957

Leading Growers at St–Joseph

Coursodon, Pierre et Gustave	07300 Mauves
Grippat, Jean-Louis	07300 Tournon
Chave, Jean-Louis	07300 Mauves
Marsanne, Jean	07300 Mauves
Trollat, Raymond	07300 St-Jean-de-Muzols
Cave Co-opérative de	
St-Désirat-Champagne	07 St-Désirat
Chapoutier, M.	26600 Tain-l'Hermitage
Courbis, Maurice	07130 Châteaubourg
Cuilleron, Antoine	42410 Chavanay
De Boisseyt-Chol	42410 Chavanay
Delas Frères	07300 Tournon
Desbos, Jean	07300 St-Jean-de-Muzols
De Vallouit, L.	26240 Saint-Vallier
Faurie, B.	07300 Tournon
Florentin, Emile	07300 Mauves
Gonon, Pierre	07300 Mauves
Gripa, Bernard	07300 Mauves
Lagnier, Georges	42410 Chavanay
Maisonneuve, Jean	07300 Mauves
Paret, Alain	42 St-Pierre-de-Boeuf
Vernay, Georges	69420 Condrieu

7

Cornas

The sight of a mature Cornas tumbling into a broad-based wine glass is unforgettable. What richness, vigour and virility are portrayed in that startling dash of colour—and the heady scent of blackcurrant and raspberry that accompanies it is sufficient to surprise the most cosmopolitan of wine tasters. Even as far back as 1763 the village priest, a M. Molin, had been moved to record: 'The mountain of this village is most entirely planted with vines which produce a very good *black* wine. This wine is much sought after by the merchants and is very heady.'

Cornas lies to the south of the main area of the St-Joseph *Appellation*, on the same west side of the Rhône, and with St-Péray marks the end of the northern Côtes du Rhône. It is a small, peaceful village that is surprisingly unchanged by busy Valence across the river. Several of the houses are made from the light-brown dried stone that is characteristic of the Ardèche and is frequently found farther down the Valley. There is no formal village centre. The piece of ground that passes for its main square is dominated by the lank spire of the church; inside, there is a memorial plaque to those fallen in the two world wars. Many of the names are from old wine-growing families that still work the slopes above Cornas.

The village's wine tradition goes back some thousand years. A Latin document of AD 885, from the canonry of Viviers, records that wine was at that time being made by an unnamed religious order. This is the first definite mention of the wine of Cornas, although it is said locally to have been appreciated by the Emperor Charlemagne as he passed through the village in 840. A good legend is virtually obligatory for any self-respecting wine community, and it is much more than probable that there was wine being made at Cornas in 840, when Charlemagne happened to be in the area!

Further evidence of Cornas's 'holy' origins comes in the register books of the St-Chaffre-de-Monastier Abbey, also in the diocese of Viviers. Here it is stated that 'a nobleman named Léotard gave to the Abbey of St-Chaffre a field measuring four *manses* and a vineyard, on the condition that the brother responsible for the order would offer his colleagues a fine annual dinner that included lampreys and big fish.' This agreement ran between the years 993 and 1014, but unfortunately it is difficult to be precise about Léotard's generosity, for the ancient measure of a *manse* has long since disappeared from use.

It does seem probable, though, that the religious orders were cultivating only small vineyards at this time; the local church documents take great care to point out with precision all boundaries and geographical situations, and the description 'a vine' occurs frequently in the old, often Latin, writings. By the time of M. Molin's enthusiasm in 1763 the scale of cultivation had evidently greatly increased, for the mountain was almost completely covered with vines.

Today the *Appellation* vineyards extend over 165 acres on the hillsides behind the village. This extent is less than in previous years, and Cornas is the one northern Rhône red wine vineyard where a happy future does not appear to be assured. As long ago as 1927, at a time when vineyards were being abandoned because there existed a shortage of men to look after them following the First World War, a local document describes the annual village wine production as around 590,000 litres: in the 1970s the most abundant harvest, that of 1973, yielded little more than one-third of this figure, about 202,500 litres. With the cultivation of the slope vines having to be performed entirely manually, there is once again less incentive for the farmer to concentrate on vine-growing; the old local saying that the *vigneron* must have '*bon dos, bon pied et bon oeil*' ('a good back, a good foot and a good eye') is all too true, and it is noticeable that at Cornas there are no growers under 35 years old bottling their own wine. The young people of the village have either turned their attentions to fruit-growing or have gone to work in Valence.

Consequently fewer than twenty of the sixty vine growers at Cornas bottle their wine; holdings are small and a man who owns both vines and fruit trees finds it much more convenient to sell his grapes off to a merchant rather than invest the money and time needed for a cellar, however small.

While the 1970s saw the growers trying to maximize their production by cultivating the more accessible land at the foot of the slopes, a 300-metre stretch between the village and the hillside where tractors can be driven, the early 1980s have heralded a return to looking after the former terraced vineyards. This is because the quality of the wine from the foot of the hillside did not rank with the standard of the wine made from farther up, and growers became aware of this once their wines were sampled at local or national tastings.

To discover just why Cornas is the northern Rhône's, and perhaps all the Rhône's, most ample, enormous-bodied wine, it is necessary to look at the soil and the climatic factors that set it apart from its neighbours. For let there be no doubt—a good Cornas 1 or 2 years old is a savage, dark wine that leaves the eye impressed and the palate coloured: even superlatives barely suffice to describe it with any justice.

First, the soil: at Cornas this is less homogeneous than in the neighbouring *Appellations* and although it contains considerable granite, other important elements are clay, limestone and sand. Much of the sand lies near the boundary with St-Péray, and it is from here that comes the most refined, quickest-ageing wine.

But probably the more important factor is the local micro-climate. Cornas is situated at a point where the Rhône Valley is very broad and the village is set well back against the Valley's western flank. It is thus quite thoroughly sheltered from the *mistral*, whose cooling force is widely dispersed across the corridor of the valley. As a result, the level of heat in the vineyards is often greater than elsewhere in the northern Côtes du Rhône, and this is directly reflected in the consistent ripeness of the grapes; their maturity no doubt helps towards the wine's unvarying intensity of colour and fullness of flavour.

For some people, however, Cornas is simply too overpowering, and in the past one or two growers have experimented with a reduced primary fermentation in order to obtain a lighter wine of more immediate appeal. The method generally used has been to shorten the fermentation from an average ten days or more to only five or six days, so that less tannin and colour will be extracted from the grapes. One of the growers who tried this different style of wine was Guy de Barjac, and he explained why he had since decided to prolong his fermentation to near its old length of time. 'I used not to ferment my grapes for more than six days, as my biggest concern was to make a wine that showed finesse. One of the great problems of Cornas is that, when young, it tends to be very coarse, and it is regrettable that pressure of demand deems that it be bottled and sold when still in its infancy. I was trying to produce a wine that could be readily appreciated at the time of its purchase, but it was the 1977 vintage that changed my mind. This wine was fine and light, but I considered that it resembled more a lesser Burgundy than a Cornas, and the last thing I wanted to do was to lose the Cornas style in my wines.'

M. de Barjac continued: 'I have therefore increased the length of fermentation again to eight days, starting with the big, full-bodied 1978 vintage. If I look back, I now realize that the six-day-fermentation wine didn't have enough tannin or quite enough body to support a respectable 8–10-year ageing. Now I have advised my friends and customers to keep some of my 1978 for the year 2000.'

M. de Barjac's fellow *vignerons* are still striving to make as full and typical wine as their forebears but in recent years have slightly modified techniques in order to make their cellar work easier. Three leading growers, Clape, Michel and Voge, have all ceased using open wood fermenting vats, preferring instead closed concrete vats in which the fermentation can be more easily controlled. However, no one destalks grapes, and both Clape and Voge favour a light crushing by foot prior to fermentation. The effect of this is to break the skins of the grapes lightly and is in no way comparable to the pressure exerted by a modern stemming and crushing machine. The grapes take longer to commence their fermentation when treated in this old-fashioned way, and a more gradual and profound extraction of the fruit occurs as a result. This is precisely what many of the growers are attempting to achieve, for the more *frappant*, or striking, their wine, the more they are pleased.

Cornas is less aged in cask than in previous times because of an ever-present demand for the *Appellation*'s tiny production. Where two years was the norm until the mid-1970s, the ageing span is now reduced to eighteen months or less, which means that it is more necessary than ever to let the wine come along quietly in the bottle.

One might expect a wine of this nature to be overpoweringly alcoholic, but not at all. It is very rare for a Cornas to exceed 13° alcohol strength, whereas a Châteauneuf-du-Pape, for instance, will often contain 14° or even a little more. The wine is thus able to attain a pleasant harmony as its initial coarseness wears off—but, alas, it is rarely given the chance to prove itself. The strongest vintages such as 1976 and 1978 will have a life-span of fifteen to twenty years, and the wine from good harvests like 1980 will certainly live for up to fifteen years. Most Cornas is not ready to drink until it is 6 to 8 years old, whatever the vintage; before that, its broad range of nuances and aromas is but barely developed, and the sensation to the imbiber can be akin to that of attempting to drink a heavy black syrup. Cornas is an unpretentious wine, but it does cry out for, and repay, long keeping; when drunk past the age of 10, it exposes a fine variety of gentle aromas, reminiscent of violets or wild flowers, so soft has the wine become.

Such a small *Appellation* boasts a tightly knit wine community where a premium is placed on dedication and hard work. There is no Cave Co-opérative in the village, and the unity and collective sense of purpose of the individual *vignerons* is all the more heartening to see. This finds unrestrained outlet in the annual Festival of the Syrah and the Roussette, held in Cornas every December, which is a worthwhile exercise in public relations: betraying much curiosity and interest, the *vignerons* spend half a day visiting cellars in other local *Appellations* and, while they may come away liberally primed, great mental note has been taken about differing techniques and attitudes towards vinification.

Cornas's best-known grower and the one who makes the best, quite exceptional wine, is M. Auguste Clape. A quiet man, he nevertheless displays a firm and discreet sense of humour and his softly spoken asides are well worth waiting for. He often wears the sort of rough wool sweater favoured by English university professors; with his glasses and grey hair, it is only to be expected that here is a man of knowledge. Indeed, he is, for M. Clape is always ready to explain his latest experiments in the cellar, or why he has slightly altered his vinification technique from one harvest to the next, all of which is done with a phlegmatic, almost scholarly air. Like the other northern Rhône champions, MM.

Chave and Guigal, he possesses the rare talent of being able to make good wine every year, whether the grape harvest has been good or bad.

M. Clape was not actually born into a wine family and only arrived at Cornas after his marriage. Perhaps it is no coincidence, therefore, that his approach to wine-making is remarkably unbridled: he experiments with ageing his wine in different kinds of wood, and in his fifties even went back to school to study the theory of viticulture at the Beaune School of Wine in Burgundy, probably the world's foremost institute of its kind.

M. Clape's experiment with the ageing of his wine in the same-sized oak and chestnut barrels in fact occurred by mistake: he meant to put all his 1973 crop in oak but mistook the identity of one of his barrels. The difference between the 'oak wine' and the 'chestnut wine' was marked; both bore a similar bouquet, but on the palate the 'chestnut wine' was dominated by the tannin emanating from the wood of the barrel. By contrast, the youthful fruit and grapiness of the 'oak wine' were much in evidence, and

M. Auguste Clape

118

this barrel appeared to have the greater future. M. Clape added that, to the best of his knowledge, wines matured in chestnut generally came round after about two years but were unlikely to attain the smoothness and suppleness of flavour of a wine matured in oak.

M. Clape's 13·5 acre vineyard has been expanded since the mid-1970s and is now one of the larger holdings in this small *Appellation*. On average, he reckons to make about 20,500 bottles of wine a year. He now sells his vintages when they are rarely more than 2 years old, which he does not consider old enough for the wine's potential to be properly developed; but he has no choice other than to comply with the wishes of his clientele. In the meantime he has established a small private cellar containing some of the best years of Cornas. The oldest he has yet drunk was a 1941, opened in 1963. Although slightly *passé* in bouquet and colour, it none the less drank very well.

An illustration of the village's long-established tradition is shown by the fact that two of its families, the Michels and the Lionnets, have been making wine there for around 400 years. M. Joseph Michel, a florid-faced man in his mid-sixties, owns 15 acres of vines, and, now that he has taken an honourable retirement, contents himself with looking after the family cellars. He is helped there by his son Robert, whose ginger-coloured hair stands out in the vineyards; at 35, Robert is the youngest family *vigneron* at Cornas and is quite frank about his preoccupation with the future of the vineyards there: 'People such as my father and Joseph Lionnet have really retired, and other good growers in the *Appellation* will retire in a short time as well. There's no young blood in sight, and that's the worrying aspect. It's not as if we can be compared with St-Joseph, where expansion is shooting ahead on the easily manageable flat ground. This is all hard work here, up the hillside in hot sun and on your feet all day, and young people aren't prepared to do it.' He shakes his head glumly.

More than half the Michels' vines are planted on the full slopes above the village, while the rest stand at the foot of the hills. The Michels firmly believe their full-slope wine to be decidedly superior to anything produced lower down the hillside—probably because the vines higher up are naturally more exposed to the sun.

The family gathers *en masse* for the *vendange* towards the end of September, and the Michels proceed to make their wine in much the same way as their ancestors: father and son churn the grapes down by foot in a large open vat before leaving the juice to ferment on the skins for ten to fifteen days. Around Easter every year they hold their own little wine fête, when all their regular customers come to collect the wine ordered the previous year and to taste the wine that has just been barrelled. The general scale of operations at Cornas is indicated by the fact that the average order placed is for only about thirty bottles.

The Michels find their way of life both varied and stimulating. As the father said: 'I wouldn't change my profession for anything. It is a good feeling to see your own wine, finished and bottled up, and then to see to whom it is going and whether it is likely to be appreciated. I used to sell almost completely to the trade, but more and more of my clients urged me to bottle it myself and sell it direct to them. What I really enjoy is having the people come to me: then I meet all sorts and nationalities. We even had a visit from a man who had read your book in Cairo, so life is full of surprises!'

A near neighbour of the Michels is M. Guy de Barjac, who looks like a French version of Robert Taylor. He has an unusual background for a *vigneron* in that he speaks three languages and has a university degree. M. de Barjac explained how he had become a wine-grower. 'My family have owned vines at Cornas for many generations, and when it came to finding a job after university my thoughts led me here. I must admit that there was the possibility of the army, but when I stopped to think, well, it's either military college or Cornas, I knew very well where I would end up.'

M. de Barjac is now making wine from nearly 4 acres of vines and has recently planted a further acre. As he works on his own, this is the absolute maximum size of vineyard that he thinks he can hope to maintain properly. And now that he has extended his fermentation back towards its old length of time, his wine is showing much better. His 1980, for instance, reveals a typical Cornas tannin, but this is not allowed to repress the soft, flowery flavours on the nose and the slowly emerging fruit on the palate.

Some of the growers also own small vineyards at St-Péray but by law must make their sparkling wine in St-Péray itself. M. Alain Voge is one such grower, and his time is consequently divided between the two villages. Like M. Clape, he is a member of St-

Péray's small but prosperous Cave Co-opérative, which carries out the vinification of his sparkling wine. In his early forties, M. Voge has a bright face and darting eyes that shine with his enthusiasm for his life as a wine-maker. He looks after his 12 acres of slope vines all by himself, which is quite some undertaking, since they are spread out all over the vineyards in about a dozen plots. Occasional but welcome help is provided by his mother, who turns out in the vineyards to help tie the vines to their stakes and lends a hand with the labelling in the cellar.

Whereas M. Voge used to age his Cornas only in wood, he has now altered the process to take in the first year in concrete vats, followed by only three or six months in cask. 'I'm aiming to make a wine that is fruitier in style than it used to be. I've also been in part compelled to do this change through my lack of storage space in the cellar. The casks take up a lot more space, and it's also been very difficult to get hold of them since we no longer have any barrel-makers round here any more. Growers here go to Burgundy for their casks these days, but just recently I managed to get some from M. Dubourg in St-Péray when his business closed down. I was well pleased with this because I don't think that our wine needs any extra tannin, and I find that the Burgundian casks, although they are very well made, give out a little too much extra tannin.'

M. Voge's Cornas is now evolving more quickly than the wine of most of the other *vignerons*, to the extent that big vintages such as the 1978 should be drunk before they are much more than 6 years old. Despite the difference in style, M. Voge still recommends that his wine should be drunk with roast meats, game or strong cheese such as Roquefort, Bresse Bleu or nicely matured goat's cheese. 'If you follow my advice,' he adds with a beaming smile, 'I'm sure you'll never have been healthier!'

Cornas Vintages

1955   Good. The wines were rather light, but had an agreeable harmony.

1956   Good. Soft, well balanced wines.

1957   A very good year. The wines were robust and fairly tannic, but have now dried out.

1958   Mediocre. Light wines.

1959 A good vintage of harmonious and well perfumed wines that are now over the top.

1960 Good. Sound wines that lacked a little elegance, but which are now finished.

1961 An excellent year. Big, full wines that held a good balance between their fruit and tannin. They have stood the test of time well, but any remaining bottles should be drunk in the next five years or so.

1962 Another excellent vintage, only a little less powerful and attractive than 1961. The wines should be drunk soon.

1963 Very poor. Extremely light wines.

1964 Very good. Sound, well-balanced wines that with ageing displayed great finesse. They are now in decline.

1965 Mediocre. Light, acid wines.

1966 A very good year. Strongly coloured wines that with age received a soft, full flavour. They should be drunk soon.

1967 Excellent. Big, heavy wines that were full of tannin when young. They have matured well and are delicious to drink at present.

1968 Poor. Very light wines.

1969 Very good. Rich, harmonious wines that were very similar to the 1959s. They will be best appreciated if drunk before 1985.

1970 Good. The crop was large, so the wines tended to lack the strength of the very best years. They have started to lose their fruity softness.

1971 Excellent: a magnificent vintage almost on a par with 1961. The wines were very full-bodied and heavily coloured. They have progressed very well and are now in prime condition. They can keep until around 1992.

1972 A very good vintage of richly coloured, richly flavoured wines that have held their attractive red colour very well. They are showing gentle age and are just beginning to dry out. To drink before 1985.

1973 Very good. A large crop of well coloured, well balanced wines. They are still in good drinking order and should live until about 1986.

1974 A medium vintage, with wines lacking in colour and flavour. The foremost growers like Clape and Michel made some good bottles, but even these are now in decline.

1975   An average year of well scented, fruity wines that need to be drunk before about 1984; with age they have blossomed well.

1976   Generally very good. A healthy harvest gave well coloured and attractively scented wines which have an equilibrium that indicates a likely life span of about twenty years. .

1977   A mediocre vintage, where the grapes were affected by rot. Lightly coloured and rather acid, the wines do not bear the stamp of good, traditional Cornas.

1978   A very good vintage. The wines have proved to be well balanced and notable for their depth of tannin, which is likely to sustain them over the next ten years at least. The growers expect them to live for a good twenty years.

1979   Quite a good vintage. The wines lacked acidity and their relative imbalance does not give them the fullness normally associated with Cornas. Some attractive bottles will no doubt emerge, but the low acidity and shortage of fruit are worrying. A vintage that may live for around ten or twelve years.

1980   Very good. Brightly-coloured wines of good intensity of fruit and tannin. They will develop attractive length with ageing, but are still very backward. The best *cuvées*, from growers such as Clape, de Barjac and Juge, should live for perhaps twenty years.

1981   A reasonable year when the wines have lacked colour but possessed attractive bouquets. Low in tannin, they are likely to advance quickly, and will be suitable for drinking in their first ten years.

Earlier Exceptional Vintages   1952, 1949, 1943

Leading Growers at Cornas

Clape, Auguste	07130 Cornas
Michel, Robert	07130 Cornas
de Barjac, Guy	07130 Cornas
Juge, Marcel	07130 Cornas
Balthazar, René	07130 Cornas
Catalon, Roger	07130 Cornas

Delas Frères	07300 Tournon
Dumien, Henri	07130 Cornas
Fumat, André	07130 Cornas
Gilles, Louis	07130 Cornas
Lionnet, Jean	07130 Cornas
Maurice, Marc	07130 Cornas
Teysseire, Jean	07130 St-Péray
Verset, Louis	07130 Cornas
Verset, Noël	07130 Cornas
Voge, Alain	07130 Cornas

8

Saint-Péray

St-Péray, the last of the northern Rhône vineyards, has a curiously confused identity, not at all akin to that of a quiet wine community. Behind the village, characterized by the soft-coloured local Ardèchois stone of some of its houses and flattered by its large market place that is shaded by irregularly spaced plane trees, the vine-covered slopes reach out and up towards the hilly loneliness of the Ardèche. Within five minutes of driving towards St-Romain-de-Lerps, Lamastre or even Toulaud to the south, the meandering road has taken the visitor into a secluded world of quiet hills, sweeping valleys and an occasional farmhouse. Sounds carry with remarkable clarity, be they the tinkling of a goat bell or the cry of a sheep separated from its flock. It is hard to imagine that on the other side of St-Péray, on the short plain that runs east of the village, the vines spread nearly into the urban confusion of Valence. They are halted by the Rhône, an impassive witness to the uneasy liaison being formed between town and country.

Such is the incongruous setting for the Côtes du Rhône's best sparkling wine. St-Péray may be little-known, but none the less its 118 acres of vineyards carry both lengthy historical and popular traditions. Thus, the still white wine attracted attention from two Roman writers: Pliny, in his *Natural History*, Book XIV, Chapters 1 and 2, and Plutarch, in Book V of his *Table Talk*.

Little is then heard of the wine until the nineteenth century, when its popularity seems to have been widespread. The young Napoleon Bonaparte was stationed as a cadet at the garrison of Valence and in later years spoke of St-Péray as his first wine discovery. Lamartine, Alphonse Daudet and Guy de Maupassant are all said to have referred to the wine in their writings, and a vaudeville entertainer called Marc-Antoine Desaugiers (1772–1827) even wrote a song entitled 'Le Voyageur de St-Péray', which went as follows:

> *A vous, je m'adresse, mesdames,*
> *C'est pour vanter le Saint-Péray.*
> *Il est surnommé Vin des Femmes,*
> *C'est vous dire qu'il est parfait.*
> *La violette qu'il exhale*
> *En rend le goût délicieux*
> *Et l'on peut dire qu'il égale*
> *Le nectar que buvait les Dieux.*[1]

The most famous story about St-Péray concerns the German composer Richard Wagner. In a letter from Bayreuth dated 2 December 1877, he wrote as follows to a leading *négociant* house: 'Will you please send me as soon as possible those 100 bottles of St-Péray wine which you offered me.' Wagner was then busy composing *Parsifal*, and it is popularly presumed by local *vignerons* that passages from this opera must have originated at the bottom of a glass of their wine.

Today the vineyards of St-Péray and Cornas border one another, and it would need a discerning eye to know where the Syrah stops and the Marsanne starts. The Marsanne is the majority grape at St-Péray and accounts for about four-fifths of all the vines. In theory, St-Péray is allowed to be made from it, the Roussanne and the Roussette grape—'in theory', because the identity of the last named has never officially been made clear.

When discussing the problem of the Roussette, some *vignerons* are apt to declare that the word 'Roussette' is merely a local term for the Roussanne vine. Others bravely suggest a difference, without being able to specify it, and say that in the past the 'Roussette' has caused great consternation to the French fraud inspectors. These gentlemen would like to see the Roussette

---

[1] *To you I address myself, ladies,*
It is to praise the Saint-Péray.
It is nicknamed the Wine of Women,
Which means that it is perfect.
The violets that it exhales
Give it a flavour of delight
And one can say that it matches
The nectar that the gods would drink.

excluded, since they claim that St-Péray should be made solely from the Marsanne and the Roussanne; the difference between the Roussanne and the Roussette is so minimal that much good time is wasted trying to find it!

One man who is able to shed light on the exact nature of the Roussanne vine is Jean-François Chaboud, who makes the best sparkling St-Péray. In 1972 he received some Roussanne cuttings from the late Dr Philippe Dufays, the viticultural expert who owned Domaine de Nalys at Châteauneuf-du-Pape, and has since been able to observe this plant's characteristics as compared with the Marsanne and the Roussanne grown at Hermitage; the latter, he avers, is distinct from the Roussanne that he is growing.

'My Roussanne is distinguished by a series of jagged edges on the leaves, which also have a lot more veins on them than the Marsanne leaves. The Roussanne grape is also more pointed than the Marsanne, and while a bunch of Marsanne will weigh a little over 1 kilo, the Roussanne gives only about half as much fruit per bunch. This Roussanne, even in a normal year, gives less juice than most other local vines and also has a lot more pips in the grapes. I find that it is extremely susceptible to attacks of oïdium and the grape juice easily risks becoming oxidized at the precise moment of harvesting. I therefore make sure that its grapes enter the press completely intact. I have 2 acres of Roussanne and in 1981 made nearly 2,500 litres of wine from them, at a degree of around 13 Gay Lussac. I sell this as still wine, but it doesn't really live much more than a couple of years, which convinces me further that this Roussanne is not the same as the one planted on Hermitage Hill. As to finding out the truth about the two vines,' he added with a laugh, 'well, I think that's a story that I shall leave to someone else, for the moment anyway.'

St-Péray and its neighbouring village of Toulaud have such widely varying soils that the growers prefer to make up one uniform wine that will be generally recognizable from year to year. Therefore it is common to blend most of the wine, as in Champagne, and to sell it without declaring a vintage. Only Chaboud among the leading growers gives his sparkling wine a year; he reasons that the wine of even allegedly indifferent vintages such as 1977 will come round in time, and that it is much more interesting for the consumer to chart the wine's progress if it carries a year and a definable character of its own.

127

Where St-Péray differs from Champagne is in the soil constituents, for there is no chalk in the ground, the dominating elements being a mixture of clay, sand and stones. In places there are patches of mountain granite and flint, which are thought to contribute to the wine's roundness.

St-Péray must by law be made exactly as Champagne, with even the yeasts used in the wine coming from that famous wine region: these are sent down in liquid form in glass jugs, or *bonbonnes*, by express train from Champagne. But it is a community that holds its own viticultural traditions very close and it is interesting that few, if any, of the growers have ever trained in Champagne or, indeed, have ever seen the inside of a *champenoise* cellar. The art of wine-making has instead been handed down from father to son over many generations and is consequently seen as a highly personalized affair. Whether M. Dupont down the road makes his wine in this or that style is not of interest to the *vigneron*; he has his own particular way of making his wine, which is therefore the right way.

In all sparkling wines a certain tartness is welcome, and the growers like to harvest early in October, while the acid level of the grapes is quite high. The grapes intended for still white wine are left for about a week longer, so that they contain more sugar and less astringency. From there the vinification procedure is as for all white wines, with fermentation taking place in concrete vats.

Around April or May after the harvest—'before the big heat of summer,' say the growers—the wine is bottled; it has a clear, almost transparent colour and no bubbles. At the moment of bottling a blend of sugar and yeasts, known as *liqueur de tirage*, is put into the wine to encourage a further fermentation; the liquid content of this mixture can be around 4 centilitres per litre, although the growers are careful not to make the wine too sweet in years when very ripe grapes have been harvested. The yeasts serve to reactivate the wine, and its renewed fermentation converts the sugar into alcohol, producing amounts of carbon dioxide as a result. The carbon dioxide gas generated has, quite literally, nowhere to run—except to the bottom of the bottle. As it slowly dissipates through the length of the bottle, bubbles appear on every side, and the wine becomes effervescent. The pressure of the imprisoned carbon dioxide is very great, and occasionally a dud or weak bottle explodes under the strain.

The bottles are then stacked in long, closely packed rows in the cellar. About a year later, with the secondary fermentation well finished, they are transferred nose-down, to wooden holders known as *pupitres*. The *pupitre* is made up of two pieces of wood, each of which contains 60 holes, which stand leaning in on one another like an inverted cone. The bottles are placed neck-first into these holders, in an almost horizontal position.

The *pupitre* is a *champenois* implement and has become more standard at St-Péray than the old local *treteau de remuage*. This is a trestle table with four trays on top of each other, a large affair 1·5 metres high, with holes for 120 bottles on each level. Only very occasionally does one see a *treteau de remuage* in a St-Péray cellar nowadays, especially since the operation of turning the bottles can generally be done only very carefully, with one hand at a time, because of the wearing away of the holes over the years.

When the bottles are put in their wooden *pupitres* or *treteaux* the wine in them is far from clear, for the secondary fermentation has brought with it a large amount of dead yeast cells and sediment. For a month the bottles in the *pupitres* are turned in pairs by a deft flick of the wrists: every day they draw nearer to the vertical, and the sediment inside them starts sliding slowly down towards the neck.

'Turning' is one of the most skilled, and least pleasant, tasks in the whole elaboration of a sparkling wine. The amateur goes into the cellar and happily turns a couple of bottles, only to see the sediment dance about in a burst of crazy merriment. The experienced *caviste* in Champagne turns as many as 25,000 bottles a day—and promptly wishes he hadn't, for turning encourages an inflammation of the wrist joints that brings on arthritis at an early age. Perhaps the end product is suitably comforting.

By the time the bottles are in a near-vertical position, the sediment is well lodged in their necks. The next operation is disgorging and corking. The bottles are placed one by one, with their necks frozen, on a rotating disgorging machine, which whips off the tightly sealed cap. The upper liquid slowly starts to run out, and with it the sediment, and the bottle is immediately topped up or 'dosed' with a mixture of cane sugar and St-Péray, half a centilitre per bottle. It is then passed straight to the corking machine, as the grower naturally does not want to lose all his good hard work and fine bubbles. Should he so desire, the grower can at this point make a *demi-sec*, or sweeter wine, through the simple addition of more cane sugar to the solution; this comes to two centilitres of *liqueur* per bottle.

Corking has usually been one of the more straightforward aspects of making any 'bubbly' wine, but times have changed. Women's fashion, the great French pursuit of *la mode*, has suddenly affected the world of wine. M. René Milliand, a *vigneron* of St-Péray, explained that the craze for women's shoes with enormous cork soles and heels has dried up the usual steady supply of high-class cork.

Good-quality corks are carefully moulded together in four segments that are joined both horizontally and vertically: this ensures an effective seal against the entry of any air and the exit of any wine. Now, with the extra demand for cork, lower-grade trees are being used, and a cheap alternative has reached the market. This is composed of only two thin strips of good, solid cork on the end, the rest being a conglomeration of tiny bits all stuck together. These tiny pieces come from the inferior trees and have a tendency to break up when the cork is being turned and taken out of the bottle. This is one problem Dom Perignon never had to consider.

After so much care and personal attention, the wine ought to be good, and it is. A St-Péray *méthode champenoise*, after three or four years in the bottle, is a smooth and rounded wine with more body, but admittedly more coarseness, than a normal Champagne. It is at that age considered to be at its best by most of the *vignerons*, although the general lack of a vintage date is clearly hampering for the consumer. Characterized by a rich, sometimes golden colour, the wine carries a certain fragrance of straw and discreet 'earthiness'. On the palate its strong grapey taste has a striking exuberance typical of a wine from the Côtes du Rhône and carries through into an agreeably lingering aftertaste. All too easy to drink at any time of the day (St-Péray acts well against even the severest of hangovers), it is best served well chilled as an *apéritif*.

One-fifth of the wine, however, is still and is generally sold under the title of *nature*. This is vinified like the other still white wines of the northern Rhône, and when made only from the Marsanne grape—as it is 90 per cent of the time—it can be drunk with great success until its eighth birthday, with little likelihood of maderization. One of the village's leading *négociants*, M. Gilles, recalled that he had once drunk a 20-year-old St-Péray *nature* with an important client: the wine was still magnificent, being golden coloured and carrying a fine nectar-like aroma. He added that the wine had played a significant part in clinching the deal in question!

Of all the Rhône Valley *Appellations*, the most provincial are St-Péray in the north and Rasteau *vin doux naturel* in the south. Neither possesses any real fame outside its immediate area, nor do they give the impression of being thriving and go-ahead. The number of *vignerons* making and bottling their own wine is restricted in both *Appellations*, and when one meets the star of St-Péray, Jean-François Chaboud, it is sad to think that a man of his ability is selling such a parochial wine, one that is likely to remain unknown to discerning wine lovers nearly everywhere.

M. Chaboud is an enthusiastic man in his early forties, just losing a little of his hair, but not through worry, for he makes, and sells without problem, the best wine in the *Appellation*. His sparkling St-Péray is the most stylized wine of all, with a robust, full flavour to it, but equally a long and attractive finish that sets it apart from many of the other wines. He considers that he bottles his wine earlier than the other growers, around the end of January, so that he can achieve a finer *mousse* than would otherwise be possible.

In front of a blazing log fire in the sitting-room of his neat house, which stands next to the cellars, he explained that his experiments with using the Roussanne grape in the sparkling wine had not been successful, 'You can see that I make a still wine from 100 per cent Roussanne, but that is the only way I can do anything with this generally difficult grape. I once tried making a sparkling wine composed half-and-half of Marsanne and Roussanne, but it simply didn't work; the wine was unbalanced, lacked acidity and simply wasn't *vif* [lively] as I would have hoped. All my *mousseux* is now made only from the Marsanne.'

He went on: 'Pierre Darona and I are the largest growers here now. I have a little over 17 acres of vines, all in the same plot in the Quartier d'Hongrie above the village. I have white clay soil there, and I find that the wine from it is fuller than the wine coming from nearer the Cornas road down on the plain. There the wines are drier and possibly a little more acid. Since the early 1970s I have worked out a way of building up terrace walls on my hillside so that I can cultivate the flat ledges mechanically; this has saved me a lot of time, as before I did all my vineyard work with horses, which are, of course, a lot slower.'

While Jean-François Chaboud lives right in the village of St-Péray, Pierre Darona's farm and cellars are tucked away on a hillside in a beautiful rolling valley that leads south-west towards Toulaud. M. Darona's family have been making *méthode champenoise* wine for at least fifty years and part-own, part-rent, a total of 22 acres of vines in the *quartier* known as Les Faures, near their home. Like M. Chaboud, M. Darona is only able to look after a vineyard of this size because he has attached three-quarters of his vines along rows of wire—which, once they are successfully trained, saves him time in their pruning and upkeep—and because he too is able to drive a tractor along the slopes and half-slopes of his vineyard.

Mme Darona explained that they were fortunate to have an alternative source of income if the grape harvest was poor and pointed from the cellar door to their clumps of apricot trees. 'As St-Péray *mousseux* must by law be left for nine months after its bottling and we leave it for twelve months, it's a great help to the family funds to have a more rapid income each year from the apricots.' The Daronas make over 80 per cent of their wine in the *mousseux* way, and it has a fine style, without perhaps showing a wholly definable local character. While M. Chaboud's wine can be drunk with certain first courses such as raw or cured ham or cold *quiche lorraine*, M. Darona's is better as a straightforward, chilled *apéritif*.

The other main vineyard owners at St-Péray are the Milliand family. The observant traveller will pick out the large and faded wall advertisement of 'Léon Milliand et Cie' on the way to Valence, and today the family owns a total of 16 acres of vines scattered in small groups throughout the *Appellation* area. This they regard as an advantage, in that it allows them to produce a desired effect in the blending of their wine. Thus there will be years when in order to maintain their usual style of a rounded wine, they will deliberately leave some of the grapes until they have started to rot, arguing that their inclusion in the wine helps to give it added body and alcohol.

The Milliands are very keen on their shooting and like to go out looking for birds and game. In this respect they are like a large proportion of the French population. A Sunday walk in the French countryside is a perilous business, with a mass of trigger-happy *chasseurs* combing the fields ready to fire off at anything that moves. Indeed, birds are few and far between, since anything with the remotest semblance of flavour is shot at, which lets out practically only magpies and sparrows!

For a village as small as St-Péray, it is surprising to find three *négociant* companies established there. Two, Eugène Vérilhac and Gilles Père et Fils, both own about 2 or 3 acres of vines, which supplement the supply of grapes they receive from small local farmers who also grow fruit and vegetables. Their St-Péray wines are respectable, although lacking the character of a private grower's. M. Vérilhac is notable for his concentration on the older, finer wines from all over the Côtes du Rhône, and his list usually contains a Cornas that is at least ten years old.

The wines of M. Gilles are less exceptional, while the third *négociant*, Paul-Etienne Père et Fils has dropped out of selling St-Péray and now trades in very ordinary Côtes du Rhône. Until 1981 there was a fourth *négociant* in the village, the agreeable M. Amedée Dubourg, whose speciality was cheaper Ardèche wines, such as the Côtes du Vivarais. He retired in that year, and as none of his seven daughters was anxious to take over the business, his cellars are now being used by the Tain-l'Hermitage Cave Co-opérative for the vinification of their sparkling St-Péray, whose annual production comes to something over 50,000 bottles.

Until the post-war years St-Péray used to be a barrel-making centre for the northern Côtes du Rhône, with a prosperous community of four *tonneliers*. Sadly, 1973 saw the retirement of the last of them, M. Vinard, who at 65 decided that he had worked hard enough and long enough all by himself.

A grey-haired, slight man who belies his years, M. Vinard explained that he took over from his father. Methods have not changed in his time, and 90 per cent of a *tonnelier*'s work remains entirely manual. The wood used has gradually altered, however, from purely oak to much more chestnut, which is taken from the Isère region east of the Rhône. Formerly the oak would come from the rest of France, Austria and Russia, but it is now both very hard to find and very expensive, with the result that some wine-growers have reluctantly had to turn towards chestnut.

A *tonnelier*'s time is divided between carrying out repairs and making new barrels. Much the hardest and most skilled work is the repairs, and it is the lack of experienced hands for this that *vignerons* most regret. To repair the area around the stopper or underneath the metal bands on a 585-litre oak barrel is a difficult operation. 'Some of the barrels I used to be sent were as much as a hundred years old,' said M. Vinard. 'It is very precise and delicate work to graft on to the grain of such old wood.'

M. Vinard found no one prepared to take over his work and realizes that his is a dying art, one that has been outpaced by the march of time. The more extensive use of metal vats was a blow for the trade, while the formation of wine Co-opératives, with their jointly owned barrels, meant that the demand from the small farmer dried up almost completely. At the same time, the reduced cultivation of the northern Rhône slopes since the inter-war years has been a further hindrance to the barrel-making trade. Now *vignerons* must buy mass-produced oak or chestnut barrels, which will never be repaired, merely replaced.

St-Péray Vintages

The white wines of St-Péray are not intended for very long keeping. As a general rule, the sparkling wine should be drunk within about six years. It is not often given a vintage, however; only J.-F. Chaboud of the top growers declares a year. The still wines are generally dated. They age a little better and can normally be drunk successfully until about 8 years old.

1964   Excellent.
1965   Poor.
1966   Good.
1967   Excellent.
1968   Mediocre.
1969   Excellent. Fruity and aromatic wines.
1970   Mediocre. The crop was very large, and the wines somewhat unbalanced.
1971   Excellent. Attractive, harmonious wines.
1972   Very good. Quite high in acid content, the wines also possessed good fruitiness and general refinement.
1973   Good. A plentiful harvest gave wines that were fruity, but sometimes a little unbalanced. Better for the sparkling wines than the still wines.
1974   Medium. A vintage that varied from grower to grower.

Some of the wines were rather 'flabby' and lacking in charm, while others possessed good bouquet and richness. The still St-Péray is now over the top.

1975 Medium. A small harvest yielded grapes that were best suited for a sparkling wine vinification. The still wines were light and fruity and should have been drunk already.

1976 Very good. Both the sparkling and the still wines were fruity and attractively coloured. The still wines have aged well and are now showing the rich and profound flavours of old age.

1977 An irregular vintage. Quite a large crop gave wines tending to be over acidic. Light styled, some have come round as their acidity has reduced, while others do not look like improving. M. Chaboud's wines are in the former group, but need drinking up.

1978 A small harvest of well ripened grapes gave correspondingly well balanced and attractive wines, with good roundness to them. The still wines will be best appreciated if drunk before 1985.

1979 A good vintage. The sparkling wines possess plenty of fruit and they have a pleasing acidity to keep them fresh. They should be drunk by 1984. The still wines are a little lacking in acidity, and should therefore be drunk soon.

1980 A large crop, whose wines were fruity with just enough depth of flavour to make them very good drinking in their first four years—the sparkling and still wines alike.

1981 Another large crop in which the wines have a tendency to be unbalanced. They have a simple fruitiness, but this is not sustained by any profound flavours. The wines should be drunk young, probably by their third or fourth birthday. Better for the sparkling than for the still wines.

Earlier Exceptional Vintages   1962, 1961, 1957, 1955

Leading Growers at St-Péray

Chaboud, Jean-François	07130 St-Péray
Darona, Pierre	07130 St-Péray
Teysseire, Jean	07130 St-Péray
Cave les Vignerons de St-Péray	07130 St-Péray

Clape, Auguste	07130 Cornas
Cotte-Vergne, R.	07130 St-Péray
Fraisse, Robert	07130 St-Péray
Gilles, Père et Fils	07130 St-Péray
Gripa, Bernard	07300 Mauves
Juge, Marcel	07130 Cornas
Mathon, Léon	07130 St-Péray
Milliand, René	07130 St-Péray
Maurice, Marc	07130 Cornas
Thiers, Jean-Louis	07130 Toulaud
Vérilhac, Eugène	07130 St-Péray
Voge, Alain	07130 Cornas

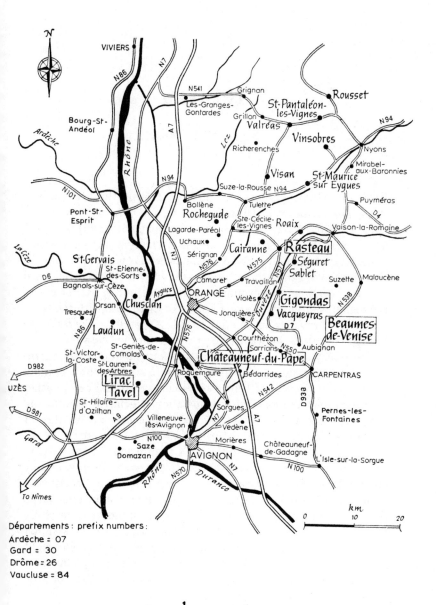

Départements: prefix numbers:

Ardèche = 07
Gard = 30
Drôme = 26
Vaucluse = 84

Southern Rhône

137

9

Rasteau

Rasteau's Grenache-based *vin doux naturel* is the least known *Appellation* wine in the Côtes du Rhône, and in many ways this is not surprising. Made on similar lines to port, with a fermentation arrested by the addition of alcohol, it is a truly heady wine with a blatant grapiness and coarseness that is not to everyone's taste. In the south of France there are several of these Grenache-based country wines, and their market is the bars and *épicier* stores of the region. Banyuls is the best known of them and, with Rasteau, one of the very few to be allowed full *Appellation Contrôlée*: to foreign eyes that represents no great distinction, however.

The village of Rasteau is situated about 20 kilometres northeast of Orange and has a typical Provençal character; a small, disordered collection of brown roofs cluster around one another near the top of a hillock, while below them the narrow streets and alleyways guard a stillness that only the occasional footfall or distant exclamation can disturb. The two social centres of the community are, for the men, the main square and, for the women, the communal *lavoir* or wash-house. In the evenings, and all day on Sundays, the beret-wearing, cigarette-smoking locals play their endless games of *pétanque*, while the housewives come out to the *lavoir* and scrub clean their family linen, standing in carefully numbered stalls like racehorses at the starting gate. In summer they are surrounded by a green spread of vines that presses right up to the village limits; in winter the little hills and plains have turned a light brown, discreetly matching the tiles on the Provençal rooftops.

It is difficult to estimate for how long Rasteau has been a wine community, for the village is noticeably lacking in documentation and local records. The first written mention of vines to have been found dates from the year 1005, when Bishop Humbert II of nearby Vaison started to rent out his episcopal vineyard to some private growers at Rasteau. Under the terms of the agreement, payment was to be given in kind, to the tune of half a hogshead of wine every year. By 1009 it is recorded that Humbert's successor, Bishop Pierre II of Mirabel, was even giving away some of the choice vines from the well exposed hill of St-Martin near the village. It is not known when the Church finally relinquished ownership of its vineyards at Rasteau.

Until 1932 there were only red, rosé and white wines made, under the title 'Côtes du Rhône'. In that year some growers started making a *vin doux naturel* from their Grenache vines, and this received its own *Appellation Contrôlée* in 1944. The late Baron Le Roy, tireless campaigner for Rhône wines and France's premier wine diplomat of this century, was a fervent admirer of the Grenache *vin doux*, and once said of it, 'We used to be lacking a pearl in the Côtes du Rhône, but Rasteau has given us one with its *vin doux naturel.*'

One may well ask why it is the Grenache, certainly not the most refined of grapes, that is used to make Rasteau. What about the other southern Rhône vines, like the Cinsault, or the now popular Syrah? Perhaps the answer to this lies in the two main properties of the Grenache grape: its wines tend to be heavily alcoholized and also age rapidly. Although a *vin doux naturel* has alcohol spirit added to it, it is obviously in the grower's interest to minimize the amount of his alcohol addition, and to maximize his natural sugar content. Another aspect of the fortified Grenache wines is that they are thought to be better the more they are aged, even to the point where they acquire a curious semi-maderized taste. This taste is called *rancio*, a word of Spanish derivation, and a *rancio* wine is considered the undoubted superior of a younger *vin doux*.

Hence the choice of the Grenache, but it is questionable whether it lends itself as effectively to making a *vin doux naturel* as the Muscat, for instance. Even a combination of the Syrah and the Cinsault, although less naturally alcoholic, would produce a wine of much greater finesse. All in all, Rasteau is a typical example of an old-fashioned *vin du coin*—one that appeals to local palates and local custom but is difficult to transport outside its immediate *ambiance*.

While the *vin doux naturel* is the only wine at Rasteau to have the right to its own individual full *Appellation Contrôlée*, there is no such thing as a defined vineyard for it. This is because the growers of Grenache within the village limits are not obliged to make *vin doux naturel* with their Grenache grapes every year; they are just as entitled to use them to make Villages wine, with its 3,500-litre-per-hectare restriction, or even Côtes du Rhône *générique*, with its higher 5,000-litre capacity. The average production for the years 1976 to 1981 inclusive was 327,500 litres, which implies that growers were taking their *vin doux naturel* grapes from 250 to 300 acres of Grenache vines.

Planted around the village, of course, are the usual Côtes du Rhône Villages vines: besides the Grenache these are notably the Cinsault, the Mourvèdre and the Syrah. Generally, the *vignerons* depend on their older Grenache vines for the *vin doux*, since they yield the most concentrated, sugary grape juice. In years of bad weather, production of the *vin doux* is evidently much restricted, as by law the Grenache grapes must contain the sugar equivalent of 15° when harvested. Thus the 1977 *vin doux* crop came to only 108,700 litres.

Most of the vines grow on what are known as *garrigues*; *garrigue* is a local term indicating a large mass of stony, infertile soil that will support vines, lavender and trees, but almost nothing else. Some of the best Grenache plots spill over into neighbouring Cairanne and Sablet and are on gentle slopes composed of heavy clay: with their good exposure these vines invariably yield well matured grapes.

Rasteau is one of the seventeen Côtes du Rhône Villages, and the harvest for these wines starts at the end of September. The Grenache *vin doux* vines are left for a further two weeks in order to achieve maximum maturity. This extra time has a significant effect on the grapes, which under the influence of the southern Rhône Valley's warmth and wind, contract into hard, sugary masses. Even in December it is possible to see on the vines healthy-looking bunches of Grenache grapes inadvertently missed during the *vendanges*. Although their skin is by then slightly shrivelled, to the taste the grapes are very sugary.

With the exception of the Cave Co-opérative, all the growers make a 'white' Grenache *doux*, that is, one vinified along orthodox white-wine methods. Thus the grapes are pressed on arrival at the cellar and are then fermented away from the skins until the density of the must reaches the desired level: this is around the equivalent of at least 15° alcohol by volume. The *mutage*, or addition of pure alcohol, is then performed, which stops the fermentation, retains the wine's sweetness, and increases the total alcohol degree to 21·5. Soon afterwards the wine is put into cask for a year or two in order to gain a little age and roundness, the former being considered particularly desirable.

To give some idea of the condition of the grapes when they enter the cellar, M. Thiérry Masson, the leading private grower at Rasteau, estimated that for his *vin doux naturel* he needed 1·5 kilograms of grapes to make a bottle of wine; for his Côtes du Rhône Villages red wine (also based on Grenache) only 1·1. The Bressy-Masson family are, in fact, the only makers of the unusually named Rasteau *Rancio* wine, which gains its title from being matured for considerably longer than the usual *vin doux*. In the old days of M. Emile Bressy, who died in 1976, the *domaine* would age their wine in cask for anything between seven and ten years, during which time a curious literally 'old' flavour, reminiscent of a table wine past its best, would be taken on. This is the esteemed *Rancio* taste, and the wine will have both a dark golden, almost crushed caramel, colour and a welcome roundness that is not evident in the less matured version. Nowadays M. Bressy's young daughter, Marie-France, and her husband, Thiérry Masson, prefer to age the *Rancio* for about five years before bottling, and the wine is still very successful.

Most of the Rasteau *vin doux* is made like white wine for one major reason: the resulting colour. As M. Andrieu, the President of the Cave Co-opérative, freely admitted: 'We are the only people to make a little red *vin doux*—it forms 7%, or about 25,000 litres of our total VDN production—because although we feel it to be the equal of the white, it is very hard to market owing to its somewhat cloudy red colour. The difference in its vinification is quite simple; we just leave the skins in the fermenting vats for three or four days at the very beginning. I think that this makes the red VDN a slightly coarser, grapier wine than the white, but at the same time, it definitely tastes less sugary—which some would consider an advantage.'

'White' is really a misnomer for the majority of the *vin doux*, for its colour is very dark gold, or almost caramel. Its bouquet, and indeed its flavour, are both sugared and full of vinosity and can

141

resemble burnt brown sugar or even marzipan: it is difficult to situate the exact sensation they give, for the fortification of the wine suppresses in large part the traditional Grenache red wine aromas and seems to leave it instead with a blend of raw grapes and alcohol that can be overbearing to sensitive palates. In the South of France Rasteau has traditionally been drunk as an *apéritif*, but is now more and more served either at the end of a meal as a dessert wine, for which it is usually chilled, or as the filler for the local melon.

The *vin doux naturel* accounts for a little under one-third of all the wine at Rasteau, the rest being made up of Côtes du Rhône Villages red, white and rosé, and Côtes du Rhône *générique* red, white and rosé. Always full-bodied and rather backward when young, the Villages red wines are similar to those of neighbouring Cairanne. Leading exponents among the private growers are the Domaine de la Grangeneuve, with an old-style, thick, robust wine with plenty of inkiness to it; Maurice Charavin, who also makes a big, old-fashioned red wine; and the Domaine des Nymphes, whose lighter style, derived from the use of grapes that have been semi-macerated for high fruit extraction, works very well. These wines are ideal for drinking between 2 and 5 years old as a rule. Meanwhile the white wine and the rosé are both considerably less impressive, and their production is very limited.

The *vin doux naturel* occupies a curious position at Rasteau, therefore, for it brings the village fame rather than fortune. The *vignerons* rely much more upon their Côtes du Rhône table wines to earn themselves a living, and realize that demand for the *vin doux* is very restricted. As M. Maurice Charavin, a member of one of the oldest wine families, observed, 'It's the VDN that I export in medium quantities—to Switzerland, Denmark and Belgium—and I find that its greatest benefit for me is its prestige. I make and sell much more Côtes du Rhône wine, on which I depend completely for my living.'

M. Charavin owns 32 acres of vines and, in addition to his *vin doux*, makes red, rosé and white Côtes du Rhône, the last from the Grenache *blanc* and Clairette grapes. He admits that he is hindered by the problem of the *rentabilité*, or viability, of his VDN, for he says: 'I leave it three or four years in cask, and it needs at least this long to take on a sort of old, partly maderized taste. If I didn't have to keep the money rolling in, I would ideally age it for twice that time, since Rasteau gains much more smoothness at a much faster rate in wood than it does in bottle. Still, I drank a 25-year-old bottle not long ago, and it was in great shape, with just the right amount of senility!'

This taste of old age is much revered in the region, and is the key to the very individual Rasteau *Rancio* of the Bressy-Masson domaine. The late M. Emile Bressy's father was one of the first growers to make a Rasteau *vin doux* in 1932 and, before the Second World War, decided with Emile to try ageing his Rasteau longer than usual. Every year a little of the *vin doux naturel* was put aside, and after six or seven years the Bressys discovered that their technique was a great success, for it endowed the wine with a smoothness on the palate that had not previously been evident; something vaguely akin to the difference in flavour between a ruby and a tawny port, perhaps.

M. Bressy was a cautious man, who needed gentle persuasion and prompting if he was to talk about his unique wine. His pride was apparent when he would state categorically: 'You'll not find another bottle with the label Rasteau *Rancio* on it; it was I and my father who started it off, and this is the only domaine making it now.'

The small cellar at Domaine de la Grangeneuve is full of *Rancio* barrels, some of which lurk, semi-forgotten, in hidden corners. All are well stoppered up and have the word '*Rancio*' written in faded chalk on their front. Around them the Côtes du Rhône barrels are easily visible, with their shininess and new chalk letters, which make them look like eager young schoolboys mixing with their sagacious elders.

One of the largest private *domaines* is owned by M. Francis Vache, who has a 62-acre vineyard at Rasteau, and also makes wine from grapes bought at Gigondas and the surrounding communities. M. Vache's family have lived at Rasteau for several generations, and he is now Mayor of the village—a restful post, one suspects. He is helped by his son-in-law, M. Faure, and together they have attempted new methods to make their Grenache *vin doux* sell: a striking new label and a simple screw-top, for instance. Their success has been limited, and M. Vache's despair is evident when he says, 'I think our *vin doux* is consistently worthy, but it just won't sell at all easily. I agree that it's not got a recognized taste like port or madeira, for example, but it's certainly enjoyed by most people round here. What are we doing wrong?'

Rasteau Vintages

The Rasteau *vin doux naturel* is not given a vintage, since it is more often than not a blended wine. Growers use their strongest, sunniest harvests to promote the wine of weak years, like 1977 or 1980, so that the customer can rely upon a consistent quality in his bottle of Rasteau.

Leading Growers at Rasteau (*vin doux naturel* and Côtes du Rhône Villages)

Bressy-Masson	
Domaine de la Grangeneuve	84110 Rasteau
Charavin, Maurice	
Domaine de Char-à-vin	84110 Rasteau
Roméro, André	
Domaine La Soumade	84110 Rasteau
Girard, Louis	
Domaine de la Girardière	84110 Rasteau
Cave des Vignerons	84110 Rasteau
Chamfort, Louis et Fils	
Domaine de Verquière	84110 Sablet
Charavin, Emile	84110 Rasteau
Charavin, Robert	84110 Rasteau
Colombet, Philippe	84110 Rasteau
Gleize, André	84150 Violès
Joyet, Paul	
Domaine des Girasols	84110 Rasteau
Liautaud, Jean	
Domaine du Sommier	84110 Séguret
Martin, Yves	84150 Travaillan
Meyer et Fils	
Domaine des Nymphes	84110 Rasteau
Nicolet-Leyraud	84110 Rasteau
Richaud, Marcel	84290 Cairanne
Saurel, S.	
Domaine de la Combe Dieu	84 La Baumette
Vache, Francis	84110 Rasteau

10

Beaumes-de-Venise

Running around the southerly end of the Dentelles de Montmirail mountains, and appearing to fuse instinctively into its olive- and vine-covered hillside, is the village of Beaumes-de-Venise. This is the home of the Muscat de Beaumes-de-Venise, undoubtedly the best of the South of France's several *vins doux naturels*, or fortified sweet wines. As the translation implies, *vin doux naturel* is a bit of a misnomer, for the Muscat de Beaumes-de-Venise and its brother wines from nearer the Mediterranean all have a little pure alcohol added to them.

Of these *vins doux naturels*—other prominent examples include Banyuls and the Muscat de Frontignan—only Beaumes-de-Venise has started to make a quiet name for itself outside France. With their alcohol strength around 21 per cent, these wines suffer from being more heavily taxed than ordinary still table wine, and a bottle of Muscat de Beaumes on a London or New York shelf is an expensive buy. In addition, only very limited quantities of the wine have been made until comparatively recently, and local demand in and around Provence has been used to taking care of most of it. Since the 1950s, however, the Muscat de Beaumes has experienced a marked upswing in renown and popularity, the growers have taken note, and the plantation of Muscat has increased to around 575 acres.

Beaumes-de-Venise itself is an old village that dates back to the early years of the Roman Empire. Taking advantage of the sulphur spring at Montmirail, the Romans established Beaumes as a small spa centre, and all sorts of their relics have since been found, such as swimming-pool walls and lengths of water piping. Also found, on the St-Hilaire hillside overlooking the village, has been a large bas-relief depicting a *vendange* scene and the treading

145

down of the harvest. The locals are naturally convinced that the grapes being trodden are Muscat, but whatever their identity, it is certain that wine has been made at Beaumes since the Roman era.

Away to the west, towards Vacqueyras, is one of the village landmarks, the church of Notre-Dame d'Aubune, which looks down on the Cave Co-opérative. It is on the approximate site of a decisive eighth-century Gallic victory over the Saracens; after the battle the Saracens were forced to take to the local hills and for months hid out in the many grottoes and caves that abound above and around Beaumes. ('Beaumes' comes from a Provençal word, *baumo*, meaning grotto, 'Venise' from the French *Venaissin*. In feudal times the village formed part of the Comtat de Venaissin, a papal fiefdom.) Every year on 8 September there is a pilgrimage to the church in celebration of this ancient victory.

By the Middle Ages Beaumes-de-Venise's wine had achieved local fame, in that the papal court in Avignon was drinking it regularly. In 1348 Pope Clement VI went as far as buying a vineyard near the village in order to secure himself a permanent supply of the wine; the property was to remain in papal hands until 1797, just after the French Revolution.

The sweet Muscat is thought by most of the growers themselves to date from no earlier than the beginning of the nineteenth century, and the small amount then made enjoyed a strong, strictly regional popularity. In 1859 the Provençal poet Frédéric Mistral referred to it in his classic work, *Mireio* (Mireille), the story of a rich girl's frustrated love for a lowly peasant. Writing in Provençal, Mistral said:

> *Lou bon Muscat de Baumo*
> *E lou Ferigoulet*
> *Alor se chourlo a la gargato.*[1]

A few years after Mistral had written these words, the vineyards of Beaumes-de-Venise were in ruins, destroyed by phylloxera. Despite the efforts of a handful of determined *vignerons*, and despite the granting of *Appellation* for the Muscat in 1945, the situation was almost at rock bottom by the early

---

[1] French
  Le bon Muscat de Beaumes
  Et le Ferigoulet
  Se boivent à la regalade.

English
  The good Muscat of Beaumes
  And the Thyme
  Should be swilled back.

1950s. There were only 100 acres of Muscat vines, split between a few small domaines, and in 1951 bad weather wiped out the whole crop: not a drop of Muscat was made in that year.

Fortunately for all concerned, a Cave Co-opérative was formed at Beaumes in 1956, which, with its spreading of costs, persuaded many of the local farmers to resume growing the Muscat wine grape, the Muscat *à petits grains*, in addition to the normal southern Rhône red wine varieties such as Grenache, Cinsault and Mourvèdre.

The Muscat is a vine of Greek origin, dating back to several centuries BC, and is now widely planted around the Mediterranean, as well as in Alsace, where it makes a dry white wine. There are many variations of it, however, and at Beaumes-de-Venise the Muscat *à petits grains* is the same variety that is used in combination with the Muscat d'Alexandrie to make the fortified Muscat de Frontignan of the French Mediterranean.

True to form, though, the Muscat at Beaumes has two sub-varieties—the *grain blanc* and the *grain noir*. The *grain noir* is the more prolific producer but by itself is considered to make a wine a little too dark in colour. One of the joys of a good Muscat de Beaumes is its appealing golden hue; to achieve this the *vignerons* rely on a combination of *grain blanc* and *grain noir*. They are grown in a surprising number of different soils all about the village, ranging between pure sand in the south, sand and stones in the east and heavy clay in the valley behind the line of hills north of the village. The effect of these combined differences on the wine is ultimately very hard to judge, for there are now so few small growers that one of the problems is that of forming a yardstick with which to evaluate the *Appellation*. In addition, the Cave Co-opérative—responsible for more than nine-tenths of the Muscat—always makes a blended wine from holdings throughout the *Appellation*. As a consequence, no one sector holds a specially esteemed reputation, and the wine is sold as straightforward Muscat de Beaumes-de-Venise, accompanied by a *domaine* name where applicable.

Beaumes-de-Venise is the only place in the Côtes du Rhône where Muscat wine grapes are planted, and the vine's liability to several different diseases has always hindered its wider cultivation. Its main complaint is oïdium, which, having taken hold of the vine, paves the way for additional attacks of grey rot; money

147

and time must therefore be spent spraying the plants with sulphur treatments—all of which adds to the *vigneron*'s overheads. While the Grenache, Mourvèdre and other customary red and rosé vines remain trouble free, the Muscat also attracts a bug called the *araignée rouge*, or red spider, which can shear the vine of all its foliage if it is not sprayed with insecticides.

Because the Muscat can be so troublesome, all the growers except M. Yves Nativelle of Domaine de Coyeux have a majority of their holdings planted with Côtes du Rhône Villages vines; these make Beaumes-de-Venise red wines, which, being of standard but not spectacular quality, do not possess their very own *Appellation* and instead form one of the seventeen Côtes du Rhône Villages. Nevertheless it is these wines and the Côtes du Rhône *générique* wines (red, white and rosé) that are the mainstay of the growers' livelihoods.

The Villages grapes, like the Grenache, Cinsault, Mourvèdre and Carignan, are harvested first, towards the end of September. The Muscat is a quick-maturing grape, but the growers leave it until mid-October, by when it is just beginning to wrinkle and harden. Its sugar content is then well concentrated and should give the equivalent of about 15° by volume.

Vinification commences on classical white wine lines. The grapes are pressed immediately, the juice run off and left to ferment at a steady pace for up to two weeks. Should the grower consider his fermentation too rapid, the vats are cooled by running water round their outside. Then comes the all-important moment of the *mutage*, or addition of alcohol. By the laws of the *Appellation*, there must be a minimum of 125 grams of sugar in each litre of the finished wine, so that a sweetness will definitely be retained. As with the making of port, the addition of the pure alcohol acts to kill all the yeast cells that are driving the fermentation. The sugar in the wine thus remains unconverted, and the wine's alcohol degree is strengthened to about 21·5.

The *mutage* is clearly a tricky business, since the *vigneron* must know exactly the state of progress of all his vats, so as to be sure when to add the neutral alcohol spirit. Some growers put in the extra alcohol all at one go, while others prefer to spread out a vat's *mutages* over several hours, thereby perhaps suppressing a potent taste of pure alcohol that can invade the wine if care is not taken. Once the *mutage* has been performed, the wine is pumped around to blend in completely the alcohol spirit, and the vats are then left for about a month to settle down. By Christmas they have accumulated a fairly large lees; the wine is then drawn off into other vats, where it stays until the early spring.

Henceforward in the vinification it is the increasing pressure of demand that takes over. The private growers are unable to fulfil their ideals about how their Muscat should be made, simply because they have normally sold the whole of one crop some months before the next one is allowed to be released. There is no dallying in such circumstances.

What all growers adhere to is the unwritten rule that their wine should be racked as little as possible, since repeated rackings deprive the Muscat of some of its extraordinarily opulent perfume. Each racking is also liable to rob the wine of up to one-fifth of a degree of its alcohol. With their wines subject to scrutiny by the National Institute of *Appellations* (INAO) from Perpignan, the growers wait to receive the right to put them on sale with the *Appellation Contrôlée* guarantee. All regional fortified wines, including Frontignan, Banyuls and Rasteau, are subject to the same control, which is normally performed around Easter following the harvest. Once approval is given, the *vignerons* are free to put their Muscat on sale.

The wine therefore receives very little ageing before it is bottled. For the large Cave Co-opérative, this is not new, for they have always liked to bottle their Muscat within six or eight months of the harvest, arguing that the wine's enormous fresh fruitiness is best appreciated in this way. But for the quartet of private growers, demand for their wine has reduced its length of ageing, and all are now selling *vin de l'année* at any given moment. In the early 1970s some were accustomed to leaving the Muscat in its concrete vats for an extra year, or occasionally even an extra three years, according to the style of wine they were seeking. Wood has never been used in the ageing of Muscat because it is believed to suppress some of the wine's tremendous bouquet and fine, translucent colour. Freshness and grapiness are above all the most desired characteristics in the Muscat, and although the very best examples of it, such as the Domaine Durban, possess great roundness on the palate, its trump card is undoubtedly its resounding, overriding Muscat sensation, something that very few other grapes can claim to possess with such potency.

There is literally no escaping the vigour of the Muscat. Even the most casual of drinkers cannot fail to remark upon its many facets: the glinting orange-gold colour, the inescapable heady bouquet, and the wine's ample flavour and long, rich aftertaste. It is a wine that makes no allowances for waverers, who may find it has too much of everything—too overpowering, too scented and too rich. For those who like it, it is uncommonly like a drug, fully worthy of Hugh Johnson's description, 'a sheer delight' (*The World Atlas of Wine*).

· Formerly drunk principally as a dessert wine, the Muscat de Beaumes is now very popular as an *apéritif*, and is a great café favourite in the southern Rhône Valley. As an accompaniment to food, it is also popular with the local Cavaillon melons. Like most *vins doux naturels*, it is generally served chilled, but too much cold can destroy its flowery bouquet. The wine's elevated alcohol degree—which can often be forgotten when drinking it, a costly mistake—ensures that its orange-tinted colour retains its depth for some years, but the Muscat cannot be regarded as a keeping wine; after five or six years it starts to lose the piquancy of its strong, grapey aromas.

The style of today's Muscat de Beaumes is in fact an evolution of an old wine that used to be made until the Second World War. In those days the sweet Muscat wine was nearly extinct, being made by a tiny number of *vignerons* whose concern was often where their next penny would come from. One such grower at the time was the late M. Jacques Leydier, whose family owns the interesting property of Domaine Durban, which makes the best Muscat of all. M. Leydier, who died in 1981, was a phlegmatic, pipe-smoking man, always ready to discuss aspects of his wine-making. His explanation of the old-style wine was as follows: 'It was a more natural wine, in that little or no *mutage* was carried out. We were not more than half a dozen making it, and what we would do would be to pick the grapes fairly late, probably after the middle of October. They were already well concentrated in sugar, but to intensify this we would lay them in bunches to dry out on straw or cane mats known as *claies*. A month or so later we would press the dried-out grapes and proceed with a normal white wine vinification. Our aim was to have as naturally sweet a wine as possible, but if the summer had been bad and the grapes had come in in bad shape, this was obviously hard to achieve. When the

Appellation Contrôlée was granted in 1945, the regulations decreed that a fortified wine of not less than 21·5° be made; that was the beginning of the Muscat de Beaumes-de-Venise as we know it today.'

With the Dentelles de Montmirail on one side of it and the massive Mont Ventoux away on another, the Domaine Durban stands well concealed, high up (at 500 metres) in some of the most forbidding countryside in the Côtes du Rhône. Rows of apricot and cherry trees add colour in the spring, while the light-brown *domaine* is given some protection from the sweeping *mistral* wind by a little batch of pine trees that stand around it. From Roman times onwards there used to be a community called Urban roughly on the site of the *domaine* and, like Montmirail, it became famed for its copious sulphur spring. When interest in this waned, however, the community declined and eventually disappeared. It was M. Jacques Leydier who bought the property in the late 1960s and who restored both it and its wine to their former eminence.

Today M. Leydier's son Bernard is running the property with the capable help of his wife Nicole, who seems firmly in control of the commercial side of things. Bernard explained more about the *domaine*: 'We also have vineyards at Gigondas, as well as Côtes du Rhône Villages vines here, but my family has always been most proud of its Muscat, which is certainly the hardest wine to vinify well. We have 22 acres of Muscat altogether, and find that it is a vine that needs a lot of care, and one that does not live very long, never much more than thirty-five years. With the highest permitted yield fixed at not more than about 1,200 litres an acre, you can see that a lot of work and worry never yields more than a little wine, especially as the grapes have to be so perfectly ripe, and without blemish, when they are harvested. My father, funnily enough, used to consider that the Muscat could age well and spoke of a 30-year-old bottle that he had drunk in 1973, which, despite bearing a slight taste of *rancio*, or light maderization, had been very fine and smooth, with only a small loss of bouquet and colour.

'Times have changed a lot since my father's day. Fashions come and go, but it's astounding to think that there was no interest at all in the Muscat after the war. Now if you come to visit me in January, for instance, you will find I have no Muscat to sell until I have been allowed to release the recently vinified wine, which means that I am a wine-maker with no wine to sell for three or four months of the year. I would like to age the wine for longer, but as you can see, there is absolutely no possibility of this.'

One of M. Jacques Leydier's colleagues in the uneasy times before the Muscat gained its own *Appellation* was M. Pierre Castaud, who comes from the oldest wine family at Beaumes-de-Venise and who, as a young man, learned to make the old-style wine with his father Louis. M. Castaud, a soft-spoken, grey-haired man in his sixties, has now retired, leaving the running of the Domaine des Bernardins to his brother-in-law, M. Maurin. He spoke about the old days: 'The pre-war wine was a less heady drink than today's Muscat, but because so much depended on the state of the grapes, we could never be sure how much, if any, we would be able to make every year. My father worked hard for the right of *Appellation*, as he saw that it would encourage a great expansion in the making of Muscat here. Once the *Appellation* was granted in 1945, we had, of course, to change our vinification methods and start adding alcohol spirit to the wine. That complicated things! We were accustomed to leaving the wine to ferment itself out, but the new laws demanded much greater vigilance over the state of each vat. When I was making the wine here I used barely to sleep for two weeks, as it is such a delicate task to know when exactly to add the alcohol. Any mistake with the *mutage* risked spoiling the whole year's crop, so at night I used to get up every two hours or so to check on how the density of the must was changing.'

The style of the Domaine des Bernardins Muscat has changed with M. Castaud's retirement. M. Castaud differed from his fellow growers in that he would press his grapes very hard before fermentation, and though this would provoke a large lees with the inclusion of odd skins in the vats, the wine gained enormously in colour and bouquet, to the extent of being the best in the *Appellation*.

M. Maurin, by contrast, uses a modern and very efficient Vaslin press but only presses the grapes relatively lightly. The Bernardins' Muscat retains an attractive gold-to-pale-orange colour but has lost the swirling bouquet, astonishing richness and cleanly defined finish that made M. Castaud's wine so outstanding. The *domaine* still gives its wine a vintage, but now that it is allowed to release the wine for sale by around the month of May following the harvest, it is always strictly the wine of the current year.

The third private grower of Muscat at Beaumes, M. Guy Rey, has also changed the style of his wine recently and, instead of ageing it for two or three years, is now selling it as *vin de l'année*. M. Rey, who lives south of Beaumes at Aubignan, owns 15 acres of Muscat vines, but even in the abundant year of 1973 these yielded no more than 84 hectolitres of wine. With such a small amount at his disposal, M. Rey cannot reach a wide market; he would obviously like to, being a hard-working and ambitious young man, but he pointed also to the hindrance of the high taxes imposed on the fortified Muscat. These are much heavier than those on ordinary, lower-degree table wine and, naturally, make the Muscat all the harder to sell. 'Making any *vin doux naturel* is hard work,' commented M. Rey, 'but when you have to contend with the foibles of the Muscat vine as well, your normal working day stretches to twelve hours. I'm sure some people must think that making fortified Muscat is like banging your head against a wall, but I do happen to like doing it!'

The private *domaines*, like Domaine St-Sauveur or even M. Nativelle's 128 acres of Muscat at the Domaine de Coyeux, are dwarfed in size by the village Cave Co-opérative. This now makes about nine-tenths of all Muscat—something like 6,300 hectolitres—and the wine is very agreeably clean and fruity tasting. It has improved recently, under the impressive drive of the young Director, M. Batigne. It is not an easy task running a Co-opérative of this size either, and some of the problems encountered in such a large winery were outlined by the technical director, M. Reboul, who succeeded the long-serving and very affable M. Paulo in 1981.

'It's quite a job co-ordinating all the different growers, for they can be very independent! We have altogether 330 members and at harvest time they obviously can't all bring in their grapes at the same time. We also vinify Côtes du Rhône Villages, *générique* and Côtes du Ventoux wines, so every day for three weeks we have 400 tonnes of grapes arriving at the Cave. It's no easy task keeping track of the progress of thirty different vats, all at different stages of development.'

Only very little Muscat de Beaumes-de-Venise used to be exported, a touching landmark being the Co-opérative's proud dispatch of twenty-five cases to New York in the summer of 1974, as well as an even smaller shipment two years before to the Rhône pioneers in Britain, Yapp Brothers. Nowadays Domaine Durban are selling a large amount of their wine to the United States, Britain and even Uruguay, and it is not unlikely that a supermarket in London will stock a *négociant* Beaumes-de-Venise, most probably from Paul Jaboulet or Vidal-Fleury. Most dispersed, obviously, is the wine of the Co-opérative, whose Muscat now sells well in Switzerland, the Low Countries, Britain, the United States and several other countries. Their sales network is aided by the easy appeal of their light and fruity Côtes du Rhône Villages and Côtes du Ventoux wines, the best of which are the reds and which can provide good value for money.

The Co-opérative gave up using corks in their Muscat bottles in 1970, and now their wine is distinguishable by its gold-coloured screw cap. Not only has this proved cheaper, but it also allows for consumption over an extended period of time. The Co-opérative's estimate that a Muscat will remain in good order for a month after opening is somewhat optimistic, but there is no doubt that the wine will lose little of its bouquet and flavour until ten days after opening. For real *aficionados* of the Muscat de Beaumes this problem should never arise, but in exceptional circumstances it will prove beneficial to keep the bottle chilled once it has been opened.

Beaumes-de-Venise Vintages

Only the Domaine des Bernardins now gives its wine a vintage and with growers selling only their wine of the year due to pressure of demand, the relevance of following which vintage to buy is lost. As a general rule, the Muscat is not a wine that ages well and the growers recommend that it should be drunk before it is about 6 years old.

Leading Growers at Beaumes-de-Venise

Leydier, Bernard	
Domaine Durban	84190 Beaumes-de-Venise
Castaud-Maurin	
Domaine des Bernardins	84190 Beaumes-de-Venise
Co-opérative Intercommunale	
des Vins et Muscats	84190 Beaumes-de-Venise

Nativelle, Yves
    Domaine de Coyeux   84190 Beaumes-de-Venise
Rey, Guy
    Domaine St-Sauveur   84190 Aubignan
Meffre, Jean-Paul
    Château des Applanats (no VDN) 84190 Beaumes-de-Venise
Domaine de Cassan (no VDN)   84190 Lafare

11

Gigondas

Close to Mont Ventoux, and blending into the low hills underneath the startling, spiky Dentelles mountains, is Gigondas, the
home of one of the southern Rhône's best, deepest red wines. A
straggling village that forms a cul de sac with its little winding
approach road, Gigondas rarely shows any signs of life; many of
the houses that huddle underneath the ruined *château* are
abandoned and decaying, while for much of the time the only
sound in the tiny *place* is the slow trickle of water from the wall
fountain; even the shop, the café, the *caveau de dégustation* look as
if they are all installed for a film set rather than for real use. Wine
communities in the Côtes du Rhône tend to be drowsy places, but
Gigondas achieves a positive state of repose.

Although the vineyards extend all around the village, most of
the wine cellars are on the strip of land between it and the River
Ouvèze, 3 kilometres or so away to the west. Gigondas has around
thirty private *domaines* that bottle their own wine, as well as two
large *négociant* companies (also vineyard owners at Gigondas) and
a small but quality-conscious Cave Co-opérative. Several of the
domaines are built on the approximate sites of Roman villas, for in
the first century AD a community of country residences was
established at Gigondas by the veteran centurions of the Second
Roman Legion, then headquartered in Orange. Relics, like
earthenware amphorae and an excellently preserved Bacchus
head, have been found between the village and the river and
indicate that the centurions were by no means teetotal. After all,
the word 'Gigondas' stems from the Latin *jocunditas*, so 'merry
city' obviously gained its name from the benevolent impact of its
wine.

It is not known how widespread the Roman vineyards were, nor whether wine-growing continued uninterrupted into the ninth century, when the next historical records are found. By that time the vineyard pattern that had evolved was one common to most of France, with the Church in possession of many of the leading *domaines* and properties and busily seeing to their untrammelled cultivation. Thus, at Gigondas the nuns of the abbey of St-André, beside the River Ouvèze, grew mainly vines and olives for their living. With the arrival of the Popes in Avignon in the fourteenth century, the superseded Bishops of Orange took to spending much of their time at St-André, where they could console themselves with the deep, heavy wine that is still made from the vines of the adjoining plateau. At the same time the Prince of Orange, in his guise as *seigneur* of Gigondas, was a substantial local vineyard owner, being credited with possessing at least sixty vineyard plots. So much did he own that he used to let out one of his foremost vineyards, the 'du Prince'. Consequently the vineyards were generally in few, but powerful, hands.

Records dating back to 1592 show that there was a small amount of well esteemed white Gigondas then being made, but the red wine had more commercial value, and most of it was regularly sold outside the community—to the chagrin of the local inhabitants. During the seventeenth century quite frequent trading was conducted with the monks of the Montmajour abbey near Arles; surrounded as they were by the Camargue water flats, the good monks found themselves in possession of plenty of rice but with no wine for their religious services. Since they held traditional ties with the abbey of St-André, there was no hesitation in selecting Gigondas as their *vin de messe*. Indeed, so well must they have appreciated the remnants of their mass wine that by the eighteenth century the abbey of Montmajour is recorded as a vineyard proprietor at Gigondas; like the abbey of Aiguebelle, near Montélimar, this holding was forfeited during the French Revolution.

The *château* of Gigondas is thought to have been built in the early part of the seventeenth century, for it was around then that the Princes of Orange used it as one of their hunting lodges. The ruins visible today represent perhaps insufficient evidence, but one can well envisage the stately rooms harbouring rollicking banquets composed of steaming game dishes, all washed down by draughts of sturdy Gigondas.

Wine-making continued steadily, if unspectacularly, into the nineteenth century, when welcome momentum was injected into the thinking and outlook of the *vignerons* by Eugène Raspail, a member of a prominent French political family who owned an estate at Gigondas. Experimenting with sulphur treatments against the growing disease of oïdium, and performing massive replanting with superior vine strains, Raspail went a long way towards placing Gigondas further up the French wine hierarchy, as well as ensuring that it was exported to a number of overseas countries. Suitably encouraged, a few growers turned to bottling a part of their wine, and the family of Hilarion Roux of Domaine Les Pallières succeeded in winning a Gold Medal at the 1894 Paris Agricultural Fair.

Despite such progress, the general practice remained that of bulk-selling both grapes and wine. There are still *vignerons* who recall how, before the First World War, horse-drawn carts laden with grapes would leave the village for some of the stately private houses of Avignon. The grapes would be vinified in private cellars under the streets of Avignon and the wine kept for personal consumption.

Until the Second World War Gigondas was often employed as a booster wine, or *vin de médecine*. Just as Hermitage used to bolster Bordeaux in times gone by, so the shippers of Burgundy would come down to Gigondas shortly after the harvest and purchase individual vats according to their likely powers of propagation. In weak Burgundy years the demand was obviously significant. Little advance in the wine community's fortunes was apparent, therefore, until the 1930s, when both Gigondas's main *négociant* companies, Amadieu and Meffre, were formed. Their presence naturally brought extra attention to the village and, significantly, helped to keep much of the local wine actually at Gigondas: formerly this wine would be sold as 'Côtes du Rhône' to merchants in Châteauneuf-du-Pape, Orange and Avignon, who showed little concern about acknowledging on their labels whether or not the wine was from Gigondas.

With an admirably united front, the *vignerons* of Gigondas at the same time took measures to ensure that, once and for all, their wine received its due recognition. Thus all cultivation of the mass-producing, slightly harsh-tasting Carignan grape was forbidden in the search for a high-grade and well constituted red wine, and growers were made to exercise more vigilance in discarding unripe, unhealthy grapes at harvest time. Patience and hard work were finally rewarded in 1971, when Gigondas received its own *Appellation Contrôlée*, and today it stands alongside Châteauneuf-du-Pape and Lirac as one of the southern Côtes du Rhône's three fully fledged red wine *Appellations*.

As the above narrative illustrates, Gigondas is a wine that has won its colours the hard way, by dint of prolonged effort, and the growers themselves take great relish in recounting the history of the wine's promotion. One unhappy consequence of the wine's progress, however, has been the spoliation of some of the wild countryside that surrounds Gigondas. Growers have sought to maximize their advance and have bulldozed and reshaped parts of the terrain so that it is capable of, but not necessarily suitable for, the bearing of vines. This is particularly noticeable on some of the once tree-clad foothills around the Dentelles mountains, but in their quest for higher production, and consequently higher income, one or two *vignerons* seem to have thrown aside all the fundamental rules of wine-making. Cold, shaded vines can be seen clustered in the lee of the Dentelles, receiving at best about four hours' sunshine a day. Such grapes that will eventually make a bottle of Gigondas will do nothing to enhance the *Appellation*'s good name.

One of Gigondas's main characteristics is its overt, very winy headiness, an element which derives in part from the preponderance of Grenache in it, and in part from the siting of the vines, which grow mainly on slopes whose gradients vary sharply. The steepest hillsides are tucked against the Dentelles, and vines are cultivated very high up them—as high as 565 metres—on rich, yellowish clay. This soil is perhaps a little lush for the Grenache vine, which traditionally likes very spartan ground, but defenders of the high-level planting point to the total absence of rot (*pourriture*) on their vines. If it snows in winter, for example, these high vines are the ones that are affected; their eventual blossoming is retarded, and they remain behind the other vines right up until the *vendanges*. This is no bad thing, say the growers, because their lower sugar content helps to balance out the high alcoholic content of the wine—one of the criticisms sometimes levelled against Gigondas.

Lower down, at about 300 metres, the medium slopes are

probably the most suitable for the vines. On a less clayey, stonier ground, which retains all moisture very well, the Grenache is in its element, along with the other permitted vines: the Syrah, the Cinsault, the Mourvèdre and the Clairette. However, the *vignerons* have recently taken steps to try to balance the composition of grapes in a red Gigondas and have therefore restricted the use of the Grenache to a maximum of 65 per cent, while either alone or all together the Syrah, Mourvèdre and Cinsault must total a minimum of 25 per cent of the content of the wine. It is from these middle-slope areas that Gigondas is said to draw its finesse and delicacy, while the partly sandy, partly stony plain around the River Ouvèze is supposed to supply the wine's typical robustness and earthiness. There are, however, no specially named growths or *climats*, and the wine is always sold simply as 'Gigondas', followed by the name of the grower's *domaine*.

Come harvest time at the start of October, the village wakes fitfully from its habitual somnolence, as temporary *vendangeurs* crowd into the only bar and walk about the tiny streets and alleys. Some of them are students; many are North Africans, who cross the Mediterranean to join their friends working full-time in France. In the vineyards the growers brief their *vendangeurs* to carry out a sorting, or *triage*, of the grapes as they go along. Anything rotten—generally between 3 and 5 per cent of the crop—is to be discarded: such grapes are either used to make a very ordinary table wine known as *rapé* or are left on the vines for the benefit of the local bird population. *Triages* are effective only if the grower himself is on hand to supervise; otherwise the back-weary harvesters are not inclined to stop to scrutinize what is going into their buckets.

As the area under vines has more than tripled in the last fifty years—to the present 2,850 acres—harvesting lasts for an extended three weeks. Again, it is noticeable that attitudes towards the treatment of the grapes before fermentation have changed in the last ten years, and more domaines are only lightly crushing their grapes, if at all. The excellent Domaine de St-Gayan, for instance, put half their grapes uncrushed into the fermenting vats, seeking, as M. Roger Meffre would say, 'to bring softness and aromas to my wine'. The Cave Co-opérative's special wine, the Cuvée du President, is made wholly from *raisins entiers* (uncrushed grapes), while all their other *cuvées* are crushed and destalked. Few *domaines* undertake destalking, however, and there seems to be a growing awareness among the *vignerons* that the correct pre-sentation of the grapes into their fermenting vats is of prime importance; formerly, the methods handed down from one generation to the next were perhaps rather too blindly followed.

Some growers, like the Cave Co-opérative, then mix their different grape varieties in the crushing pump before filling the fermenting vats; others, mindful of the fact that the Grenache and Mourvèdre grapes reach maturity at different times, ferment the different grape varieties in separate vats and assemble them only the following spring. The difference between the two types of wine is very hard to discern.

Gigondas has such a long viticultural history that not all the fermenting vats are made of the usual concrete or enamel. Some of the older *domaines* have stone vats built into the rock walls, and the Domaine de St-Cosme is still using some seventeenth-century vats that were burrowed into the rock below ground-level.

After the grapes have fermented for one or two weeks, the wine is racked off and left to develop its malolactic fermentation. The following spring it is generally put to mature in cask; the *vignerons* adhere to a local saying that when the first flowers appear on the vines, then is the time to transfer the wine to the barrel. In the past, ageing in cask has lasted for about two years, or even more in the case of the most traditionally minded *vignerons*, but a reassessment of technique has occurred since the mid-1970s, so that several *domaines* are now ageing for a maximum of one year in cask. Among these figure three of the best *domaines* in the *Appellation*—St-Gayan, Longue-Toque and Les Goubert. All are making wines of greater finesse and complexity of flavour than most of their neighbours. Meanwhile, traditionalists such as the Domaines Les Pallières continue to age their wine for almost three years in wood; the effect of this is less overpowering than might be thought, for the Roux brothers bottle only their best vintages, those that are likely to be enhanced by such treatment. Their wine remains one of the best in the *Appellation*.

Once bottled, Gigondas needs a further two or three years to develop a true harmony between its bouquet and its strong flavour. Always a wine of great depth of colour, it can startle the uninitiated with its near-black inkiness and its surging bouquet. The aromas of the bouquet are hard to define, for there goes with the raspberry or blackberry fruitiness a certain elusive, earthy scent not unlike fresh black truffles; perhaps the smell of a forest after an autumnal rainstorm would be a pleasantly poetic way of putting it.

The French call this sensation a *goût de terroir*, and its force on the bouquet continues on to the palate, sometimes bringing with it, in addition, a little intriguing spiciness. A Gigondas has great profundity of flavour but not always the well formed richness to make it a balanced wine; perhaps this rather discordant aggression is one of its main charms, for refinement and sophistication would appear to be uneasy parties to a bottle of Gigondas. All in all, it is one of France's biggest wines, never to be idly quaffed, and one that demands conscious effort on the part of the drinker. Bright summer days are not for Gigondas; its required companions are the fireside of winter and the glow of a hot dish of game.

Gigondas is not a *vin de garde* in the style of the northern Côtes du Rhône Syrah wines, but the best vintages should live for between twelve and fifteen years. The ideal ages to drink it between are 5 and 8, when it will be mellow but certainly not tame. It is often compared with its southern neighbour, Châteauneuf-du-Pape, but does not attain the other wine's complexity or comparative finesse: Gigondas generally has a deeper colour and often betrays its alcohol more.

A little rosé and white wine is also made at Gigondas, although since 1971 the latter has not had the right to its own *Appellation Contrôlée* and is now sold as 'Côtes du Rhône'. As elsewhere in the region, the white-wine grapes are principally the Clairette, the Bourboulenc, the Grenache Blanc and the Ugni Blanc, with a little Picpoul; they make a wine of high alcohol content and uneven finish that has a marked tendency to oxidize after two or three years, like many run-of-the-mill southern wines. To be drunk very well chilled, white wine made at Gigondas is really a novelty—one that, served blind, can easily be used to trip up the experienced taster. The rosé's grape composition, like that of the red wine, is controlled, with the stipulation that a maximum of 60 per cent Grenache and a minimum of 15 per cent Cinsault must be used. It is superior to the white, but the hot climate so beneficial to the red tends to betray the rosé by endowing it with an excessive alcohol content of around 14°. In a light wine like rosé such a heavily sugared must has an unbalancing effect—not only on the wine but also on the head of the drinker. Not all the *domaines* make a rosé, and there is no doubt that Gigondas is best appreciated when it is red.

The village's largest wine-maker is the *propriétaire-négociant* Gabriel Meffre, who, in company with Pierre Amadieu, has played a direct part in furthering the prosperity of Gigondas. Meffre is, in fact, the resounding success story of modern French viticulture, and his large bulk-carrying tankers are a now familiar sight to even the most casual of French *autoroute* users, as his wine is sent in every direction across the country.

M. Gabriel Meffre himself is a native of Séguret, the neighbouring village, while his wife was born in Gigondas. The son of a modest viticultural family, he shrewdly recognized the southern Côtes du Rhône as a region that, although little-known, was full of potential for the grower who was prepared to expand. In 1930 he bought the Gigondas Domaine de Daysse, and 50 acres of vines, and by 1936 had become a *négociant* in his desire to market as much wine as possible. M. Meffre then found his progress slowing down, but the stagnation of the war years soon disappeared, and in 1946 southern France suddenly found itself encumbered with masses of surplus army material, mostly American, for which the resale market was, not surprisingly, very small. Seizing his opportunity, M. Meffre stepped in and bought up a whole fleet of bulldozers, earth-shovellers and heavy-duty vehicles, with the idea of using them to carry out vast new vineyard plantations. His capital outlay was, of course, small, and in the same year he transformed the Domaine St-Jean, near Travaillan. Situated on the huge, infertile Plan de Dieu flatland that extends west away from Gigondas, this *domaine* had been abandoned after the German occupation, and its nearly 100-acre vineyard had fallen into a wretched condition. Meffre set to work with his machinery to such effect that today this *domaine* boasts nearly 550 acres of long rows of well kept vines.

Meffre's ex-army machinery was largely the reason for his rapid success: whenever he bought *domaines* that had mostly slope vines, he was able to enlarge them by bulldozing any obstructive hills into a favourable south-facing position, and where *domaines* were on flat ground, it was again no problem to bulldoze away the scrub and few trees capable of coexisting with the vine on such poor terrain. Expansion therefore knew no bounds, particularly on the already mentioned Plan de Dieu, where Meffre & Company now owns six *domaines* and over 1,750 acres of vines.

Meffre is now the largest owner of *Appellation Contrôlée* vines in France, with more than 2,100 acres. The company's showpiece is the splendid, curiously styled eighteenth-century Château de Vaudieu at Châteauneuf-du-Pape, but this, sadly, is not inhabited. They also own the imposing sixteenth-century Château de Ruth near Ste-Cécile-les-Vignes.

The present massive size of the Meffre operation can be judged from the fact that only 13 per cent of all the wine it handles comes from its own vineyards. With sales of some 3,800,000 hectolitres a year (four or five times the total annual harvest of the whole of Châteauneuf-du-Pape), Meffre is the factory of the Côtes du Rhône. Bulk-carrying tankers stand outside the Gigondas cellars all day, every day, as the wine is shipped abroad for dispersal right around the world. At this level of output, quality is clearly not the finest, but the Gigondas Domaines des Bosquets and La Chapelle generally produce sound wine.

The man behind this impressive story, Gabriel Meffre, is a tanned sturdy man who looks as if he would be tough both in and out of business. By contrast, his younger son, Christian, thin and bearded, has about him a studious air, as befits a young man with a law degree. While he is charged with the commercial side of the business, his elder brother is responsible for the smooth running of all their machinery, which comes to more than 100 tractors, lorries and . . . bulldozers.

Opposite Meffre is the village's other *négociant* company, Pierre Amadieu, which is smaller and older. M. Amadieu was the first grower to follow the example of Hilarion Roux and bottle a good part of his wine. Since the firm's foundation in the 1920s he has thus been able to build up a strong network of sales to restaurants all over France, and this is one of the main sides of his business.

The Amadieu family owns two *domaines* at Gigondas, La Machotte and Le Romane, whose 200-acre vineyards are advantageously sited on the slopes of the narrow valley that runs between Sablet and Gigondas. M. Amadieu's son, Jean-Pierre, an enthusiastic young man who specializes in the vinification of their wines, explained how they treated their Gigondas estates: 'We have a flock of about 1,000 sheep which we bring down from the mountains to near Gigondas in summer; their dung is excellent for the vines and seems to help thwart bad attacks of rot. We do have to corral them in, however, as otherwise they'd be off everywhere and we'd never be able to find their obliging offerings!'

M. Amadieu also makes a fairly respectable Côtes du Rhône and Côtes du Ventoux but justly reserves special treatment for his very good, old-fashioned style Gigondas, which is aged in wood for over a year. The ageing cellar is in a very novel setting, away to the north-east of Gigondas, in an old railway tunnel on the disused Orange to Buis-les-Baronnies line. The company bought the tunnel at an auction in 1955 and has ranged along its 165 metres 160 large oak barrels, or *foudres*.

Meffre and Amadieu are Gigondas's largest landowners; generally, the *Appellation*'s other domaines are much smaller and much older. One of the most interesting is the Domaine St-Cosme. Its present owner, M. Henri Barruol, is a small, energetic and entertaining character, who stumbled into being a *vigneron* through marriage—and has no regrets at all in either department: 'I used to be a full-time wood carver,' he explained, 'and after marrying and moving to Gigondas, I learned a lot about wine from an old schoolfriend who is a local oenologist. That was nearly twenty years ago, and now, with the benefit of hindsight, I'm really glad I kept up wine-making at St-Cosme.'

It is just possible that M. Barruol has in his possession some of the oldest fermenting vats in France. When he was enlarging his cellar thirty years ago he unearthed some small vats of some 1,000- and 4,500-litre capacity that had been carefully built into the soft stone walls of the cellar. These had been put one on top of the other in staircase fashion, on four levels, with a top-to-bottom height difference of 5 metres. The system operated with great logic, and racking of the wine would be performed by simply letting it run down little communal channels to the next lowest vat. About 1 metre up the walls of each vat the stone wall is inset to accommodate the wooden planks which would be used to prevent the must from overflowing during the primary fermentation. With this restraining barrier over the vats, all *remontage*, which today is carried out with pumps, would be encouraged quite naturally. The fermenting wine would push upwards, unsuccessfully, and so churn itself over.

Unfortunately, M. Barruol is unable to indicate the precise age of these vats: 'I have had experts here, and they are all undecided—or unprepared to commit themselves. The vats definitely date from at least the eleventh century, but since the *domaine* is on the site of an old Gallo-Roman villa, it is very possible that they are much older still. After all, the Romans made plenty of wine here at Gigondas.'

Most of the Gallo-Roman treasures and relics found at Gigondas have been in the grounds of another viticultural property, the Domaine Raspail-Ay, which stands right beside the main D7 road. The old estate used to be much larger, but sadly, in accordance with the French law of equal right of inheritance, it was split into four parts. One of these, comprising 44 acres of vines, is owned by M. François Ay, who in the working of his vineyards has discovered all sorts of glass and earthenware relics, including completely intact second-century tumblers and long-stemmed glasses that were presumably used for wine drinking.

M. Ay is a tall, well built man who, in his role of President of the *Syndicat des Vignerons*, has the unenviable task of keeping the peace over issues such as new vineyard exploitation and the consequent change in the face of the countryside. He is very well read and much interested in history, and related a story of how the family vineyard had almost fallen into abandonment during the nineteenth century: 'After phylloxera the Raspail family found themselves hard-pressed to finance the replanting of the entire vineyard, which had not then been split into four. However, they did own one valuable asset, a marble statue called the Diadumenos of Vaison-la-Romaine. This they had acquired for virtually nothing, and they determined to try to sell it to save the vineyard. The Louvre in Paris hemmed and hawed but wouldn't buy it, and just as the Raspails thought all was lost, the British Museum stepped in and bought the Diadumenos. That was in 1869, and with the British money the Raspail family were able to restore their vineyard. The statue is still in the British Museum, but I have never seen it.'

In such a small community it is not surprising that the Mayor is usually a *vigneron*, and the owner of the Domaine de Longue-Toque, M. Roger Chapalain, is one such person, although he has recently handed over the running of his very good domaine to his son, Serge. M. Chapalain is a great, balding, jovial man who until 1962 was a full-time army officer. His interest in wine-making stems from a convalescence spent at his father-in-law's house at Gigondas after the Second World War; thereafter M. Chapalain resolved to take all his leaves from the army at the time of the *vendange*. With a comparatively late start in wine-making, he holds a less old-fashioned philosophy than several of his colleagues. He pointed out the essentials of his technique: 'The vinification here is not wholly traditional to Gigondas, for we use an adapted maceration system, leaving two-thirds of the grapes uncrushed before fermentation. There are more growers now vinifying on *raisin entier* lines, and I have also seen them come round to our idea of restricted ageing in wood, never more than a year, since Serge and I are trying to make a wine that is less hard and more supple than the customary Gigondas.' The Chapalains are fulfilling their aim with flying colours, since the Longue-Toque wines have become very impressive: dark, almost black in colour, their bouquet is reminiscent of blackcurrants. On the palate they possess a finely balanced combination of fruit, acidity and tannin and seem to have escaped the overt domination of the Grenache that can make these southern wines rather blatant. They should be left for five or six years to develop their harmony.

On his army travels around the world, had M. Chapalain encountered any singular wines? 'Well, yes; in the African republic of Chad there is a small amount of wine made by the missionaries for their church services. I don't know whether it was due to divine inspiration or what, but they somehow managed to come up with two crops of grapes every year!'

One of the leading and most typical of the traditional wines of Gigondas comes from the 62-acre Domaine Les Pallières, owned by the family of Hilarion Roux and run by the two brothers Pierre and Christian. The Roux family were the first bottlers at Gigondas back in the 1890s, and today they continue to bottle only their very best vintages. Thus their 1968 and their 1975 did not qualify for bottling and instead were sold off in bulk to *négociants*. The Pallières vineyard is in the north of the *Appellation*, on the way towards Sablet, and the vines are hidden away at over 200 metres. The Roux brothers are almost as retiring as their vines, and it takes a major local wine fair to draw Pierre out into the public eye. Extremely diffident, he is convinced that Pallières should remain faithful to its custom of presenting well-aged, ruby coloured wines that, by the time they are released for sale, have completed a considerable part of their evolution; a vintage such as the 1978 was not generally released until the spring of 1982, for instance. The wine that reaches the bottle is therefore always interestingly made up of a beguiling spicy fruitiness; memories of peeping into father's box of Havana cigars come back when considering the bouquet and the wine's overall strength of flavour and persistence of plum-like aftertaste make it the ideal accompaniment for roasted red meat, powerful cheese like Roquefort or Stilton and all game—notably the local speciality, *marcassin* (young wild boar), or hare.

Accompanying the Domaines of Pallières, Longue-Toque and Les Goubert in the top four at Gigondas is Roger Meffre's consistently excellent Domaine St-Gayan. M. Meffre works with his son, Jean-Pierre, and their 35-acre vineyard stands on the plain of clayey soil topped with broken chalkstone on the way to Sablet. The *mistral* wind regularly comes flying down the plain to pummel their vines, among which those that are Syrah can be identified by their training along lengths of wire, as is stipulated in the *Appellation* rules at both Gigondas and Châteauneuf-du-Pape. This method is called 'Royat', being an ordinary Gobelet pruning with the wire led through the sturdy vine shoots, and helps to channel the extra abundant vegetation that the Syrah always carries.

Although they follow the *Appellation* rules about how much Grenache and Syrah should be used in making their red and rosé Gigondas, the Meffres do not seem entirely convinced that the southern Rhône is the optimum home for the Syrah. As Jean-Pierre, a lanky, friendly boy in his early twenties, commented: 'There is a certain controversy going on about the suitability of the Syrah down here in the Vaucluse *département*, because the Syrah isn't all that easy to vinify well. If fermentation isn't just right, the wine can acquire a nasty taste that we call—no disrespect to your country—a *goût de pommes anglaises*. Why we should call it English apples, I don't know, but it is rather the same taste that you find if you leave the wine too long on its lees and is especially noticeable on the bouquet.'

The Meffre family has been at this property since 1400, and Roger recalled that the style of wine made by his father was tougher and longer-lived than the wine he is now making. 'Equally, twenty-five years ago there was no Syrah on the domaine, and now the proportion is up to nearly 20 per cent,' he explained. 'I'm also ageing in cask for a shorter time, preferring to leave the wine in concrete vats for a year and a half, and then rounding it off with between six and twelve months in wood.' M. Meffre is another *vigneron* who achieves his stated aim of making a more accessible, more easily drinkable wine, for although the Domaine St-Gayan red is always a big wine, it carries with it an interesting complexity of tannin, acidity and strong fruit flavours. M. Meffre finds the scent of truffles in his wine, while to others it is blackcurrants with, before the wine is 6 or 7 years old, a deep tannin firmly locked in. His top vintages, like the 1978 and the only slightly less good 1979, can easily live for twelve years.

The other leading *domaine* at Gigondas is a small property, only 13 acres, but it also makes wine from vineyards at Sablet and Beaumes-de-Venise. The Domaine les Goubert is owned by the Cartier Père et Fils but is run on a daily basis by Jean-Pierre Cartier—not surprisingly, since the smiling-eyed M. Cartier *père* has difficulty remembering his age but, when pressed, admits to around 75. The Les Goubert vineyard is planted with predominantly Grenache, backed up by the other three recommended vines, Syrah, Mourvèdre and Cinsault, and is close to the better-known Domaines of Raspail and Pesquier, south-west of the village itself. The cellars are very well kept and neatly laid out, and the Cartiers like to age their red Gigondas in their 550 litre *demi-muids*, the Cuvée Réservée receiving six months more than the ordinary-label wine. Both are well made, the Réservée being darker and more traditionally styled than the rather lightly fashioned ordinary Gigondas. A young *domaine*, whose vines are mostly only 20 years old, Les Goubert is likely to become better known during the 1980s.

The very smallest landholders at Gigondas are represented by the Cave Co-opérative, which is close to being the best in the Côtes du Rhône. It has an average yearly production of 10,500 hectolitres of all wine, including Côtes du Rhône and table wine as well as Gigondas, which is a tiny figure by comparison with the enormous, mass-producing Co-opératives all around it. An intimate concern, it is spotlessly and meticulously run by the busy M. Andrillat and shows that, if due care and control are exercised, Co-opératives can actually make good wine.

The cellars are distinguished by a series of well maintained *foudres*, each holding 150 hectolitres of maturing wine. Once these Swiss and German barrels contained beer, which was in no way a drawback, since all brewery barrels are lined with a pine resin that keeps the beer out of contact with the wood. When the Co-opérative bought their inexpensive ex-beer barrels, therefore, they simply planed off the pine resin and converted them to take the wine of Gigondas.

The Co-opérative's wines are thoroughly consistent and are led by the good but rather overpriced Cuvée du President. Along with the wines of Pierre Amadieu, Maurice Archimbaud at the Château de Montmirail, Roland Gaudin at the Domaine du Terme, Roger Combe at L'Oustaou Fauquet, and François Ay at the Domaine Raspail-Ay, they form a solid second division of honestly made, reliable wines that help to propagate the good name of Gigondas.

Gigondas Vintages

1959   Very good.

1960   Mediocre.

1961   Very good.

1962   Very good. Wines of notably good balance.

1963   Poor.

1964   Excellent. Very full bodied wines.

1965   Poor.

1966   Good. The wines were sound, but a little lacking in charm and finesse. They are now very old.

1967   Excellent. A powerful vintage, with the wines possessing good balance and bouquet. They are now fading away.

1968   Poor.

1969   Excellent. The wines were rich and harmonious, and their general elegance made them very good for drinking in their first ten years.

1970   Very good. An enormously strong vintage, high in alcohol and tannin. Some of the wines were rather harsh, but the best of them, from domaines such as Les Pallières, St-Gayan and the Château de Montmirail, were quite outstanding. They are drying out with age, and should be drunk soon.

1971   Excellent. Well coloured, full bodied wines with a better overall balance than many of the 1970s. They have passed their best, but present good examples of a Grenache-based wine that has stood up well to the test of time.

1972 Very good. Wines with a deep colour and agreeable strength, whose good acidity level has helped them to age very well. They should be in good order until around 1985.

1973 A disappointing year. A very large crop gave lightly coloured wines of variable quality.

1974 Generally a mediocre vintage. Some quite full bodied *cuvées* were made, but many of the wines were lacking in richness and degree. They are not generally showing very well any longer.

1975 Poor. A small harvest of light wines that were short on colour and bouquet.

1976 Very good. A dry summer gave wines that have become very charming. Ruby-coloured, they are striking through their well developed, flowery bouquets and their general well founded harmony. The wines do not hold much tannin and will be splendid for drinking until around 1984.

1977 Quite a good year, although there are some unbalanced wines from the smaller domaines. The better wines, such as those from Les Pallières and L'Oustaou Fauquet, were not very deeply coloured but were agreeable for their supple style and good length of finish. They are now showing the aromas of old wine and should be drunk by about 1984.

1978 Excellent. A sunny October rounded off a fine summer's ripening for the grapes, and the wines possess a bright red colour, a slowly opening 'cigar box' spicy bouquet and a firm richness on the palate. Very well structured, these wines will live for a good ten to twelve years. Note the Domaines du Terme and St-Gayan.

1979 Very good. Well coloured wines that are only marginally less full than those of the 1978 harvest. Good, complex bouquets and agreeable fruitiness backed by lingering amounts of tannin make this a very charming vintage that will continue in good order until at least 1987. Note the Domaines de Longue-Toque and Les Goubert.

1980 A very large crop of good wines that are already showing well. They are evenly coloured, with a bouquet that is developing well; although somewhat short on tannin, their acidity indicates that they are likely to age surprisingly well, given that they are not noticeably full-bodied. By around 1986 there could be some very good bottles.

1981 A reasonable vintage, marked by a very dry autumn, which unbalanced the grapes' ripening. Some growers have made wines rather low in acidity that will be suitable for drinking within 5 or 6 years, while others have succeeded in producing some robust and classically styled *cuvées* that will age well. In the latter group are the Domaine Les Pallières and the Domaine Les Goubert.

Earlier Exceptional Vintages   1955, 1949, 1947

Leading Growers at Gigondas

Meffre, Roger	
Domaine St-Gayan	84190 Gigondas
Chapalain, Serge	
Domaine de Longue-Toque	84190 Gigondas
Roux, Hilarion, Les Fils de	
Les Pallières	84190 Gigondas
Cartier, Jean-Pierre	
Domaine Les Goubert	84190 Gigondas
Amadieu, Pierre	84190 Gigondas
Archimbaud, Maurice	
Château de Montmirail	84190 Gigondas
Ay, François	
Domaine de Raspail-Ay	84190 Gigondas
Cave des Vignerons de Gigondas	84190 Gigondas
Combe, Roger	
L'Oustaou Fauquet	84190 Gigondas
Gaudin, Roland	
Domaine du Terme	84190 Gigondas
Barruol, Henri	
Domaine St-Cosme	84190 Gigondas
Bezert, Pierre	
Domaine de la Tuilière	84190 Gigondas
Boutière, Raymond et Fils	
Domaine du Pesquier	84190 Gigondas

Burle, Ed
    Les Pallieroudas   84190 Gigondas
Chassagne, F. et Fils
    Domaine du Pourras   84110 Sablet
Chastan, André et Fils   84100 Orange
Chastan, Fernand
    Clos du Joncuas   84190 Gigondas
Chauvet, Bernard
    Le Grapillon d'Or   84190 Gigondas
Chauvet, Edmond
    Domaine Le Péage   84190 Gigondas
Domaine de Cassan   84190 Lafare
Faraud, Jean-Pierre   84190 Gigondas
Faravel, Antonin
    Domaine La Bouissière   84190 Gigondas
Fauque, Jean-Claude
    Domaine St-Pierre   84150 Violès
Gorecki, J.
    Le Mas des Collines   84190 Gigondas
Gras, André
    Domaine St-François-Xavier   84190 Gigondas
Lambert, Pierre
    Domaine de la Mavette   84190 Gigondas
Meffre, Gabriel
    Domaine des Bosquets   84190 Gigondas
Meunier, Laurent
    La Gardette   84190 Gigondas
Pascal
    Domaine de Grand Montmirail   84190 Gigondas
Quiot, Pierre
    Domaine des Pradets   84190 Gigondas
Richard, Georges
    Domaine La Tornade   84190 Gigondas
Roux, Charles et ses Fils
    Château du Trignon   84190 Gigondas
Roux, Georges et Jean
    Domaine Les Chênes Blancs   84190 Gigondas
Veyrat, Pierre
    Château St-André   84190 Gigondas

12

Châteauneuf-du-Pape

Known the world over, Châteauneuf-du-Pape is a worthy centrepiece for the Côtes du Rhône. The old papal village that straddles a hillock 16 kilometres from Avignon possesses a certain and memorable aura, for not only does the name fire the imagination but the ruined castle tower too, with its broken walls recalling a splendour and magnificence long since departed. It was to this small village that the first of the Avignon Popes, Clement V, would make his way in the early fourteenth century, humbly seated on his mule and ever anxious to inspect his vineyard: in the words of the Provençal poet Félix Gras, in his 'Cansoun dou Papo Clément V':

> *Lou Papo Clément cinq, d'assetoun sus sa miolo,*
> *S'envai veire sa vigno, amount a Casteu-Nou;*
> *Porto dins sa saqueto, em' uno bono fiolo,*
> *Un taioun de jamboun, de pan e quauquis iou!* [1]

Clement had been installed as Pope in 1309. With relations badly strained between the King of France and the Papacy of Rome, and with Italy battle-torn by religious strife, he had no hesitation in choosing to remain in his native France. Besides, he was from

---

[1] French
Le Pape Clément cinq, assis sur sa mule,
S'en va voir sa vigne, là-haut à Châteauneuf;
Il porte dans son sac, avec une bonne fiole,
Un morceau de jambon, du pain et quelques oeufs!

English
Pope Clement the Fifth, seated on his mule,
Goes off to see his vines, up there at Châteauneuf;
He carries in his bag, along with a good flask,
A piece of ham, some bread and eggs!'

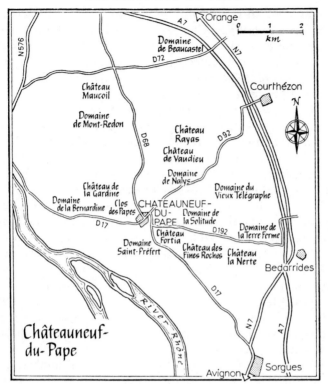

Châteauneuf-du-Pape

Bordeaux, was fond of his wine and had already planted his own vineyard there, now known as Château Pape-Clément, in the Graves region. History relates that Clement had a few vines planted 'near Avignon', but it was really his successor, Pope John XXII, who was responsible for the development of Châteauneuf-du-Pape's fortunes.

John was clearly a financially minded Pope, and by setting in order the papal treasury was able to enlarge the modest official residence in Avignon. But he was a romantic too and longed to retire from the oppressive summer heat of busy Avignon to the tranquillity of the surrounding countryside. A formal country residence was sought, and his choice fell upon Châteauneuf, which already contained the foundations of a large castle ruined in 1248. Between 1318 and 1333 the 'new château' was built. It was a monster construction, even by the affluent standards of the time,

175

and Pope John was only able to move into it one year before his death. His new castle, or Châteauneuf, usefully performed a dual purpose; not only was it intended as a summer residence, but it also formed part of a protective line of castles around Avignon. The villages of Bédarrides, Sorgues, Noves and Barbentane completed the circle.

Pope John used the 25 acres that went with the *château* for growing vines and olives, both of which were already exploited by the local inhabitants. He found the range of fruit that could be grown was restricted by the lack of a regular water supply to his new domaine, and it was the vines and olive trees that best adapted themselves to the partially arid terrain.

John's vineyards became the best-known in the village, but the community had been growing vines for at least 150 years before his arrival, as is witnessed by a document revealing that in 1157 Gaufredus, the unlikely-named Bishop of Avignon, congratulated one Frédéric Barberousse on the lands and vines that made up Châteauneuf. However the first mention of the wine itself comes in the year 1320, when a regular traffic of full barrels of wine from Châteauneuf to the Palace of Avignon was reported, and of empty barrels on the way back, a journey which in those days would have lasted about four hours.

The Châteauneuf vineyard, although quoted as numbering 3·3 million vine plants in 1334 (today this would represent a surface area of some 2,500 acres), belonged to a mass of small owners, and so John was unable to furnish all the wine needed for the papal feastings held in Avignon. Recourse was made to the nearby village of Bédarrides, today part of the Châteauneuf-du-Pape *Appellation* area, for an annual delivery of 1,550 litres. Even this was still inadequate for the papal palace, if a menu of the year 1324 is anything to go by. A gargantuan feast was then held to celebrate the marriage of the great-niece of Pope John and comprised, *inter alia*, 55 sheep, 690 chickens, 580 partridges, 270 rabbits, 8 pigs, 4 wild boar, 40 plovers, 37 ducks, 50 pigeons and many other diverse delicacies.

The official papal stay at Avignon lasted from 1309 to 1378. It was a time of tremendous prosperity for the previously humble city, and the papal bounty generously extended itself to the neighbouring countryside. Even up till 1410, when the differences with Rome were healed and only one Pope was thereafter recognized, Châteauneuf received beneficial papal attention, and its castle was maintained in tip-top order. The vineyard, on the other hand, underwent a few ups and downs, as of all Pope John's successors only Innocent VI (1352–1362) and Benoît XIII (1394–1423) really interested themselves in its progress and satisfactory upkeep, and Benoît exiled himself to become Anti-Pope in 1403.

Thereafter, one assumes, the vineyard lapsed into local obscurity, without perhaps producing a quality of wine capable of attracting the attention of kings and nobles, for no further documentation on the wine of Châteauneuf-du-Pape exists before the eighteenth century, evidence of the inevitable decline in the village's fortunes after the return of the papacy to its seat in Rome. In 1562 the *château* had been badly damaged by the marauding Huguenot Baron des Adrets, but its dungeon and one tower had remained intact—until a fateful day in August 1944, when the retreating German forces contrived to blow it in half as they abandoned their encampment there.

The wine that we now know as Châteauneuf-du-Pape has not long held that name. Even into the early nineteenth century it was known within France as 'Châteauneuf-Calcernier'—indicating the limestone deposits that were once exploited close to the village. The wine sold abroad during the eighteenth century went for the most part under the name of *vin d'Avignon*; it was taken up the Rhône by barge in 265-litre barrels and dispatched from Lyon to all destinations, including England and the United States. The leading wine to be exported at that time was that of the Château de la Nerte, which was sold under its own name.

The wine of La Nerte was the first Châteauneuf to be bottled, an enterprising practice that had started in 1785. Shortly after the Battle of Waterloo in 1815, the Domaine de la Solitude was also bottling a little of its wine and these two estates directly helped the growing reputation of the local wine. By 1822 the wine of La Nerte was considered the best of 'Châteauneuf-Calcernier' by the wine writer Dr A. Jullien, but it was not quite the same style of wine that we know today. Dr Jullien wrote: 'Well-coloured, the wines of La Nerte have a softness and agreeableness: the best moment to drink them is at the height of their maturity, after three or four years.' He also mentioned the wines of La Fortiasse (Château Fortia) and Clos St-Patrice, but it was La Nerte which undoubtedly led the field. While just one principal quality of wine seems to have been made from the different grapes being cultivated in the area, it is evident that such famous names as La Nerte and Fortia formed only a tiny part of the whole vineyard. In 1800 the Châteauneuf-du-Pape area was said to hold 1,650 acres of vines, and in 1817 2,025 acres. The 1847 holding at La Nerte and Fortia together was reported as 54 acres, which evidently made them a tiny part of a very large plantation, for these figures do not include the villages of Courthézon and Bédarrides, which are today part of the overall Châteauneuf-du-Pape *Appellation* area. If these two villages and part of Orange are included in the vineyard returns for 1817, then the approximate equivalent of today's *Appellation* area comes to no less than 4,800 acres.

By 1860 the wine of La Nerte was the most expensive of all Châteauneuf-du-Papes because of the heavy demand for it both in France and abroad. The village vineyards were continuing to flourish at around the 2,000-acre mark, but all progress was abruptly halted by the onset of phylloxera. Desperate *vignerons* tried flooding the flat ground and spraying novel chemical mixtures on to the vines but to no avail.

Not surprisingly, many growers abandoned hope and turned to the full-time cultivation of cherries, almonds, apricots and olives. The village, as a result, had two large olive mills up until the First World War, and its cherries found a confirmed market in England, where they were held in great esteem. Reconstruction of the vineyards was cautiously started in 1878 but then accelerated to reach a figure of 2,125 acres by 1913. Before the Second World War the community of Châteauneuf itself possessed over 3,775 acres of vines, and today the whole *Appellation* area has reached a virtual saturation point of 7,600 acres.

Châteauneuf-du-Pape occupies a notable niche in the history of modern viticulture, for it was there in 1923 that the first regulating laws were devised for table wines. These are now known as the laws of the *Appellation Contrôlée* in France and have since been copied by German, Italian and Spanish wine-growers. The aim of the Châteauneuf-du-Pape *vignerons*, led by the late Baron Le Roy of Château Fortia, was to safeguard their wine from trafficking and general abuse, and to this end they drew up a charter containing six stipulations. These ran as follows:

178

1. A completely natural delimitation of the area to be planted with vines was proposed; only land capable of bearing lavender and thyme was to be cultivated, these two plants preferring an equally poor soil to the vine.
2. Only specifically named grape varieties would be allowed to be planted.
3. The training and pruning of the vines was to be regulated.
4. The wine was to contain a minimum alcohol degree of 12·5. (This is still the highest minimum level in all France.)
5. At harvest time there was to be a *triage*, or sorting of the grapes. At least 5 per cent of the crop had to be discarded, this to ensure the inclusion of only healthy, well-ripened grapes.
6. No rosé wine was to be made, and wine that failed to pass a tasting panel would not be sold as Châteauneuf-du-Pape.

For their time these laws were monumental. Their efficiency is well judged from their almost unchanged existence more than sixty years later, and they now form the basis of the national laws of *Appellation d'Origine*, themselves only adopted in 1936.

Such exemplary vigilance over their wine was repeated by the *vignerons* in a municipal decree of 1954. Flying saucers had just come to people's attention, and the village decree firmly stated:

Article 1. The flying overhead, landing and taking off of aeronautical machines called 'flying saucers' or 'flying cigars', of whatever nationality they may be, is strictly forbidden on the territory of the commune of Châteauneuf-du-Pape.

Article 2. Any aeronautical machine—'flying saucer' or 'flying cigar'—that lands on the territory of the commune will be immediately taken off to the pound.

Châteauneuf-du-Pape has never been a large village and today has not more than 3,000 inhabitants. Being the home of such a well-known wine, as well as the unofficial capital of the Côtes du Rhône, it bustles with activity and movement for a large part of the year. Tourists drawn by the magic and renown of its name wander through the sloping, confined streets, sometimes pausing to ring the doorbell of a *vigneron* who has a sign announcing the sale of wine outside his house. Side by side, beret-wearing Frenchmen and robed Arabs linger around the tiny village square and fountain, which cluster beside the main road through the

The Pope's Castle

village. Arabs from North Africa now form a large proportion of the vineyard personnel and are housed in simple quarters on the large domaines or in little houses in the village when they work for smaller *propriétaires*.

The Pope's castle used to stand just at the top of the village, and its solitary corner tower now makes an easily recognizable local landmark. From the tower the view is immense: vines on all sides, set into a spartan ground full of large cream and rust-tinted stones. Clusters of trees denote the old-established wine *domaines*. Across to the south-west the Rhône curls away in a beckoning sweep. Meanwhile, the village below continues on its daily path, just occasionally giving an indication of its wealth and importance when a smart local car dashes past a lumbering vineyard machine.

The variety of good vines at Châteauneuf-du-Pape is greater than in any other French vineyard, and altogether thirteen different grapes are allowed to go into the wine. Few *domaines* now actually possess the complete range, but most growers still rely on a combination of seven or eight. What is more, they honestly believe in the individual contribution of each kind of grape: 'Drop that grape and you'll lose such and such a nuance in the wine,' they say emphatically.

The handful of *vignerons* who grow all thirteen vines have tracked down some of the lesser plants only with difficulty. After the phylloxera attack some of the vines—like the Picardan and the Muscardin—all but disappeared, and it was a revived interest in seeing how the wine would turn out when made with all thirteen that brought them out of total obscurity.

The full list of vine varieties contains most of the Côtes du Rhône 'regulars'. It is: Grenache, Syrah, Mourvèdre, Cinsault, Counoise, Vaccarèse, Terret Noir and Muscardin (all red grapes), and Clairette, Bourboulenc, Roussanne, Picpoul and Picardan (all white grapes). (The Grenache Blanc and the Terret Blanc are also planted.) The first four vines are the most widely planted, while the Muscardin and the Counoise in particular are rarely found anywhere else, the former seemingly being unique to Châteauneuf-du-Pape. Its origin is obscure, but one of the village's most prominent theorists, the late Dr Philippe Dufays, was always adamant that it bears no resemblance to the Muscat or Muscadet family.

Baron Le Roy of Château Fortia is a supporter of the Muscardin, as he explained in the following terms: 'You know, we'd be better off here if we replaced the Cinsault with the Muscardin. The Muscardin doesn't produce a lot, makes a wine of low degree and spreads out over the soil, preventing tractors from passing freely between the vines, all of which combine to put people off it. But I believe that it gives a freshness on the palate and helps the wine to achieve elegance.' Like Baron Le Roy, François Perrin of Domaine de Beaucastel is not in favour of the Cinsault, for he invariably finds that it gives a rather mean-tasting, thin wine. From tasting individual vats of Muscardin at Domaine de Mont-Redon and various individual vats of Cinsault around the *Appellation*, it would seem that these views are sensible. Neither Muscardin nor Cinsault give their wine much colour, and indeed a $2\frac{1}{2}$-year-old wine of either grape has a marked strain of orange tints in its already pale red. However the Muscardin possesses a welcome crispness that accompanies its light fruit, in contrast to the rather flat-tasting, thin wine of the Cinsault.

The equally little-known Counoise, like the Grenache, comes

from Spain. Pope Urban V (1362–70) was presented with some cuttings of it by a Spanish vice-legate called Conejo, and the French subsequently altered the vine's name to 'Counoise'. Only a very few domaines now cultivate it, but it has strong support from Baron Le Roy, who considers it one of the best grapes at Châteauneuf-du-Pape. François Perrin has it planted at Domaine de Beaucastel and believes that a *cuvée* of Vaccarèse and Counoise together can form the good, firm backbone for a classically styled Châteauneuf. Individually, they do not display this firmness. Again, Domaine de Mont-Redon have been experimenting with single vats of less-known grapes, and a 2-year-old Counoise showed a red to light purple colour, with a peppery bouquet that is said to be typical of the grape, and a fruit somewhat reminiscent of loganberries on the palate. If the *vignerons* as a whole ever adopt Baron Le Roy's enthusiasm for the Counoise, they will find that it is a hardy plant, very resistant to rot, and one that is harvested at the end of the *vendanges*, just before the Mourvèdre.

In the last century a lengthy study on the likely contribution of each grape was carried out by a Commandant Ducos, and it is still interesting to read his findings, even though there will never be any consensus among the growers as to what proportion and blend of grapes will make an ideal vat of Châteauneuf-du-Pape. Ducos imagined his ideal vat and recommended that it contain grapes in the following proportions: 20 per cent Grenache and Cinsault, to provide the wine with 'warmth, liqueur-like sweetness and mellowness'; 40 per cent Mourvèdre, Syrah, Muscardin and Vaccarèse, to give it 'solidity, durability and colour, accompanied by a straightforward, almost thirst-quenching flavour'; 30 per cent Counoise and Picpoul, to supply 'vinosity, charm, freshness and accentuation of bouquet'; finally, 10 per cent Clairette and Bourboulenc, to bring 'finesse, fire and sparkle' to the wine.

Commandant Ducos's flowery recommendations—which do not include all thirteen varieties—have been eroded this century for one main reason. Just as with Gigondas, Châteauneuf-du-Pape was for many years sold to Burgundian merchants as a 'booster' wine, to provide the northern wines with body and alcohol in weak years. The wine would be sold by the vat shortly after the harvest and would be shipped straight up to Burgundy to perform its medicinal transformation. Seeing such an assured market before them, growers at Châteauneuf were encouraged to plant much more Grenache, a plant that gives a high-degree wine. Even after the Second World War individual vineyards that comprised 80 or 90 per cent Grenache were not uncommon.

Today there is a perceptible move away from such an imbalance. Châteauneuf-du-Pape is now famous in its own right, while many growers feel that in order to keep an evolving clientele happy, they must produce a wine that is easier to drink and less alcoholic. The Syrah, which had been successfully planted at the Domaine Condorcet in 1878, is now very fashionable, along with the Cinsault, while the Mourvèdre, which is inclined to produce somewhat 'hard' wines, is less in favour. Meanwhile, the amount of Grenache planted averages between 60 and 75 per cent of any vineyard. Those growers who bottle their own wine tend to have smaller amounts of Grenache than the mixed-culture vine-growers, who will sometimes have almost entirely Grenache-filled vineyards cultivated next to their cherry and olive trees. Such mixed-culture growers generally sell their grapes to merchants.

The *Appellation* area is not confined to Châteauneuf-du-Pape but runs out from the village towards the neighbouring com-munities of Orange, Courthézon, Bédarrides and Sorgues. Nearly everywhere there is to be seen its most characteristic feature, the large, smooth stones that always make a vivid impression on the visitor. These red and cream coloured stones, varying in size from the equivalent of a Provençal tomato to that of a very well grown melon, are not alluvial deposits from the Rhône, as is the popular belief, but are the deposits left by very ancient Alpine glaciers that descended across France until halted by the Rhône to the west of the village.

The stoniest land of all is to the north and north-west of Châteauneuf-du-Pape; the vines on the domaines of Mont-Redon, Les Cabrières and Château Maucoil appear engulfed in a sea of stones, leaving the clay soil underneath barely visible. As a general rule, it is true to say that the more stones there are, the higher the maturity of the grapes will be, for the stones act to absorb the heat rays of the sun and reflect them back on to the vines. In mid-summer, for instance, the stones remain warm to the touch until long after sundown.

While the stones help the vines to ripen, they also directly hinder the working of the vineyards. Before the introduction of machinery around 1950, all wooden implements like ploughs had to be metal-reinforced, and today wear and tear on even the most robust modern machines is no less considerable. New vine plantation, in particular, is a slow, painstaking process. Most of the young vines are trained against wooden stakes to save them from being buffeted by the southern *mistral* wind, and the drilling of two holes for the plant and the stake is very slow work on such unyielding ground.

Not all the *Appellation* is so profusely covered in stones, though. In the southern part, near the Domaines St-Préfert and Condorcet, the land is more gravelly and so produces lighter, slightly less alcoholic wines. Then to the east and north-east, in the direction of Bédarrides and Courthézon, the land becomes alternatively more sandy and more clayey but still retains many of the stones. Well sited *domaines* here are those of Beaucastel, Solitude and Vieux Télégraphe.

With three quite distinct soil types inside their vineyard area, many of the smaller growers are happy to have their vines spread out in different plots, or *parcelles*: this gives them ample opportunity to blend into a single vat grapes that differ in sugar content and maturity. Such blending was traditionally much valued by the Popes, according to M. Paul Avril, of the Clos des Papes: 'The Popes used to receive their taxes in kind from the local *vignerons*, and so installed one giant *cuve* into which went all the different wine. They were always delighted to find that the assembled wine from this *cuve* was of a consistently high standard,' he concluded.

Apart from the Syrah, which grows along wires, all the vines are trained in the usual Gobelet style, with a broad spacing of 2 metres between each plant to permit the passage of vineyard machinery. The combination of sun and wind that is typical of the southern Rhône climate means that for the most part the vines are disease-free. Their principal blight remains the *pourriture*, or rotting of the grapes, and still no effective answer has been found to this.

Until 1869 Châteauneuf-du-Pape, like many French wine villages, respected a *ban des vendanges*, which regulates the opening date of the harvest to greatest common benefit. In olden days it used to be decided either by a committee of growers or, more often, by a local landlord or *grand seigneur*, since the custom dates back to the fifteenth century. In the days when many taxes and rents were paid in wine, the feudal landlords had no interest in receiving unripe grapes from their tenants on the land and so instituted the *ban* or public proclamation permitting the start of harvesting. By the eighteenth century the intention was more to give all growers an equal chance of making and selling their wine under similar conditions, and anyone who harvested before time was fined five *livres*, although his crop was not confiscated, as was decreed at nearby Cairanne. The official day of harvesting, according to local records, was most commonly a Monday, Sunday being excluded on the grounds that it should be consecrated to rest and what is obscurely termed 'offices'.

In 1962, at the instigation of M. Pierre Lançon of Domaine de la Solitude, the *ban des vendanges* made a comeback at Châteauneuf-du-Pape. The ceremony now takes place in the cellars of the village *château*, and with great pomp a cross-section of the grapes is tasted. If they are judged to be ripe, a public declaration is cried out, allowing the start of harvesting two days later, generally around 20 September. A carefree dinner then follows.

When the *vendange* starts, the streets of the village swarm with activity, and a barely concealed feeling of excitement pervades the atmosphere. For three or four weeks Châteauneuf-du-Pape looks like a wine village—and smells like one. Open doors reveal newly washed barrels, lengths of rubber piping and churning presses. From even the quietest alleyways drifts a smell of fermenting must. Outside one or two cellars mounds of grapes are laid out on large tables, and are slowly sifted through by stooping workers. This is the *triage*, or rejection of at least 5 per cent of the grapes, that was initiated in 1923 along with the other quality controls. In bad years over one-quarter of the crop will be set aside by the most conscientious growers, the inferior grapes going towards an ordinary table wine. Generally, the *triage* is performed in the vineyards, although strict supervision is necessary as not every picker is able to perceive the difference between a good and a bad grape. To help, they are sometimes provided with two containers (often green and red to denote the difference) for the healthy grapes and the discard, or *rapé*. In a difficult year like 1975 some domaines such as Mont-Redon will send their pickers through the vineyards three times in an attempt to harvest each grape variety according to its maturity. Generally the first grape to be harvested is the Syrah, which suffers from the rains that often fall in the last week of September.

When the *vigneron* finally receives the harvest at his cellars, he knows that the weeks ahead will be full of worry and pre-occupation. With wines based on a single grape, the grower can happily watch over the progress and development of one 'child'; at Châteauneuf he must administer care and attention to widely differing 'children'—some vats filled with high-degree Grenache juice, others filled with softer white-grape juice and still others containing rich, highly scented Syrah juice. The grower must use his native wizardry to know when and in what proportions to assemble the vats and, above all, must ensure that his final wine is well balanced.

Nowadays such a thing as a 'typical' Châteauneuf-du-Pape is hard to find. This is because the vineyard is in a near-constant state of flux, with growers experimenting with alternating combinations of the thirteen grape varieties and with differing methods of vinifying them. The traditional Châteauneuf-du-Pape that would be fermented for a month or more and then aged for five years is now virtually a ghost from the past; growers simply cannot afford to keep their wine off the market for so long. This is partly why more white wine is being made, and it is now also possible to encounter four or more different types of red Châteauneuf that will please strictly according to the personal taste of the imbiber.

The majority of the *vignerons*, however, still like to vinify their wine broadly following the long-accepted methods taught to them by their fathers and grandfathers; only the duration of fermentation and the time left for ageing in wood have changed. Thus the must will ferment for two or three weeks, and by the spring the wine will all have been transferred to wooden ageing casks. After a stay of twelve months to two years, the wine is prepared for bottling. Most *domaines* prefer to fine and filter their wine before releasing it for sale, so that the client is presented with an entirely clear bottle.

Obviously, variations exist. Some growers like to carry out the *égrappage*, or destalking, of their grapes before fermentation. This is supposed to lower the wine's acid level slightly, because of the absence of the acidity in the stalks and stems. Equally, if a rich, long-lived and strongly coloured wine is sought, some or all of the juice from the second pressing will be added: Domaine de Beaucastel round off their wine in some vintages in this way, while

186

Château Rayas, formerly one of the very best and most traditional *domaines*, have always added all the second-pressing juice.

At present the greatest difference of opinion concerns the handling of the grapes prior to fermentation. In the most traditional, high-quality *domaines* such as Vieux Télégraphe, Fortia and Beaucastel, their owners prefer to crush their grapes ever more lightly, if at all. Domaine du Vieux Télégraphe leave 30 per cent of their grapes intact, crushing the rest only lightly; Château Fortia leave some grapes intact; others, notably their Syrah, are crushed by foot, and the majority are compressed by a carefully set modern crusher that will not break up the pips; Domaine de Beaucastel actually leave as much as 80 per cent of their grapes intact but then follow their own *vinification à chaud* method, whereby the outside of the grapes is immediately heated at 80 °C in order to extract the colour and the aromas inside the skin. This is followed by a cooling to 20–25 °C, at which temperature a steady two- or three-week fermentation takes place.

In all instances growers are attempting to maximize the finesse and balance of their wine without overweighting it with the extracts of heavily crushed stalks, stems and pips, all of which bring extra amounts of tannin and acidity which can critically upset the wine's balance. Their course is a logical one, since they also want to retain what they regard as the traditional Châteauneuf-du-Pape character without diminishing it in any way.

Two other eminent *domaines*, those of Beaurenard and Nalys, are also using mainly *raisins entiers* or uncrushed grapes—Nalys completely and Beaurenard for half their crop. However, their point of departure is their rapid preparation of the wine after its fermentation. M. Coulon at Beaurenard ages his wine for between six and nine months in cask, so that generally most of it is bottled within the year following the harvest. It is immediately striking for its racy fruit, but it also possesses underlying tannin that gives it welcome backbone. Nalys too give their red wine only a short stay in cask and bottle, most of it within fifteen months after the harvest, also with generally good results on much the same lines as Beaurenard.

One or two other growers also believe that today's pump-operated crushing machines can be over-effective and that an over-mashed pulp tends to enter the fermenting vats. They have therefore turned completely away from the *foulage* and towards a form of vinification by maceration with the help of carbonic gas. Under this method, the grapes are piled directly from the vineyard into their vats, where the sheer force of weight breaks up the bottom layers and heats them up through the natural compression arising from the presence of so many grapes in a confined space. The vats are filled with carbonic gas, and in these circumstances, as fermentation gets under way, a maximum of fruit is extracted as opposed to a more normally balanced equation of fruit, tannin and acidity. This wine comes out much lighter in style than usual, and although it may not be 'typical' of Châteauneuf-du-Pape, it is both marketable and readily drinkable within a year or two, no doubt to the satisfaction of these growers' bank managers.

The main exponent of this *macération carbonique* style of vinification is M. Pierre Lançon of Domaine de la Solitude, who explained his own particular method: 'What I want above all from my wine is bouquet and finesse. I attach less importance to colour and body, which you could say were the most typical characteristics of a red Châteauneuf-du-Pape. I use an adapted *macération carbonique* formula, whereby I leave the uncrushed grapes to ferment slowly for a week in vats filled with carbonic gas. Under the action of the carbonic gas the grapes start to ferment within their skins, but to avoid giving the wine a purely *macération carbonique* taste—a simple fruitiness like that found in the wines of the Beaujolais—I then run off the juice and let the grapes ferment in the normal way for another two weeks. This permits the wine to regain its own Châteauneuf-du-Pape character. At the end of these three weeks of fermentation, I run the wine off and press the left-over pulp three or four times. I generally add the juice of the first three pressings to give the wine slightly greater richness and then leave it to complete its malolactic fermentation. By the New Year it is normally in the maturing casks, where I leave it to age for a little over six months.'

The striking point about M. Lançon's technique, which he started in 1954, is its rapidity. His Châteauneuf-du-Pape is ready for bottling within the year following the harvest, but of late his *macération carbonique* formula seems to be stripping his wine of much of its guts and character. Until the mid-1970s the wine of la

Solitude was always good and reliable, with agreeable fruit when young, which developed into a fine richness after about five or six years. Presently the *domaine* seems to be going through an unsettled period.

Old timers would gruffly say that these hastened-along wines were not the real Châteauneuf, but while the 'real' Châteauneuf can be blandly talked about, it is an unfortunate fact of life that it is a wine unknown to many. When found outside the immediate vicinity of the production area the wine is often false, mixed or diluted. Perhaps it is the innate charm of the name, easily pronounceable, but a lot more 'Châteauneuf-du-Pape' is drunk than is ever made.

The *vignerons* themselves are well aware of—and worried about—this situation. M. Paul Avril, ex-President of the *Syndicat des Vignerons*, delivered the surprising fact that only 25 per cent of all Châteauneuf-du-Pape is bottled at the village, the rest being sold in bulk. 'In the medium term it would obviously be desirable to enforce compulsory bottling within the *Appellation* confines, as has been done in Alsace,' he said. 'But it's worth remembering that 80 per cent of all Alsatian wine was bottled in their region prior to their ruling. Our task is much harder, but that doesn't lessen our determination. It's been shocking to taste some of the bottles of Châteauneuf-du-Pape brought back from abroad by visiting *vignerons*, and we're fed up with seeing the wine and its name blatantly trafficked.'

At its best, Châteauneuf-du-Pape is indeed a majestic wine. Its alluring colour is reminiscent of rubies, while its powerful bouquet seems to nurture the many herbs and wild flowers that grow scattered about the hills and plains around Avignon. The bouquet remains intriguingly complex, however; its warmth certainly never deserts it, but the nuances within it can vary subtly during the course of drinking a bottle. The late owner of one of the best *domaines*, M. Jacques Perrin of Domaine de Beaucastel, used to put it like this: 'I can tell you that some of Châteauneuf-du-Pape's characteristic aromas resemble irises, violets and roasted almonds, for instance, but then we could turn to another bottle from another vat or another vintage and find that the predominating sensations were perhaps truffles, laurel and local herbs. In addition, these may alter the longer the wine is exposed to the air, so you can't really talk in black-and-white terms about what a

Châteauneuf-du-Pape should specifically resemble—all of which, of course, adds to the wine's enticement!'

On the palate traditionally made Châteauneuf-du-Pape is wholehearted and enveloping, the sort of wine that staves off the cold on wintry nights. Generally rather tannic until its fourth or fifth birthday, the wine thereafter 'straightens out', until its commanding elements of fruit, alcohol and richness are well fused. This power and harmony will be retained in outstanding vintages such as 1978 for twelve to fifteen years, but in no sense can Châteauneuf-du-Pape be considered a 'stayer' along the lines of the Syrah-based northern Côtes du Rhône wines. The presence of so much fast-maturing Grenache precludes that, and the wine is ideally drunk between 6 and 12 years old, the lower figure being applicable in sound or good vintages like 1976 and 1980 and the higher figure applying to the best vintages like 1967 and 1978. The main exceptions to this rule are the wines of the Domaines de Beaucastel and Vieux Télégraphe, Château La Nerte and Clos de l'Oratoire des Papes, which in their most powerful vintages will live for around twenty years. The wines of Domaine de Mont-Redon and Château Rayas dated before 1976 are also capable of such longevity. Mont-Redon have since lightened the style of their wine, seeking greater suppleness and more immediate drinkability, while Château Rayas has gone into a sad decline following the death of its exceptional owner M. Louis Reynaud.

One of the main reasons for drinking a Châteauneuf-du-Pape before it is too old is that as its richness fades so its high alcohol content is unmasked. The strong heat of the South of France invariably gives it an alcohol level of between 13° and 14°—a good two degrees more than a Bordeaux, for instance—and this can make the wine somewhat blatant in style if put alongside its aristocratic Bordelais rivals. However, when compared with any other famous southern wine, such as Chianti Classico, Barolo or Rioja, there is little doubt that Châteauneuf-du-Pape reveals the greatest overall balance and finesse, well in keeping with Alphonse Daudet's description of it as 'the Wine of Kings and the King of Wines'.

Before the Second World War the *vignerons* instituted a personal bottle to represent their *Appellation*, and this is used by most of the private *domaines* and growers. The bottle is the classic Burgundy shape but has embossed below its neck the old papal coat of arms, surrounded by the words *Châteauneuf-du-Pape Contrôlée*. Only owners of vineyards who have bottled their wine at their *domaines* are permitted to use this attractive bottle, so all wine from the *négociant* trade comes in the usual plain bottle. As a reliable yardstick for buying a good, genuinely made bottle of Châteauneuf, this embossed bottle serves an admirable purpose for the consumer.

With such a powerful, full-bodied wine as Châteauneuf-du-Pape, it is best to serve strongly flavoured food that will enhance and complement it. Thus any game, red meat dishes or a good wintry stew are ideal. Cheese, too, is a good companion for the red wine, notably the stronger varieties such as Camembert, Roquefort and Stilton, or any goat's cheese or garlic-based cheese such as Gaperon or Boursin.

Although quite rarely found abroad, a little white Châteauneuf-du-Pape is made, which constitutes just over 2 per cent of the total production, or some 1,800 hectolitres. There have been exciting developments in the vinification of this wine in the last few years, as growers have striven to get away from the old, heavy style of wine that was always prone to an early oxidization. The selection of grapes used for it remain much as before—the Clairette, Bourboulenc, Roussanne, Grenache Blanc and Picpoul—but enterprising domaines such as Nalys, Père Caboche and Font-de-Michelle are now vinifying at very reduced temperatures in order to extract maximum fruit and crisp freshness from their white grapes. M. Jean-Pierre Boisson, the young and keen son of the owner of Domaine Le Père Caboche, explained his particular technique: 'I use a combination of the Grenache Blanc, Clairette, Bourboulenc and a very little Picpoul. As the Grenache Blanc has a tendency to oxidize when it experiences the least exposure to air, I aim to perform a low-temperature fermentation and rapid bottling. This means that after pressing I leave the juice to settle for eighteen hours in concrete vats, then transfer it to stainless steel tanks for fermentation at a controlled temperature of 14 °C. Under this control fermentation lasts for about a month; I don't let the malolactic occur because we are in a region where the white wines tend to be a little flabby and lacking in acidity. To stabilize the wine, I then leave it at minus 5 °C for two weeks, which precipitates the tartarics to the bottom. After filtration, it is bottled a little after the middle of November. A wine like this, very fresh and immediately aromatic, should be drunk young, certainly within two years.'

The white wines, notably from the Domaine de Nalys, but also from Le Père Caboche, Domaine de Mont-Redon and Domaine Font-de-Michelle all represent this racy new style with great success. They display interesting fruit aromas—peaches or even peach stones and pineapples spring to mind—they are attractively coloured, with even yellow tints in them, and yet behind the young fruit and colour is a considerable Châteauneuf richness which, after a year or so in the bottle, develops into a lengthy and satisfying finish. The Domaine de Nalys white in particular deserves to be better-known.

Other interesting white wines at Châteauneuf-du-Pape come from the Domaine de Beaucastel, Château Rayas before the 1976 vintage, Domaine de la Terre Ferme and Domaine Jean Deydier et Fils. The Beaucastel and Rayas wines can age extremely well, although François Perrin of Beaucastel pointed out a pheno-menon observable in his white wines that is also sometimes apparent with the best white wines at Hermitage from growers such as Gérard Chave: 'You can taste my white wines when a year or two old, and you'll see that they have a balanced acidity and that their aromas and general weight indicate a long life ahead. But suddenly I give you a 3- or 4-year-old bottle, and you say, 'What is this resin taste in the wine? And the bouquet's aromas, as opposed to flourishing, are very suppressed.' Your analysis is correct—the wine has a form of oxidization passing through it, carrying it from its youth into a state of honourable old age. This often occurs with my whites when they are between 3 and 7 years old.' And to prove the point he pulls out a bottle 11 years old, followed by one that is dated 1956. The first wine, packed with rich straw-gold colours and an intense concentration of almost flower-like aromas on bouquet and palate, improves with about twenty minutes' aeration and is notable for its lovely clean aftertaste. The 1956, all gold, its flavours reminiscent of old Burgundy, at 26 still possesses remarkable richness but begins to dry out towards a Château Chalon style of wine after twenty minutes. Beaucastel white is made from 80 per cent Roussanne and 20 per cent Grenache Blanc, while the Rayas white comes from the Grenache Blanc and the Clairette, with, in old vintages ending in the 1960s, occasionally a little Sauvignon and Chardonnay. However, like its red wine, the Château Rayas white from 1976 onwards has become unreliable.

Unlike the main regions of Burgundy and Bordeaux, Châteauneuf-du-Pape has never received an official ranking of its vineyards. About a dozen *domaines* lead in acreage and quality of wine, however, and these are supported by a massive network of over seventy smaller growers who look after their own bottling and selling. In the past ten years the number of *vignerons* who have turned towards bottling at their properties has increased, and there is every likelihood nowadays of finding an honestly made and very sound bottle of wine from just such a small grower in a liquor shop in London or New York.

The largest *domaines* remain the standard-bearers for the *Appellation*, though; Mont-Redon, Beaucastel and Château de Vaudieu own vineyards that come close to, or barely exceed 200 acres, which means that the running of these or other *domaines* is never delegated, as can often be the case in Bordeaux. Each owner is therefore totally responsible for his wine. Furthermore, the *vignerons* are determined to maintain the *status quo*. The vineyards are rigorously protected against development; only local *viticulteurs* are permitted to build within the *Appellation* limits, and even their projects are closely scrutinized by all the councillors, from the Mayor (generally a *vigneron* himself) downwards. The story is told of a hapless foreigner who came to Châteauneuf to develop a small vineyard; after experiencing enormous difficulty in obtaining a regular water supply for his house and other similar impediments, he decided to give up and leave. The *status quo* survived.

DOMAINE DE MONT-REDON

The largest estate at Châteauneuf-du-Pape, and possibly the best-known one abroad is the Domaine de Mont-Redon, which has a 235-acre vineyard. This has belonged to the Plantin family since 1921, and when they bought it there were no more than 5 acres under vines. Large tracts of wooded land were cleared away and replanted with all thirteen of the permitted vine varieties. The *domaine* is now run by M. Didier Fabre and M. Jean Abeille, M. Plantin's grandsons, and is one of the showpieces of Châteauneuf-du-Pape, with healthy, carefully tended vineyards and a spotless efficiency inside the cellars.

Mont-Redon lies in isolated country in the north-western corner of the *Appellation*, in what is one of the oldest wine *quartiers* of the region. A document of 1344 speaks of the vines of Mourredon, Les Cabrières—the adjoining vineyard—and Bois Renard, now the Domaine de Beaurenard. Unlike Château Rayas, for example, with its fine, siliceous soil, all these properties, which are on the higher plateau of Châteauneuf-du-Pape, are distinguished by their typical local terrain of masses of rounded stones.

Didier Fabre is a bearded man with a learned air about him; in discussing his vineyard he is almost as phlegmatic as an Englishman. He has been very keen to set Mont-Redon apart from the old-fashioned, heavy wines that used to typify Châteauneuf-du-Pape *rouge* and explained his attitude in simple terms: 'I don't want our wine to have more than about 13·7° of alcohol, since we are trying to make wine that people can enjoy and, above all, drink rather than look at. Our 1977 would be a case in point: the vintage was not particularly good, but our wine was very harmonious and is nice to drink even five years later—*un vin sympathique*. With up to 400 hectolitres (53,000 bottles) a year, we are also now the largest vinifiers of white Châteauneuf, which we make from the full selection of white grapes allowed.'

The red wine of Mont-Redon is always given a closely supervised vinification, starting with a light crushing and destalking, performed on their modern cellar equipment. Fermentation is performed at a slightly lower temperature than normal (25 °C), and the wine is aged initially in the *domaine*'s fat-looking 17,500-litre barrels that are carefully arranged in the first ageing cellar, the one where all the assembling of different *cuvées* is undertaken. Thereafter the blended wine is matured in casks half this size in the second ageing cellar and is bottled a little before its second birthday.

While Mont-Redon is now making very acceptable wine in off-years, the lightening of its style seems to have robbed it of some of its highest qualities in the best vintages, such as 1978. There is perhaps just a little lack of body and less depth of flavour now than when one looks back to the legendary big-vintage wines from the domaine, such as 1961, which, over twenty years later, is still stunning. Overall the wine remains good or very good, but traditional Mont-Redon drinkers are warned of the alteration in style, which may not be to everyone's taste.

Apart from its very good white wine, the domaine is also proud of its *eau-de-vie*, or alcohol spirit made from the distilled grape *marc*. A certain amount of the spirit is always taken by the state as a form of tax (it is particularly used in hospital surgery), but the *domaine* keeps the best of what remains and ages it in small 670-litre oak casks. Two thousand bottles of this '*Marc de Châteauneuf-du-Pape*' are made every year and go out to a small, regular clientele. The *eau-de-vie* is strong stuff, having an alcohol content of 42 per cent, and is best drunk as a *digestif* at the end of a meal.

CHÂTEAU DE LA NERTE

The *château* that was formerly most famous in the history of Châteauneuf-du-Pape is now no longer so well-known. Château de la Nerte, which dates back to 1599, has undergone considerable ups and downs during its long history as a wine estate. It was first brought to eminence by its early owners, the de Tulle family from Piedmont; always eager to commercialize their wine as widely as possible, the de Tulles had by 1750 started exporting it to Germany. By 1785 they had gone a step further and were selling their wine in bottles to European countries and in barrels to the United States, notably to the city of Boston. This represented a considerable advance in the fortunes of the vineyard, for documents of the time point to the great difficulties experienced by the de Tulle family in selling their wine in the early part of the century.

La Nerte gained in stature throughout the nineteenth century, partly, no doubt, thanks to the antics of its old dashing owner, the Marquis de Villefranche. He moved freely in the high society of Paris and, when questioned on his activities, invariably claimed that his wine infinitely prolonged man's capacity for enjoyment. His sales technique was, of course, impeccable, and the wine of La Nerte came to grace many an important table.

But then fortunes changed dramatically. Phylloxera destroyed the vineyard and temporarily the *domaine*'s reputation was lost. A new owner from Marseille let the replanted vines decline into near abandonment, and by the outbreak of the Second World War the wine of La Nerte had virtually ceased to exist.

The recently retired manager of the estate, M. René Derreumaux, arrived in 1941 to try to rekindle the vineyard's former fortunes and glories. But work was slow to begin: 'The Motte family bought La Nerte at a public auction in 1941, and no sooner had they turned their thoughts seriously to rebuilding the vineyard than the German *Luftwaffe* arrived to take over the *château* as their local Operations Centre. The *château* and its outbuildings were occupied until August 1944, when the British Air Force relieved us in a really pinpoint raid: I shall never forget their accuracy in dropping twenty-two bombs on the outbuildings and leaving the château untouched,' added M. Derreumaux.

Directly after the Liberation serious work was started on the transformation of the old cellars and the vineyard. The estate now has 143 acres of vines in one of the most renowned parts of Châteauneuf-du-Pape; the *châteaux* of Fortia and Fines Roches and the Domaine de la Solitude are the bordering vineyards. Only a little over one-quarter of the crop is ever bottled, something like 55,000 bottles, which is a far cry from the days when La Nerte was the entire region's pace-setter. Under M. Derreumaux's son, also called René, La Nerte has started to make about 6,500 bottles of white wine from the Clairette grape alone, while the red remains perhaps the most striking example of traditional Châteauneuf-du-Pape that exists. Except in uneven years like 1977, the Nerte red wine is massive—inky-coloured with only pale stripes of red visible, high in alcohol and backward-tasting owing to the immense amounts of tannin in the wine. M. Derreumaux *fils*, a lean man of around 50, is very enthusiastic about the *domaine*'s wine and, as technical director, has also instituted a special *cuvée*, the Cuvée des Cadettes, which is made in the better vintages like 1978 and 1979. This is truly black wine, very heavy and not necessarily the sort of drink that would appeal to light, Beaujolais-style *habitués*—for a start, it possesses 4° or 5° more alcohol. All the La Nerte reds are still aged for up to three years in cask and, despite their power and vigour, display attractive blackcurrant flavours. This style is somewhat anachronistic these days and suggests that La Nerte should be put in the category of wines to be drunk safely sitting down and in winter time, when the cold has to be kept at bay.

CHÂTEAU RAYAS

The saddest event at Châteauneuf-du-Pape in the 1970s was the death in 1978 of M. Louis Reynaud, the extremely able and slightly eccentric owner of Château Rayas. The Reynaud family used to be notaries in the Provençal mountain town of Apt, and their connection with Châteauneuf-du-Pape started in 1894, when M. Reynaud's father decided to retire there, in the process buying the *château* and the land that went with it. There were a few vines, but M. Reynaud senior was content simply to potter about among his cornfields, olive groves and cherry orchards. His son Louis, on the other hand, was greatly attracted by the idea of having his own vineyard and accordingly went off to agricultural school in Angers to learn his trade. On his return he planted 38 acres of vines and in 1922 set about making his own wine.

M. Louis Reynaud's attitude to the rules and regulations of his *Appellation* was unorthodox, but even when he was in his late seventies the kindly exterior, twinkling eyes and soft voice did not conceal his challenging and unerring belief in quality at all costs. Under his direction the average yield from the Château Rayas vineyard was only about 800 bottles an acre, half the normal figure for Châteauneuf-du-Pape. He would leave his red wine to age in cask for four to five years, with at the most one racking a year, merely saying, 'Disturb the wine as little as possible; age it in cask, then leave it for two years in bottle, by which time you can sell a wine that is ready to drink.'

Although he was clearly a believer in tradition, M. Reynaud also revelled in his little foibles; he called Rayas *Premier Grand Cru* on its labels, in spite of the fact that no such designation exists or has ever existed at Châteauneuf; then he would experiment with grape varieties not listed in the permitted group of thirteen, so that both the Burgundian Pinot Chardonnay and the Sauvignon grape would sometimes 'slip' into his white wine, along with the Grenache Blanc and the Clairette. The general effect was to make nonsense of the axiom that southern white wines oxidize easily: the richly flavoured whites of Château Rayas would need at least five years to show their true colours!

Until 1955 M. Reynaud also made a sweet white wine similar to a Sauternes, and this became extremely popular with a small, informed clientele in the United States. When the liberating

American forces arrived in Avignon in 1944, a group of connoisseur soldiers from Boston shocked the proprietor of a well-known restaurant by asking for the sweet white wine of Château Rayas. The unhappy proprietor could not hide his blushes and shamefacedly had to admit that he had never heard of this local wine!

M. Reynaud would make his red Châteauneuf-du-Pape from just three grapes, the Grenache, Syrah and Cinsault, and the combination in his hands was devastating. Rayas red wines had outstanding character, tremendous elegance and smoothness of bouquet, the latter sometimes recalling the scent of violets. Very long-lived, they were justifiably rated as probably the very best wines of the southern Rhône Valley.

However, having built his temple, Louis Reynaud failed to show anyone how to maintain it. One of his sons was born slightly retarded, and the other was never given formal instruction in making good and healthy wine. Just why Louis performed his vinification or his ageing of the wine in a certain way was clearly never explained, and his son, Jacques, is busy ruining most of the cuvées that lie in the now unkempt cellar of Château Rayas. Basic errors like failing to perform a regular ouillage and failing to clean the barrels properly are bad enough, but continuing to age the Rayas red for three to four years in cask when, according to the son, the wine is now only made from the quick-maturing Grenache, is criminal and distressing. The decline in the wines of Rayas, in its sister Châteauneuf-du-Pape Pignan and in the formerly excellent Côtes du Rhône domaine Château de Fonsalette commences with the second bottling of wines of the 1976 vintage. It is a tragedy to have to speak of Château Rayas in this way, for Louis Reynaud's smile and softly intoned, 'Yes, there are some pretty things in life,' delivered when tasting a fabulous vintage of Rayas together, are what one prefers to remember about this kind and remarkable man.

DOMAINE DE BEAUCASTEL

The domaine now making the longest-lived of all Châteauneuf-du-Papes is Beaucastel, owned by the Perrin family and run by the sons of the late M. Jacques Perrin, François and Jean-Pierre. Its 200-acre vineyard is situated on the eastern side of the *Appel-*

M. François Perrin

lation, near Courthézon, and contains all thirteen grape varieties. Named after a Huguenot, Pierre de Beaucastel, the property has grown vines since at least 1832, and the recent transfer of it to M. Perrin's sons, following his death in 1978, shows that *domaines* can continue, and at the very least thrive, if the next generation is properly shown what to do.

François Perrin looks a little like Tom Courtenay. In his late twenties, he wears thin wire glasses and is meticulous in his delivery of information and explanation about Beaucastel. His father Jacques commenced their special *vinification à chaud* process for their red wine, and his talent was such that good wine was made in moderate vintages, 1968 being a case in point. François explained that for this he fermented by grape variety, and that for the red wine he used only the nine permitted red grapes. These are assembled in the spring following the harvest. Thereafter the wine is aged in the neat Beaucastel cellars, where the 5,500-litre casks, with their smart red edges and gleaming varnish finish, have stood since François' great-grandfather's time. Beaucastel then cause local farmers a problem by suddenly approaching them for 400 to 500 eggs when it is time to fine the wine, and, after as light a filtration as possible, the wine is bottled, normally near its second birthday. François Perrin is very concerned about the effect that filtration can have on a wine and in this respect is closer to the attitudes of Californian wine growers than to those of Châteauneuf-du-Pape *vignerons*. 'It's all up to the customer. If he will bear with us and accept that a wine with a deposit is likely to have greater depth of flavour and a wider range of aromas, then I can send out unfiltered wine. But many people are just not informed, so that I cannot compromise restaurant owners, for instance, by selling them unfiltered wine which may be complained about by their customers. My private customers here—they are different, I'm glad to say.'

Beaucastel red is always a wine of supreme character but is often one that is not easy to drink when young, since it needs a long time to develop in the strongest vintages. At tastings of young Châteauneuf it will not necessarily figure highly, the word 'dumb' often being used against it, as its fruit has not emerged from behind a mask of tannin. There is a sensation of cherry or of blackcurrant-inspired fruit, but this and the complexity of the bouquet will show well only after at least six or seven years. This is particularly true of the excellent 1970, 1978 and 1979 vintages, all of which can live for up to twenty years without difficulty.

The vineyards of the Domaine du Vieux Télégraphe

CHÂTEAUNEUF-DU-PAPE

DOMAINE DU VIEUX TÉLÉGRAPHE

Another important *domaine* with a growing reputation for top-class Châteauneuf-du-Pape is the 123-acre Domaine du Vieux Télégraphe, which draws its name from a site on the plateau near Bédarrides where in 1793 Chappe, the inventor of the optical telegraph system, built a tower to help him in his experiments. Henri Brunier and his sons grow four grape varieties—the Grenache (75 per cent), the Syrah (15 per cent), the Cinsault (5 per cent) and the Mourvèdre (5 per cent)—on this windswept plateau, covered in heaps and heaps of the smooth round Châteauneuf stones, which here are more purple-tinted than usual.

M. Brunier has modernized his cellars in striking fashion, and Vieux Télégraphe can boast one of the most streamlined and logical vinification processes in the whole *Appellation*. His receiving holders for the harvest run along rails set between two lines of fermenting vats, so that he can empty the same load in different

M. Henri Brunier

vats, should he so wish. He never destalks, and about 30 per cent of the grapes enter the stainless-steel fermenting vats uncrushed, the rest receiving only a very light crushing. Fermentation will last no more than ten or twelve days, after which M. Brunier transfers his wine to concrete vats in order to provoke the malolactic fermentation as soon as possible—stainless steel being too cold for this. 'Not only have I altered my technique at the beginning of the vinification,' continued M. Brunier, 'but I am now only ageing my wine in oak for a year; seven or eight years ago I would leave it for two years, but that extra time was bringing in more oxidization

201

than any positive elements. Sometimes I now take my wine out of the cask and leave it before bottling in enamel-lined vats; this can give it five years' extra life, as well as retaining its fresh aromas better.'

Henri Brunier is a small, trim man in his fifties, with an easy manner and a relaxed smile that charm his many foreign visitors. Wine-making at the *domaine* was started by his grandfather, Hypolite, in 1900, and soon afterwards he was bottling his own wine and taking it to the fairs in Germany, Belgium and Switzerland. The family are proud that they won a Gold Medal at the first National Culinary and Gastronomic Exhibition held in Paris in 1927, and now that both M. Brunier's sons are helping him, one on the oenological side and the other on the commercial side, the outlook for this *domaine* looks very promising. Of especial note are the 1978 and the 1980 vintages; the former shows the charm of good Châteauneuf all over it, and the bouquet is akin to the opening of a spice or cigar box. It is a wine that will live until about 1990. The 1980 is a great success, in a vintage that is not considered outstanding, and its fruit aromas are described by M. Brunier as resembling blackcurrants and mulberries. Very well balanced, it too will live for ten or twelve years.

The following are some of the other important *domaines*, vinifiers and *négociants*.

DOMAINE DE BEAURENARD

A seventh-generation wine *domaine* owned by M. Paul Coulon, who is helped by his eager son, Daniel, in the running of the 70-acre vineyard that stands north of the village. Four grape varieties are used—Grenache (70 per cent) and Syrah, Mourvèdre and Cinsault (all 10 per cent each). Half the harvest is lightly crushed, the rest not at all, and this helps M. Coulon to achieve his aim of making 'a wine that is pleasant to drink'. The Coulons bottle their wine when it is between 6 and 15 months old, and it invariably displays tremendous charm and ample blackcurrant-inspired fruit. It is always very well balanced and, according to the strength of the vintage, should be drunk between 3 and 8 years old. The best recent vintage has been the 1980. The Coulons also make a Côtes du Rhône *générique* at their other *domaine*, La Ferme

Pisan, and this is fresh quaffing wine that should be drunk very young.

Domaine de Beaurenard,
P. Coulon & Fils   84230 Châteauneuf-du-Pape

CAVES EUGÈNE BESSAC

A *négociant* company that stands inside rampart-type walls near the centre of Châteauneuf-du-Pape, Bessac deals in the wine of both the northern and the southern Côtes du Rhône. At harvest time the company buys grapes and newly made wine and matures them in its extensive underground cellars. The wines are well vinified and consistent in quality; the Châteauneuf-du-Papes are the most impressive.

Caves Eugène Bessac   84230 Châteauneuf-du-Pape

CAVES ST-PIERRE

Founded in 1898, this is a *négociant* company that also owns some vineyards at Châteauneuf-du-Pape. Its most notable wines are its Châteauneuf-du-Pape Domaines des Pontifs and Condorcet, its Côtes du Rhône Château de Bastet and Château d'Aigueville, and its Tavel. These are all reasonable wines, with the Côtes du Rhône representing the best value.

Caves St-Pierre   84230 Châteauneuf-du-Pape

LE CELLIER DES PRINCES

This is Châteauneuf-du-Pape's only Cave Co-opérative. Founded at Courthézon in 1924, it has 180 members holding vineyard plots at Châteauneuf-du-Pape. Attempts are being made to reduce the traditionally very high Grenache content in its wine, and a '*vigneron* bonus scheme' operates to encourage the planting of different grapes like the Syrah and the Cinsault. The wine is soundly made, although a little lacking in personality.

Le Cellier des Princes   84350 Courthézon

DOMAINE CHANTE-CIGALE

This is a 99-acre *domaine* run by M. Christian Favier and his father-in-law, M. Noël Sabon. The vineyard is split up into about thirty plots and is dominated by the Grenache (80 per cent), with the difference made up of Syrah (10 per cent), Mourvèdre (5 per cent) and Cinsault (5 per cent). It was the grandparents of M. Favier who gave the *domaine* its 'singing grasshopper' name; no actual site at Châteauneuf carries this name. The wine is made in an extremely traditional way, with an extended three- or four-week fermentation following the crushing of 70 per cent of the grapes. Emphasis is placed on ageing in cask, with a minimum of eighteen months normally, which can rise to four years in the case of vintages like the 1976. Only red wine is made, and it is sound, middle-range Châteauneuf, without the sparkle and height of character offered by the best *domaines*. Perhaps it is given too much time in wood, to the detriment of the wine's fruit and subtlety of flavour.

Domaine Chante-Cigale,
  Sabon-Favier   84230 Châteauneuf-du-Pape

LES CLEFS D'OR

Jean Deydier and his son Pierre make very good, traditional wines from an old family vineyard of 62 acres. The red wine has a very typical Châteauneuf-du-Pape character, showing good complexity of flavour, and is usually strongly scented and full-bodied. Wines made up until the late 1960s could live for up to twenty years, but nowadays it is better to drink the Clefs d'Or red before it is 12 years old. The white wine is one of the better ones in the *Appellation* and, made from the Grenache Blanc and Bourboulenc, should be drunk young. The Deydiers also own a 30-acre Côtes du Rhône vineyard called the Domaine de Beaumefort at Mondragon.

Les Clefs d'Or,
  SCEA Jean Deydier et Fils   84230 Châteauneuf-du-Pape

CLOS DE L'ORATOIRE DES PAPES

The property of the Amouroux family, this 100-acre vineyard is grouped to the north-west of Châteauneuf-du-Pape. It is an all-female affair, run by the *Veuve* Amouroux and her daughters. The wine has always been classically made, with an ageing of at least two years in cask, and has generally been one of the best to be found: richly flavoured and long-lived, it has in the past been a fine example of the 'traditional' Châteauneuf-du-Pape. In the late 1970s the wine did not match its usual very high standards.

Clos de l'Oratoire des Papes,
  Ets L. Amouroux   84230 Châteauneuf-du-Pape

CLOS DES PAPES

The Clos des Papes is the old papal vineyard directly behind the village *château* and is easily distinguishable through the Burgundian-style wrought-iron gate that stands at its entrance. It forms part of the 75 acres of vines owned by M. Paul Avril, whose family provided Châteauneuf-du-Pape's first consuls and treasurers from 1756 until 1790. M. Avril is an enthusiastic grower who sets out to make a traditional but not too heavy style of wine. This can be very good, although some vintages lack consistency.

Clos des Papes,
  Avril, Paul et Régis   84230 Châteauneuf-du-Pape

CLOS DU MONT-OLIVET

The three sons of the late M. Joseph Sabon make an excellent old-style Châteauneuf-du-Pape from 42 acres of vines, some of which were planted before the First World War. As with the Clos des Papes, the vines grow in scattered plots, with the result that a compilation, or *assemblage*, of the different grapes has always to be made. The 1967, 1976 and 1978 vintages have been exceptional, with the full depth of flavours expected from high-class Châteauneuf-du-Pape. Often backward until its sixth year, Clos du Mont Olivet can generally be kept, providing cellaring conditions are stable, until around its fourteenth year.

Clos du Mont-Olivet,
  Les Fils de Joseph Sabon   84230 Châteauneuf-du-Pape

LA CUVÉE DU VATICAN

This 42-acre vineyard is owned by M. Félicien Diffonty, the ex-Mayor, an alert man who has always enjoyed being involved in the village's affairs and projects. His family have been wine-growers for several generations, and his brother Rémy owns the Domaine du Haut des Terres Blanches. The Cuvée du Vatican red is a good example of a traditional, soundly made and agreeable *domaine* wine that just lacks the class to take it into the top rank.

La Cuvée du Vatican,
    Diffonty & Fils   84230 Châteauneuf-du-Pape

DOMAINE DURIEU

Paul Durieu owns 50 acres of vines near the Domaine de Mont-Redon and cultivates the Grenache, Syrah, Mourvèdre, Cinsault and Counoise. Curiously, he found that the domaine used not to have enough Grenache to be fully balanced, and soon after taking over the property from a relation, he planted 17 acres with the staple Châteauneuf-du-Pape grape. A young, pleasant man, M. Durieu believes that Châteauneuf should strike a balance between the very light style, as practised by *domaines* like La Solitude, and the old, heavier style, as displayed by La Nerte. Thus he commences fermentation without crushing or destalking, relying on his must pump to break about half of the skins before the bunches enter the enamel-lined fermenting vats. He likes to store his wine in concrete vats after giving it a brief spell in wood, so that 'something ready to drink' can be sold. M. Durieu is bottling only about 30 per cent of his production, since he has been spending his spare money on putting his vineyard in order. He will be increasing his bottling run slowly in the future. As one of the few young men to have taken over a *domaine* at Châteauneuf-du-Pape in recent years—without inheriting it—he deserves to succeed in what is initially a very capital-intensive exercise. The Domaine Durieu red is a good wine that achieves the owner's stated objectives, and the 1978 and 1980, wines of good balance and considerable richness, will help to make the *domaine* better-known. M. Durieu also makes a Côtes du Rhône from his 62-acre vineyard on the Plan de Dieu, near Camaret.

Domaine Durieu, Durieu, Paul   84230 Châteauneuf-du-Pape

CHÂTEAU DES FINES ROCHES

One of the old leading names at Châteauneuf-du-Pape, the Fines Roches estate totals 135 acres of vines that grow around the rather Hollywood Gothic style *château* that dates from the late nineteenth century. Some of the wine is made by an adapted *macération carbonique* vinification, which produces a correct, but uninteresting wine. The *cuvées* that are made in the traditional way have recently improved in quality, and it is possible that this *domaine* is emerging from a protracted spell in the doldrums. The 1979 vintage was a success with the wine that was kept longest before being released for sale—a matter of two years.

Château des Fines Roches   84230 Châteauneuf-du-Pape

CHÂTEAU FORTIA

This *château* and the 70-acre vineyard surrounding it are the property of the Baron Le Roy de Boiseaumarié, the son of the man responsible for the initiation of the vineyard laws in 1923. The *château* is very close to the village but nestles behind a protective group of trees on a tiny hillock at the head of the vineyards. Baron Le Roy displays amazing enthusiasm about all aspects of the history and geology of the vineyards at Châteauneuf-du-Pape and recently experimented by piling up some inferior Grenache crop in a well exposed position half a metre above the ground; to his satisfaction the evaporation of the liquid in the grapes resulted in a gain of 1·3° in five or six days.

The first record that vines were being cultivated around the old house dates back to 1763, and when the residence was enlarged into a *château* around 1815, a splendid vaulted cellar with walls nearly 2·5 metres thick was added on. Nowadays the vines grown at Fortia are Grenache (80 per cent), Syrah (10 per cent), Mourvèdre (3 per cent), Counoise (2 per cent) and a total of 5 per cent for the white grape vines Roussanne, Grenache Blanc and Clairette. Château Fortia makes red and white wines, but it is the red that is more striking; it is a memorable wine, always highly scented and full of finesse, which is made in an entirely traditional way.

The 1976, 1978 and 1980 vintages have all been very successful and are notable for their balance and elegance. The charm and character of the Château Fortia red place it among the best three at Châteauneuf-du-Pape, and it should generally be drunk before it is 10 or 12 years old.

Château Fortia, Baron Le Roy   84230 Châteauneuf-du-Pape

CHÂTEAU DE LA GARDINE

The Château de la Gardine lies to the west of Châteauneuf-du-Pape, not far from the Rhône. When bought by M. Gaston Brunel after the Second World War, its 20-acre vineyard was in a state of near-abandonment. M. Brunel slowly built it up to its present size of 135 acres and now works with his sons in making a red wine that is typical of its *quartier*, slightly light in colour and body, due perhaps to the light, possibly unpropitious soil of the vineyard, whose top layer is only ever between 20 and 40 centimetres deep. This leaves the vines susceptible to drought in long, dry summers. The wine of La Gardine comes in a special *château* bottle: this is brown and misshapen, and has embossed below its long, slender neck the words: 'Château de la Gardine Mise du Château'.

Château de la Gardine,
  Brunel, Gaston   84230 Châteauneuf-du-Pape

CHÂTEAU MAUCOIL

Adjoining the Domaine de Mont-Redon is the 55-acre Château Maucoil, which is owned by M. Pierre Quiot, now almost an octogenarian and certainly the oldest active grower in Châteauneuf. The property once served a profitable purpose for the Prince of Orange, who appropriated it in 1571 and then sold it off ten years later. M. Quiot and his wife also own another Châteauneuf-du-Pape *domaine*, the Clos St-Pierre, as well as the Gigondas Domaine des Pradets and the Côtes du Rhône Clos des Patriciens. The wine of Château Maucoil is the best of them all but tends to be light and lacking in the wholehearted character expected of a *domaine* Châteauneuf-du-Pape.

Château Maucoil, Quiot, Pierre   84100 Orange

DOMAINE DE NALYS

Following the death of Dr Philippe Dufays in 1978, this *domaine* has been split up a little and now covers 124 acres instead of its former 200 acres. Dr Dufays, until 1955 a practising doctor, was an intelligent man deeply interested in all aspects of viticulture and was renowned for his studies on the Châteauneuf-du-Pape grape varieties and for his wit in talking about them. The full range of thirteen grapes is grown at the *domaine*, with the red wine

208

dominated by the Grenache (55 per cent of the total plantation) and by the Syrah (18 per cent). This is made in the modern accelerated manner, with only uncrushed grapes being loaded into concrete vats for fermentation. After a short stay in wood, the wine is bottled a total of fifteen months after the harvest. On the bouquet it betrays its overtly fruity, maceration origins, but there is also a softness, with just a little tannin, holding the wine together at the very end, which make it quite successful in its own right. M. Pelissier, the *oenologue*, is aiming to make a rounded, easily accessible wine, and believes that the reds should be drunk by the time they are 5 to 8 years old.

Nalys also makes Châteauneuf-du-Pape's most successful white wine from the full selection of white grapes headed by the Grenache Blanc (6 per cent of the total vineyard) and the Clairette (5 per cent). Very refined, with an ample bouquet sometimes reminiscent of peaches, it possesses the style and finesse of a white Burgundy. It is best drunk before it is 3 years old.

SCI Domaine de Nalys   84230 Châteauneuf-du-Pape

PÈRE ANSELME

The largest *négociant* business in Châteauneuf-du-Pape wines, Père Anselme buys annually a little under one-tenth of the village's production. This is then matured in its cellars for two to three years. In 1956 the company created its own special bottle, the 'Fiole du Pape', whose shape is distorted and which can be covered in an artificial dust in order to simulate great age. Père Anselme deals mainly in wines from all over the southern Côtes du Rhône, and these, apart from their best *cuvées* of Châteauneuf-du-Pape and their good Côtes du Rhône Villages Séguret, are usually sound without being particularly inspiring.

Père Anselme   84230 Châteauneuf-du-Pape

DOMAINE DU PÈRE CABOCHE

This 74-acre vineyard is owned by Théophile Boisson and is actively run by his son, Jean-Pierre, a very enthusiastic and open-minded young man. The name of the property, derived in an amusing way, dates back to the alliance of the Boisson and the Chambellan families in 1772, when Jean-Louis Boisson from Jonquières married a Chambellan daughter. The Chambellans, like many families at the time, had two occupations: they were both *vignerons* and the village blacksmiths. The occupation of blacksmith merited them the nickname of *Caboche*, which is a horse's plated shoe, and thus the name of the *domaine* was created.

Their vineyards are mostly grouped together, the largest plot being their 42 acres on the Plateau de la Crau, between Vieux Télégraphe and Nalys. The predominant vine is the Grenache (70 per cent), followed by the Syrah (10 per cent), while the Boissons' interest in making white wine is illustrated by the 15 per cent of the vineyard that is accounted for by Clairette, Grenache Blanc and Bourboulenc. The family pick their grapes in especially shallow buckets, so that as far as possible the grapes arrive intact at the cellars, located in the village. Thereafter all the grapes except the Syrah are lightly crushed, M. Boisson considering that the Syrah contributes better fruit when vinified whole to start with, and fermentation takes place in stainless steel vats that have been installed since 1973. Following an active fermentation of ten to twelve days, the wine is left for two more days on the *marc* to obtain the tannin extracts and is then transferred to concrete vats to help start the malolactic fermentation. After a filtration comes ageing in barrels for one to two years, the length of time varying according to the style of the vintage.

The red Père Caboche can be quite a successful wine, although it does not perhaps possess the full, splendid depth of classic Châteauneuf-du-Pape. It is not a long-lived wine, eight years being adequate for its ageing, and is upstaged by the very good Père Caboche white wine, whose vinification has been discussed earlier.

Domaine du Père Caboche,
   Boisson, Théophile   84230 Châteauneuf-du-Pape

PRESTIGE ET TRADITION

Prestige et Tradition is an association of ten growers who share bottling and storing premises. Their vineyard holdings are not generally large, averaging between 20 and 30 acres, and for this reason it has proved all the more economical for them to divide the overhead costs necessary for bottling and holding stock. These are traditional smaller growers' vineyards, with heavy emphasis placed on the Grenache, and the style of wine made is mostly time-honoured—backward and tannic when young, with a deep black cherry colour, which straightens out by the sixth or seventh year in the best vintages. The practitioners of this approach are MM. Barrot, Jean and his nephew Lucien, Boiron and Michel. The last three *domaines*—the Cuvée de Tastevin, the Bosquet des Papes and the Vieux Donjon—are generally the best of the grouping. A lighter style is sought by MM. Jeune, Laget, Mestre and Pécoul, while the very modern approach is undertaken by MM. Lançon and Revoltier—their wines are fruity without great depth and tannin.

Barrot, Jean
   Cuvée du Hurlevent   84230 Châteauneuf-du-Pape
Barrot, Lucien
   Cuvée du Tastevin   84230 Châteauneuf-du-Pape
Boiron, Maurice
   Le Bosquet des Papes   84230 Châteauneuf-du-Pape
Jeune, Jean
   Clos de la Cerise   84230 Châteauneuf-du-Pape
Laget, Pierre
   Domaine de l'Arnesque   84230 Châteauneuf-du-Pape
Lançon, Pierre
   Domaine de la Solitude   84230 Châteauneuf-du-Pape
Mestre, Jacques
   La Cuvée des Sommeliers   84230 Châteauneuf-du-Pape
Michel, Père et Fils
   Le Vieux Donjon   84230 Châteauneuf-du-Pape
Pécoul Frères
   La Cuvée des Bosquets   84230 Châteauneuf-du-Pape
Revoltier, Joseph
   Le Vieux Chemin   84230 Châteauneuf-du-Pape

LES REFLETS

This is an association of growers founded in 1954 to bottle, condition and store the wine of each grower under the same roof. Since its inception Les Reflets has done much to further the name of Châteauneuf-du-Pape, led by the three excellent *domaines* Les Cailloux, Chante-Perdrix and Clos du Mont-Olivet (*q.v.*). The wine of all these *domaines* is made in the traditional manner, richness of flavour and an extended longevity being paramount. Les Cailloux is perhaps the most feminine of the three, always bearing a typical, swirling bouquet that is full of different herbal nuances; the Chante-Perdrix is the biggest, most full-blooded wine, regularly aged in cask for up to three years, but a wine that is not overpowered by such treatment. The Clos du Mont-Olivet fits nicely between these two in style. The remaining wines are generally well made and typical of the *Appellation*, with the exception of the Domaine de la Solitude, which is nowadays lighter than ever and consequently less impressive than before.

The members of Les Reflets are:

Brunel, Lucien	
Les Cailloux	84230 Châteauneuf-du-Pape
Descarrega, Charles	
Les Cabanes	84230 Châteauneuf-du-Pape
Girard, Robert	
Cuvée du Belvedère Le Boucou	84230 Châteauneuf-du-Pape
Lançon, Pierre	
Domaine de la Solitude	84230 Châteauneuf-du-Pape
Nicolet Frères	
Chante-Perdrix	84230 Châteauneuf-du-Pape
Sabon, Les Fils de Joseph	
Clos du Mont-Olivet	84230 Châteauneuf-du-Pape

DOMAINE DE LA SOLITUDE

The 400-year-old Domaine de la Solitude, in the ownership of M. Pierre Lançon, is a practitioner of the 'modern' Châteauneuf-du-Pape and concentrates the vinification of its wines along adapted *macération carbonique* lines. M. Lançon, a busy and public-spirited man, seems to have lightened his red Châteauneuf in the past ten years, for wines such as the 1979 and 1981 have been almost rosé-coloured and contrast sadly with former excellent vintages like the 1969 and 1971, which lived for at least ten years. There is also a Solitude white, made from Clairette and Grenache Blanc, which now represents almost one-tenth of the production.

The *domaine* first bottled part of its wine in 1815, when the then owner Paul Clair Martin returned from the Battle of Waterloo with the highly prized Croix de la Légion d'Honneur. He proceeded to work full-time on his vineyard and in 1827 despatched five 265-litre barrels to Greenwood and Butler of England. Although the *domaine* was then making both white and red wines, the English preferred the red and would receive what was termed '*Vin Rouge de la Solitude*', a name that had already appeared on the first bottle labels.

Domaine de la Solitude,
    GAEC Lançon Père et Fils   84230 Châteauneuf-du-Pape

DOMAINE DE LA TERRE FERME

Owned by the Bérard family, the Domaine de la Terre Ferme has 150 acres of vines in the east of the *Appellation*, near Bédarrides. The Bérards are also *négociants* in some of the other southern Côtes du Rhône wines, which are carefully selected by M. Pierre Bérard, well-known locally for his tasting expertise. The House is best regarded for its red and white Châteauneuf-du-Pape, however, upon which M. Bérard has some interesting views: 'You must use *maćeration carbonique* on the Syrah and the Mourvèdre but not on the Grenache; this allows you to make a wine that will age but also one that is quite light in style and which can be drunk easily, without overpowering the drinker.' The Terre Ferme reds are generally darkly coloured, with almost burnt-chocolate aromas and quite a full, heavy southern flavour—a little blatant in style and lacking the finesse of the leading *domaines*. The white, fermented at under 20 °C, is quite fresh and acceptable and should be drunk within the year following the harvest.

Domaine de la Terre Ferme,
    Bérard Père et Fils   84370 Bédarrides

CHÂTEAU DE VAUDIEU

This is a striking eighteenth-century *château* whose property runs next to Château Rayas. The wines have an old-established reputation which in the past placed them in the front rank of Châteauneuf-du-Pape. Owned by the family of Gabriel Meffre of Gigondas since 1955, its vineyard has been enlarged to 185 acres. Nowadays some of the *cuvées* are made in a lightened style, which robs them of what character they previously possessed, and it is sad that wines such as these should be mainly exported, for they give the foreign purchaser an unrepresentative picture of the type and quality of wine that is being made at Châteauneuf-du-Pape these days.

Château de Vaudieu,
    Meffre, Gabriel   84230 Châteauneuf-du-Pape

Châteauneuf-du-Pape Vintages

The vintage chart that follows is intended as a broad guide to the whole of Châteauneuf-du-Pape. It is very difficult to be exact for the whole *Appellation*, since its large size means that vintages can differ substantially from one area to the next. Results vary too according to which grape varieties are grown, the method of vinification and the time for ageing in the wood as practised by different *domaines*. As an extra guideline, therefore, specific *domaines* have occasionally been quoted.

1955 A very good vintage. The wines were both richly flavoured and well balanced. They are now generally over the top.

1956 Generally a very mediocre vintage. Disappointing, light wines.

1957 A very good but tannic year that took a long time to come round. The wines are now past their best, with the fading of their colour and flavours bringing an unmasking of the alcohol.

1958 A very poor vintage.

1959 A very good year, although lighter and less complete than 1955 or 1957. The wines failed to match the very high standards of the northern Côtes du Rhône, but certain vineyards—notably Château Rayas—produced excellent red and white wine. The reds softened out very well with ageing but should now be drunk without delay.

1960 A very ordinary year. The wines were considered undistinguished by many of the growers, and only the very best were ever bottled.

1961 A superb vintage, the best after 1945, and only possibly rivalled by the 1978 since. The wines fulfilled many *vignerons'* highest expectations: rich in colour and flavour, they had tremendous balance and grace, and the most traditionally made, such as Beaucastel, Rayas, Mont-Redon and Clos de l'Oratoire des Papes, are still very much alive, with the prospect of several years more in which to heighten still further their lovely complexity.

1962 A very good year that was inevitably overshadowed by 1961: the crop was large, but the wines were powerful and well balanced. They should be drunk soon. A notable year at Château Rayas.

1963   Extremely poor.

1964   An excellent vintage of limited quantity. The wines were very full and well coloured, and are now thoroughly softened out. They should ideally be drunk before around 1986. An outstanding year at the Domaine de la Solitude.

1965   A weak, disappointing vintage.

1966   Very good. Sound and quite full bodied wines, although they lacked a little of the all-round charm of the 1964s and 1967s. They are beginning to tire, but the biggest wines, such as those from Clos du Mont-Olivet and Beaucastel, are still in good shape.

1967   An excellent vintage; with 1978, the best since 1961. Very tannic and full of dark promise in their youth, the wines have developed a many-sided fullness and harmony. Splendid wines from nearly all the recommended *domaines*; those that stand out as still showing extremely well are Rayas, Jaboulet's Les Cèdres, Lucien Brunel's Les Cailloux, Beaucastel, Mont-Redon and Clos du Mont-Olivet.

1968   Mediocre. Generally light wines.

1969   A good and, in places, very good year. The quality of the wines varied according to which *quartier* they were from, but some of the best, such as Château Fortia and Les Clefs d'Or, were well rounded and pleasant to drink in their first ten years.

1970   An excellent vintage, although not quite up to the standard of 1967. Strongly scented and rich in flavour, the wines have now advanced to show some of the damp, truffly flavours of age. The more traditional *domaines* should prove very enjoyable until around 1988.

1971   Generally a very good vintage. The classically made wines have come along very well and should be good for drinking until around 1986, since their fruit is in some cases just beginning to disappear. Wines made in the lighter style, like those from the *domaines* of Beaurenard, Nalys and La Solitude, were particularly successful.

1972   Good. The wines were well perfumed and generally charming. They are well evolved and should be drunk quite soon.

1973   A very large crop inevitably tended to reduce quality and the vintage can only be termed 'medium to good'. The wines were often lacking in colour and bouquet, and only occasional bottles will still be in good order.

1974 Good. The wines were generally well perfumed and well balanced. Their agreeable combination of fruit and tannin will make them suitable for drinking in their first ten years. Wines from *domaines* like Beaucastel and Rayas will live a little longer.

1975 Generally a poor vintage. Certain parts of the *Appellation*, such as the Domaine de Beaucastel, were affected by hail, while those growers who were able to harvest normally found their wines deficient in colour and body. By contrast, wines made in the modern style, such as those from the *domaines* of La Solitude and Nalys, proved very good for early drinking.

1976 A good vintage, but one whose wines are of varying quality. A harvest that looked like being excellent was spoilt by rains during September, and while some wines are rather light on the palate, others seem to be low in acidity. The vintage has not worked out as well as was hoped, and the best wines, such as those from Château Fortia and Domaine de Mont-Redon, are likely to be well evolved by around 1984–5.

1977 Quite good. The wines have proved better than expected with some ageing, and although they are light in colour and depth of flavour, some attractive *cuvées* have developed. Most of the wines will be good for drinking before they are about 8 years old.

1978 Excellent. Certainly the best vintage of the decade, the wines have an intense black-cherry colour with great lustre to it and on the bouquet are still pretty tannic, with a mixture of fruit and flower sensations beginning to emerge. Very well balanced, there is so much depth of rich flavour on the palate that traditionally made wines will live for at least fifteen to eighteen years. Notable wines from Vieux Télégraphe, Fortia, Beaucastel, La Nerte, Les Cailloux, Les Clefs d'Or and Le Bosquet des Papes.

1979 A sound vintage of light-styled wines that will prove excellent drinking in their first eight years. They are generally very well scented, and although some *domaines* came up with unbalanced *cuvées*, the best wines, such as those from Domaine de Nalys, Beaucastel, Beaurenard, Montpertuis and Château des Fines Roches, show great charm through their simple fusion of fruit and tannin.

1980   Generally a very good vintage. The wines are darkly coloured despite the large harvest and promise to give a great range of aromas on the bouquet. There is a good, discreet support of tannin and these well balanced wines will be in tremendous order around 1984–7. Note the wines of Domaine du Vieux Télégraphe, Beaurenard, Cuvée de Tastevin and Château Fortia. Very complete, well balanced white wines from Domaine de Nalys and Domaine de Mont-Redon.

1981   A difficult year, marked by drought during the summer. The crop was small and the wines are rather low on colour, degree and acidity. Although it is early days, they do not seem apt for long keeping, and their lack of balance could lead to the making of some disappointing bottles. Quite good for the whites, although a lack of acidity has made some of them a little 'flabby'.

Earlier Exceptional Vintages   1954, 1952, 1949, 1947, 1945, 1944, 1942, 1937, 1934, 1929. With bottles of this age much depends, first, on who made them and, secondly, on where and how each bottle has been kept. Some of the wines of the *domaines* of Beaucastel and Rayas, for instance, are still in tremendous order, whereas old wines from the *négociant* houses will often have passed their best. Moreover, if the wines have been stored from an early date in the colder, more northerly climate of Britain, they are likely to have aged more slowly than those that have remained near the scene of their production.

There follows an extensive list of the principal growers who bottle their own wine at Châteauneuf-du-Pape. The authors have decided to stick their necks out and nominate which they consider to be the best properties under the headings First Growth, Second Growth and Third Growth.

FIRST GROWTH

Château Fortia
   Baron Le Roy   84230 Châteauneuf-du-Pape

Domaine de Beaucastel
  Pierre Perrin   84350 Courthézon
Domaine du Vieux Télégraphe
  Henri Brunier et Fils   84370 Bédarrides

SECOND GROWTH

Château La Nerte   84230 Châteauneuf-du-Pape
Clos du Mont-Olivet
  Les Fils de Joseph Sabon   84230 Châteauneuf-du-Pape
Domaine de Beaurenard
  Paul Coulon & Fils   84230 Châteauneuf-du-Pape
Les Cailloux
  Lucien Brunel   84230 Châteauneuf-du-Pape

THIRD GROWTH

Chante-Perdrix
  Nicolet Frères   84230 Châteauneuf-du-Pape
Les Clefs d'Or
  Jean Deydier et Fils   84230 Châteauneuf-du-Pape
Domaine de Mont-Redon   84230 Châteauneuf-du-Pape
Domaine de Nalys   84230 Châteauneuf-du-Pape

Other Leading Growers in the Châteauneuf-du-Pape
Appellation

84370 BÉDARRIDES

Bérard, Père et Fils
  Domaine de la Terre Ferme
Gonnet, Fils d'Etienne
  Domaine Font-de-Michelle

84230 CHÂTEAUNEUF-DU-PAPE

Amouroux, Ets. L.
  Clos de l'Oratoire des Papes
Armenier, Élie et Philippe
  Domaine de Marcoux

Arnaud, Louis et ses Enfants
  Domaine de Cabrières-les-Silex
Avril, Maurice
  Domaine Le Père Caler
Avril, Paul et Régis
  Le Clos des Papes
Avril, Vve Geneviève
  La Font du Pape
Barrot, Jean
  L'Hurlevent
Barrot, Lucien
  Cuvée du Tastevin
Boiron, Maurice
  Le Bosquet des Papes
Boisson, Théophile et Fils
  Domaine du Père Caboche
Bonneau, Marcel
Brunel, Gaston
  Château de la Gardine
Chapoutier, M.
  Domaine de la Bernardine
Château des Fines Roches
Chausse, Henri
  Quartier des Terres Blanches
Comte de Lauze, Jean
Descarrega, Charles
  Les Carbanes
Diffonty et Fils
  Cuvée du Vatican
Diffonty, Rémy
  Domaine du Haut des Terres Blanches
Durieu, Paul
  Domaine Durieu
Fabre, Henri
  Domaine de la Tour St-Michel
Favier-Sabon
  Domaine Chante-Cigale
Féraud Fils
Geniest, Louis
  Mas St-Louis

Girard, André
Girard, Robert
   Cuvée du Belvedère Le Boucou
Grangeon, Etienne
   Domaine du Cristia
Jacumin, Pierre
   Cuvée de Bois Dauphin
Jeune, E.
   Domaine du Grand Tinel
Jeune, Gabriel et Fils
   Domaine de Montpertuis
Jeune, Jean
   Clos de la Cerise
Laget, Pierre
   Domaine de l'Arnesque
Lançon, Pierre
   Domaine de la Solitude
Laugier, René
   Domaine de la Roquette
Marchand, Jean
   Domaine du Bois Dauphin
Mathieu, Charles
Mayard, Roger et Fils
Meffre, Gabriel
   Château de Vaudieu
Mestre, Charles
   Le Chêne-Vert
Mestre, Jean-Claude
Michel, Père et Fils
   Le Vieux Donjon
Pécoul Frères
   La Cuvée des Bosquets
Quiot, Jerome
   Château de Vieux Lazaret
Quiot, Pierre
   Château du Vieux Lazaret
Raynaud, Pierre
   Domaine des Sénéchaux
Revoltier, Joseph et Fils
   Le Vieux Chemin

Reynaud, Jacques
  Château Rayas
Riché, Claude
Sabon, Roger et Fils
Serre, C.
  Domaine St-Préfert
Trintignant, Mme Jean
  Domaine Trintignant
Usseglio, Pierre
Usseglio, Raymond

84350 COURTHÉZON

Co-opérative Vinicole 'Le Cellier des Princes'
Jamet, Jean-Paul
  Clos de Val Aouri
Melia, Charles
  Château de la Font du Loup
Sabon, Aimé
Sinard, Robert et Fils
  Domaine St-Laurent

84100 ORANGE

André Jean
  Domaine de St-Anaclet
Bernard, Michel
  Clos Grange Neuve
Chastan, André et Fils
  Domaine de la Jaufrette
Chastan, René
  Quartier Palestor
Chastan, Yves
  Quartier Palestor
Daumen, Arnaud
  Domaine de la Vieille Julienne
Jaume, Roger
  Domaine des Chanssaud

84700 SORGUES

Drapéry, André
  Domaine du Grand Coulet

13

Tavel

Tavel, the finest rosé area of France, stands on the west bank of the Rhône 16 kilometres north-west of Avignon and 40 kilometres north-east of Nîmes. It is in the *département* of the Gard, and the crossing of the river brings with it a marked change in the face of the countryside. The 'market-garden' aspect of the Vaucluse *département* across the river—watered, productive green fields bordered by windbreaking rows of cypress trees—has abruptly disappeared. In its place the eye sees, above all, aridity: parched columns of vines, and austere rocky hillocks with little but a dried-out brush capable of growing on them. West of Tavel the sparseness increases, and the land becomes a maze of small valleys and woods, with groupings of vines encircling the many, semi-forgotten villages.

Tavel fits into the pattern of the countryside. It is a tiny place and has an admirably narrow main street running through it. Sleeping dogs increase the narrowness, but the passing traffic respectfully organizes itself to steer right around them. On either side of the road little houses lean jumbled together, their brief balconies adorned with picturesque climbing flowers. The air of a wine village seems to be lacking, though: most of the main growers live outside the village, and it is only at the end of a long, hot day, when thirsty tractor drivers roll in from the fields, that Tavel gives a clue as to its true identity. With the long rays of the last sun lancing down the main street, the busy swallows looping overhead and the vineyard workers idly chatting in little groups, Tavel at last comes alive.

When wine was first made at the village is not clear. Records are patchy, but it is known that King Philip le Bel (1268–1314) once passed through Tavel on one of his grand tours of the kingdom.

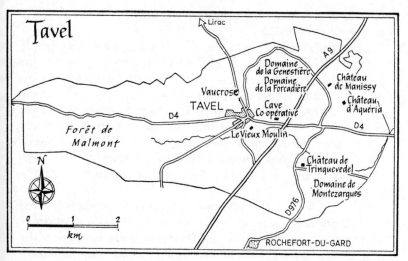

Without dismounting from his horse, he lustily drained a goblet and exclaimed, 'There is no good wine except for Tavel!' Later the poet Ronsard (1524–85) is said to have described the wine of Tavel as *sol in amphora*, but although *vignerons* are fond of this reference to their wine, they are unable to point out the work in which it figured.

Meanwhile, Tavel had graduated from early fame at the papal table in Avignon to regular appearances at the Versailles Court of the Sun King, Louis XIV (1638–1715). The custom was to ship the wine from the local port of Roquemaure, now the unofficial centre of the Lirac *Appellation*. Considerable quantities were sent beyond the immediate territory, all passing under the name of 'Côtes du Rhône' rather than Tavel. Recognition of the wine's place of origin seems to have come only in the mid-eighteenth century: in a communication of 1765 a cardinal in Rome requested the Archbishop of Avignon to secure 'more of that wine of Tavel' for their annual rendezvous the following year.

One of the legends that grew up with the wine at this time was that it was extremely durable. No journey was considered too long for it, and the port of Roquemaure handled a large proportion of overseas shipments, for Italy, England and even the Indies. The prevailing taste then was for drinking wines such as Tavel when they were quite old, which was just as well, for the Tavel must have aged very quickly when taken on prolonged sea journeys in only very small casks.

Throughout the eighteenth century and later Tavel was strictly defended by its *vignerons*. Careful rules were drawn up, such as the prohibition of the entry of all outside grapes and wine, on the grounds that their presence in the community could not enhance, and would probably only harm, Tavel's reputation. A *ban des vendanges*, or official date of harvest, was also fixed rigorously every year. This became a useful ploy for the *seigneur* of Tavel, who always decreed himself a three days' start on his fellow *vignerons*. There was never, of course, any arguing with the mighty *seigneur*!

By 1828 Tavel was in full prosperity, and its vineyards covered nearly 1,800 acres. Most of the plots were on the series of little hills south and west of the village, and their slope wine was some of the best that could be found in the locality. Alas, the phylloxera attack reduced the whole vineyard to almost nothing, and the harassed growers were forced to replant on all the chalk-sand flatlands immediately next to the village; these were nearer than the hillsides, and although the wine was less good, they could be worked more easily and more cheaply. The hillside area, covering some 620 acres, went largely uncultivated until 1965, when concerted action by many of the villagers led to their using bulldozers to clear out the scrub on the slopes that had generally been regarded as infertile. The chalky soil that was revealed was covered in masses of white and crumbly flat stones, and this ground has since lived up to its old reputation as being one of the best areas of Tavel. The *parcelles* are much smaller than those on the Vallongue plateau, and many belong to members of the Cave Co-opérative, which is one of the most celebrated in France.

Inspiration for the total clearance of the hillsides had stemmed from a similarly successful action performed on the Vallongue, which lies north of the village, in 1957. At that time Tavel's name was well established in the United States, but with the vineyard totalling no more than 495 acres, growers found they did not have enough wine to serve their other home and foreign markets properly. The Vallongue, a well exposed raised plateau, seemed ideal for their purposes but was thickly wooded and established as a paradise of rabbits, hares, partridges—and, of course, French marksmen. It must have been a heartrending decision for some of the *vignerons* who had grown used to their regular plates of game, but good sense prevailed and the ever-united wine community undertook to follow the example of Gabriel Meffre of Gigondas and bulldoze into shape nearly all the plateau. Now there are long rows of vines on the Vallongue, which stretch away towards distant clutches of cypress windbreaks; with their uneven heights and shapes the far-off trees resemble a ragged band of part-time soldiers. Right away to their north-east the further side of the Rhône Valley is visible, with the Dentelles de Montmirail and Mont Ventoux shimmering blue-grey some 30 kilometres distant. The view from the Vallongue is one of the best of the southern Côtes du Rhône vineyards, and the feeling it gives early on a summer's day is almost ethereal.

As a result of all this activity, the vineyards now extend over 1,875 acres, which is as complete as they have been since the early years of the nineteenth century. Altogether nine different grape varieties are allowed in them. These are headed by the Grenache, which by the rules cannot exceed 60 per cent of a *vigneron*'s plantation, and by the Cinsault, of which there must be at least 15 per cent. In recent years there has been a slight trend away from the Grenache, as growers seek to make a wine of lessened alcohol content. A little 14° Tavel is still made, especially from the clayey, stone-covered Vallongue, and in such a wine the fruit is often marred by an all-pervading sensation of alcohol—pleasant for some, maybe, but robbing the wine of its balance. The Cinsault is now regarded as the vine capable of 'smoothing out' this defect, and its plantation has consequently increased to 20 or 25 per cent of the whole vineyard.

The Grenache and Cinsault are the natural bases of Tavel, and the growers rarely make use of the full complement of vines available to them. The other seven are, in rough order of importance, the Clairette, Bourboulenc, Syrah, Mourvèdre, Picpoul, Carignan (not more than 10 per cent of this is permitted) and Calitor, which is slowly disappearing from use.

The Syrah and the Mourvèdre have been permitted only since 1969, and their presence in or absence from a Tavel rosé makes a lively subject for conversation among the wine-making fraternity. These grapes undoubtedly inject colour and a little extra body into the rosé, but perhaps that is a contradiction in terms. M. Georges Bernard, of the excellent Domaine de la Genestière, considers that even a small percentage of either grape is sufficient to dominate the wine, and it is certainly true that wines such as those of Jacques Lafond from Domaine Corne-Loup and the Cave Co-opérative itself display more red in their colour and possess a 'darker', perhaps less really clean-cut taste than do M. Bernard's wines. A subjective evaluation of this nature should not hide the fact that both the Corne-Loup and Cave Co-opérative wines are very good; it is all down to personal preference.

Most of the vines are ideally suited to growing in Tavel's hot, dry and windy climate, and the greatest vineyard menace in the past has surprisingly come from the local rabbits. These raiders gladly ate up many neglected vines during the Second World War and in the post-war years turned their attentions to all the newly planted young vines—so much so that they virtually became Tavel's public enemy number one. Their assault was particularly severe at the Château de Manissy, which is run by a religious order. Perhaps it was specially invoked divine providence that brought on the myxomatosis attack of the 1950s, for the Château now has an eminently thriving vineyard!

At the time of the *vendanges*, around the middle of September, it is the fast-maturing Cinsault grapes that are picked first, followed by the Grenache. The *vignerons* then proceed on their orthodox rosé vinification, which is simply an abbreviated version of making red wine and not, as some people believe, a question of adding red and white wine together! Thus the brilliant pink colour is attained from a preliminary maceration of the grapes which lasts for one or two days: piled up together in the vats, the grapes gradually crush each other, thus lightly breaking their skins and liberating some of their juice. The vats, normally enamel-lined, are specially cooled during the maceration by conducting running water around them, since the growers do not want fermentation to get properly under way. The object at this stage is merely to extract the necessary colour without any of the accompanying tannin.

The temperature at which the maceration is undertaken is most easily controlled through the use of stainless-steel tanks, and *domaines* like Le Vieux Moulin of the Roudil family and La Forcadière of Armand Maby are now firmly committed to this new technique. Armand Maby, the ex-Mayor of Tavel and always a prominent member of the wine community, explained why: 'The grapes often come in from the vineyards at a temperature of around 25 °C, so I have to cool them the moment they enter my cellars or else I'd end up with a red wine on my hands. I therefore cool them in the stainless-steel tanks which I bought recently and which allow for a far closer temperature control than the old concrete vats. As I take the temperature down to around 15–18 °C, I leave the grapes to macerate for two or three days. I'd like to macerate as low as 12 °C, but I find that difficult to achieve and sustain.'

So pleased is he with his tanks that M. Maby is also fermenting his rosé in stainless steel, while at this point of the vinification the Roudils turn back to using enamel-lined vats. A third style is favoured by the well-known Château d'Aquéria, who ferment a little of their wine in concrete vats and the majority in 40- to 50-hectolitre wooden casks. Their wine is very good, if a little darker and more robust than M. Maby's very fresh and attractive Domaine de la Forcadière. Once again, we are talking about an *Appellation* that is making a very high standard of wine, and only personal preference can really decide between wines of the quality of Château d'Aquéria, Domaine Le Vieux Moulin and Domaine La Forcadière.

After about two days' maceration, the grapes are removed from their vats or tanks and pressed lightly to provide more juice. Fermentation then gets quickly into top gear away from the skins and lasts for about a week, until very little sugar remains. One of the most agreeable aspects of a Tavel rosé is its clear-cut, dry flavour, and to achieve this the *vignerons* like to ferment nearly all the sugar out of the must. The malolactic fermentation follows soon after, and by January the young wine starts to be bottled so that its youthful freshness can be appreciated.

One fallacy that has for some reason always accompanied Tavel is that it is a keeping wine, a *vin de garde*. No rosé can pretend to be a *vin de garde*, and no rosé was ever designed to be. If a *vigneron* sought to make a *vin de garde*, he would make a red wine with tannin in it, not a pink wine without tannin. That said, there do exist quite sharply differing attitudes among the growers towards the question of maturing Tavel. At the Château de Manissy, for instance, the monks of the Sainte Famille leave their wine to age for a year in underground wooden barrels. M. Leveque, of the Seigneur de Vaucrose, is another grower who will age his wine for over a year and not release it for sale until it is nearly two years old. The effect of ageing and storage on such a pure and uncomplicated wine as Tavel is not particularly pleasant, for much elegance and freshness tends to be lost.

The other, majority school of thought favours early bottling, with the wine never being put into wood. The Domaine Le Vieux Moulin used sometimes to mature its wine in cask for two or three months, on the grounds that this could provide a little extra bouquet, but has abandoned this procedure in order to keep its wine as fresh and lively as possible. Now all the leading *domaines*, like Genestière, Forcadière and Vieux Moulin, adhere to this early bottling and their wines are invariably a racy pink colour, light, refreshing and all too easy to drink too much of.

One of the recurring problems of rosé wines is that of their image. They are commonly criticized as being a kind of half-caste: neither red nor white, they are too light and trivial for many lofty wine drinkers, who see them as the product of some illegitimate and rather clandestine union. Tavel can safely be set quite apart from all such charges. It has immense refinement and fully justifies its reputation as the leading rosé in France, if not the world. The pyramid underneath it is shaky, though, for too often are rosés no more than pink water, like the product of a red-wine vat that went wrong. This is especially true of many Languedoc, Provençal and even Portuguese rosés.

So where does Tavel score over all its rivals? For a start, it possesses an unaccustomed and totally agreeable depth; this is supported by a great, clean fruitiness and length of bouquet. It may be a light wine, lacking the complexities of its neighbour Châteauneuf-du-Pape, but it is none the less very complete: underneath all the superficial fruit and charm there is a substantial finish. A young Tavel is a lustrous pink and entrances the eye and the palate with its satisfying simplicity. Its elegance is startling and is an asset that sets it out in a class of its own.

A little over 55 per cent of all Tavel is made at the Cave Coopérative, whose foundation in 1937 did much to help the small cultivator, previously completely dependent on the *négociant* trade for selling his wine. There are now 140 members under the President, M. Barrelet, and the wine sets a fine example for Coopératives everywhere. It is consistently good, without perhaps being the best at Tavel, but, above all, has a recognizable character of its own, and unlike the wine of many co-opératives, does not give the impression of having come out of a factory. Beside the Co-opérative the private *domaines* are few and small.

CHÂTEAU D'AQUÉRIA

One of the largest, Château d'Aquéria, possesses about 105 acres of vines. It is a splendid seventeenth-century house completely surrounded by its vines, and lies in beautifully secluded countryside north-east of Tavel. Before it run unbroken views of vineyards and distant hills that shine a hazy green under the southern sun. Its shaded garden and broad stone stairways make it into a sort of dream *château*, all the more so because there are well stocked cellars to go with it.

Château d'Aquéria rosé was one of the first French wines to appear in the United States after the ending of Prohibition. Indeed, its speed in establishing a foothold in the United States market was largely responsible for the early surge of popularity there for Tavel rosé, a popularity that has never deserted the wine. The man who achieved this was M. Jean Olivier, the long-standing owner of Château d'Aquéria who died in 1974. M. Olivier, who was a close friend and contemporary of another great local wine character, the late Louis Reynaud of Châteauneuf-du-Pape's Château Rayas, had several friends from New York and Boston who had tasted and enjoyed his wine on trips to Europe in the late 1920s. In 1932, after the lifting of Prohibition, he promptly arranged a shipment of his wine to be sent off to them. The word was gradually spread around, and the wine grew so much in renown that Château d'Aquéria came to reserve the large part of its production for America alone. Today the Château is run by M. Olivier's son-in-law, M. Paul Debez, and his son Vincent, and they are making good wine, perhaps a little more full-bodied than the finest, freshest styles but none the less very sound. They still use wood in the cellars, in part to ferment and in part to round out some of their wine with a six-month ageing. The Château also makes a small amount of good red Lirac.

CHÂTEAU DE MANISSY

Along the road from Aquéria stands an anonymous old Provençal *mas*, or farm, and it is here that live the monks of the Sainte Famille, a religious order for people of late vocation. Founded in

Holland at the end of the nineteenth century, the order soon afterwards began to look out for overseas bases, and in France it came upon the Château de Manissy which was already a wine *domaine*. This did not deter the monks from settling down at Manissy, since their late-conversion philosophy means that they group together men of a large variety of skills. Wine-making is, unfortunately, neither a common nor an easy occupation to learn, though, so the first monks had to endure all the trials and tribulations of learning from scratch an entirely new trade.

There are seven monks living full-time at the Château, and they receive regular visits from foreign brother monks, who are often called upon to help in the 70-acre vineyard. The chief *caviste*, or cellar master, is always a member of the order, and the present one, Frère Roger, has spent over twenty-five years at Manissy gradually acquiring all the skills necessary to make their rosé. But he is by no means complacent, for he says: 'It's very hard work making this wine but also extremely pleasing to be faced with the challenge. As our wine is very rounded from ageing for a year in wood, I think it is best drunk no more than chilled in summer (about 10 °C) and at room temperature in winter (the old room temperature before central heating of about 15 °C).'

The brothers of Manissy are calm, gentle people, well able to accept the vagaries of the world. Wine-making is often temporarily put aside when weatherbeaten old tramps wheel up on misshapen bicycles, seeking refuge and solace from the outside world. All are courteously attended to; never is a word of exasperation uttered. The tramps sometimes come complaining of the tremendous heat and their terrible thirst, clearly in the hope of a quick glass of Manissy Tavel. When satisfied, their rough faces are transformed into delighted smiles—surely a fine testimony to the restorative powers of the wine.

LE VIEUX MOULIN DE TAVEL

One of the few *domaines* to have its cellars right in the village itself is Le Vieux Moulin de Tavel, which makes very good wine. The owner, M. Gabriel Roudil, is grey-haired and slight but possesses a toughness and resilience that stem from over forty-five years of hard outdoor work. He is now keeping a watchful eye on his three sons, who look after the daily cellar and vineyard work, and admits that this is a far cry from his grandfather's time, when the family employed fifteen full-time workers. The French laws of equal family inheritance have since reduced the property to just over 100 acres at Tavel and 17 acres in the Lirac *Appellation*. M. Roudil is thorough and painstaking over his wine but concedes that luck can just occasionally help out a *vigneron*. In 1973, for instance, it was his small grandson who pointed out the need for an early harvest; near the middle of September M. Roudil had taken him out to show him the vines and by chance had given him a Cinsault grape to eat. 'I waited for his grimace at the grape's bitterness, but instead he just asked for another one. I knew then that I had to harvest straight away, mobilized everyone and everything I could find, and the next day the *vendange* had started,' said M. Roudil. His alacrity was well rewarded, for he managed to avoid the disastrous rains that helped to spoil many later-picked southern crops.

DOMAINE DE LA GENESTIÈRE

The best Tavel of all comes from a completely restored *domaine* just outside the village, M. Georges Bernard's Domaine de la Genestière. His wine is outstanding, the very epitome of what a crisp, dry rosé should be. Beautifully pink in colour, it has a perfect balance of fruit and finesse which makes it a joy to drink. So delicious and easy to drink is it, though, that one bottle is never enough.

M. Bernard owns 86 acres of vineyards at Tavel and 25 at Lirac and is one of the growers who feels that the presence of the Syrah and the Mourvèdre is intrusive in a rosé. Consequently his Tavel is made up of 50 per cent Grenache, 20 per cent Cinsault and the remainder from a mixture of Carignan, Clairette, Picpoul and Bourboulenc. With a brief maceration—a minimum of twelve and a maximum of twenty-four hours—he is seeking a thoroughly well balanced wine that is never too alcoholic; his wines rarely surpass 12°, in contrast with some of the lesser lights of the *Appellation*. He believes that a good Tavel is already fine to drink by January following the harvest but restrains himself a little and puts his year's production out on sale after Easter, under the Domaine de la Genestière and his second label, the Domaine Longval.

M. Bernard is a robust and energetic man who leads a very private life, to the point of appearing sometimes to be on the fringe of the wine community. His *domaine* has been faithfully restored

M. Georges Bernard

with authentic eighteenth-century timberwork, and he has built a hall in Andalucian style that transports the visitor to the very gates of Granada and Seville. His other love is horses, and he relaxes by riding his thoroughbreds around the Gard countryside. He is very proud of his young daughter, who is learning to fight bulls from horseback, as is the custom in Portugal and Mexico, but in fights in which the bulls are not put to the sword. In this case the greatest emphasis is placed on the rapidity and manoeuvrability of the horse, and the rider's skill in understanding and controlling the horse is paramount.

As with most of the *vignerons* at Tavel, M. Bernard prefers to drink his wine before it is two years old but has no doubt that it stands up admirably to travel, even when young. In more peaceful days his wine would regularly go as far abroad as Cambodia, where it was always well received. M. Bernard also believes that Tavel can be drunk successfully throughout a meal; with a wine of his class this is certainly true, for it partners well both meat and fish. Particularly good dishes to accompany Tavel are oysters and lamb or veal: the wine's dryness makes for an excellent combination, while it is also delightful with classic picnic dishes such as *quiches* or light pastry-covered onion or leek tarts.

Interestingly, M. Bernard finds that Orientals have a distinct soft spot for Tavel. Apart from his Cambodian sales, he finds a large market for his wine in Chinese restaurants in Paris. Of his 150,000 bottles sold annually to the capital, more than 55,000 are taken by the Chinese, and their orders are increasing all the time.

Also featuring among M. Bernard's impressive list of clients are the Brazilian airline Varig and the famous London store Harrods.

Other *domaines* of interest include the following.

DOMAINE DE LA FORCADIÈRE

Owned by the ex-Mayor of Tavel, M. Armand Maby, the vineyards comprise 109 acres. The family also owns the 50-acre Domaine de la Fermade at Lirac, while M. Maby's son-in-law, M. Christian Amido, also possesses some vineyards. M. Maby is a very up-to-date winemaker, and the style of his wines has evolved in the past few years; he seems to recognize that Gardois wines are never going to be long stayers, so he is making well balanced, easily accessible reds and excellent, fruity rosés that should be drunk before they are 4 years and 2 years old respectively. He is a friend of Gérard Chave at Hermitage and of young François Perrin of the Domaine de Beaucastel at Châteauneuf-du-Pape, and the three meet regularly to discuss ideas and new techniques.

CHÂTEAU DE TRINQUEVEDEL

A viticultural *domaine* since before the French Revolution, this attractive soft stone *château* with its smart white shutters stands a little to the east of the village, on the way towards Rochefort-du-Gard. The property comprises about 60 acres of vines; when bought by the Demoulin family in 1936, the vineyards were in very poor condition, being mostly planted with low-grade hybrid vines. In 1960 M. Demoulin started to bottle his wine, and it is now exported to Britain and the United States. It can be very good but is a little lacking in consistency.

PRIEURÉ DE MONTÉZARGUES

Further down the Rochefort road from Trinquevedel and hidden in a small gully that overlooks the plain running across to Villeneuve-lès-Avignon, is the Prieuré de Montézargues, one of the lesser-known properties at Tavel. The 74-acre vineyard is run by the children of the late Louis Allauzen; situated on the flank of a low hill, the principal vines are the Grenache, Cinsault, Carignan and Picpoul, which grow in mainly sandy soil.

The Allauzens are young and charming, keen to do well in what was essentially the occupation of their father on his own. They use

233

stainless-steel tanks for a one-night maceration and store their wine in underground concrete vats for up to eighteen months before releasing it for sale. They bottle only 10 per cent of their production, the rest going to *négociants*, reflecting Mlle Allauzen's comment: 'We're not very good at commerce, but we do try to make good wine.' The Montézargues rosé, in its best vintages (such as 1978), is an agreeable wine, although its fruit lacks a little freshness due to its prolonged storage. Were there to be a strong demand for the wine in its bottled form, which would necessitate an earlier bottling, Montézargues would become one of the better wines in the *Appellation*: the promise is there.

DOMAINE MÉJAN-TAULIER

An approximately 70-acre vineyard run by M. André Méjan, the son-in-law of the late M. Valéry Taulier. They have planted no Syrah and aim to make a light style of Tavel which is not, however, put on sale until at least nine months after the harvest.

La Protectrice de Tavel

Tavel Vintages

Vintage lists are of secondary importance at Tavel, where the rosé should definitely be drunk young. Most of the *vignerons* are emphatic about this, and their wine supports their views: light and fruity, it is no way intended for consumption more than two or three years after the harvest. The exceptions to this are the Château de Manissy and the 'Seigneur de Vaucrose'; the former is aged in wood, while the latter is stored for two years before release, so that if one's taste is for deep-orange, dried-out wines, then these *domaines* are of interest. Recent vintages have been:

1962 Very good.
1963 Poor.
1964 Good.
1965 Very good.
1966 Very good.
1967 Very good.
1968 Mediocre.
1969 Mediocre.
1970 Good.
1971 Excellent.
1972 Good.
1973 Excellent.
1974 Good.
1975 Mediocre.
1976 Very good.
1977 Mediocre.
1978 Very good.
1979 Very good. The wines had a pleasing freshness behind their fruit, but have now lost their brilliance.
1980 Very good. The wines were clean-tasting, with tremendous fruit and roundness. Their balance was generally exceptional. Note the Domaines de la Genestière and la Forcadière, whose wines should be drunk by the summer of 1983.
1981 Good, although like neighbouring *Appellations* Tavel suffered from a prolonged drought that hindered the development of the grapes. The wines are lighter and a little more acid than the 1980s, and should be drunk before they are 2 years old.

Leading Growers at Tavel

Bernard, Georges	
Domaine de la Genestière	30126 Tavel
Maby, Armand	
Domaine de la Forcadière	30126 Tavel
Roudil, Gabriel et Fils	
Le Vieux Moulin de Tavel	30126 Tavel
Olivier, Société Jean	
Château d'Aquéria	30126 Tavel
Cave Co-opérative des Grands Crus de Tavel	30126 Tavel
Lafond, Jacques	
Domaine Corne-Loup	30126 Tavel
Allauzen,	
Prieuré de Montézargues	30126 Tavel
Amido, Christian	30126 Tavel
Charmasson-Plantevin	
Les Trois Logis	30126 Tavel
Château de Manissy	30126 Tavel
Demoulin, F.	
Château de Trinquevedel	30126 Tavel
Fraissinet, Les Filles de	30126 Tavel
Lafond, Jean-Pierre et Fils	
Domaine Roc-Epine	30126 Tavel
de Lanzac	30126 Tavel
Lefèvre, Edouard	
Domaine de Tourtouil	30126 Tavel
Leveque	
Seigneur de Vaucrose	30126 Tavel
Méjan-Taulier	
Clos Canto-Perdrix	30126 Tavel

14

Lirac

If the rosé of Tavel possesses a rival, then it is its neighbour, Lirac. Although relatively unknown and quite certainly under-appreciated, Lirac makes consistently good and sometimes out-standing rosé; always fruity, well balanced and distinguished, the rosé has in the past brought the *Appellation* what little fame it has ever known. Drinking habits are now slowly changing, though, and many people who might have drunk rosé all through a meal now prefer to have a bottle of white followed by a bottle of red. Growers have seen the demand for their rosé fall away dramatically since about 1973 and have consequently turned much more towards the red, now the most widely made wine at Lirac.

The *Appellation* takes its name from one of four small villages that lie in a ring near the Rhône about 16 kilometres north-west of Avignon. Lirac itself is an unmemorable place, with severe stone houses looking on to a spartan main square that lacks even the slightest motions of everyday life. The other villages are a little more *mouvementé*, notable Roquemaure, which stands right beside the Rhône 6 kilometres east of Lirac. Vines were grown here, and extensively in the neighbouring area, in the thirteenth century, but the first firm evidence of a wine transaction is not before 1357; then the papal Court, under Innocent VI, purchased twenty casks from a Roquemaure merchant called Guillelmi Malrepacis and also drew on stocks of wine available from St-Laurent-des-Arbres.

Roquemaure is first identified in literature in the texts of Livy ('The War with Hannibal'), since it is deduced that Hannibal sent his elephants across the Rhône on rafts at Roquemaure, although Livy makes no mention of the part of the Rhône that was crossed. It was obviously a perilous operation, for apart from the alarm of the elephants at not finding themselves on *terra firma*, there were hordes of noisy Gauls waiting on the eastern bank. Later, when his troops were contemplating the crossing of the Alps with some despondency, Hannibal harangued them in a famous speech that spoke of their exploit of 'taming the violence of the mighty Rhône'. Crossing the Alps and fording the Rhône were obviously the two most difficult physical feats that he accomplished on his journey from Spain to Italy.

Roquemaure's easy accessibility and convenient situation next to the Rhône attracted both farming and commercial interests, and the local wine-makers were active in the defence of the quality of their wine and in ensuring that their market was not upset by intrusions of wine from other regions. Thus in the early eighteenth century the panel, or consuls, of Roquemaure refused to allow Châteauneuf-du-Pape to pass for a local wine, saying that it was only very ordinary and that it also bore a prejudicial *'goût de terroir'*—bold words indeed!

The protection of the wine of Roquemaure, and of that of the surrounding Gard *département*, was formalized in 1737, when a royal decree for the first time named different wine-making areas under a grouped title, that of La Côte du Rhône. The decree specifically mentioned all the four villages that today make up the Lirac *Appellation*—Roquemaure, Lirac, St-Laurent-des-Arbres and St-Geniès-de-Comolas—as well as Tavel, Orsan, Chusclan and Codolet. All these *'véritables bons crus'* were to have the letters 'CDR' burned on to their barrels, along with the vintage year of the wine, while no wine from outside this region was to be stored at Roquemaure, whose port was a busy shipping centre for the Gardois wines to Britain, Holland and Germany.

By 1774 Roquemaure was the principal wine-producing community of the Gard *département*, figures of that year showing that altogether 1,226 *muids* (barrels) of 675 litres each were made there, with the next most important village, Laudun, producing only 772 *muids*.

The other two villages in the *Appellation*, St-Laurent-des-Arbres and St-Geniès-de-Comolas, lie north of Roquemaure, just off the Orange–Nîmes main road. St-Laurent is easily the most striking village of the four, with a well preserved fortified church dating from the twelfth century: its tower and walls are a local landmark, visible for some distance all around. During the early part of the nineteenth century Pauline Malosse de Casal, the elaborately named owner of the Domaine du Sauvage, exported wine from St-Laurent through the Mediterranean port of Sète to destinations as far away as Britain, Holland and even the United States. This *domaine*, and its wine Vin du Camp d'Annibal, have since disappeared without trace.

St-Geniès is the most unfortunately sited village of the four, for it lies near a large, smoky steelworks and spends many of its days enveloped in a sort of unhealthy morning mist. The *mistral* wind blows the factory fumes south towards St-Geniès, and the effect of this semi-perpetual haze on the surrounding vineyards can only be harmful: it is noticeable that the grapes ripen less quickly with this smoky barrier between them and the sun.

Even though its wines have not been widely heard of, Lirac has one great claim to fame in the history of French viticulture. It is a dubious honour: phylloxera is said to have started there in about 1863. By all accounts the then owner of the Château de Clary, which has remained a wine *domaine* to this day, was a great experimenter and innovator and would take delight in making the most unlikely wines from his vineyard: these included ports and madeiras. One day he tried planting some Californian vine cuttings to see how they would fare at Lirac, but this time he had made a grave miscalculation. The American vines, being resistant to the phylloxera insect, carried plenty of the little creatures in their roots. The defenceless French vines were easy prey for them, and Clary's vineyard was promptly devoured by the phylloxera, which went on to ravage most of Europe's vines. Other tales may be told about the outbreak of phylloxera, but the Lirac growers strongly believe in the authenticity of this one.

Lirac was granted its own *Appellation Contrôlée* in 1945, but the vineyard was then less than a third of its present size (now about 1,525 acres), and most of the wine would be sold in bulk to merchants. Fame and fortune thus continued to elude it, and it was not until the early 1960s that its popularity began to pick up from almost nothing. Then the arrival of several families from Algeria marked the turning point. Expelled with nothing to their names, the ex-colonists were determined to retrieve their situation. Having bought *domaines* throughout the *Appellation*, they set out to gain a better price for, and a wider distribution of, their wine by selling it bottled. Lirac stalls appeared at all the major French wine fairs, and little by little spread greater knowledge

239

and appreciation of these agreeably uncomplicated wines.

Much of the land bought by the ex-Algerian settlers was wooded and uncultivated, and it was a major task to make it fit for vines. One of the best examples of this recent plantation is the plateau that runs west of Roquemaure; here the vines date from 1962, and their terrain closely resembles that of Châteauneuf-du-Pape, being covered with piles upon piles of smooth, rust-coloured stones. These range from the size of a potato to that of a water melon, and, strewn all over the generally sandy vineyards, they perform well their function of radiating heat on to the vines. The sudden open spaces of these young vineyards come as a surprise in the generally rather scrub-covered countryside; as one stands on this plateau on a clear day amid the intense light summoned by the driving *mistral* wind, the eye is dazzled, both by the pale shades of the soil and by the long, distant view across the Rhône Valley.

Apart from the Roquemaure plateau, most of the other *Appellation* vineyards are on gentle slopes that run away from the respective village centres; with their sound exposure, the grapes generally ripen up well under the southern heat. Out of keeping with most of the Côtes du Rhône, though, Lirac has a large amount of Cinsault vines, most of which were planted in the rapid expansion of the early 1960s; these undoubtedly contribute much towards the native softness noticeable in many of the red wines. Of course, the Grenache remains the majority grape, and the Syrah and the Clairette are also well planted. During the 1970s the Mourvèdre's plantation increased, as some growers such as Maby at La Fermade and Lombardo at Domaine du Devoy have sought to give their wines a little extra staying power and depth.

Other grapes to be found within the *Appellation* are the slowly disappearing Carignan, which is not anyway permitted to make up more than 10 per cent of the vineyard, the Ugni Blanc (the grape used in the making of Cognac, where it passes under the name of St-Emilion), the Bourboulenc, the Calitor, the Picpoul and the Maccabéo. This last grape is exceptional to Lirac and is thought by the growers to add something special (never defined) to the wines.

The *vendanges* come towards the end of September, although there are some *vignerons* who prefer to start as much as two weeks earlier, aiming to make white and rosé wines that are fruity and tart. The red wine is vinified along traditional lines, although not all the growers like to crush and destalk their grapes before fermentation; the trend towards *raisins entiers*, which is discernible in the more progressive *domaines* of Châteauneuf-du-Pape, is also evident at Lirac, notably with the leading *domaine*, Château St-Roch, which leaves its grapes to macerate for six days before fermenting the juice from them. A steady fermentation of between four and eight days follows, and after racking the wine will generally be left in enamel-lined vats; rarely is it put in wood. Most of the growers are seeking to accentuate the fresh style of their wine. Exceptions of note are Georges Bernard's Domaine de la Genestière, which is aged for eighteen months or so in cask, and the Domaine du Château St-Roch, where the Verdas leave their wine six months in barrel 'to help to develop the bouquet'.

Lirac is the best red wine in the Gard *département*, and it is most interesting to see how these west bank wines differ radically in style from the east bank wines of the Vaucluse *département*. The strong, sometimes harsh *goût de terroir* evident in wines such as Cairanne or Vacqueyras is noticeably absent at Lirac, where the reds are lightly styled, fruity and easy to swill back without too much thought. They are not the sorts of wine that will make a strong initial impression on a first-time Rhône drinker, being dwarfed by their neighbours, the Vaucluse or even the Drôme wines, into a sort of downbeat modesty. Certainly, the less good examples that one finds outside France lack any sort of backbone of flavour, and this is the risk that the wine runs if it is not well made. The best *domaines*, including Château St-Roch, Château de Ségriès and La Fermade, usually produce wines that display the attractive harmony and light fruit—akin almost to a plum jam— that make them good for early and uncomplicated drinking. Such wines, although never very dark-coloured, have such an embracing softness about them—on the bouquet and the palate—that they are delightful to drink even in the summer, when other more heady wines have been discarded until the arrival of the autumn breezes. Taken slightly chilled, they can be delicious with cold meats and pâtés.

The rosés, meanwhile, are vinified in the same way as Tavel, with just a brief maceration to gain a little colour and then about a week's fermentation. Dazzling pink when young, a good Lirac rosé can aspire to be the peer of a Tavel: refined and delicately fruity, the wine is invariably well balanced and not over-alcoholic—this last factor stemming in part from the abnormally high amount of Cinsault grapes that go into it. It is also fortunate that at Lirac there exists none of the folklore of Tavel that endows rosés with legendary ageing power: the wine is therefore bottled within about six months, and the *vignerons* firmly believe that it should not be drunk when more than 3 or 4 years old.

Not more than 3 per cent of all the wine is white, and this too is made along orthodox lines, with a preliminary pressing and fermentation of seven to ten days. It is a surprisingly good wine that is slightly neglected by its makers, who claim that they only bother with it in order to satisfy the demands of their friends and to keep themselves amused. Best drunk within eighteen months, it has a fruitiness and natural roundness sometimes missing from the lesser whites of Châteauneuf-du-Pape, for instance, and makes a good, refreshing *vin d'apéritif*.

Lirac as a whole, therefore, produces good, very drinkable wines whose price is well in keeping with their quality. While *Appellations* like Gigondas and Cornas have seen their prices soar in the late 1970s, the *vignerons* of Lirac have been either unable or unwilling to force their price up substantially, which, when one is talking about a light, drinking wine, is surely the only course to take. Nevertheless, it remains difficult to comprehend why Lirac has never enjoyed greater renown. One reason may well be that the vineyards set on the rocky *garrigues* around Roquemaure were abandoned not only after the phylloxera attack but also, for a second time, between the two World Wars, when farmers preferred simple, low-outlay cultivation such as olives or minor forestation.

Thus between the establishment of *Appellation Contrôlée* in 1945 and the arrival of the ex-Algerian *vignerons* in the 1960s, there were only three private wine *domaines* at Lirac. They were the Château de Ségriès, the Château de Clary and M. Antoine Verda's very good Domaine du Château St-Roch: the first took up its own bottling only in the early 1970s, but even today Clary's wine is sent to a merchant nearby for both bottling and marketing, and as a result loses an unquestionably valuable 'Château-bottled' identity, which can be extremely useful in promoting the name of an obscure *Appellation*.

The owner of the Château de Ségriès is the Comte de Régis, Lirac's longest-serving *vigneron*, who has looked after the family

242

vineyard for over sixty years. Now an octogenarian, the Count remains fit and young in spirit for his age, and together he and his wife make a splendid *vieille France* couple—very polite, very charming and not at all taken aback by the eccentricities of the modern age. The Count explained how he had become a wine-grower: 'Wine has not always been my family's main occupation, as the Château de Ségriès used to produce mainly corn. After phylloxera the vineyards were enlarged, but my father suddenly died when I was 10. What would you have done . . .? I didn't really have much choice but to keep the vineyard going and to see that my five younger brothers and sisters were adequately cared for.'

The Ségriès vineyard now covers over 50 acres and is expanding with the aid of the Count's enthusiastic son, François. The Count himself was President of the Growers' Association of Lirac for over thirty years and played a prominent role in seeing that the area obtained its own *Appellation Contrôlée* shortly after the Second World War. Now he is happy to lead a quieter life, residing mainly in his fine old town house in Nîmes but keeping an eye on his son's work at his Lirac and Bandol *domaines*, as well as checking up on his wife's property in the Mâconnais region, north of Lyon. Since the second half of the 1970s the red wine of Château de Ségriès has improved, drawing itself away from its former over-light and straightforward style towards a more substantial and complex make-up. In this aromas like gentle spices are detectable on the bouquet, and a necessary backbone of tannin holds the wine together on the palate, making it one of the better and more long-lived samples in the *Appellation*. The 1978 Ségriès red was a very good, solid wine that will live for six to eight years and whose style is therefore more interesting than some of the light, early bottling *domaines* whose wines need to be drunk before they are 3 years old. Eighty per cent of the Ségriès wine is red, and the Château also makes a sound rosé and a very respectable white, the latter being clean and fruity and a good advertisement for the underestimated whites of Lirac.

The Château de Clary too is owned by a senior member of the wine community, M. Marius Mayer. This rambling *domaine* stands in secluded country beside the dense forest of Clary, north of Tavel, and because second-century Roman relics, like wine decanters, goblets and amphorae, have been found in its grounds, M. Mayer is convinced that it is the oldest wine *domaine* in the region. Certainly, the wine has been sold abroad for a long time; in the eighteenth century 600-litre barrels of Clary were regularly shipped from Roquemaure to Switzerland, Germany and Britain. The wine intended for France would also be shipped from Roquemaure and would travel by way of the country's many canals. This lively enterprise flourished for some decades but was abruptly halted when the *château*'s owner, the Comte de St-Priest, was guillotined by the *révolutionnaires* in Montpellier.

M. Mayer bought the property in the 1930s and has since doubled the size of its vineyard to 136 acres. He related: 'In olden times the occupants of Clary could drink their own wine with all the game of the Forest of Clary—wild boar, deer and so on. I now have to content myself with hare, partridge and quail, but that's no hardship!'

The arrival of the ex-Algerian settlers, who are known in France as *pieds-noirs*, stirred Lirac from this easy tranquillity and provided the area with badly needed momentum. The *pieds-noirs* wine-growers found vineyard cultivation and cellar techniques less evolved by several years than those practised on the large estates of North Africa, and their enthusiasm and uninhibited outlook greatly stimulated the worldwide marketing of the wines of Lirac. One of the first families to settle was that of M. Charles and Mme Marie Pons-Mure; like many others, this stalwart pair, now both approaching their eighties, were forced to abandon their Algerian properties when independence was granted in 1961. Mme Pons-Mure had been running a wine *domaine* of over 850 acres in the highly esteemed area of Oran: 'I had completely replanted the entire vineyard since the Second World War, so you can well imagine my feelings when we had to leave—with nothing in our pockets,' she said.

Her husband went on: 'I used to pilot myself about in a small plane in Algeria, so once we had arrived in France I decided to take a chance on hiring one and scouting out several likely wine areas. From the air I find it is much easier to spot and assess the potential of rural land, and this was what led me to Lirac, as I'd noticed the possibilities of the wooded plateau near Roquemaure. The land was bought cheaply because it was wooded and, once bulldozed flat, was planted with vines.'

Mme Pons-Mure resumed; 'Charles started making wine from 30 acres of vines that I'd bought, and we decided to send some to the International Wine Fair at Mâcon in order to try and get our names on the map. The only problem was that we didn't have a *domaine* name by which we could be identified. At the time I was living in a tumbledown house that was slowly undergoing repairs, so I thought I would use the name "Castel Oualou" as a joke. [*Castel* is Provençal for 'castle' and *oualou* means 'there is no' in Arabic.] Well, that was all very well,' she continued, 'and the wine won medals at the 1962 Mâcon Fair, which meant that the name of "Castel Oualou" started to become known. One day, though, the official name inspectors came along and asked to see my castle. When I told them there wasn't one and that the castle pictured on my label came from *Snow White and the Seven Dwarfs*, they weren't at all amused. They made me print a cross through the Snow White castle, and the label has stayed that way ever since.'

Mme Pons-Mure's Domaine de Castel Oualou now covers 133 acres, and her wine comes in the light, quaffable style that is most typical of Lirac reds. In good-quality vintages the wines are attractively cherry-coloured and delicately balanced, the overriding impression being one of fruitiness. However, this style falls down in lesser years such as 1980, when the colour of the wines is almost transparent, and their lack of balance and astringency is grating. Castel Oualou also make a predominantly Syrah-based *cuvée*, which is a little more robust and certainly more interesting in the weaker vintages.

Charles Pons-Mure also vinifies in the light, easy-to-drink style at his Domaines de la Tour at Lirac and de la Blaque in the Low Alps. His craggy face looks well travelled, and the air he carries of adventurer-cum-intellectual remind one of that intrepid Scot, Fitzroy Maclean. Indeed, it would be no surprise at all to bump into M. Pons-Mure in the Caucasus of Russia or on a Western Isle in Scotland, as he is a rare and memorable character; for ten years champion yachtsman of North Africa, he has also on more than one occasion won the four-day tour of Algeria, driving Peugeots and Panhards around the desert.

Both M. and Mme Pons-Mure make some of Lirac's best 'light-style' wine, and their frequent winning of medals at important wine fairs has done much for the *Appellation*'s reputation. Their interest in Lirac extends beyond their own *domaines* too, for Mme Pons-Mure's brother, M. Louis Rousseau, is another leading wine-grower. M. Rousseau, an energetic, highly capable man, arrived at Lirac via Algeria and Uruguay. He explained how he had become such a globetrotter: 'In Algeria my business was livestock breeding and cereal growing, but after the first Algerian rebellion of November 1954, I thought that things could only get worse. Consequently, I went off with some friends to South America to see what possibilities there were in that part of the world. We hired a taxi for a month and visited most of the interesting Uruguayan estates. The result was that I returned with my family in 1956, having sold everything in Algeria, and was once more breeding sheep and Hereford bulls. Around 1963, when Uruguay's economy had really started to crack up, I came back to France and bought vineyards at Laudun and then Lirac. With my son, Alexis, I now make red and rosé from those two *Appellations*; I think they're quite typical for the region, as I like to make them as soft and elegant as I can.' M. Rousseau's wines generally live up to his description of them, for they are light, but well balanced and fruity—also in the forefront of the 'light-style' wines.

Close family connections continue elsewhere in the *Appellation*, for Mme Pons-Mure's son-in-law, the enterprising Jean-Claude Assémat, owns the 89-acre vineyard Les Garrigues. M. Assémat also sells his wine under the Domaines des Causses and St-Eynes labels and varies his method of vinification between a customary short fermentation and the use of *macération carbonique* for certain *cuvées*. His ordinary Lirac is put on sale a little more than one year after the harvest and, like nearly all the 'light-style' wines, is quite refreshing, without being particularly spectacular. More interesting is his pure Syrah wine, which carries more substance.

The best *domaine* at Lirac is undoubtedly the Domaine du Château St-Roch, owned by Antoine Verda and now jointly run by his well qualified sons Jean-Jacques, who looks after the cellars and vinification, and André, who runs the vineyards. Jean-Jacques, a dark, bespectacled young man in his late twenties, explained how the Domaine had been created: 'My father started his career as a merchant at Châteauneuf-du-Pape but considered that this side of the Rhône held more potential for someone wanting to own vineyards. Consequently, he set about buying lots of land on the *quartiers* that are named Lescarce, Le Devès and La Pesade, all set on the gentle hills around Roquemaure. By 1955, he had bought almost 100 acres, of which only 20 already bore vines, but these were themselves very run down. Our first wine was made in 1960 from just 5 acres of young vines, and slowly we increased the replanting to cover all 100 acres. Our grape mix is much as it is elsewhere at Lirac, with the Grenache complying with its minimum 40 per cent requirement, the Cinsault accounting for 23 per cent, the Syrah and the Mourvèdre 13 per cent each and the difference made up of white grapes.'

Darting enthusiastically around the well laid out cellars of St-Roch, Jean-Jacques continued, 'Lirac is known as a fruity wine, but I feel that it needs a little more development than that, which is why we like to leave it for about six months in our 4,000-litre oak barrels here. This develops its bouquet and helps to give it a bit more solidity. As a result, I would say that our best vintages like the 1978 and, to a slightly lesser extent, the 1976 can live for six to eight years.' St-Roch make 80 per cent of their Lirac in red, 19 per cent in rosé and 1 per cent in white, and it is the red that is justifiably most alluring. A wine of tremendous harmony, it has a little more depth and complexity than most of the Lirac reds, which is quite essential if these wines are not to remain semi-forgotten and somewhat nondescript. The opening up of other sources of light red wine, ranging from Iron Curtain countries to Australia, South Africa, South America and, of course, jug wine from the United States, means that wines like the 'light-style' Liracs are an endangered species, not only through the risk of duplication but also through the danger of carrying a higher price as a consequence of being made in a high fixed-cost country such as France.

Finally, mention should be made of a wine to look out for in the future and of one to be avoided. The 86-acre Domaine du Devoy is owned by M. Joseph Lombardo, an ex-wine-grower of Tunisia, whose 500-acre property there was nationalized in 1964. M. Lombardo has been at Lirac since 1969, and his *domaine* is beginning to produce sound wines from the young vineyard on the plateau between Roquemaure and St-Laurent-des-Arbres. However, a near-neighbour of his, the Cave Co-opérative of St-Laurent-des-Arbres, founded in 1931 and the largest single wine house in the *Appellation*, makes wines that are extremely variable and sometimes highly disagreeable.

Lirac Vintages

Most of the red wine of Lirac is made in a light, overtly fruity style, and these wines are suitable for quite early drinking—at anything between 2 and 5 years old. The slightly weightier wines, such as the Châteaux de St-Roch and Ségriès, as well as some of Armand Maby's *cuvées*, can be kept for up to eight years or so, but would not improve after six years. The rosés are made to be drunk young, and when more than 4 years old often show signs of maderization. The whites should also be drunk young.

1955   Very good.

1956   Good.

1957   Good.

1958   Good, the wines were well balanced.

1959   Poor.

1960   Generally mediocre, although there was an outstanding red at Château de Ségriès.

1961   Excellent. Wines of tremendous balance and finesse.

1962   Good.

1963   Poor.

1964   Very good. Robust, long-lived red wines.

1965   Poor.

1966   Very good. Well perfumed, 'complete' wines of great charm.

1967   Good, although the wines were surprisingly quite considerably inferior to those from Châteauneuf-du-Pape across the river.

1968   Mediocre.

1969   A mediocre vintage. The wines were disappointingly light.

1970   Very good. Full-bodied and tannic red wines.

1971   An excellent year. The reds were very well balanced and charming.

1972   Good. The reds were quite well coloured and light and easy for early drinking.

1973   Generally good. The rosés were light and fruity, while the reds proved suitable for drinking in their first five years. An exceptional year for the white wine of Château de Ségriès.

1974   Good. The reds and rosés were both attractively coloured and soundly balanced. The reds are now over the top.

1975 Mediocre. A small harvest containing some indifferent wines. The reds were marginally better than the rosés.

1976 Very good. The red wines held great bouquet and overall finesse, and their tannin support enabled the heavier wines to progress well. Those such as Domaine du Château St-Roch should now be drunk up, as they have no room for improvement. Very good, attractively fruity rosés that showed very well for a little over two years.

1977 Generally a poor vintage, characterized by light, rather dull wines. Too much rain meant that the grapes were ill-formed and consequently acidity was high in many *cuvées*. Nevertheless, the Château de Ségriès succeeded in making a very good red wine that should now be drunk for best appreciation of its ageing, spicy aromas.

1978 A very good vintage indeed. The growers' prayers were answered, and perfect weather during ripening led to a fair-sized crop of healthy grapes. Notable for their good deep colour and remarkable balance, the red wines of the lighter style are quite ready to drink, but wines such as the Domaine du Château St-Roch will be good until around 1985. The rosés were also very successful.

1979 A good vintage, although one that has given charming, feminine wines that will be suitable for early consumption. The red wines are well perfumed and bear an easy fruitiness. Note the wine of Domaine du Devoy and the Syrah wine of Castel Oualou. The rosés were reasonably attractive but suffered from the same lack of depth as the reds, thereby being a little unbalanced.

1980 Mediocre. The reds were light, often very unbalanced and acidic. Not many good *cuvées* have been made, even by the better growers; the best examples are rather thin and not even charming like the 1979s. Better for the rosés, which were fruity and held greater relative depth of flavour.

1981 Another uneven vintage; again, one that was better for the rosé wines than for the reds. A rainy summer brought high acidity, and the hope is that some of the weightier reds will come round after around three years' ageing. The rosés are for early drinking.

Earlier Exceptional Vintages   1952, 1949, 1947, 1945, 1943

Leading Growers at Lirac

Verda, Antoine et Fils
  Domaine du Château St-Roch 30150 Roquemaure

de Régis, François
  Château de Ségriès   30150 Lirac
Lombardo, J.
  Domaine du Devoy   30126 St-Laurent-des-Arbres
Maby, Armand
  La Fermade   30126 Tavel
Pons-Mure, Charles
  Domaine de la Tour de Lirac 30126 St-Laurent-des-Arbres
Pons-Mure, Marie
  Domaine de Castel Oualou   30150 Roquemaure
Roudil, Gabriel et Fils   30126 Tavel

Amido, Christian   30126 Tavel
Assémat, Jean-Claude
  Les Garrigues   30150 Roquemaure
Cappeau, Y. et C.
  Domaine du Sablon   30150 Roquemaure
Cave Co-opérative de
  Roquemaure   30150 Roquemaure
Cave Co-opérative des Vins
  de Cru Lirac   30126 St-Laurent-des-Arbres
Cregut, E. et J.
  Domaine de Cantegril   30150 Roquemaure
Degoul, R.
  Château de Bouchassy   30150 Roquemaure
Duseigneur, Jean
  Domaine Duseigneur   30126 St-Laurent-des-Arbres
Fuget, Robert
  Château de Boucarut   30150 Roquemaure
Granier, Achille
  Domaine de la Croze   30150 Roquemaure
Leperchois, Emile
  Les Carabiniers   30150 Roquemaure
Mayer, Marius
  Château de Clary   30150 Roquemaure
Méjan, André
  Domaine Méjan   30126 Tavel

Nataf, Edmond
  Domaine de Maillac   30150 Roquemaure
Olivier, Société Jean
  Château d'Aquéria   30126 Tavel
Rousseau, Louis et Fils
  Domaine Rousseau   30290 Laudun
Rousseau, Pierre
  Domaine de la Claretière   30150 Roquemaure
Sabon, Roger
  Domaine Sabon   30150 Roquemaure
Testut, Philippe   30150 Lirac

15

Côtes du Rhône Villages

The idea of the Côtes du Rhône Villages started in 1953, when the National Institute of Appellations of Origin (INAO) determined that four Rhône communities were making wine worthy of carrying a higher status than the ordinary 'Côtes du Rhône' label, now often referred to as Côtes du Rhône *générique*. These communities—Gigondas, Cairanne, Chusclan and Laudun—were not considered sufficiently good to be allowed to join the select band of full *Appellation* wines—Châteauneuf-du-Pape, Côte-Rôtie, Cornas and so on—but were clearly superior to the mass of wines sold under the simple 'Côtes du Rhône' title. Rules were therefore laid down governing the grape varieties that they would be permitted to use; the minimum alcohol strength of their red wines had to rise from 11 per cent to 12·5 per cent; and less wine per acre was to be made.

The four communities complied with these regulations and, in return, were allowed to sell their wine as 'Côtes du Rhône', followed by the village name: 'Côtes du Rhône Cairanne', for instance. In this way it was hoped that a definite and recognizable identity would be promoted for each village. In 1955 Vacqueyras joined the group, followed in 1957 by Vinsobres. In 1967 it was decided to give all the communities a common title: the example of the Beaujolais was heeded, and the Côtes du Rhône Villages came into official being.

In 1982 there were seventeen communities within the Côtes du Rhône Villages, the most recent promotion being that of Beaumes-de-Venise for its red wines in 1976. All are permitted to sell their wine under their own Village name, and when the wine of neighbouring 'Village' communities is blended, this has the legal right to be sold as plain 'Côtes du Rhône Villages'. One of the founder members, Gigondas, was raised to full *Appellation* status in 1971, and in the years to come others should follow suit—provided the INAO sorts out how exactly it wants to encourage a better quality of wine.

To explain: the INAO allows growers to make 3,500 litres of Villages wine per hectare (1,400 litres per acre), which, in years of abundance and subject to strict control by tasting, can be extended to 4,200 litres. Any remaining wine that the grower may make from his vineyard has to be sold as *vin de pays*—put brutally, as swigging wine to be sold in corner stores or local cafés. However, that same grower can disregard the Villages wine rules, which also dictate that the red should have a minimum degree of 12·5, and choose to make 5,000 litres from each hectare of his vineyard, at a degree of 11, and sell it as Côtes du Rhône *générique*—at a marginally lower price than the Villages, but with the security of receiving an *Appellation* price on 5,000 litres per hectare. Some very good *domaines*—Claude Jaume at Vinsobres is one and Rey-Mery's Domaine des Treilles near Valréas is another—have opted to forget about making Villages wine if some of it has to be sold as *vin de pays*, and elected to make all their wine as plain Côtes du Rhône, receive an *Appellation* income on 5,000 litres per hectare, and be done with it.

What would undoubtedly halt this disturbing trend would be a decision by the INAO to allow growers to sell wine in excess of 3,500 litres per hectare and up to 5,000 litres per hectare as ordinary Côtes du Rhône. Certainly, it is hard to rationalize that 4,200 litres in an abundant year can be classified as superior Côtes du Rhône Villages, while another 800 litres from the same vines can only be termed modest *vin de pays*, several quality and price categories lower. In such circumstances the growers' attitude is understandable, and it is to be hoped that consideration will be given to this matter by the authorities: otherwise the philosophy and objectives of the Villages category will be eroded.

The 1982 list of Villages was:

Beaumes-de-Venise (other than the Muscat)
Cairanne
Chusclan
Laudun

Rasteau (wines other than the *vin doux naturel*)
Roaix
Rochegude
Rousset-les-Vignes

Sablet   Vacqueyras
St-Gervais   Valréas
St-Maurice-sur-Eygues   Vinsobres
St-Pantaléon-les-Vignes   Visan
Séguret

CAIRANNE

Sixteen kilometres north-east of Orange is the tiny village of
Cairanne, one of the top communities included in the Côtes du
Rhône Villages category. It is set on the top of a gently rising
hillock and, with its raised bell-tower dominating the straggling
village rooftops, is easily visible for miles around on the surrounding plain. From Cairanne the view once more emphasizes the
marked contrast that exists between the southern and northern
Côtes du Rhône: the vineyards cover a massive area, stretching
south for 10 kilometres towards Gigondas, and then another 10
kilometres west towards Rochegude. Their only interruption
comes from the occasional little village or row of hills—otherwise
it is a land completely given over to the vine and to the wind.

The open spaces of the wine plain south of Cairanne are an easy
prey for the legendary *mistral* wind, and it is hard to imagine a
more desolate scene than when it is blowing as hard as it can
through these exposed vineyards. In winter it is freezing; fully
muffled workers toil unhappily over the vines, striving to keep
both footing and sanity intact as the wind buffets them. The
French have a word, *énervant*, that they use often when talking
about the *mistral*: it is not chosen lightly, for the wind really does
sear the nerves, particularly when it has been blowing non-stop for
three days and nights.

Cairanne is one of the older villages of the Vaucluse *département*,
although it is not known when wine was first made there. The
discovery of a neolithic cemetery near the village indicates that
there was a habitation there from at least 2,000 BC, and traces of a
Roman *castrum* have also been found in the vicinity. With wine
being made by the Roman centurions resident at Gigondas, it is
not improbable that other parts of the region also held vineyards,
although undoubtedly on a very limited scale.

By the fourteenth century village decrees mention vineyards, and at the start of the fifteenth century there are known to have been over 130,000 vine plants—which would work out at a 100 acres or so these days. Little else is known about Cairanne's vinous past around this time, for in the sixteenth century the village became fully involved in the wars of religion, due probably to its advantageous setting on the top of a small hill. Rival armies fought constantly for its possession, and in 1589 the whole village was even held to ransom for 35,000 *écus* (a lot of money, so the locals say) by the Huguenot general Lesdiguières; this gentleman was no mean dealer, since the following year he had turned on his tracks and was holding Huguenot communities to ransom.

In the nineteenth century Cairanne's wine had a good reputation, for the asking price per hectolitre in 1817 was quoted as 35 francs, higher than Châteauneuf-du-Pape at 30 francs and considerably higher than all neighbours such as Rasteau, Roaix and Ste-Cécile-les-Vignes. The vineyard then amounted to about 350 acres, and expansion of it has continued ever since, particularly since the First World War. This thriving wine area is now distinguished by its progressive and well organized Cave Co-opérative and a collection of very good and reliable private *domaines*. The Co-opérative and most of the private cellars stand near the D8 road in what is known as the new village; the old village on top of the hill was largely abandoned in the years following the wars of religion and, sadly, has never been restored.

The Cave des Coteaux de Cairanne was founded in 1929 and has 260 subscribers who contribute towards a production of over 5,850,000 litres of wine every year. It is one of the larger, but also one of the best Co-opératives in the Rhône Valley; its present director, M. Lacrotte, and his technical assistant, M. Coulouvrat, are set on establishing the name of Cairanne both inside and outside France and are therefore continuing the forward-looking policy that the Cave has long held. All their Villages wine, generally around 1,485,000 litres a year, is bottled by them, for instance. When the Co-opérative started bottling some of their wine in 1957, ripples of scepticism went all around the tradition-conscious Côtes du Rhône. Even today the belief persists that it is not worth the while of the small *vigneron* to bottle and sell his own wine; many growers still prefer to sell off their wine in bulk and so avoid the additional costs of bottling, labelling and packaging. As the bottled wine has roughly twice the value of the same wine in bulk, it is difficult to understand why this stubbornness persists in many places.

Almost half the Cairanne vineyards are planted on the clayey slopes north-east of the village, and from this *quartier* comes the best wine—fine and rounded. The *garrigues* area south of the village accounts for another 35 per cent of the vines; this is a stony, meagre soil that manages to support only vines, lavender and the odd juniper tree. It extends down towards the village of Travaillan and the lonely Plan de Dieu plain, as well as across to Gigondas and the Montmirail mountains. Wines from the *garrigues* are normally high in alcohol degree, very coloured and tannic, and need three or four years' ageing to acquire a certain finesse.

A combination of these two wines is what is most usually sold as Cairanne, and the result of the blend is not disappointing. Richly coloured, often resembling the attractive brightness of black cherries, the red wine of Cairanne has a bouquet of rich, burnt spices and blackcurrant fruit flavours that in the most powerfully styled *cuvées* lead it to resemble the Châteauneuf-du-Pape of a traditional lesser grower. A big, mouth-filling wine, the best examples of it come from the Alary family at L'Oratoire St-Martin, the Brussets' Domaine des Travers and from the Cave Co-opérative's Réserve des Voconces. Such wines as these are best drunk between 3 and 6 years old.

In keeping with current tastes, the Co-opérative is now making a Cairanne *Primeur*, as has been done for some time in the Beaujolais. Here fermentation never exceeds three days (the best Villages wine is left to ferment for more than a week and spends up to two years in concrete vats and wooden barrels prior to bottling). The wine is hurried into the bottle by mid-November and is consequently very light, virtually all fruit and no tannin. By Easter following the harvest, *Primeur* wines are generally over the top, and their raw, young grape taste does not appeal to every palate. Because this is not one of their leading 'prestige' wines, the *vignerons* tend to make use of their less good vineyards, near the River Aigues, for it.

A little quite reasonable rosé is also made, although it is in no sense the equal of the red wine. Both it and the red are founded on the Grenache grape, while some of the growers also amuse themselves by making small quantities of white wine. This is often very passable and comes from four principal grapes, the Clairette, the Marsanne, the Grenache Blanc and the Ugni Blanc. Although it has a slight tendency to maderize quickly, when in good order it displays an agreeable light straw colour and a fine, lengthy finish.

In terms of quantity, Cairanne is easily dominated by its Cave Co-opérative, but there are none the less some very interesting private *domaines*. Perhaps the foremost is the Oratoire St-Martin, which is owned by the Alary family. The 85-acre vineyard makes an excellent deep-bodied red wine that normally needs two or three years to fuse its fruits and tannins successfully, in addition to very good rosé and white wine. It is run jointly by two brothers with the help of their sons. One of the brothers, Bernard, recalled that his family had always lived at Cairanne but had had a surprising number of different occupations. 'Cairanne had its own silk factory between 1860 and 1890, and my great-grandfather was a large-scale silk-worm breeder,' he said. 'He also extensively cultivated the garance plant, which makes red dye, and at that time had no vines at all. One day nylon was invented, which was a blow for his silk-worms, and then the French army gave up using red trousers. My grandfather was left totally high and dry and as a result went back to the vineyards, which he had given up when the silk trade was going so well. You can see from all this that the face of the countryside has been constantly evolving over the last hundred years.'

Another good private *vigneron* is M. André Brusset who, in company with his son, looks after the 75 acres of the Domaine des Travers. By contrast with M. Alary, he favours a swift vinific-ation; he includes the stalks during his four-day fermentation, however, and also adds some of the second-press wine, which always makes his Cairanne full-bodied and quite tannic. M. Brusset then likes to age his wine for around two years in cask, which in less good vintages can be rather overpowering for the wine; 'I like to use wood in the old-fashioned way,' explained M. Brusset, 'because that way you get a full, velvety wine that will age well in the bottle.'

Leading Growers at Cairanne

Alary et ses Fils
  L'Oratoire St-Martin   84290 Cairanne

Brusset, André et Fils
    Domaine des Travers   84290 Cairanne
La Cave des Coteaux de Cairanne 84290 Cairanne
Aubert, Max
    Domaine de la Présidente   84290 Ste-Cécile-les-Vignes
Beaumet, Père et Fils
    Domaine de St-Andéol   84290 Cairanne
Calatayud, Jean
    Domaine du Grand-Chêne   84290 Cairanne
Delubac, Père et Fils
    Domaine de la Fauconnière   84290 Cairanne
Grignan, Raoul
    Domaine du Grand-Jas   84290 Cairanne
Jullian-Gap
    Domaine d'Aeria   84290 Cairanne
Pierrefeu, Gérard et Fils
    Domaine Le Plaisir   84290 Cairanne
Plantevin, A.
    Domaine de la Gayère   84290 Cairanne
Rabasse-Charavin
    Les Coteaux St-Martin   84290 Cairanne
Richaud, Marcel
    Le Bon Clos   84290 Cairanne
Zanti-Cumino
    Domaine du Banvin   84290 Cairanne

CHUSCLAN

The famed rosé village of Chusclan stands in unexpectedly green
countryside north of Laudun and 11 kilometres west of Orange.
Its vineyards are on the narrow plain that runs north between the
west bank of the Rhône and the Laudun hills as far as Bagnols-
sur-Cèze. The River Cèze, full only after the torrential rains of
early spring, runs right past the village, and as a result the
countryside around Chusclan has an unaccustomed luxury in its
colour.

Chusclan was one of the first four villages to be named in a
decree of 1953 that permitted it to use its village name on its wine,
in addition to the usual 'Côtes du Rhône' title. The area that is

now allowed to make Chusclan, in fact, extends over the neigh-bouring communities of Orsan, Codolet and St-Etienne-des-Sorts, but none of these three in any way matches the quality of the wines that come from Chusclan itself.

Wine relics have been found that date from the first to the fifth century AD, so it is reasonable to suppose that wine was being made at Chusclan by the Romans, even if there was no parti-cularly large encampment around the village. Later on it was the Church, in the form of a Benedictine community, that assured Chusclan's prosperity as a wine-producing community. The monks' priory, which has since disappeared, supported a good-sized vineyard from the tenth century up until the Revolution, and in 1550 the parish register described the village vineyards as covering 200 acres.

At the same time, the local aristocratic family, the Counts of Grignan, also owned a renowned vineyard at Chusclan. The Grignans, a powerful and politically very nimble family, suc-ceeded in having their wine served at the royal table for many years. A clever concession was made to the monarchy by naming a section of their vineyard the 'King's Garden', and the practice was also established that whenever a ruling monarch was travelling in the area, he should be presented with several barrels of Chusclan. It is unlikely that the wine then being made was rosé; the one firm record of the Grignans' sly approach speaks of a present of four casks of white Chusclan given to Louis XIII when he was visiting Pont St-Esprit, 16 kilometres away, in 1629. Antiquity also mentions a sweet dessert wine of Chusclan, but precise references to it are untraceable, and the *vignerons* themselves are unaware of its existence.

An export trade was started at an early date, most probably due to the initiative of the Grignan family. In 1748 some wine was sent off to two Dutch merchants, and in 1788 there was a dispatch to England: in both cases the quantity sold is not known. Then, in 1811, a memorandum from the Academy of the Gard (probably in Nîmes) speaks of trading with Germany, Russia, Denmark and Sweden. In most instances the port of embarkation was Sète, 130 kilometres away on the Mediterranean coast.

Chusclan has therefore known a quietly prosperous past, which seems to have reached its summit around the time of the Napoleonic Wars. In 1812 the wine of Chusclan was fetching the

highest price of any of the Gard *département* communities, Tavel
and Lirac included. And in 1813 its vineyards numbered 1,000
acres of vines, only a little less than today.

At the start of the twentieth century, however, Chusclan
seemed to be marking time; it lacked a bottling and sales outlet for
its wine. This was corrected in 1939, when M. Joseph Rivier
founded the Cave Co-opérative de Chusclan. Now 134 members
cultivate about 1,340 acres of *Appellation* vines, under the
guidance of M. Rivier's successor, M. Jean Grangeon. Their best
rosé, the Cuvée de Marcoule, is named after the French atomic
station next to the village and comes in an attractive flute-shaped
bottle. Meanwhile a red wine has been made since 1961, and
whereas this represented nearly half the production in the early
1970s, now it accounts for 80 per cent with rosé sharply reduced to
13 per cent and white at 7 per cent. M. Rivier recalled why he
thought this turnabout had occurred: 'The name and fame of
Chusclan are founded on its rosé, and nowhere more so than in the
United States. But lately we've been encountering a resistance to
rosé from people who no longer want to drink it all through a meal.
Instead they now prefer a white wine followed by a red, which of
course leaves no room for the rosé.'

Chusclan rosé—made mainly from the Grenache and
Cinsault—is a delightful wine, superior in its class to the red, and
it is sad that it should be overlooked in this way. The Co-opérative
make their rosé to be drunk fresh and young, when all its fruit and
youthful vigour can be amply enjoyed. It has a pleasing pink-
orange colour, an agreeable roundness and a surprisingly clean,
dry aftertaste. Occasionally it can be a little too heady, with
around 14° alcohol by volume, and this can slightly unbalance the
wine's general harmony. None the less, the best Chusclan *cuvées*
outclass all the other Côtes du Rhône Villages rosés and can stand
with pride within reach of those of Tavel and Lirac.

The red wine is made from the customary selection of Côtes du
Rhône grapes, with the addition of one purely local plant, the
Camarèse. Fermented for about five days, and aged in cask for just
three or four months, it is a light-bodied, quite acceptable wine for
early drinking. It is not spectacular, but when at its best the wine
possesses a softness typical of its region and can be drunk
successfully until about its fourth birthday. The white wine,
meanwhile, has been made only since the mid-1970s, and the style

aimed for is fresh and lively, as befits a low temperature fermentation wine.

Leading Growers at Chusclan

Caves des Vignerons de Chusclan	30200 Chusclan
Cave Co-opérative de Codolet	30200 Codolet
Cave des Vignerons de St-Etienne-	
des-Sorts	30 St-Etienne-des-Sorts
Cave Co-opérative d'Orsan	30200 Orsan

LAUDUN

Laudun is one of the four oldest Côtes du Rhône Villages, having been allowed to use its name on its wine since 1953, when Gigondas (now a full *Appellation*), Cairanne and Chusclan were similarly promoted. It is also one of the Gard *département*'s oldest vineyards, for amphorae dating from 300 to 200 BC have been found on the Plateau du Camp de César immediately behind and above the village. Admittedly, these could have contained olive oil, but it is noticeable that around Laudun the vine has always been much more commonly cultivated than the olive.

The village is set against the hillside formed by the plateau cliff, and its vineyards spread out around and below it. The less important communities of St-Victor-la-Coste and Tresques are also permitted to share the Laudun *Appellation*, but their wine does not match up to that from Laudun itself. These are real 'backwater' villages that lie in the rambling, deserted hills south and west of Laudun; it requires a definite detour to visit either of them, and the uninhibited wide-eyedness of the locals when they see a stranger speaks for itself.

Probably the first organized wine-making at Laudun originated with the building of a medieval castle at the village, and in 1375 wine was sent from Laudun, via Codolet on the Rhône, to the papal cellars in Avignon. The date of this castle, which has long since disappeared, is not known, and the next reference to the wine surfaces in a local document of 1557. In this a M. Olivier de Serres is reported as describing 'the old Château of Laudun in Languedoc' as producing '*très-excellent vin*'. Obviously, the aristocratic

261

family inhabiting it had useful contacts overseas, for in 1561 a shipment of *vin de Laudun* was sent to a customer in Rome.

Thereafter the village wine continued to grow steadily in stature and renown. During the reign of King Henry IV (1589–1610), royal prospectors were sent to the South of France to seek out suppliers of silk for the ladies of the Court; there was then a flourishing silk trade at Laudun, but the prospectors found themselves equally charmed by the country wine and consequently returned to Paris laden with both commodities. Much of the wine at this time was white, and very highly regarded, for when King Louis XIII visited the region in 1629, he was presented with a barrel of white Laudun.

During the eighteenth century the wine's success naturally encouraged an enlargement of the vineyards, and in a register of 1774 Laudun was deemed to be the region's second largest producer of wine—after Roquemaure, but ahead of Tavel, for instance. By 1800 its vineyards totalled 1,750 acres and were mainly situated on the slopes immediately around the village. The plain below that runs eastwards was reserved for cereal plantation. Even then it was the white wine that continued to draw praise, and in 1816 the respected chronicler A. Jullien gave it warm mention in one of his books. By strange contrast, the red wine was barely ever spoken of, for the 1892 *Dictionnaire géographique et administratif de la France* also only mentioned the 'light, sparkling white wines of Laudun' in its brief description of the Gardois wines.

Today Laudun is quite a big, bustling place, since many of the nearby factory workers live there. Some of its old-world Provençal charm has therefore been lost, as the core of the old village is surrounded by an abrupt ring of modern houses. Wine and industry seem more or less compatible, however, and the village vineyards are still well cultivated.

Laudun's red, rosé and white wines are made mainly by three Cave Co-opératives (two near Laudun and one at St-Victor) and by a handful of private growers. The white wine, made from the Clairette and Roussanne grapes, continues to be well thought of and is unquestionably one of the best of the southern Rhône whites—second only to the leading names at Châteauneuf-du-Pape. Fortunately, it manages to escape the staleness that so quickly invades many regional white wines, and its simple freshness and pleasing fullness will last in abundance for two or three years. Pale straw-coloured, it is a wine that suits nearly all fish dishes.

The red remains the most widely made wine, and the very good Cave des Quatre Chemins makes five times more red than white, for instance. When they come from a good supplier, Laudun reds are very good; they have a bright red-purple colour and are generally well balanced, with a nicely constituted combination of fruit and spicy flavours. They are not wines intended for quiet sipping; their strength and depth of flavour make them suitable to be drunk with red meats and cheeses. The most notable vinifiers at Laudun are the Cave des Quatre Chemins, the Domaine Rousseau and the Domaine Pelaquié. The wine of all three is harmonious and good for drinking up until about its fourth or fifth birthday.

This is a change for the wine of the Pelaquié family, however. Until 1976 this *domaine* made a near-legendary wine under the guidance of old M. Joseph Pelaquié, the grandfather of the two boys now in charge of the *domaine*, Luc and Emmanuel. When he died M. Pelaquié had been with the Cave Co-opérative of St-Victor for fifty-five years, since he co-founded it in 1921, and he had instructed his grandsons to make their wine in precisely the old manner. Thus there would be a fermentation in contact with the skins for at least a month, as had been the practice in Châteauneuf-du-Pape when M. Pelaquié was a young man. Then, after anything from two to four years in cask, the wine would emerge with an enormous colour and extremely high tannin content, which, according to M. Pelaquié senior, would allow it to live for forty or fifty years '*sans aucun problème*'.

Now his grandsons have changed the style of vinification to be more in keeping with current-day attitudes, and with a massive replanting programme taking place in their 124-acre vineyard, they are no longer ageing their wine in cask, since they consider that this would give them too much extra work at a very busy time. Grenache will continue to be their basic vine, accounting for 60 per cent of the plantation, backed up by the Syrah, Mourvèdre, Cinsault and Counoise for the red wine. The brothers also find that they have a lot of work in the cellar matching up the wines from the three different plots that form the total vineyard. Although all the vines are on slopes, some grow on sandy soil, others on a combination of sand and clay and others on a gravelly top soil. The first vintages have been quite successful and have won some medals at wine fairs, while the *domaine* is also making a little very good white wine, whose freshness and pear-like aromas make it ideal for summer drinking.

Not a lot of rosé is made at Laudun, but the best of it is very good, almost on a par with better-known Chusclan. Its leading vinifiers are the Cave des Quatre Chemins and the Domaine Rousseau.

Leading Growers at Laudun

Rousseau, Louis et Fils	30290 Laudun
Cave des Quatre Chemins	
'Le Serre de Bernon'	30290 Laudun
Pelaquié, Luc et Emmanuel	30290 St-Victor-la-Coste
Estournel, Rémy	30290 St-Victor-la-Coste
GAEC Michel	
Domaine St-Pierre	30300 Tresques
Cave Co-opérative de St-Victor-la-	
Coste	30290 St-Victor-la-Coste
Cave des Vignerons de Laudun	30290 Laudun

ROAIX AND SÉGURET

Roaix and Séguret are two very attractive medieval villages, both lying near the Ouvèze river that runs southwards past Gigondas and across the Plan de Dieu plain. Linked since 1960 by a communal Cave Co-opérative near Séguret, they received the Villages *Appellation* in 1967.

The Ouvèze Valley is an old wine-producing area and was mentioned as such by Pliny in Book XIV of his *Natural History*, written around AD 77. Vine-growing was certainly an active pastime in the medieval era, for Séguret's local grandee, the Comte de Toulouse, was a noted vineyard owner in the thirteenth century. Very little else is recorded in later history about the making of wine at these villages, although we know that in 1817 only 45 acres of vines were formally declared as giving a harvest at Roaix; while Séguret had nearly 200 acres of vines, the value per hectolitre was noticeably higher at Roaix—28 francs as opposed to

20 francs. Mind you, the wine of Gigondas was going for only 22 francs a hectolitre in that year, so surely there must be hope for these small vineyards in the next century!

Nowadays the vineyards of both villages are generally grouped into small plots, as most of the *vignerons* also cultivate a wide range of fruit and vegetables; lately one or two growers have set up on their own, away from the generally all-embracing influence of the Cave Co-opérative, and one in particular, Nadine Latour, has shown what this area can produce by dint of careful vineyard and cellar control.

Séguret gives perhaps the best general view of the main southern Côtes du Rhône vineyards, for it is a village almost precisely sculpted into a rocky hillside that faces due west towards Orange. In summer the plain below becomes an enormous stretch of green that contains the leading Villages and Côtes du Rhône *domaine* wines of the Vaucluse *département*.

The red wine of the Cave Co-opérative of Roaix-Séguret is not particularly distinguished, and a better idea of the wine of these two villages can be derived from the two or three private *domaines* that in the last ten years have commenced their own bottling. Quite full-bodied and possessed of a cherry-red hue, these wines are attractively formed, very much in the mould of constant drinking companions rather than anything more grandiose. Those of Nadine Latour and Fernand Chastan should be drunk within three or four years. Meanwhile, a little white wine is made from the Grenache Blanc and the Clairette grapes, but it is no better than average.

Leading Growers at Roaix and Séguret

Chastan, Fernand	
Les Garrigues	84190 Gigondas
Lambert, Florimond	84110 Roaix
Latour, Nadine	
Domaine de Cabasse	84110 Séguret
Liautaud, Jean	
Domaine du Sommier	84110 Séguret
Meffre, Gérard	
La Fiole du Chevalier d'Elbène	84150 Violès
Cave Co-opérative de Roaix-Séguret	84110 Séguret

ROCHEGUDE

Rochegude lies in dense vine country 8 kilometres south-east of the industrial town of Bollène. Easily recognizable from a distance because of the outline of its elegant seventeenth-century *château*— now a luxury hotel—the village appears to stand guard over the massively arranged rows of vines that line up in every direction before it. The vines are 70 per cent Grenache, with the complement made up principally of Cinsault, Carignan, Syrah and Mourvèdre, and the nearly 2,000 acres of vineyards reach out across a short plain towards Suze-la-Rousse in the north and Ste-Cécile-les-Vignes in the east.

In the last century a different style of wine from today's red table wine was responsible for bringing the village a certain fame. The Marquis d'Aquéria imported some vine plants (which varieties are not specified) from Jerez and commenced making a white wine that would be sold when six years old; so famous did it become that Thomas Jefferson is said to have sent George Washington a few bottles.

Today it is the Cave Co-opérative, formed only in 1958, that bears the responsibility of harbouring the village's reputation. Around 32,500 hectolitres of all wine are made every year, and under the Villages denomination, which was granted in 1966, only red wine is allowed to be sold. Well scented, it is one of the better Villages wines, bearing a wholly welcome softness and concentration on fruitiness. The destalking of the grapes before fermentation (*égrappage*) and a flexible attitude to maturing in cask may well contribute towards this: thus very tannic wines receive a little over six months in cask, while the lighter vintages are kept for only a month or two in this way.

Ordinary Côtes du Rhône rosé and white wines are also made but can be fairly rough.

Leading Grower at Rochegude

Cave Co-opérative Vinicole de
    Rochegude   26130 Rochegude

SABLET

Sablet, the neighbour of Séguret and Gigondas, is a classic old fortified village. Extending away from its neat Romanesque bell tower, which incongruously tells the right time, its winding concentric streets and tunnelled archways lead through to splendid views on every side: the singularly shaped Dentelles Mountains, the long green ridge of umbrella pines that ends in the bumpy hillocks above Séguret and the massive Plan de Dieu wine plain. Promoted to Villages status in 1974, Sablet lives by its wine: under his counter the butcher has almost as good a collection of wines from the local *domaines* as has the village tasting *caveau*, while even the litter bins exhort passers-by to drink the red and rosé wines of Sablet!

Sablet used to be a papal possession and by the early sixteenth century was producing wine on a steady basis. By 1833 435 acres around the village contained vines, but the main local products were then the olive and the garance dye plant. Most of the wine was drunk by the villagers themselves.

The village gained prominence in the late nineteenth century, when a M. François-Frédéric Leydier of Sablet invented a machine for grafting American vine root stock on to French vines. This helped to halt phylloxera, which was then at its height, and M. Leydier's vice-like machine became a widespread bestseller.

As its name implies, Sablet is surrounded by mainly sandy ground. The success of the local vines on such sandy soil led to new plantations and experiments being tried along the Camargue coast west of Marseille, and today the Camargue produces large quantities of very respectable wine in addition to its traditional rice.

Sablet's Cave Co-opérative, 'Le Gravillas', was founded in 1935 and makes an acceptable red Villages wine. For long the centre of vinous attraction, it has been surpassed in recent years by the blossoming of several private *domaines* that have started to produce better, more stylized wine. One of the more unusual is M. Louis Chamfort's Domaine de Verquière, for while the trend of late in the Rhône has been away from prolonged ageing in cask, M. Chamfort has stuck doggedly to an extensive cellar ageing, so much so that in early 1982 he was still selling his 1975 vintage. M. Chamfort, an intelligent and active man in his early sixties, has done much to secure Sablet's Villages promotion by busily researching the community's past history, which he freely admits has not been exactly action-packed! Now, however, his wine seems to be losing its 'good drinking' tag and exchanging it for a 'curiosity' billing. It is made principally from the Grenache, Mourvèdre and Cinsault grapes which are grown on the 75 acres of vines that he has scattered around Sablet but is now put on sale when to most ordinary palates it is already oxidized; the brown colour and dried-out flavour tell their tale. This seems wasteful because the wine is in essence good but just too old.

In the past Sablet's other leading *domaine* has been the Château du Trignon, owned by M. Charles Roux, who, like several of the Sablet growers, also has a vineyard at Gigondas. The red wine is generally very sound, reflecting the style of Sablet wines, which tend to be a little more supple and feminine than their beefy neighbours from Gigondas. Their lighter red colour and occasionally strawberry-like flavour make them good partners for simple meat dishes or poultry, and they are best drunk before they are 4 years old. Names to look for, in addition to the Château du Trignon, are the Grangeons' Domaine du Parandou, Paul Roumanille and René Bernard.

Leading Growers at Sablet

Arène, Luc	
Domaine de la Marsane	84110 Sablet
Bernard, René	84110 Sablet
Chamfort, Louis et Fils	
Domaine de Verquière	84110 Sablet
Chassagne, F. et Fils	
Domaine du Pourras	84110 Sablet
Chauvin Frères	
Domaine Le Souverain	84110 Sablet
Grangeon, M. et Fils	
Domaine du Parandou	84110 Sablet
Roumanille, Paul	84110 Sablet
Roux, Charles	
Château du Trignon	84110 Sablet

ST-GERVAIS

Five kilometres or so north-west of Bagnols-sur-Cèze is the village of St-Gervais, which was promoted to Côtes du Rhône Village status in May 1974. It is an unassuming little community, made up of a clutter of tiny, light brown houses all built out of the local soft stone; some of the streets are said by the locals to be the width of a car, but the scarred walls testify to the trapping of all larger models. Bordered to the north by the outhills of the Ardèche, this somnolent village looks out across the short valley of the Cèze. There, a winding line of trees denotes the curling progress of the river, and the light green colours of the vines form a simple contrast with the dark green hills beyond the river. It is a world that could come from an artist's canvas, and odd splashes of red are occasionally added to it by fields of gently waving poppies.

St-Gervais's past has gone largely unrecorded, but *département* archives mention the fact that wine was being made there around the seventeenth century. By 1789 the local aristocrat, the Marquis de Guasc, was reported even to be bottling some of his wine, but this practice was terminated shortly afterwards when he ended up on the guillotine.

Today most of the vineyards run down from the hills behind the village and on to the river's edge. As is normal for this part of the Gard *département*, they are subjected to extremes of both heat and wind. In summer the *mistral* wind can be so violent that fierce flurries of dust coil constantly over the vines. Tractor drivers take to wearing thick goggles for protection against the dust and look for all the world like pioneer aviators.

Altogether there are 500 acres of *Appellation* vines, mainly Grenache and Cinsault. A lot of replanting has been undertaken since the early 1960s as the growers have worked hard to attain their Village status, and now there are very few low-grade or common vines to be found in the local clay–limestone soil.

Most of the wine is made by the village Cave Co-opérative, with only two private *domaines*. The Co-opérative, founded in 1924, groups together 158 members—not a bad number for a village of only 500 inhabitants! In winter it is sometimes almost deserted, as most of the *vignerons* are out pruning their vines, and the unwary visitor is likely to be surprised by the sight of M. le Directeur, Henri Roux, zooming up to the entrance of the Co-opérative on his ancient but admirably efficient bicycle. M. Roux has been with the Co-opérative since 1953 and has been responsible for helping the village to commence exporting its wines to Belgium and Holland. The Co-opérative red and rosé wines are generally pretty good, although their greatest fault is that they can be too light-bodied. The best *cuvées* are supple, well coloured and agreeably fruity, with a suggestion of blackcurrants; these reds should be drunk before they are 5 years old.

The Co-opérative's red wine is vinified on purely traditional lines, and, having been aged in concrete vats (the Co-opérative does not own any barrels), it is bottled roughly eighteen months after the harvest. In contrast to this, there is a private *domaine*, M. Guy Steinmaier's 64-acre Domaine Ste-Anne, which makes its wine with the sole intention of extracting as much fruit as quickly as possible from the grapes, which enter the vats whole. M. Steinmaier calls his process '*sémi-carbonique*', for he leaves the grapes to macerate for up to twelve days in closed vats. He relies on the Grenache (50 per cent) and the Syrah (20 per cent) as the main constituents of his wine, which is left in concrete vats for six to twelve months before bottling. Soft and fruity, his St-Gervais red is an attractive wine. He is also making a Côtes du Rhône *générique* white wine and has been experimenting with the plantation of all the Rhône 'classics'—the Bourboulenc, Roussanne, Marsanne, Clairette and Viognier. Such enterprise deserves its rewards, and M. Steinmaier already has a wide restaurant following in the region.

The red and rosé of St-Gervais are still very little-known even inside France itself. This situation should surely change, however, for even if their quality falls a little below the high standards of nearby Laudun and Chusclan, they are superior to some of the older-established Côtes du Rhône Villages from across the Rhône.

Leading Growers at St-Gervais

Steinmaier, Guy et Fils	
Domaine Ste-Anne	30200 St-Gervais
Cave Co-opérative de St-Gervais	30200 St-Gervais
GAEC Les Frères Pailhon	
Domaine Le Baine	30200 St-Gervais

ST-MAURICE-SUR-EYGUES

St-Maurice-sur-Eygues is a tiny, nondescript village, with a token fountain plonked down in its middle, that lies halfway along the main N94 road from Bollène to Nyons. Most of the community's life revolves around its Cave Co-opérative, which has 175 members. The River Eygues flows just south of the village, and most of the vineyards are situated on short slopes that line the northern part of the Eygues valley. As usual, the majority of the vines are Grenache, and can form as much as 80 per cent of the total plantation.

The wines of St-Maurice are generally of a reasonable quality. The Villages reds are given just three months in cask, less than used to be the case, and are all the better for it. They have a soft fruit flavour and honey-like sensation on the palate and, in the better vintages like 1979, are very acceptable. Some *cuvées* of the Co-opérative's Côtes du Rhône *générique* are aged for longer in wood, and these wines reflect more the traditional concept of the area as a producer of heavier-styled wines. The rosés are light and pretty unmemorable, while the little white wine made under the ordinary Côtes du Rhône label is typical of its region in being rather undistinguished.

Leading Grower at St-Maurice-sur-Eygues

Cave des Coteaux de St-Maurice-
    sur-Eygues   26650 St-Maurice-sur-Eygues

ST-PANTALÉON-LES-VIGNES and ROUSSET-LES-VIGNES

The villages of St-Pantaléon-les-Vignes and Rousset-les-Vignes are the two most north-easterly Côtes du Rhône Villages and are set against a ring of forbidding mountains that separate them from the early alpine settlements south of Die. The countryside at the foot of these mountains is suddenly verdant, for it is criss-crossed by a network of life-giving mountain streams. Many *vignerons* are therefore able to grow all their own vegetables and occasionally sell them further afield to regional markets.

As the village names imply, it is the vine that is predominant.

Until 1948 both villages made a wine known as Haut Comtat, but in that year the denomination was changed to the straightforward title of 'Côtes du Rhône'. In 1969, St-Pantaléon was promoted to Villages status, and Rousset followed suit in 1972. Now both wines are vinified at the Cave Co-opérative of St-Pantaléon, founded in 1960 and presided over since 1973 by the affable M. René Bernard. All the wine that the 220 members want bottled goes on to the Cellier des Dauphins bottling centre at Tulette.

Most of the vines are grown on flat clay and limestone ground all around the two communities. In places there are plots of vines on sloping land, and these grow on a mainly gravelly surface. Some 60 per cent of the vines are Grenache, and these are followed in importance by the Carignan, the Cinsault, the Syrah (on the increase) and the Mourvèdre. The Carignan is not used in the Villages wines, while M. Bernard interestingly gave the view that the Mourvèdre was not at its best in these vineyards near the alpine foothills.

A little over 180,000 litres, which represents the best wine from the two Villages, is bottled every year. This amounts to about 240,000 bottles, which leaves the Cave Co-opérative with little sales or export latitude. Their Villages red wine is vinified in a traditional way but is never aged in cask. Neither is it ever very dark-coloured, like the big Vaucluse Villages wines from places like Vacqueyras and Cairanne, and it is softer in style too. It should be drunk before it is 4 years old, with red or white meats, but preferably the latter—veal or pork, for example. The ubiquitous gastronome Curnonsky was acquainted even with the wine of St-Pantaléon, and in one of his diaries he praised it highly.

The Co-opérative also make a Côtes du Rhône *générique* blend, which they age in 225-litre casks, all smartly laid out underneath their bottle store and bought from a Burgundian cooperage. These wines are also respectable. As for the little rosé made, the best advice is that it should be avoided, while the recently launched white Côtes du Rhône, made from Grenache Blanc, Clairette and a very little Bourboulenc, would benefit in the first instance from its vines being more mature.

The Cave Co-opérative is the only producer in these two villages bottling any of the local wine; there are four private growers in St-Pantaléon, but they send their wine to merchants, while all the growers in Rousset belong to the Co-opérative.

Leading Grower at St-Pantaléon-les-Vignes and Rousset-les-Vignes

Union des Producteurs de
St-Pantaléon-les-Vignes et
Rousset-les-Vignes   26230 St-Pantaléon-les-Vignes

SÉGURET *see* ROAIX AND SÉGURET

VACQUEYRAS

Lying on the main D7 road between Gigondas and Beaumes-de-Venise is the village of Vacqueyras, the home of one of the best red Côtes du Rhône Villages wines. With many of its vineyards directly bordering upon Gigondas, it is not surprising that the general quality of Vacqueyras's wine is high; there is also a long-established tradition to help the village, since records show that as far back as 1414 there was an 'extensive' vineyard in the immediate neighbourhood. Little else has ever been recorded about the local wine, except that in the late sixteenth century a municipal decree had to be passed authorizing the full-scale protection of the vineyards from attacks by itinerant goats. Curiously, these animals were more partial to the ripening grapes than were the village children, and the legislation against them was suitably severe.

The village has had a quiet past, and when reminiscing the *vignerons* invariably turn to the story of Vacqueyras's most illustrious citizen, the Provençal troubador, Raimbaud. Born in 1180, the son of the village idiot, Raimbaud possessed great musical talent and charmed many a noble lady to his bedside with his deeply entrancing madrigals: indeed, these were of sufficient quality to secure him a royal appointment as Governor of Salonica. Alas, Raimbaud's success was brief, for he was killed in 1207 when fighting the Turks. The village is very proud of this rags-to-riches story, and in honour of it the Cave Co-opérative was named 'Le Troubadour' upon its foundation in 1957.

Vacqueyras's red wine surpasses all others in the Côtes du Rhône Villages with the exception of Cairanne. It is vinified mostly in the traditional way, although some growers, like the Cave du Troubadour and the Domaine des Lambertins, have taken to using the *macération carbonique* method for a part of their wine.

The *Appellation* has more private bottlers than any other Village, which makes for an interesting variety in the style and quality of the wines. Among the best *domaines* are Roger Combe's Domaine de la Fourmone, Edouard Dusser-Beraud's Château des Roques, Le Parc Alazard Père et Fils' Domaine de la Colline St-Jean, Domaine Pascal Frères, A. Chastan et Fils' Domaine de la Jaufrette and Arnoux's 'Le Vieux Clocher'. All these *domaines* make wines of good quality and elegance, it being particularly worthwhile to compare the Fourmone and the Château des Roques side by side: the former with its emphasis on balance and a flowery, perhaps violets-inspired flavour, the latter with the dark brooding *goût de terroir* aromas commonly associated with this area and a tremendous cherry black hue, a wine to accompany strong meat or game and not to be touched until its fourth year. Both are very good wines and quicken the wine lover's pulse with the knowledge that the even better Gigondas and Châteauneuf-du-Pape are now not very far away.

Roger Combe of Domaine La Fourmone is an exceptional man, for he speaks Provençal fluently and also writes poetry in the local dialect. This he learned from his family, at a time when there were no organized classes in the village schools, and he is proud enough of his region and origins to put Provençal phrases on his labels; thus his Vacqueyras label carries the words '*Raco Racejo*', which means that the race perpetuates or that the father and son resemble each other. In this respect he is fortunate to have both his son and his daughter helping to make and sell the family wine, made from 40 acres at Vacqueyras and 22 acres at Gigondas. Although he vinifies in a classical manner, his light crushing of the grapes plays up his intention of achieving an elegant style of wine. He is also uncommon among Vaucluse growers in his decision not to fine or filter following a six- to twelve-month ageing in cask. M. Combe makes a little rosé and white in ordinary Côtes du Rhône but justifiably concentrates his efforts on his red, which he considers should be drunk by the time it is 6 or 7 years old in the case of Gigondas and 4 or 5 years old in the case of Vacqueyras.

Wines from the majority of the other *domaines* carry a strong

274

purple colour and are big boys indeed, with a powerful depth of flavour that is typically found in wines of this area of the Vaucluse *département*. In the wine of a lesser grower this *goût de terroir* can amount to a definite harshness on the palate. The best wines, however, have a striking complexity of burnt flavours, spices and a scent that some growers consider akin to raspberries. When drunk between 4 and 7 years old, they display much softness and length of finish but should not be kept much longer, as a marked fading deriving from the high percentage of Grenache sets in. Fortunately, it is the red that forms the large part of the wine at Vacqueyras, since the rosés and whites can be utterly unreliable and should be generally avoided.

Leading Growers at Vacqueyras

Combe, Roger et Fils
  Domaine La Fourmone   84190 Vacqueyras
Dusser-Beraud, Edouard
  Château des Roques   84260 Sarrians
Archimbaud-Vache
  Clos des Cazaux   84190 Vacqueyras
Arnoux et Fils
  Le Vieux Clocher   84190 Vacqueyras
Bernard, Albert et Lucien
  Domaine de la Garrigue   84190 Vacqueyras
Cave des Vignerons 'Le Troubadour'   84190 Vacqueyras
Chastan, A. et Fils   84100 Orange,
  Domaine de la Jaufrette   Bois Lauzon
Dusserre-Audibert, Jean
  Domaine de Montvac   84190 Vacqueyras
Faraud, Jean-Pierre
  Domaine du Pont du Rieu   84190 Vacqueyras
GAEC Le Parc Alazard Père et Fils
  Domaine de la Colline St-Jean   84190 Vacqueyras
Lambert Frères
  Domaine des Lambertins   84190 Vacqueyras
Marseille, Pierre
  Domaine de Chantegut   84260 Sarrians
Mayre, Rémy
  Le Mousquetaire   84190 Vacqueyras

Mourre, Gilbert
   Domaine Le Colombier   84190 Vacqueyras
Pascal Frères   84190 Vacqueyras
Ricard Père et Fils
   Domaine du Couroulou   84190 Vacqueyras
Ricard, Jean
   Cave Jean Ricard   84190 Vacqueyras
SCA Le Clos de Caveau   84190 Vacqueyras

VALRÉAS

Strategically placed on the top of a hill, and protected by a ring of mountains to the north, east and south, Valréas is on the N541 road, about 25 kilometres east of Donzère and the Rhône. It is a compact town, built within the confines of a circular boulevard and against the slope of its hillside. At the top of the hill stand a fine twelfth-century church and a renovated eighteenth-century *château*. The church possesses a splendid organ, originally built in 1506, on which young enthusiasts are allowed to practise freely, and some of its oldest corner towers are respectfully dedicated to St Vincent, the patron of wine-growers.

Valréas used to be one of four villages that formed a papal enclave inside France from 1317 until 1791; even today the four villages—Valréas, Grillon, Richerenches and Visan—have maintained their separate identity, for all are officially situated in the Vaucluse *département* even though they are completely surrounded by the *département* of the Drôme. This represents quite an anomaly for the French administration, which ever since the establishment of the *Code Napoléon* has organized its *départements* to be neatly adjacent with one another: in this case, however, history and precedent have prevailed.

During the fourteenth century the Popes resident in Avignon were given to casting rapacious looks over the surrounding countryside, and whenever possible land acquisitions were made at suitably nominal prices. Consequently, in 1317 the sharp-minded Pope John XXII retrieved the extravagant Dauphin of France from financial ruin by paying him 6,000 *livres* for the village of Valréas. In 1320 Pope John continued his good work and succeeded in actually being given Richerenches: this usefully extended his property outside Avignon and gave him another source of wine, for the Knights Templar had for 200 years been making wine from their base there.

By 1383 the papacy had bought the other two villages of Visan and Grillon and found itself with a 200-square-kilometre enclave conveniently situated about 65 kilometres from Avignon—a very useful fallback if ever trouble should arise in the papal city. The wisdom of this acquisition was amply demonstrated a little later, when the papacy returned definitively to Rome and yet the papal enclave remained intact on French territory, an undoubted bugbear to successive French monarchs. It was not until 1791 that the enclave finally returned to French hands, following the victory of the revolutionary army from Avignon over the gathered enclave forces at Sarrians, near Carpentras.

Wine has long been made at Valréas and in its early days was largely the responsibility of the Church. A statement by the Bishop of Vaison-la-Romaine in 1262 mentioned the vines of Valréas, and later documents of 1298 and 1316 point to the quite extensive cultivation of the vine around the village. By the start of the nineteenth century Valréas had become one of the largest wine-making communities of the Vaucluse *département*, with its vineyards covering nearly 1,325 acres.

Today Valréas makes wine—and cardboard boxes. Almost half the town works in the carton industry, which originated in the last century when boxes were needed for transporting the silk thread that was produced locally on an extensive scale. And still the inhabitants possess a strong sense of an identity apart: in 1974 they formed a grouping known as the Union of Wine Growers of the Enclave des Papes. This is a centre that bottles Cave Co-opérative and private *domaine* wine from anywhere within the old papal territory. There is a strict rule that no outside wine is allowed, as the *vignerons* are anxious to emphasize their separate nature.

The Valréas vineyards now cover 3,500 acres, and all the important Côtes du Rhône grape varieties are included in the plantation. Many of the vines grow on gentle inclines, rather than full slopes, and it is noticeable that the soil can change quite sharply from one plot to the next. Generally, there is a mixture of clay and limestone, with a sprinkling of rounded pebbles on the surface. This sparse ground is ideal for vines, as well as for olive trees and lavender plants, which are grown in lesser numbers.

Valréas possesses a well-known Cave Co-opérative under the capable direction of M. Georges Amic, who talked about the progress made since its foundation in 1928: 'We've come a long way since then,' he said, 'when our annual production was 9,900 hectolitres. Today we make on average over 90,000 hectolitres, of which about half qualifies for Côtes du Rhône *générique* and 4 per cent, or 3,825 hectolitres, qualifies for Valréas Villages. The granting of the Villages status in 1967 was a great boost to our 500 members, and they are now much more inclined to undertake "progressive" replanting in their vineyards. By "progressive" I mean that plants like the Syrah and the Cinsault are more in favour than the Carignan; they may produce less, but they give a better class, softer wine.' The red wine of the Cave Co-opérative 'La Gaillarde' fits into the category of reasonably made wines from large-scale sources that are quite frequently available in the southern Rhône. It should not be kept more than about four years, however.

Valréas has a number of thriving wine *domaines* that are helping to spread the *Appellation*'s name to a wider public, of which the most interesting is undoubtedly Le Val des Rois, owned by M. Romain Bouchard, who comes from the famous Burgundian family that has been making wine since 1681. 'The trouble was that there were too many of us,' said M. Bouchard, a lean man in his fifties, whose ruddy-brown face testifies to an outdoor life in the vineyards. 'I was the first of the family to leave Burgundy, and until 1964 actually grew oranges in southern Morocco, which I expect raised a few eyebrows at home! When I came back to France, I did a brush-up wine course near Lausanne and bought this domaine, Le Val des Rois. Most of the vines were over 50 years old, so I replanted from scratch using the Grenache, Syrah and Cinsault at a novel distance of 3 metres apart, so that I could work the slopes with machinery. I have also recently planted a little Gamay on the higher vineyards, at 400 metres, and am very pleased with the result—these vines have given a wine with an enormous blackcurrant aroma.'

M. Bouchard's Val des Rois domaine covers 30 acres and runs alongside the Vinsobres property that now belongs to Thiérry Bouchard, his brother. He regards wine as just as much an intellectual as an agricultural challenge and calls himself the

'Provençal surgeon from a Burgundian family'. By this he means that his vinification process runs along Burgundian lines, whereas in the vineyards he generally follows the local customs. Hence he destalks all the grapes before fermentation, which itself never lasts more than six days. His Villages wine from Valréas may spend up to one year in enamel-lined vats before bottling; he has given up ageing it in wood, seeking a very steady evolution of the young fruit flavours, and will go as far as making a rendezvous to drink a bottle of his best vintages like the 1978 after ten years. Supple and easy to drink, these wines have more distinction than most of the traditionally made local Villages wines.

M. Bouchard thinks that there lies a very subtle difference between the wines of Valréas and Vinsobres, where he used also to own a property. He described it in the following way: 'I believe this difference is most apparent in the respective wines' fruit. A Valréas seems to me vaguely evocative of flowers on its bouquet, while a Vinsobres red wine has more a suggestion of blackcurrants. But you wait and see, I'll confuse the lot of you—and probably myself—when I start integrating some Gamay into my Villages wine. Ten per cent is allowed, and I am coming round to the view that here the grape variety plays perhaps a more important role in the constitution of the wine than does the soil make-up.'

A little Valréas rosé is made in addition to the red wine, mainly by the private *domaines*. A fairly dry and fruity wine, it is good for relaxed summer drinking. A selection of the *domaine* wines is available at the Château de Simiane, which is the *Mairie* at Valréas, and here visitors are able to taste and discern the radical difference in style that exists between the lighter, fruity approach of Le Val des Rois and the old-fashioned, woody type of wine made by Léo Roussin at his Domaine de la Fuzière. Between these two come the sound *domaines* of Grands Devers and La Prévosse.

Leading Growers at Valréas

Bouchard, Romain
    Le Val des Rois   84600 Valréas
Bonnefoy,
    Notre Dame de Vieille   84600 Valréas
Davin, Henri
    Domaine de la Prévosse   84600 Valréas

Gras, André	
Domaine de St-Chetin	84600 Valréas
Laurent, Maurice	84600 Valréas
Pouizin, Pierre	84600 Valréas
Roussin, Léo	
Domaine de la Fuzière	84600 Valréas
Sayn, André	
Cours de la Recluse	84600 Valréas
Sinard, René	
Domaine des Grands Devers	84600 Valréas
Cave Co-opérative	
'La Gaillarde'	84600 Valréas

VINSOBRES

Vinsobres is a typically dormant little brown Provençal village, full of narrow streets, gossiping old-timers and softly flowing fountains. Situated about 30 kilometres east of Bollène along the course of the Eygues Valley, it is one of the more senior Côtes du Rhône Villages, having been allowed to use its own name on its wine since 1957. Its main point of interest lies in its two Caves Co-opératives; these stand some way out of the village, which is thereby deprived of the activity of everyday life, though this matters little to the inhabitants of Vinsobres, who nearly all work in the vineyards anyway.

Vinsobres is an old wine village. Around the fourth century AD Vinsobrium is thought to have been in the hands of the Voconces tribe, who would make wine from the sloping fields around the village. References to this wine, and the fact that it was later mostly made by the Church and local *seigneur*, appear in local documents throughout the Middle Ages; then, in 1633, the Bishop of Vaison-la-Romaine, one Monseigneur de Suarès, came up with a quotation that has never been forgotten by the grateful people of Vinsobres, so conveniently suited is it to the world of twentieth-century advertising. The Bishop's words were:

> *Vin Sobre ou Sobre Vin*
> *Prenez le Sobrement.*[1]

[1] *Sober Wine or Wine of Sobriety,*
Take it soberly.

280

What is most noticeable about this saying is that it only rhymes when spoken in a strong Provençal accent, whereby the final words become 'vaing' and 'sobremaing'!

During the eighteenth century the vineyards extended to as many as 520 acres, a figure that held constant and even rose slightly before the attack of phylloxera, which was apparently more severe than normal at Vinsobres. Vineyard reconstruction did not begin on any scale until 1905, but it gradually accelerated and today has reached the healthy size of around 3,000 acres, spread chiefly over an 8-kilometre strip either side of the River Eygues.

The older Cave Co-opérative, the 'Vinsobraise', was founded in 1949 and now has 300 members, who contribute towards an average total of 75,000 hectolitres of wine, from ordinary table wine up, every year. Over three-quarters of this wine is red, and most of it is sold by the Cellier des Dauphins bottling and marketing centre at Tulette, 15 kilometres away. Usually it passes under the ordinary 'Côtes du Rhône' label, without the 'Vinsobres', and is of a very medium standard.

In 1959 a second Co-opérative, the Cave du Prieuré, was formed. This concerns itself solely with ageing and selling the Vinsobres Village wine, some of which is already exported to Switzerland, Germany, Belgium and Britain. The Co-opérative takes in the wine from its ninety-five *vigneron* members around Easter after the harvest and ages it in both large and small casks. Ageing of the wine lasts for up to two years; it is difficult to escape the feeling that this is too long. Often the red wine of the Prieuré tastes rather 'stewed' or hot and even seems to smell of wood; it would possibly be more suitable to age it for under a year, as some of the private *domaines* do with their wine, which is often clearly better balanced.

Situated in and around the Vinsobres *Appellation* area are about six private *domaines*, but because of a change in the *Appellation* laws that occurred during the mid-1970s, the best of them is no longer making Vinsobres Villages wine. M. Claude Jaume, a forward-thinking man with an impeccable, modern cellar, explained why: 'Before I could make 35 hectolitres per hectare [1,400 litres per acre] of Villages wine that would obviously fetch higher Villages rates, as well as being able to sell excess production up to 50 hectolitres as Côtes du Rhône

281

générique: so, 35 hectos of Villages and 15 hectos of *générique*. Now I am no longer allowed to sell the excess above 35 hectos as anything other than *vin de pays*, for which I get much less money. I therefore prefer to produce my 50 hectos per hectare and sell them all as Côtes du Rhône *générique*, and be done.'

M. Jaume's attitude is one that is both understandable and ever more common in the southern Rhône Valley. The rules do not seem to be encouraging quality in this instance, for it is with the more indifferent wine-makers that extra production of Côtes du Rhône *générique* becomes out of place in an area already bursting at the seams with this class of wine.

Of those *domaines* that still make and bottle Vinsobres Villages wine, the better ones are the Domaine les Aussellons and the Domaine du Coriançon. It is their red wines that are of most interest, for although a little rosé is made by most of the growers, it is not usually very distinguished, tending to be over-alcoholic and needing maximum cooling in order to be more or less palatable. Even less white wine is made, and this is often very uneven.

Leading Growers at Vinsobres

Ezingeard
    Domaine les Aussellons   84110 Villedieu
Vallot, François
    Domaine du Coriançon   26490 Vinsobres
Bouchard, N.
    Domaine de la Bicarelle   26490 Vinsobres
Durma, Fernand
    Domaine St-Vincent   26490 Vinsobres
Vallot, Xavier
    Domaine des Escoulaires   26490 Vinsobres
Vinson, Jean
    Domaine du Moulin   26490 Vinsobres
La Cave du Prieuré   26490 Vinsobres
Cave Co-opérative 'La Vinsobraise'   26490 Vinsobres

VISAN

Inside the Enclave des Papes and 22·5 kilometres north-east of Orange is the charming old village of Visan. Once noted for its *château*, which was destroyed in the sixteenth-century wars of religion, the medieval village stands on a small hill a little apart from most of today's habitations. A series of narrow stone archways lead into the sandy-coloured upper part of the village, where stands a cluster of crooked old houses, some festooned with climbing wisteria and vine plants, others connected to one another by shaky-looking overhead passages. These circular streets and neat archways are impressive reminders of the well guarded prosperity of former ages, when first one single family owned the whole village, then it was divided between the Baux and Dauphin families. By the fourteenth century it was the Church that possessed most of the village, including its already flourishing vineyards.

It is thought that wine-making extends even further back in history, for when the Cave Co-opérative was being built in 1937, several coins, pots and jars dating from the time of Augustus and Hadrian were unearthed. It is not certain that these pots and jars were used for wine, of course, but the local *vignerons* typically have no doubts about it!

By 1250 a village wine press was spoken of in contemporary archives, and at roughly the same time the church of Notre Dame des Vignes was built near the road to St-Maurice-sur-Eygues. Tucked away in a tiny grove of evergreens in the middle of a vineyard, the church undoubtedly drew its name from its location. Even today it has a deep significance for the local wine-making community, and every year on 8 September there is a pilgrimage to it. Three religious masses are performed, and there is a general blessing of the vineyards. Out of respect for the pilgrimage, the *vignerons* of Visan never do any work on that day, and many of them take part in the services and the carefree buffet that follows.

Wine-making at Visan for many years revolved almost entirely around the village Cave Co-opérative. Although this was not founded until 1937, wine had been made on its premises for forty years previously. In 1897 the local Delaye family decided to expand their cellars in order to cater for a larger production and took over a site on the edge of the village. By 1912 the private cellars were extremely well equipped, with novel glass-lined vats being used for fermentation and storage of young wine and the old wooden barrels serving to mature all the red wine. Sales outlets were no problem, since M. Delaye ran a successful restaurant in the suburbs of Paris; by the outbreak of the First World War his *vin des Côtes du Rhône* had become very popular in the capital.

Before 1937 most of the local growers had started to send their grapes to M. Delaye, and when he died in that year a group of eighty-eight of them bought the Cave from his widow. The cellars were once more expanded, and today there are 365 contributors to the Co-opérative, which is directed by the capable M. Jean Ordener.

Out of a total annual crop of about 100,000 hectolitres, the Cave makes roughly 10,000 hectolitres of Visan Villages wines, which are all vinified apart in an adjoining building. M. Ordener explained the advantage of this set-up: 'This allows us to select carefully all the harvested grapes according to which part of the vineyard they have come from. You see, we use most of the slope grapes for our Villages wines: these are generally riper and more healthy than the grapes from the plain vines. Our members have also increased their plantation of the Syrah in recent years, so that I would estimate that as much as 30 per cent of our Villages wine is made up of it, while Grenache has decreased to 60 per cent of the blend. Cinsault and Mourvèdre are the other principal grapes used.

'We are now also vinifying around 2,500 hectolitres by the *macération carbonique* method, for which it's really essential to have grapes that are in prime condition. Because of this, I'm very careful about using *macération*, as I tend to feel that it has become too popular too quickly.'

Since the second half of the 1970s the Co-opérative's thunder has been stolen by two *domaines* who have set out to bottle as much as possible of their very good wine. The Domaine de la Cantharide is exceptional, in that it is owned and very actively run by a girl in her twenties, Janine Roux. Dark-haired, charming and blessed with a winning smile, she emerged from pruning the vineyards in the teeth of a savage January *mistral* gale to explain part of the tale behind her *domaine*. The fact that she was five months pregnant seemed not to slow her down in the slightest: 'I designed the cellar in 1977 and decided to start bottling some of our harvest straight away. I didn't want to get too carried away with bottling all the crop, especially in indifferent years like 1981, when the wines lacked acidity, so ideally we bottle around 60 per cent of our wine. The vineyard runs all around the little chapel of Notre Dame des Vignes, which I think should bring us some good luck, and our vines extend as far as the line of low hills that separate Visan from the Eygues Valley.

'Our soil here is mainly clay, and my husband and I have both found that grapes grown on this soil don't seem to lend themselves to the *macération carbonique* process. We undertake a traditional fermentation, with no destalking and a very light crushing just to break the grape skins a little. We vinify in stainless-steel tanks and leave the wine at least two years in concrete before bottling.'

The Cantharide vineyard is three-quarters composed of Grenache and Syrah, and their best *cuvées* are those composed of Grenache-Syrah and Grenache-Mourvèdre. These show a brilliant red colour and their lurking raspberry fruitiness is backed up by an agreeable tannic firmness that makes them a cut above the normal local Villages wine. Watch out for Cantharide and Janine Roux!

The other domaine, Clos du Père Clément, is owned by M. Henri Depèyre and his sons, who displayed a rare reluctance, bordering on total suspicion, to answer any questions about their neatly laid-out property. Their smart *domaine* house is 300 years old, and its varnished doors and shutters point to a recent restoration, while the vineyards, set in a mainly clay soil, carry a rose at the end of each row. Their vineyards were planted in stages from 1972 onwards, and now they bottle all their Visan Villages, which is 100 per cent red wine. Like the Domaine de la Cantharide, they ferment in stainless-steel tanks, but only put their ordinary Côtes du Rhône *générique* in cask; the Villages red is stocked in underground concrete vats for two years before being released for sale.

Since 1979 one quarter of their wine has been made by *macération carbonique*, but the traditional blends are much more interesting. As a reflection of the area, they are very fruity, the sensation being one of raspberries, but there is also the presence of tannin at the end to give the wine a little more punch.

All the Visan red wines reflect the strong heat that is generated in the local countryside during the summer months and consequently carry an alcohol degree that runs from 12·5 to 14. However, this does not overwhelm the well made wines of the Domaines Cantharide and Père Clément, whose best recent vintages have been the 1978 and 1979. These should be drunk before they are 5 or 6 years old.

Visan obtained its Villages status in 1966, and red, rosé and white wines are sold under that name. The red is much the best wine, for the rosé often lacks balance through being too alcoholic and rather hard-tasting, while the white wine is largely un-distinguished. The Cave Co-opérative says that some of its members have just started to plant Bourboulenc vines, but only an optimist would see this as rescuing what is a very mediocre wine.

Leading Growers at Visan

Laget-Roux
    Domaine de la Cantharide   84820 Visan
Depèyre Frères
    Clos du Père Clément   84820 Visan
Domaine de Costechaude   84820 Visan
Cave Co-opérative
    'Les Coteaux de Visan'   84820 Visan

Côtes du Rhône Villages Vintages

1955   Excellent.
1956   Poor.
1957   Very good.
1958   Good. Wines that were generally well balanced.
1959   Only mediocre. The wines tended to be too light.
1960   Mediocre. Undistinguished, light-bodied wines.
1961   Excellent; full-bodied, sound wines.
1962   Good; the wines were lighter than the 1961s, and so unfortunately suffered by unfair comparison.
1963   Very poor.
1964   Very good. Strong, tannic wines.
1965   Poor.
1966   Good. The wines were supple and well balanced.
1967   Excellent. A really strong-bodied vintage, the wines had abundant bouquet and great all-round charm.
1968   Very poor. Light wines.
1969   Very good. Sound, appealing wines.

1970   Excellent. Very full wines, with ample bouquet and strong appeal.

1971   A very good vintage. Pleasant, quite full wines that were better in the Gard *département* than in the Vaucluse or the Drôme.

1972   Generally a good year. The red wines were quite rich and possessed good balance.

1973   A mediocre vintage. The wines tended to be unevenly coloured and lacking in fullness.

1974   An average year. The wines were generally lacking in colour, and were sometimes low in alcohol content. The Gard *département* wines were on the whole a shade better than the others.

1975   Poor. Both the reds and the whites suffered from lack of balance and lightness of colour.

1976   Good. The red wines developed quite well, although they possessed less staying power than was at first thought likely. The most backward wines from Villages like Cairanne and Vacqueyras are now losing some of their fruit.

1977   Poor. Most of the wines were lightly coloured and deficient in flavour, despite there being only a small harvest. The reds should by now have been drunk.

1978   Very good indeed. The vintage was successful throughout the Villages area, with the growers around Vacqueyras, Cairanne and the best *générique* growers from the Drôme *département* obtaining some really full blooded *cuvées* of big, slow-maturing wine. Such wines as these are good for drinking now, and will remain in good order until around 1984–5.

1979   Very good in most of the Côtes du Rhône area. The Vaucluse *département* came up with the best wines, which possess perhaps a little more charm than the harder 1978s. They will be good for drinking up to about 1984. Slightly less successful in the Gard *département*, where the wines were sometimes rather light.

1980   A variable vintage. There were some very good wines made by the better growers, but also too much low end of the market wine that was pale and weak. The leading *domaines* in the Vaucluse and the Drôme succeeded in making well balanced wines with good richness and follow-through, while the Gard *département* growers' wines were characterized by a good harmony and an easy accessibility of style that deem them good for drinking in their first three years.

1981   Generally a difficult year. The summer weather was variable all over the Rhône Valley, and many of the wines have resulted out of balance and rather lacking in depth. An unmemorable vintage, one that should be drunk without ceremony before 1984.

16

Côtes du Rhône

Côtes du Rhône is the best-known wine in the lower Rhône Valley because, quite simply, it accounts for over 80 per cent of all the *Appellation* wine made between Vienne and Avignon. This represents the region's backbone but not its pennant. Most Côtes du Rhône is an unpretentious country wine that is sometimes very good, sometimes very bad but nearly always pretty drinkable. It is also the wine of the small grower—the farmer whose family have long tilled their own little plot of ground, producing vegetables, fruit and staple family needs, as well as a little wine to wash it all down.

Such small growers today put their trust in their local Caves Co-opératives, which since the 1920s have directly aided the fortunes of the many little 'Clochemerle'-type villages all over southern France. The Co-opérative has at the same time become an important social unit, a forum and point of contact for the whole community, and, according to its far-sightedness, a prestigious link with the outside world, be it in France or overseas.

Among the whole range of Co-opératives, which in the Rhône Valley number just over sixty-five, there are a handful that are very good, a lot that are respectable and others that barely deserve to have their product called 'wine'. The very good Co-opératives, such as those at Gigondas, Tavel, Cairanne and Laudun, are often rightly known for their principal *Appellation* or Villages wine, but they serve a valuable purpose in helping to break down the consumer's somewhat natural resistance to wines that come from one mass source, as they inevitably must when emanating from a Cave Co-opérative. Meanwhile, since the mid-1960s there has been a perceptible change in attitude in many Co-opératives, which have made themselves much more efficiently organized than ever before. Qualified wine chemists are employed in the more prominent Co-opératives, and marketing and sales know-how seems to have risen directly in proportion to the quality of the wine.

The Côtes du Rhône *Appellation* differs from the Villages in that it is less demanding over how much wine may be made per acre, how much alcohol the wine must contain and what grapes should be allowed to be grown. Thus the Côtes du Rhône (called locally the *Appellation générique*) is permitted to produce a maximum of 5,000 litres per hectare (equivalent to 2,699 bottles per acre), whereas the Villages are restricted to 3,500 litres per hectare (equivalent to 1,889 bottles per acre). Obviously, the less wine that is drawn from a given unit of land, the more concentrated and better it will be.

Plain Côtes du Rhône wines need only contain 11 per cent alcohol by volume, while the Villages are fixed at 12·5 per cent for the red wines and 12 per cent for the rosés and the whites. There is, of course, nothing to stop the *vigneron* from making a wine of naturally higher degree: one of the best ways of doing this is by growing higher-grade vines like the Grenache or the Syrah, which are the backbone grapes of the southern and northern Rhône respectively. Thus growers making red wine in the Villages category must use a maximum of 65 per cent Grenache and a minimum of 25 per cent of one, two or all three of the Syrah, Cinsault and Mourvèdre, all of which are regarded as 'improver' grape varieties. No such demand is made of the *générique* growers, who must merely conform to growing a wide selection of vines termed 'noble' as opposed to hybrid, at the same time restricting their Carignan plantation to under 30 per cent (10 per cent for the Villages); the Carignan is the mass-producing vine found all over the Midi and Languedoc regions of France. Its wines are not distinguished and can often be hard and sharp-tasting.

The laws on vineyard plantation are sensible and well balanced, for it takes decades first to change country people's outlook and then to enact such a change when as complicated and extended a task as replanting a vineyard is considered. In such circumstances room has still been left for the individual who may wish to pursue his hunch or his whim over what vine goes well in what soil, so that a Côtes du Rhône *générique* can still be made from grapes such as the Picpoul, Roussanne or Viognier if it is white, or from the

Gamay, Pinot Noir or Terret Noir, for instance, if it is red. Decreeing that a minimum total of 25 per cent should come from three good-quality grapes in the making of Villages red wine is likewise intended to reflect on growers who will also be making *générique* wines. They do not have to grow all three grapes, however; not every grower may agree that the Syrah is necessarily suited to the southern Rhône valley, with particular reference to parts of the Vaucluse *département*, but then some current schools of thought in California imply that the vine is the all-important factor and the soil it grows in only secondary. Such is the appealing diversity of opinion that will maintain wine-making as a thoughtful and challenging art, to which there is no pat solution, for centuries to come.

It is also worth mentioning that the Côtes du Rhône *générique* region has not as yet been successful in making rosé and white wines of the general quality of the reds. The whites, in particular, are generally very mediocre and have an alarming tendency to 'go off'—to turn dark yellow and taste stale—within a year or two of their harvest. Admittedly, no switched-on grower is necessarily going to devote his life, time and money to cracking the problem of white Côtes du Rhône, but tasting of even the best white Châteauneuf-du-Papes and Lauduns does indicate that this area seems less well equipped to produce white wine than either reds or rosés. While the rosés are generally superior to the whites, with them much depends on the geography of their place of origin and the skill of their vinifier. The Gard *département* is certainly the best area for rosés.

Below are mentioned a random cross-section of Côtes du Rhône *domaines*, *négociants* and Cave Co-opératives. Since the early 1970s there has been a gratifying advance in the number of *vignerons* prepared to undertake their own vinification and bottling, and although some fairly awful surprises are in store for the dedicated investigator, many good discoveries can be made. The choice now, in the early 1980s, is so much larger that importers should have no justification for not quoting a good private Côtes du Rhône *domaine* on their list. While the Vaucluse *département* still produces the richest, most complex wines with great depth of flavour and punch, the Gard *département vignerons* have been the most active in recent years in combining a new independence from the Cave Co-opératives or the *négociants* with a concerted drive to make their own wines individually and, if necessary, to sell them collectively. The style of the Gardois reds will never make them world-beaters, for they lack the all-embracing sturdiness of the reds from across the Rhône, but their softness and balance ensure that there is a ready audience for them among people who prefer to drink lighter wines in the Beaujolais vein.

The best Côtes du Rhône comes from the *domaines*, with the occasional exception of a top-class *propriétaire-négociant* house such as Paul Jaboulet or Guigal, whose whole range of wines is known to be reliable. However, such wine is not always easy to find, partly because some *domaines* produce only limited quantities of wine, partly because wine traders and importers prefer in this modern age to deal with just one source of supply for their Rhône Valley wines, one for their Bordeaux region wines and so on. Thus in addition to the *domaines*, the *négociants* listed are all based in the Côtes du Rhône region and sell by the bottle directly to the consumer. Much Côtes du Rhône that is available throughout the world today will obviously not be mentioned in this brief report: it is bought by merchants all over France and Europe, shipped to them in bulk-carrying tankers or lorries and does, occasionally, emerge in the bottle with its composition a little altered. 'Go to the source' must be the cry: those *négociants* that are based in the Rhône Valley itself provide easily the best wine in this category. Failing such a supplier, it is best and simplest to purchase Côtes du Rhône from one's best-known, most reputable local shipper.

DOMAINES

Both the style of vinification and the finished wine vary substantially from one place to another when considering such a large category as Côtes du Rhône *générique*. For this reason the *domaines* have been subdivided by *département*.

The Ardèche Département (prefix 07)

This is an embryonic area for *domaine*-bottled Côtes du Rhône wines. M. Herberigs has been bottling for over ten years and makes a steady, quite well balanced red wine. For a long time he

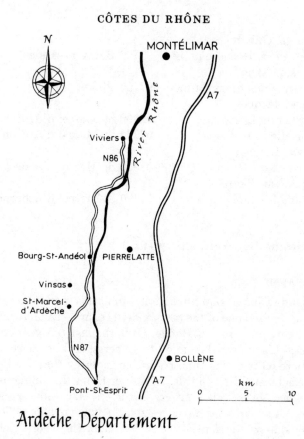

Ardèche Département

was the only grower in the area to be making and bottling and selling his wine, but in the past five years he has been joined by a handful of keen growers, mainly around the attractive village of St-Marcel-d'Ardèche, which lies equidistant between Pont-St-Esprit and Bourg-St-Andéol. Also worth noting is the wine of M. Rodolphe Goossens of Domaine de l'Olivet near Bourg-St-Andéol. Unfiltered and briefly aged in cask, it presents an interesting combination of fruit and backbone that is rather unusual for this region of normally light wines.

LEADING CÔTES DU RHÔNE DOMAINES IN THE ARDÈCHE DÉPARTEMENT

Goossens, Rodolphe
    Domaine de l'Olivet   07700 Bourg-St-Andéol

Herberigs, Gilbert
   Château de Rochecolombe   07700 Bourg-St-Andéol
Grangaud, Alain
   Domaine des Fines Grunes   07700 Vinsas
Sabatier, Jacques
   Le Plan de Lage   07390 St-Marcel-d'Ardèche
Saladin, Louis et Paul   07390 St-Marcel-d'Ardèche
Terrasse, R.
   Domaine du Roure   07390 St-Marcel-d'Ardèche
Thibon, Jean-Pierre
   Mas de Libian   07390 St-Marcel-d'Ardèche

The Drôme Département (prefix 26)

CAVE JAUME

M. Claude Jaume is an intelligent, ambitious man of around 40 who has devised one of the best modern cellars seen anywhere for the making of Côtes du Rhône. Over the last ten years he has increased his vineyard from 50 to 67 acres, and he concentrates now more on red wine than before, considering that the Eygues Valley is most suited to this. In former times the Jaume family also owned several olive groves, for in the dry and very sunny Eygues Valley area the olive tree and the vine are able to flourish side by side on the gentle slopes that flank the river. The very severe weather of 1956 unfortunately killed off many of the olive trees, however, and now the *vignerons* tend their much reduced olive groves only as a very minor sideline.

M. Jaume has invested his future in the latest equipment for his cellar—stainless-steel fermenting tanks and horizontal presses that can be set with great accuracy—and is making one of the best, most drinkable Côtes du Rhône reds to be found in the Valley. The emphasis is on balance and a fruity, accessible style which is cleverly backed by the tannin and alcohol lent by the presence of around 15 per cent Syrah. His wines should really be drunk by the time they are 3 or 4 years old, with just a little attention given to the fact that they reflect the abnormally temperate climate of the area through an alcohol degree that varies between 13 and 14.

Cave Jaume, Claude et Nicole Jaume   26490 Vinsobres

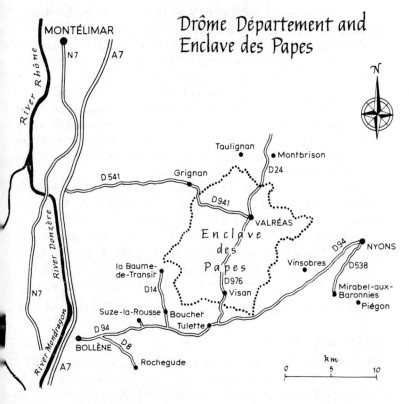

Drôme Département and Enclave des Papes

CHÂTEAU DE L'ESTAGNOL

Just north of Suze-la-Rousse and its commanding twelfth-century castle, which now houses the Université du Vin, is the Château de l'Estagnol. Its 180-acre vineyard stands in ground that over the years has been cleared of woody thickets and briars to make way for vine plantation. The vineyard is divided up into tree-ringed plots, which are all interconnected by tracks cut through the woods and scrub, while the appearance of the stark modern cellar building has been partly softened by the Rhône Valley's boldest display of pop art. Adorning the side wall are eagles, wild horses, tractors, bulldozers and a bottling line—all swooping, running or looking busy.

This is novel country for the vine. Until 1936, when M. Chambovet bought the property, the main local products were barley, wheat and sunflowers. Now it is the Grenache that is predominant, along with five other traditional Rhône vines.

Four-fifths of the wine is red, of which a small part is made by the *macération carbonique* process. The rest is fermented for five days and then left to age in wood for a few months, a reduction in the tendency in the mid-1970s to age in cask for eighteen months. It is generally a very sound wine, although the change in style has not necessarily benefited it, placing it more on a par with many correctly made but not inspiring wines that come under the Côtes du Rhône title. Nevertheless, it is well balanced and supple and should be drunk before it is 4 years old.

The white wine, made entirely from the Bourboulenc grape, is definitely one of the best white Côtes du Rhônes to be found. Fruity, crisp-tasting and well constructed, it should be drunk within two years of the harvest and is an excellent partner for seafood. The rosé is the least eminent of the three wines but reflects credit on its *domaine* by always being well vinified.

SIAP

    Château de l'Estagnol   26130 Suze-la-Rousse

CHÂTEAU LA BORIE

The splendid Château La Borie stands among woods and vines 3 kilometres north of Suze-la-Rousse. Once the possession of the Princes of Orange, it is today owned by M. Emile Bories, whose name, curiously enough, bears absolutely no connection with the property.

M. Bories arrived in France from Algeria in 1963 and boldly decided to replant almost the whole of the *château*'s vineyard. Seven different vines were used, including initially the Alicante, of Spanish origin, and the Counoise, more often found at Châteauneuf-du-Pape, where it has a strong following among leading wine-makers such as Baron Le Roy. Great emphasis was placed on the Syrah, and it constitutes over one-fifth of the 175 acres of vines.

The Château La Borie red wine is vinified in the traditional way, although it is never actually aged in cask. Bottled within the year following the harvest, it usually straightens out a little afterwards and is perfect to drink when 2 or 3 years old. The presence in it of the Syrah is well illustrated by the strong colour,

and the wine's general harmony and length of finish place it among
the leading Côtes du Rhône wines.

A word of caution should be added, however; none of the wine is
estate-bottled, and two blends are sold—one being Château La
Borie and the other being Domaine La Borie. The latter wine is a
disappointment when compared with the Château La Borie wine,
often being light in both colour and taste.

Bories, Emile
    Château La Borie   26130 Suze-la-Rousse

DOMAINE A. MAZURD ET FÍLS

The Mazurd family owns 185 acres of vineyards extending
through the villages of Tulette, Bouchet, Visan and Valréas and is
a typical case of a grower leaving a Co-opérative in order to branch
out on his own—in the case of the Mazurds, with great success.

The Mazurd cellars are on the edge of Tulette, a nondescript
place that looks south to the Aigues Valley and a long tree-topped
ridge of hills that partially hide the vast presence of Mont
Ventoux. It is open vine country with, as usual, the emphasis on
the Grenache; this accounts for 70 per cent of the Mazurd vines,
the difference being made up of 15 per cent Syrah, 10 per cent
Cinsault and 5 per cent Carignan. Some of their Grenache are 65
years old, and, according to M. Mazurd, a busy, grey-haired man
in his early sixties, they provide an ideal backbone to his wines.

The Mazurds perform an unusual vinification for their red
wines, which account for 95 per cent of their total production.
Starting with uncrushed *raisins entiers* entering carbonic gas-filled
vats, they undertake a rapid *macération carbonique* fermentation
and then place the wine for racking purposes in concrete vats.
Maturing is completed over the course of anything from one to
two or more years in cask, depending on whether M. Mazurd is
making a Côtes du Rhône or a Côtes du Rhône Villages and on
whether it is his Grenache-Syrah blend (called Mazurka) or his
100 per cent Grenache (titled *Cuvée* St-Quenize).

The red wines of Domaine Mazurd are very successful, for they
show an alluring fruitiness which is backed by a substantial finish.
In this respect their style is more reminiscent of a strong-bodied
Vinsobres wine, which should be drunk in winter with stews or hot
meat dishes: good country wine to suit good country food would

be an apt description for them. They are not particularly long-lived, five years being a maximum longevity.

Domaine A. Mazurd et Fils   26130 Tulette

DOMAINE DU PETIT BARBARAS

This is a first-rate *domaine* owned by M. R. Feschet, who, like his neighbour M. Mazurd, was a member of two Caves Co-opératives, in this case those of Suze-la-Rousse and the Costebelle at Tulette, until building his cellars in 1976.

The Feschets own over 70 acres of vines on the stony-topped, clay-soil plateau that runs due east of Suze-la-Rousse beside the main D94 road. The vines are principally Grenache and Cinsault, backed up by Syrah with a little Carignan, and obviously do well at this higher than usual exposure, around 150 metres.

Ninety per cent of the wine is red, and full-bodied and attractive it is too. Bright purple in colour, it has a richness of flavour and a strong blackcurrant-inspired taste that stand up well to the tannins and spicy aftertastes that the wine leaves when drunk before it is 3 years old. A very good wine to accompany roast beef or autumn game birds, it is well worth while looking out for.

Feschet R. et Fils
Domaine du Petit Barbaras   26130 Bouchet

DOMAINE DE LA TAURELLE

At the top end of the Eygues Valley, and set against a charming backdrop of fruit trees and lavender plants, is the Domaine de la Taurelle. The local village, Mirabel-aux-Baronnies, is one of those settlements perching on a hillock, distinguished by the church and its spire at the top and by the circle of stone-walled houses protecting it at the bottom.

The vineyards stand at over 240 metres here, and most of the trees bear witness to the force of the *mistral* wind, their trunks bent in a variety of theatrical-looking poses but all in the same direction. Mme Roux and her friendly son, Christophe, cultivate 49 acres of vines on slopes running away from their well-sited *domaine*, the varieties in order of importance being Grenache, Syrah, Carignan and Cinsault. They make traditionally styled red Côtes du Rhône, which receives a short time in cask and is left to develop its full potential in bottle. Cherry-coloured, it is a wine of immense power and tannin in strong vintages such as 1978, while in years like 1977 and 1979 most notable are its balance and softness of flavour, which seems most to resemble apricots or plums. The Rouxs recommend that their red wine should be drunk before it is 5 or 6 years old; they also make a little white and rosé, which are of secondary interest.

Roux, Mme et Fils
    Domaine de la Taurelle   26480 Mirabel-aux-Baronnies

DOMAINE DES TREILLES

This is a very attractive *domaine* whose restored soft-stone manor house has belonged to the Rey-Mery family since 1772. It stands beside the D10 road running from Valréas to Montbrison and is one of the most northerly Côtes du Rhône *domaines* in the lower half of the Rhône Valley.

M. Rey is one of the jokers of the area, an instantly likeable man with a broad tweed cap tilted spectacularly over his left ear and an anecdote always at the ready. An ex-rugby player for Valréas ('They carried me off in my last match after I had played most of the game with a broken shoulder—feel it, feel it!'), he retired when he was 39, since when all his activities have been channelled into looking after his 57-acre vineyard as well as his asparagus and olive tree plantations.

Eighty-five per cent of their vines are Grenache, with Syrah, Clairette, Cinsault and Carignan making up the complement. They grow on a mixture of sandy and stony ground near the *domaine* and running into the Valréas *Appellation* area, but, like other growers, M. Rey is no longer interested in making Villages wine if he is to be limited to 35 hectolitres a hectare for it. His normal crop is about 50 hectolitres a hectare, and he prefers to make all his wine as Côtes du Rhône *générique*, with its *Appellation* price, as a result.

The red wine receives just under a year's ageing in cask in the *domaine*'s pre-Revolution vaulted cellars, and half of it is bottled. Full-blooded, with an alcohol degree generally around 13·5, it bears a bright purple hue and displays ample fruit on both bouquet and palate. The scent is, in fact, almost akin to violets, a description that M. Rey would gladly accept about his wine, since he is convinced that it is anyway capable of bestowing life-giving

M. Rey

properties on people and animals. 'My grandmother lived until she was nearly 100, and my mother is still going strong at 93. Then take the case of our dog. He used to suffer from epileptic fits until one day he licked up some wine that had spilt into a bronze pan. Now we give him a daily ration of wine in this bronze pan, and he has never had another epileptic fit.' In the face of such evidence, there is only one recommendation—try the wine of Domaine des Treilles!

Rey, R. et Mery
 Domaine des Treilles   26230 Montbrison-sur-Lez

LES ASSEYRAS

Robert Blanc is a keen *vigneron* who looks after 47 acres of vines split into two properties, one of them near his house above Tulette and the other inside the Valréas vineyard area. Based on 90 per cent Grenache, with support from the Syrah, Carignan and just a little Cinsault, he makes mainly Côtes du Rhône *générique* with a small proportion of Villages for good measure.

 M. Blanc has been bottling his wine since the mid-1970s and is used to giving it a quick three-month stay in 225-litre casks before release. He feels that the quality is enhanced by his vines being in large part on slopes and by there being a substantial amount of old Grenache plants as well. Certainly, he is succeeding in making an excellently fruity and soft style of wine, whose steady red colour and hint of tannin are more evocative of a Gard *département* wine. His Côtes du Rhône is preferable to his Villages (which can be a little too pitchy or 'cooked') and is good for drinking with white meats or poultry.

Blanc, Robert
    Les Asseyras   26130 Tulette

OTHER CÔTES DU RHÔNE DOMAINES IN THE DRÔME DÉPARTEMENT

Couston et Monnier	
Domaine de la Tour Couverte	26130 Tulette
Le Terroir St-Rémy	26130 La Baume-de-Transit
Bourret, Pierre	
Domaine de Roquevignan	26130 Rochegude
Tourtin, Mme Louis	
Domaine du Gourget	26130 Rochegude
Bérard Père et Fils	
Domaine de la Berardière	26130 Tulette
Domaine La Serre du Prieur	26130 Suze-la-Rousse
Domaine Ste-Marie	26130 Suze-la-Rousse
Estève, Jean-Pierre	
Domaine du Bois Noir	26130 La Baume-de-Transit
Gautier, Jean	
Château de Lignane	26130 Suze-la-Rousse
Ginies, Gilbert	26480 Piégon
Pinet, Joseph	
Domaine Chastelle	26230 Taulignan
Pradelle, R. et Fils	
Domaine du Jas	26130 Suze-la-Rousse
Trutat, Bruno	
Les Davids	26 Livron-sur-Drôme

The Gard Département (prefix 30)

CHÂTEAU DE BOUSSARGUES

Set in over 500 acres of woodlands just off the main D6 road that runs west of Bagnols-sur-Cèze to Alès, the Château de Boussargues has over 55 acres of vineyards that were planted in the early

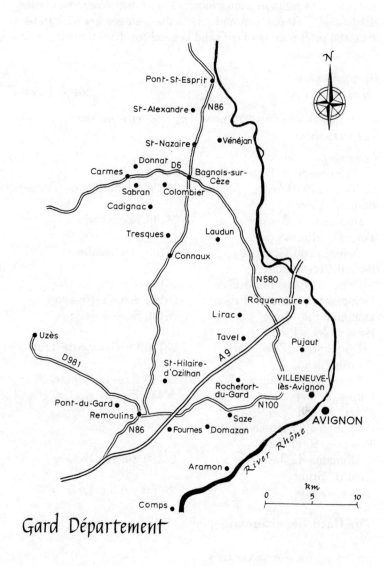

N

Pont-St-Esprit

St-Alexandre

N86

Vénéjan

St-Nazaire

Donnat

D6

Carmes

Bagnols-sur-
Cèze

Sabran

Colombier

Cadignac

Laudun

Tresques

Connaux

N580

Roquemaure

Lirac

Tavel

Pujaut

Uzès

D981

A9

St-Hilaire-
d'Ozilhan

VILLENEUVE-
lès-Avignon

Rochefort-
du-Gard

N100

Pont-du-Gard

AVIGNON

Remoulins

Saze

N86

Fournes

Domazan

River Rhône

Aramon

km

0   5   10

Comps

Gard Département

1970s by Mme Chantal Malabre. The attractive *château* has been very well restored, having been in the family for about eighty years, and the Malabre-Constants also cultivate asparagus as well as keeping several hives of bees.

The principal vines are the Grenache, Syrah, Carignan, Cinsault and Ugni Blanc, and vinification is commenced by using *raisins entiers* in order to endow the wine with as much fruitiness as possible. The red, rosé and white Côtes du Rhône are all bottled for early drinking, and Mme Malabre is keen on selling her wine as far afield as she can, having relied on bulk sales to *négociants* until 1981. The Boussargues red is a typical Gard wine, with an innocuous fruitiness and pleasant accessibility that make it sound, if not outstanding.

Malabre-Constant, Chantal
Château de Boussargues   30200 Colombier

CHÂTEAU DE DOMAZAN AND CAVEAU DU CHÂTEAU DE DOMAZAN

The 74-acre Château de Domazan vineyards are run by M. Christian Chaudérac, a lean, grey-haired but athletic-looking man in his early thirties. The Chaudéracs have been at Domazan for many years, and their *domaine* dates back to the fourteenth century; sacked during the Revolution, its lands were subsequently divided up so that the vineyard accompanying it today is relatively small.

Ninety per cent of their wine is red, made from only 50 per cent Grenache, with more concentration than usual on the Syrah (25 per cent of the plantation) and on the Cinsault (20 per cent). Most of the vines at Domazan are cultivated on a plateau which holds terraces of alluvial stones covering a light top soil, although near the village entrance there are some sandy *quartiers*.

A commendable *esprit de corps* is detectable at Domazan, where five of the growers have grouped themselves together to form a selling organization called the Caveau du Château. They are all young men who realize the importance of selling to a wide variety of markets and have already sent wine to Britain, the United States, Belgium and Germany; they refuse to sell in bulk, which is often sought after at giveaway prices by Swiss customers.

The Château de Domazan red wine is bottled one year after the harvest, following storage in concrete vats, and carries a racy wild-fruit bouquet that could have come off a hedgerow. Quite pale in colour, its pleasing mixture of fruit and acidity makes it an excellent summer wine for drinking before it is 3 years old.

The other four members of the Caveau du Château de Domazan are all making wine worthy of attention. There is Jean-Paul Arnaud of Domaine des Roches d'Arnaud, whose wine, red-purple in colour and bearing a bouquet that is herbaceous and surprisingly lingering and complex for the area, has a Mourvèdre-inspired style of firm fruit. There is Daniel Charre of Domaine du Sarrazin, whose wine more typically shows an attacking wild fruit flavour, and whose light balance makes it ideal for drinking within two years of the harvest. There is Serge Gallon of the Mas d'Eole, who makes a light and quite fruity wine, as pale as one would expect from some areas of the Gard. And, finally, there is Louis Reynaud of Domaine Reynaud, whose Côtes du Rhône is red cherry, with a hint of vanilla on the bouquet; its soft fruit is well held together by just a trace of tannin.

Chaudérac, Christian	
Château de Domazan	30390 Domazan
Arnaud, Jean-Paul	
Domaine des Roches d'Arnaud	30390 Domazan
Charre, Daniel	
Domaine du Sarrazin	30390 Domazan
Gallon, Serge	
Mas d'Eole	30390 Domazan
Reynaud, Louis et Fils	
Domaine Reynaud	30390 Domazan

CHÂTEAU DE FAREL

The Château de Farel at Comps, about 18 kilometres south-west of Avignon, is the most southerly domaine in the Côtes du Rhône. A 62-acre property, it is owned by M. Pierre Silvestre, the Director of the General Union of Côtes du Rhône *Vignerons*, who looks after their interests from Avignon.

The vineyard is based on the Grenache, with the Syrah, Mourvèdre, Cinsault and Carignan also present, and grows in a mainly clay soil which is topped by round alluvial deposit stones. M. Silvestre ferments in a classical manner in concrete vats and, according to the position of his stocks, ages his wine in large oak barrels for a few months before putting it out on sale.

Nine-tenths of the wine is red, and although never particularly strong-coloured, it has an agreeable balance and finish. It is best to drink the wine young, for some of M. Silvestre's Grande Réserve *cuvées* appear to have received an overpowering ageing in wood, which upsets their balance. A little rosé and white are also made.

Silvestre, Pierre
    Château de Farel   30300 Comps

CHÂTEAU DE RIBAS

This charming *château* was bought, presumably on favourable terms, after the Russian Revolution, following which event the previous owner had been bankrupted after being dispossessed in his native country. M. Michel Vignal is the grandson of the purchaser and is keen to make his wine better-known; as a result he has invested in stainless steel tanks and bottling equipment and, since the 1979 vintage, has been bottling wine that formerly he would sell off to merchants.

The vineyard amounts to 11 acres, set south-west of Laudun and characterized by the smooth alluvial stones that are the hallmark of Châteauneuf-du-Pape. However, M. Vignal's vinification method is open to some criticism, for while there can be no doubting his well-intentioned enthusiasm, it seems strange that he should choose to vinify his wine in concrete vats and then leave it to 'age' in stainless-steel tanks for one year. Stainless steel is not recognized or intended to be a medium for storing wine, and indeed the effect is apparent on the wine of the Château de Ribas, which tastes hard and astringent, despite showing some promise on the bouquet. This is an example of the changing mentality that is evident in the Rhône Valley but which, when badly channelled, can lead to unfortunate results.

Vignal, Michel
    Château de Ribas   30290 Laudun

DOMAINE DE L'AMANDIER

This is a very well run *domaine* set beside the main Bagnols to Alès road, on the edge of a tiny hamlet called Carmes. It has nearly 50 acres of Côtes du Rhône vines and another 25 acres of table-wine grape varieties. The Pages family have been making wine at Carmes for over 150 years, and a living testament to the healthiness of the life is M. Gaston Pages, the most spritely 86-year-old in the Rhône Valley, who trots round his vineyard and cellars pointing out matters of interest to visitors.

His son, Urbain, looks after the *domaine* on a day-to-day basis and has been responsible for replanting the vineyard with a relatively low percentage of Grenache and higher than usual quantities of Syrah and Cinsault. He is also experimenting with Cabernet Sauvignon and with Syrah for his *vin de table*, which could give interesting results in years to come. The vines are all trained along wires and are immaculately kept.

Eighty per cent of the wine is red, 10 per cent rosé and 10 per cent white, the last being made from the Ugni Blanc, the Grenache Blanc and the Bourboulenc. Since 1978 the *domaine* has been bottling almost all its wine; the red is stored in concrete for one year and in bottle for another year before its release on sale. In the courtyard of the *domaine* M. Pages *père* is happy to open the door of an ordinary-sized room which is crammed full of bottles undergoing their year's ageing—an incredible 60,000 altogether.

As a result, the red wine of Domaine de l'Amandier is ready to

M. Gaston Pages

drink in the year after it is put on sale; it has quite an attractive, almost sweet, fruitiness and a pleasant length of finish—good but not great wine. The rosé is supple with a clean fruit flavour and is good to drink with spicy Chinese food, while the white, fermented at low temperature in the Pages' stainless-steel tanks, is crisp-tasting and should be drunk before it is 2 years old.

Pages, Urbain
  Domaine de l'Amandier   30200 Carmes

DOMAINE DE COCOL

Hidden at the end of a track among trees in a vale north of Donnat is the 74-acre Domaine de Cocol. Its proximity to the River Cèze allows the owner, M. Jean-Paul Sabot, to cultivate pear and apple trees as well as his vines. Since the late 1950s M. Sabot, a smiling and healthy-looking man in his early forties, has been gradually replanting his vineyard, so that it is now based on no more than 30 per cent Grenache, a total of 35 per cent being accounted for by the Syrah and the Cinsault. M. Sabot is intending to plant the Picpoul, Bourboulenc and Clairette so that he can also make a white wine.

His cellar is distinguished by eight large barrels that are unusually shaped—long and rather flat, with a slight tapering at one end only. M. Sabot, obviously proud of them, explained: 'The barrels belonged to the French Railways and were used for transporting wine all over France on the goods wagons of the SNCF. That is why they are this curious shape, so they wouldn't fall off on the railway. The largest holds 20,500 litres and the smallest 14,000 litres, and my father bought them off the SNCF in 1947. Despite opposition from the young *oenologue* advising me, I am using them to age my wine for ten months or so.'

M. Sabot would sell his wine to *négociants* until the 1980 vintage, and although he is now selling barely 10,000 bottles a year, he aims to increase this figure sharply in the future. Certainly, his wine reflects its *raisin entier* fermentation and its Gard *département* origins, showing a bright red cherry colour and a softness on the palate that sustains the initial fruity attack. Like most of its neighbouring wines, it is best drunk before it is 3 or 4 years old.

Sabot, Jean-Paul
  Domaine de Cocol   30200 Donnat

DOMAINE LE HAUT CASTEL

Two or three kilometres north-west of Bagnols-sur-Cèze is the Domaine Le Haut Castel. The smart light stone *domaine* and its cellars are at the top of a small hillside and look out over the vineyards and the peaceful Cèze Valley that lies beyond.

In the last ten years the size of the vineyard has been almost doubled, to reach 64 acres, some of which lie within the Chusclan *Appellation* area. However the Arène family feel the same way as many growers in the Rhône Valley in choosing not to make Villages wine with its permitted lower quantity per hectare, so that any extra wine must be sold off as *vin de pays*. They are therefore happy to make red, rosé and white Côtes du Rhône *générique*; most of the wine is red, and its soundness speaks well for M. Arène's old-style vinification methods, which include a nearly two-year ageing in cask. Generally rich and well balanced, the wine has a firm purple colour and a substantial, long finish. Also popular with the *domaine*'s British and Dutch customers is the white wine. Made from the Clairette, Grenache Blanc, Picpoul and Bourboulenc, this is bottled in the spring following the harvest.

Arène, Augustin
  Domaine Le Haut Castel   30200 Bagnols-sur-Cèze

DOMAINE DES MOULINS

M. André Payan, the owner of the 75-acre Domaine des Moulins at Saze, is an intense, bearded man who typifies the new zeal to be found among young wine-growers in the Gard *département*. His *domaine* has been in the family for over fifty years, but he has modified the composition of the vineyards since his father's day so as to accommodate as much as 40 per cent Syrah, of which he is a great fan.

The vineyards run between Saze and Domazan and are distinguished by the deposits of smooth round stones that lie on top of compacted clay soil. M. Payan completes his vineyard with extensive planting of Grenache (40 per cent) and with Mourvèdre, Cinsault, Clairette and Carignan.

In the past few years his attitude towards his red wine has

changed, in part prompted by demand from his customers, so that he admits that he is now making a softer, less robust style of wine. The accent is on fruit, and he feels that the Syrah is a grape admirably suited to achieving this. The Moulins red wine, generally a steady purple, certainly lives up to M. Payan's intentions, for a wild raspberry scent is followed by a lingering fruitiness on the palate whose fresh style is very appealing.

The *domaine* red and rosé have been bottled only since the 1980 vintage, and it is likely that the enterprising M. Payan will be rewarded with an extensive overseas clientele in the years to come, for he is making the sort of fruity and uncomplicated wine that is delicious to drink at any time, in not always moderate quantities.

Payan, André
Domaine des Moulins   30650 Saze

DOMAINE DE LA RÉMÉJEANNE

This 62-acre vineyard is owned by M. François Klein, a ruddy-complexioned, silver-haired man in his late fifties who arrived in the Gard in 1961 from Morocco, where he had managed a 2,500-acre wine *domaine*. Having done his studies at agricultural college in Morocco, he was keen to experiment in an area of France that he considered underrated in viticultural terms—very much the same sort of reaction felt by the ex-Algerian residents who are now making wine at Lirac.

M. Klein's vineyards are very spread out, in some fifty plots, and are mainly composed of Grenache (40 per cent) and Syrah (25 per cent), backed up by Cinsault and Carignan, which thrive in his largely sandy ground. Only red wine is made, on cellar equipment that is old but spotlessly kept. This includes a vertical press, made in Lyon about fifty years ago, and an old hand piston pump now driven by a small electric motor which transfers the wine from one vat to another: somewhat Heath Robinson in appearance, perhaps, but M. Klein insists that such machinery, if in good working order, is just as capable of handling the wine gently as any modern equipment.

After a five- to seven-day fermentation in concrete, M. Klein stores his wine once again in concrete for eighteen months to two years and, after bottling, does not release it for another four or five months. It shows very good rich fruit, with a typical Gardois softness and roundness that continues into a long aftertaste. Well constructed, it has great charm and is good for drinking until it is about 4 years old.

The *domaine* also grows asparagus, cherries and figs, and M. Klein has recently enthusiastically stepped into the export field with the dispatch of a small shipment of his wine to Chicago. Keep an eye open for it.

Klein, François
Domaine de la Réméjeanne   30200 Cadignac

DOMAINE DE LA ROUETTE

A 42-acre property, this domaine belongs to the Guigue family, who have been wine-makers since the seventeenth century. This does not stop them from using modern vinification methods, and the white and rosé are fermented under controlled temperature in stainless-steel tanks. The rosé, light and inoffensive, is certainly the better of the two wines.

The red wine is made from about 45 per cent Grenache, supported by Syrah, Cinsault and Mourvèdre, and the Guigues like to vinify this by *macération carbonique* in underground concrete vats. The wine is then aged for a year or two in barrel, the length of stay being determined by the weight of demand for the *domaine* wine at any one time. Lightly styled but attractively fruity, it represents good middle-range Côtes du Rhône in the noticeably soft style of Gard wines.

Guigue, Père et Fils
Domaine de la Rouette   30650 Rochefort-du-Gard

MAS CLAULIAN

St-Alexandre is the first community south of Pont-St-Esprit and is an attractive circular village whose appearance gives the hint of fortified Provençal villages to be found further down the valley. As one stands surrounded by pine-clad hillsides and vineyards, and with scattered olive trees growing in the rolling countryside, the pulse quickens at the prospect of Provence not far away.

The Herbouze family arrived in St-Alexandre from Morocco in 1962, and their 30-acre vineyard has been built partly on pine-covered woodland that was cleared to create today's terraces. Claude Herbouze, an enterprising man in his early thirties, is now making the *domaine* red wine on the basis of uncrushed grapes, which he leaves to macerate in enamel-lined or concrete vats. Headed by the Grenache and the Syrah, his wine is then stored in vats for one to two years before half of it is bottled. It has a respectable quality, with a sound red colour and fruity attack on the palate, which indicate that it is good for drinking before it is 4 years old.

The Herbouzes are concentrating their sales efforts on France, for they work on their own and do not find it easy to sell in bottle further afield. This is an oft-repeated state of affairs in the Rhône Valley, one that is a bar to more *domaines* going out on their own and bottling. As it is, the Herbouzes rely on Claude's sister-in-law in Brittany to hold a little stock for them, and this family aid has helped them sell to a wider public.

Herbouze, Claude
   Mas Claulian   30130 St-Alexandre

OTHER CÔTES DU RHÔNE DOMAINES IN THE GARD
DÉPARTEMENT

Allauzen
   Château de Valpinson   30130 St-Alexandre
Castay et Johannet
   Domaine de Signac   30200 Bagnols-sur-Cèze
Chinieu, Jean-Claude
   Domaine de Lindas   30200 Bagnols-sur-Cèze
Coste, Pierre
   Domaine de Laplagnol   30130 Pont St-Esprit
De Serésin, Père et Fils
   Domaine de Bruthel   30200 Sabran
Fabre, René
   Domaine des Coccinelles   30390 Domazan
Imbert, Père et Fils
   Domaine de Lascamp   30200 Cadignac
Juls, Joel
   Château du Bresquet   30200 St-Nazaire
Meger, Lucien
   Domaine des Boumianes   30390 Domazan
Payan, Achille
   Domaine du Cabanon   30650 Saze

Pons, Dominique
    Domaine des Cèdres   30200 St-Nazaire
Poudevigne, André
    Domaine de la Crompe   30390 Domazan
Riot Frères,
    Domaine des Riots   30200 St-Michel-d'Euzet
Rique, Pierre
    Domaine de Roquebrune   30130 St-Alexandre
Robert, Alain et Fils
    Vieux Manoir de Frigoulas   30130 St-Alexandre
Sabatier, Roger
    Domaine de l'Espéran   30130 St-Alexandre
Simon, Francis
    Domaine du Moulin du Pourpré 30200 Sabran
Tarsac, Jacques
    Domaine St-Jacques   30200 St-Michel-d'Euzet
Valat, André
    Château St-Maurice-l'Ardoise   30290 Laudun
Verda et Fils
    Domaine Cantegril-Verda   30150 Roquemaure

The Vaucluse Département (prefix 84)

CHÂTEAU DE FONSALETTE

This 37-acre vineyard is under the same ownership as the Château
Rayas and Pignan at Châteauneuf-du-Pape and has therefore
undergone the same drastic changes that have occurred in the
wine of the other two *domaines* since the death of their expert
owner, M. Louis Reynaud, in 1978.

The *domaine* was built up between 1945 and 1955, as M.
Reynaud experimented to see which vines were best suited to
Fonsalette's terrain. Eventually he decided upon the Grenache,
Syrah and Cinsault for the red wine and the Grenache Blanc and
the Clairette for the white.

Wines from this *domaine* labelled before the year 1976 are still
worth looking out for, since they were made with the same
attention and ability that M. Louis Reynaud would bring to bear
on his famous Châteauneuf-du-Papes. The red, with its deep
purple colour and overwhelming sensation of blackcurrants on

BOLLÈNE

D8

Villedieu

D 938

Puyméras

Ste-Cécile-les-Vignes

VAISON-LA-ROMAINE

Mondragon

Cairanne

Lagarde-
Paréol

Rasteau

Uchaux

Entrechaux

Mornas

Sérignan-
du-Comtat

D975

D977

Sablet

N7

Travaillan

La Baumette

Suzette

Camaret

Violès

Lafare

A7

ORANGE

D7

Jonquières

Beaumes-
de-Venise

D 938

D 950

Aubignan

Loriol-
du-Comtat

Châteauneuf-
du-Pape

CARPENTRAS

River Rhône

D 942

Sorgues

Entraigues

Vedène

D6

Morières

A7

Châteauneuf-
de-Gadagne

l'Isle-sur-la-Sorgue

AVIGNON

N

km

0   5   10

Vaucluse Département

both bouquet and palate, bore a fruitiness and refinement that recalled wines such as good Fixin or Gevrey-Chambertin; it could live for up to twelve years.

The white too was exceptionally good, with a soft straw colour, immense richness and a long 'honeyish' aftertaste. Delightful to drink between 4 and 6 years old, it has now become of academic interest, except to those who chance upon a pre-1976 bottle.

Reynaud, Jacques
    Château de Fonsalette   84290 Lagarde-Paréol

CHÂTEAU GOURDON

Two or three kilometres north of Bollène is the striking Château Gourdon, built in 1780 and distinguished by its one lonely spire. Owned by Mme Sanchez-Gauchet, her son and daughter, it has a 95-acre vineyard based on Grenache and the classic southern Rhône collection of vines. These grow on a light, partly sandy soil, which is also suitable for the extensive asparagus cultivation that the family undertakes. Indeed, they believe that the asparagus is a crop ideal for resting land between taking out and planting vines.

Château Gourdon appears in red and rosé Côtes du Rhône; the red is vinified traditionally with storage for one year in concrete vats before being put on sale. Only about one-quarter of the production is bottled, and this is sound enough: its sturdiness and the tannin hiding behind the early suggestion of fruit mean that it is suitable to drink when it is 3 or 4 years old.

Sanchez et Gauchet
    Château de Gourdon   84500 Bollène

CHÂTEAU DU GRAND MOULAS

This is an enterprising new *domaine* whose cellars are set in the unlikely surroundings of Mornas, a huddled little village that stands right on the main N7 road between Bollène and Orange. It is owned by the Ryckwaert family, who are of Flemish origin but who in reality are almost nomadic, having been in Algeria from 1820 until the early 1960s, when they arrived in France.

The *domaine* is run by two brothers, Yves, who looks after sales and finance, and Marc, who is responsible for the viticulture. Both are in their early thirties and have their time fully spent directing their wine and fruit interests. Yves explained more about how the *domaine* had started to make wine: 'We left Algeria with virtually no money, so that although we had grown vines and fruit there, we couldn't consider starting up a vineyard with all the necessary cellar installations. Instead we chose to go into low-investment fruit trees—apples and pears—of which we now have 160 acres and an export-orientated business.

'Having banked a little money, our father bought about 130 acres of heavily wooded, sloping country at Uchaux, just behind the Château de St-Estève, in fact. We had a tremendous task clearing this land and so far have 57 acres under vines, which we hope will rise to 72 acres in due course. The problem is that much of this land is simply too ravinous and too dense to clear to our satisfaction.'

Marc continued: 'We've planted 66 per cent Grenache and the rest Syrah, and we made our first wine from these vines in 1978; there is a slight problem with the vineyards lying 11 kilometres from our cellars here at Mornas, but we spread the grapes out in 400-kilogram fruit crates so that they are not crushed during transportation. Then we ferment virtually unbroken grapes, starting with an extended maceration in stainless-steel tanks, and are at present bottling the wine six months after the harvest. In time we would like to buy some 4,000-litre barrels to give the wine about six months' ageing in wood, but we don't want to detract from the extremely fresh style of wine that we're making.'

Grand Moulas Côtes du Rhône succeeds in fulfilling its makers' objectives, for it is admirably fruity, with a fresh but not superficial tang to it which denotes the presence of one-third Syrah in it. As the Ryckwaerts decide when to harvest according to the acid and not the sugar levels in their grapes, they tend to restrict the alcohol degree to some extent, which is of great importance in a wine of this nature. Thus their Côtes du Rhône is generally around 12°. It is a wine of such a summery disposition that the authors' personal preference is to drink it lightly chilled but in substantial quantities.

Yves Ryckwaert is also very proud of his *eau-de-vie* made from pears, something which they distil after they have the apple harvest out of the way. A busy life they lead, but one that seems sure to be successful.

Ryckwaert, M.
Château du Grand Moulas   84350 Mornas

CHÂTEAU MALIJAY

Château Malijay is one of the most resplendent of all Côtes du Rhône *domaines*. Situated about 8 kilometres east of Orange, it stands in the middle of some prolific wine-producing country, near the villages of Jonquières and Violès. An old *château* was built on the site around the eleventh century, but this was almost completely destroyed towards the end of the eighteenth century. A new *château* was then constructed, using stones from the old building, by the Seigneur Baron de Malijay. The Baron also kept up the estate vineyards, which had been cultivated from the fifteenth century onwards.

Today the *château* belongs to M. Jean-Louis Nativelle, an energetic and forceful man who has modernized the cellars so that they are now one of the efficient large-scale wine businesses in the Côtes du Rhône. The vats are stainless-steel; the wine is closely and scientifically looked after; and bottling is performed under sterilization so as to prevent the entry of any foreign bacteria into the wine.

The vineyards cover 460 acres and are mainly composed of Grenache, Cinsault, Carignan, Counoise and Syrah, although the Mourvèdre and Clairette have recently been added. The *château*'s average annual production is very high—around 9,000 hectolitres—and the style of both the red and the rosé is extremely light. Of course, this is the sort of wine that followers of trends now want to drink, and in this respect the Château Malijay red is par for the course: very pale, it has adequate fruit on the bouquet and just enough length to give it some appeal. It should ideally be drunk before it is about 2 years old. The rosé is a good, clean wine, whose lightness is no hindrance. Drunk chilled, within the year following the harvest, it will liven up a summer's afternoon.

M. Nativelle also owns the eleventh-century farm called Mas St-Louis, and both its wine and that of Malijay are widely exported—so widely, in fact, that one of the authors has actually sipped Malijay *rouge* while the guns and cannons fired off around him during a *coup d'état* (*manqué*) in the South American republic of Surinam.

Nativelle, Jean-Louis
　　Château Malijay　　　　　　　　　　　　　　　　84150 Jonquières

CHÂTEAU DE ST-ESTÈVE

Eight kilometres north of Orange, in rolling, wooded countryside, is the Château de St-Estève. The 625-acre estate has belonged to the Français family since 1804, but it was not until the start of this century that any vines were grown on it. Even then its principal occupations continued to be its forestry, sheep farming and silk-worm rearing.

In 1953 M. Gérard Français-Monier, a former French diplomat, decided to do away with his 50 acres of common vines and to increase the whole vineyard to what is today 135 acres of nothing but noble Rhône vines. These are led by the Grenache, followed by the Syrah, Cinsault and Mourvèdre, while for the white the Grenache Blanc, Roussanne and Clairette are used, although an experimental 2·5 acres of Viognier were planted in 1981.

M. Français is helped by his intelligent and progressive-thinking son, Marc, who, with his spectacles and corduroy trousers, looks every inch the thoughtful *vigneron*. Their vineyard techniques are modern: they run a covering of black plastic along the rows of young vines and estimate that their development is in this way speeded up by as much as one or two years. M. Français *père* explained the reasoning behind this method: 'The plastic strip has holes punched in it around the foot of each vine so that humidity can never build up underneath it. The strip therefore acts to retain pure heat around the vine roots and, of course, eliminates the need for weeding, since grass is not able to grow underneath it. With vines treated like this, I am able to harvest a decent crop of grapes after two years; they make a table wine which I can sell off straightaway and so have a yield from my capital much more quickly than usual. The gains from this method are both agricultural and commercial.'

The red, rosé and white wines of St-Estève are very well vinified, and their good quality is firm evidence of the Français' up-to-date policies. The principal red wine, the Grande Réserve, receives a six months' ageing in cask, but as it is half made from long-lasting Syrah, this treatment enhances its style and helps to develop the roundness of its bouquet and flavour. A well struc-tured wine, its tannin content allows a strong vintage such as the 1978 to live up to eight years. With less robust vintages such as the 1979, the wine repays keeping for about four years.

317

The Français' other red wine *cuvée*, the Cuvée des Deux Perdreaux, is not aged in cask and is intended for more rapid drinking, the wine being by nature less full-bodied. Meanwhile the *château* is making a very good white wine, which, fermented at around 12 °C, shows a likeable, fresh green fruit taste and a harmony that make it an ideal companion for fish dishes served during the hot summer months. The rosé, made by the classic brief stay on the skins technique, is the least good wine of the three.

Français-Monier
Château de St-Estève   84110 Uchaux

DOMAINE DE LA CHAPELLE

This seventeenth-century *domaine* stands on a small plateau overlooking Châteauneuf-de-Gadagne, a quiet village nearly 10 kilometres east of Avignon. The vineyard was acquired in 1955 by M. Marcel Boussier, a short, affable man in his early sixties, who was determined to produce the good wine he knew the country around Châteauneuf-de-Gadagne to be capable of. Châteauneuf-de-Gadagne had possessed a respected vineyard as far back as the fourteenth century but had subsequently fallen sharply from prominence. With its stony soil strongly resembling that of Châteauneuf-du-Pape, M. Boussier saw no reason why he should not be able to make wines of a very high standard.

From their 25 acres of vines, headed by nearly 50 per cent Grenache, Marcel and his art college-educated son, Claude, concentrate on making wine of as high a quality as possible. They vinify the red wine in the traditional way, ageing it in cask for eighteen months. It is generally a very powerful wine, possessing a deep colour and bouquet to match, and is best drunk when it is about 3 years old; in this way it will have rounded out and cast aside some of its high initial tannin content.

About one-tenth of the wine is rosé, and this is bottled one year after the harvest. Fresh and well scented when tasted from the vat *chez* Boussier, it suffers from not being bottled earlier.

Boussier, Marcel et Claude
Domaine de la Chapelle   84470 Châteauneuf-de-Gadagne

DOMAINE DE L'ESPIGOUETTE

Many of the 50 acres of the Domaine de l'Espigouette are sited on the vast open space of the Plan de Dieu, and with no Cave Co-opérative at Violès, many of the local growers choose to vinify and bottle their own wine.

M. Edmond Latour is one such man; grey-haired and friendly, he explained that he has been bottling his wine since the mid-1970s and was hoping to be in a position to bottle all his harvest by the mid-1980s. He is helped by his son, who has attended wine school at Mâcon, and together they make their red wine based on the Grenache, Cinsault and Syrah, which are fermented together rather than being assembled vat by vat at a later stage.

Their red Côtes du Rhône is somewhat pale-coloured but carries an interestingly spicy bouquet, something like the *goût de terroir* in a wine like Cairanne. The fruit on the palate is similar to plums, and its subdued nature indicates that the wine should be drunk before it is 3 years old.

White and rosé wines are also made at Domaine de l'Espigouette, but neither is exceptional.

Latour, Edmond
Domaine de l'Espigouette   84150 Jonquières

DOMAINE DE LA GIRARDIÈRE

Louis Girard left the Cave Co-opérative at Rasteau and undertook his first bottling with the 1979 vintage. His red Côtes du Rhône is made mainly from Grenache, of which there are some very old plants growing on his 49-acre vineyard. Fermented traditionally, it is a deep rich red, with a powerful blackcurrant-inspired bouquet. On the palate there is a good balance of tannin and acidity, and the wine's concentrated fruit flavour makes it suitable for considered wintertime drinking.

The Girard family also make a little Rasteau *vin doux naturel* from their Grenache vines, and this too is very good. It displays a surprising finesse, and the bouquet is particularly striking, with aromas such as marzipan in evidence.

Girard, Louis
Domaine de la Girardière   84110 Rasteau

DOMAINE MARTIN

Formerly called the Vignoble du Plan de Dieu, this 87-acre property has been in the Martin family since 1905. It stands just outside Travaillan, on the edge of the vast stony plain known as the Plan de Dieu, and the *domaine*'s vines are split into small lots that grow all around the village; their terrain is the same throughout—the massive bed of small stones that has been nurturing vines on and off since the thirteenth century.

During the 1970s Jules Martin's sons, Yves and René, introduced the Syrah to the vineyard, and this now forms 10 per cent of the plantation. The Grenache accounts for 60 per cent, the Cinsault for 10 per cent and the Mourvèdre for 5 per cent, while the remainder of the vineyard is composed of Carignan, Grenache Blanc and Clairette.

The style of their red wine is therefore full-bodied, with a rich earthiness and depth of colour that can remind one of red Gigondas. René, the brother in charge of vinification, ferments their red for about a week, and it is then matured in oak for around eighteen months. His wine is lighter than that of his father Jules, and nowadays he estimates that the *domaine*'s best vintages, such as 1978 and 1979, should be drunk up to 5 years old.

A little rosé is made, and now that this is bottled less than a year after the harvest, it is more able to display a pleasant freshness. The Martins also make some white wine—only 6,500 bottles a year, but it is a well balanced, clean and fruity drink. First made in the 1980 harvest, it is something which the sons are keen to develop as they continue to reduce the Carignan plantation in the vineyard.

Jules Martin, who first bottled the family wine in 1952, has now retired, but a good *vigneron* is hard to keep down, and he can be seen in the neighbourhood making deliveries to local customers. He leaves the commercial side of the domaine to Yves; married to a Rasteau girl whose dowry was some Grenache vines from that village, he has been making a Rasteau *vin doux naturel* which is aged in wood for two years and is pale pink as opposed to the normal gold colour. It appears that he must take some more lessons in *vin doux naturel* from his young wife.

Martin, Jules et ses Fils
Domaine Martin   84150 Travaillan

DOMAINES MEFFRE

The Gigondas company of Gabriel Meffre, the largest owner of *Appellation* vines in France, is the proprietor of altogether six

Côtes du Rhône *domaines*: the Domaines du Plan de Dieu, La Meynarde and St-Jean at Travaillan, the Domaine de l'Abbaye de Prébayon and the Domaine du Bois des Dames at Violès, and the Château de Ruth at Ste-Cécile-les-Vignes. The wines of all six *domaines* are good and fairly regular, the best probably being the Château de Ruth; they fill the need for middle-range Côtes du Rhône but lack the individuality to be something exceptional.

Domaines Meffre   84190 Gigondas

DOMAINE MITAN

This small but very good *domaine* of 25 acres is near the village of Vedène, about 10 kilometres from Avignon. It is very much a one-man show, with M. Mitan looking after everything himself, from the vineyards, to the cellars, to the sales of his wine.

The vineyards are set on clayey slopes and are composed of four vines, the Grenache, Cinsault, Syrah and some recently planted Mourvèdre. M. Mitan makes his wine on traditional lines, and after a year's ageing in oak it bears a strong colour and agreeable richness of flavour. It also possesses a softness and finesse that are unusual for wines of the Côtes du Rhône *générique* category.

Less than one-quarter of the wine is rosé, and this too is well made. Its strong pink colour and fullness of taste make it reminiscent of one of the good Gard *département* rosés such as Chusclan.

Mitan, Frédéric
Domaine Mitan   84270 Vedène

DOMAINE DES RICHARDS

A 45-acre *domaine* whose vineyard is made up of Grenache, Syrah, Carignan and Ugni Blanc, this property has belonged to the Combe family for three generations. Like some of their neighbours, they ceased selling their wine in bulk to *négociants* in the early part of the 1970s and are now bottling a successful, richly flavoured Côtes du Rhône red. Vinified along traditional lines, this is aged in approximately 1,500-litre barrels for one year and is very good: darkly coloured, with a touch of black cherries in its aspect, the wine has a raspberry-inspired bouquet of fine depth. There is the flavour of wild raspberries on the palate which continues into a long follow-through, and the Domaine des Richards red should ideally be drunk when it is 3 years old, when extra softness has been gained.

The Combe family, not to be confused with the affable Roger Combe at Vacqueyras, are rather suspicious of foreign visitors and would only release the additional information that they make 10 per cent rosé and 5 per cent white wine.

Combe, Pierre
Domaine des Richards   84150 Violès

DOMAINE STE-APOLLINAIRE

This 37-acre property is set on slight slopes at a height of about 300 metres on the outskirts of the attractive little village of Puyméras, which lies enclosed by the foothills of the Low Alps about 8 kilometres north-east of Vaison-la-Romaine.

Puyméras is surrounded by vines and fruit trees, the latter bent and looking south with one regard in deference to the incessant *mistral* wind. Local articles dating back to 1380 speak of vines being grown in the village, while in the fifteenth century more than 250,000 plants (about 200 acres in modern terms) were said to have been cultivated at Puyméras.

Frédéric Daumas and his wife are a young couple dedicated to planting and tending their vineyards and making their wine by what they term 'bio-dynamic' methods. Thus, rather in the guise of followers of Rudolf Steiner, they will look at the cosmos before replanting vines and will study the lunar cycles before pruning them for instance. This is not as way out as it may sound when one takes into account how important the lunar cycle was considered to be in the last century among merchants in Bordeaux trying to decide when was the most propitious moment for bottling their wine. The pressure exerted through the position of the moon in relation to the earth was regarded as capable of altering bottle levels: less wine would be needed to fill a bottle when the moon was full, for instance.

Matters change a little when it comes to 'leaving the wine alone' in the cellar, however. While a refusal to put down chemical fertilizers in the vineyards is a laudable and positive move, the refusal to use any sulphur dioxide (SO_2) in the wine in order to kill the inevitable bacteria present in it means that the simple pleasure of opening a bottle of wine and drinking it is suppressed. Thus the

Daumas are uneasy if someone visits their cellars without warning, wanting to taste their wine. Why? The answer is that the wine needs at least two hours' aeration if it is to work off the lingering gases that have built up through the failure to kill certain living elements in the wine. Sulphur is to some a contentious weapon to use on a wine, which is not surprising when one tastes some of the more blatant examples of ignorantly made peasant wine that can be found, but it is necessary if only to keep the wine's equilibrium—necessary in small doses, that is.

M. Daumas relies on the Grenache and the Syrah as his principal vines, and the Syrah makes its presence well felt in his Cuvée d'Apolline Côtes du Rhône. Although not heavily coloured, it carries bags of tannin behind the initial fruit and is a wine good for drinking until it is 5 years old. Like the *domaine*'s *cuvée* of pure Syrah, which has a soaring fruit sensation on the palate, it must be opened at least two hours in advance of drinking, and even then may not be capable of throwing off its locked-up gases and early mustiness.

Daumas, Frédéric
Domaine Ste-Apollinaire   84110 Puyméras

DOMAINE ST-MICHEL

This 30-acre domaine is in the charming, almost perfectly restored hamlet of Uchaux, remarkable for the neatness and symmetry of its soft Provençal stone dwellings. Uchaux lies north of Orange on the way to Rochegude and is surrounded by vineyards and thickly wooded countryside. The better vineyards are on the sloping ground at Uchaux, where the soil is predominantly sandy, although most *domaines* such as St-Michel also have plots on the clay soil plain below.

M. Nicolas relies on just three vines—the Grenache for half his plantation and the Syrah and the Cinsault for a quarter each. He likes to vinify his grapes in uncrushed or *raisin entier* form, and after a rapid fermentation of a week or so he stores his wine in concrete for about two years. He has been bottling part of his crop since 1981 and is happy with this move away from dependence on *négociants*.

He makes only red wine, which, bright red in colour, carries a respectable bouquet and a reasonable length of finish. As it stands, it is an honest example of correct Côtes du Rhône, and just possibly it is the sort of wine that would be enhanced by a stay of under half a year in cask.

Nicolas, Jean
Domaine St-Michel   84110 Uchaux

DOMAINE ST-PIERRE

The 63 acres of vines belonging to this *domaine* are spread out over Violès, Gigondas and Vacqueyras, the result of intermarriages over three generations. It is the property of M. Jean-Claude Fauque, a very keen and ambitious grower who has a penchant for fast sports cars—not quite the *vieille France* picture of the country wine grower!

M. Fauque depends on Grenache and Syrah, with a little help from some very old Carignan plants, to make his red Côtes du Rhône. This is vinified traditionally and spends one year in cask. It is a very good wine indeed: bright purple, the bouquet shows the *goût de terroir* characteristics of the better wines from this part of the Vaucluse, recalling damp truffles; the depth of fruit and tannin indicate a well structured and superior wine that is suitable for drinking before its fourth birthday.

The *domaine* also makes quite a good Gigondas and a less appealing Côtes du Rhône rosé. Its future appears to be in good hands, with M. Fauque's son studying at Wine School in Bordeaux.

Fauque, Jean-Claude
Domaine St-Pierre   84150 Violès

DOMAINE DU VIEUX CHÊNE

This 46-acre *domaine* has its vineyards split into three holdings, around the villages of Travaillan, Sérignan and on the Plan de Dieu. It is run by two young brothers, Jean-Claude and Dominique Bouche; Jean-Claude, a wiry-looking, thoughtful man in his early thirties, is a biology and chemistry graduate of Marseille University and admits that it took him a few years to go into wine, because 'I didn't want to spend the rest of my life driving a tractor for eight hours a day.' He then graduated from Montpellier Wine School and soon discovered how wrong his conception of wine-making had been.

He is now completely involved in the subject and has the unbridled attitude of a young educated man. The *domaine*'s vines are mainly Grenache (about 75 per cent), with 15 per cent Syrah; the difference is made up of Cinsault and the comparatively rare Muscardin. The grapes are fed into the stainless-steel vats by way of a conveyor belt so that they enter almost completely un-crushed; following an extended maceration and fermentation at controlled temperatures, the wines are stored for about fifteen months in concrete vats until bottling.

The Bouche brothers made their first wine in 1978, before which date their father had been sending the grapes to the Cave Co-opérative at Sérignan. They make two differently styled *cuvées* every year, the fresher, almost strawberry-flavoured one being called Les Capucines, and the sturdier, more traditional one entitled Haie aux Grives. The latter is perhaps more interesting, with greater complexity in its red-black colour and more length provoked by the higher Syrah content. Of course, the brothers would suggest purchasing both wines at once, so that the Capucines could be happily drunk while the Haie aux Grives was getting itself ready to be drunk. Both are good wines, and it is worth keeping an eye open for them.

Bouche, Jean-Claude et Dominique
   Domaine du Vieux Chêne   84150 Camaret

PLAN DEÏ

This curiously named *domaine* represents 35 acres of what used to be the 270-acre Château La Meynarde, which was dispersed in 1979, when Gabriel Meffre bought the major portion of 112 acres plus the Meynarde name. The vines run across the Plan de Dieu, notable for its immense size and for its heaps of small alluvial stones, and are an interesting mixture of 65 per cent Grenache, 25 per cent Mourvèdre and 10 per cent Counoise.

Jean-Marie Lobreau sells his wines under two names, Plan Deï and La Vignonnerie; a 35-year-old Burgundian, he was the wine-maker at La Meynarde until the dispersal of the property, and for his Plan Deï *cuvée* he ferments the grapes at no more than 20 °C in stainless steel, adding the finishing touches to the wine with a brief ageing in oak. The wine has a brilliant blackcurrant lustre to it, and the analogy with blackcurrants continues on to the fruit flavour shown on the palate, which is supported by a welcome amount of tannin. By contrast, the *cuvée* La Vignonnerie is a fruity, soft wine, with only a medium red colour, as it is made from almost 100 per cent Grenache. It should be drunk within a year or so of the harvest.

Lobreau, Jean-Marie
    Plan Deï   84150 Travaillan

SOCIÉTÉ DES GRANDS VINS DE CHÂTEAUNEUF-DU-PAPE ET DES CÔTES DU RHÔNE

This sizeable company owns several *domaines* in Châteauneuf-du-Pape and the Côtes du Rhône, the most famous being the Château des Fines Roches at Châteauneuf-du-Pape. The Côtes du Rhône wines in general tend to lack flair and can be very humdrum, the sort of wine that raises false hopes when found on a supermarket shelf at an interesting price. This is very sad because some years ago the quality of the *domaine* wines used to be very fine. Today the firm's two leading Côtes du Rhône *domaines* are the Château du Bois de la Garde and the Château du Prieuré St-Joseph.

SGVC   84230 Châteauneuf-du-Pape

OTHER CÔTES DU RHÔNE DOMAINES IN THE VAUCLUSE DÉPARTEMENT

Alessandrini, Vincent
    Domaine Bois Lauzon   84100 Orange
d'Arnaudy, J.-P.
    Château de La Serre   84800 L'Isle-sur-la-Sorgue
Autard, Paul
    Domaine Autard   84350 Courthézon
Barbaud, Jean Paul
    Domaine des Favards   84150 Violès
Biscarrat, François
    Domaine de la Guicharde   84430 Derboux
Biscarrat, Louis
    Château du Grand-Prébois   84100 Orange
Boyer et Fils
    Domaine de Bel-Air   84150 Violès
Brun, Pierre
    Domaine de la Cambuse   84110 Villedieu

Charasse, Claude et Associés
  Domaine de St-Claude   84110 Vaison-la-Romaine
Combe, Pierre
  Domaine de Tenon   84150 Violès
Coulon, Paul et Fils
  La Ferme Pisan   84110 Rasteau
Damoy, Julien
  Domaine de la Renjarde   84100 Sérignan
Daniel, Guy
  Domaine La Bastide St-
  Vincent   84150 Violès
Daussant, Eric
  Domaine de Grand Plantier   84270 Vedène
Deforge, Jean
  Domaine Jean Deforge   84470 Châteauneuf-de-Gadagne
Farjon, Albert
  Les Grands Rois   84290 Ste-Cécile-les-Vignes
Faurous, Henri et Fils
  Domaine Le Grand Retour   84150 Travaillan
Garagnon, Paul
  Domaine du Gros-Pata   84110 Vaison-la-Romaine
Gargani, R.
  La Fauconnière   84 St-Romain-de-Mallegarde
Gleize, André
  Vignoble Gleize   84150 Violès
Gonnet, Cohendy et Fils
  Domaine La Berthète   84150 Camaret
Groiller, M.
  Domaine de Boilauzon   84150 Travaillan
Jaume, Alain
  Domaine du Grand Veneur   84110 Orange
Jullien et Fils
  Domaine de l'Aigaillons   84 Suzette
Martin, Hélène et Fils
  Domaine de Grangeneuve   84150 Jonquières
Maurizot, Charles
  Domaine Les Roures
  du Plan de Dieu   84150 Travaillan
Meffre, Gérard
  Château La Courançonne   84150 Violès

Perrin, Pierre
  Cru de Coudoulet, Domaine
  de Beaucastel   84350 Courthézon
Sahuc, Abel
  Domaine de la Grand' Ribe 84290 Ste-Cécile-les-Vignes
Saurel, S.
  Domaine de la Combe Dieu 84 La Baumette
Serguier, Yves et Fils
  Clos Simian   84110 Uchaux

NÉGOCIANTS

BELLICARD

Founded at Mâcon in 1889, this house moved a large part of its business to Avignon in 1920. It owns no vineyards, and although its wine is bought shortly after the harvest—in November—none is actually brought to the company cellars until the following spring. Half the wine is from Caves Co-opératives, and half from small *vignerons*.

Their two best-selling wines are the Côtes du Rhône *générique* and Tavel. The red Côtes du Rhône is a very good wine, well-coloured and full-flavoured, with just a hint of *macération carbonique* about it. The Tavel rosé is generally a sound wine with adequate fruit in it, but can sometimes be a little hard or metallic.

LE CELLIER DES DAUPHINS

The Cellier des Dauphins at Tulette acts as a bottling and marketing centre for ten local Caves Co-opératives. These are the Co-opératives of Ste-Cécile-les-Vignes (Cécilia), Nyons, Rochegude, St-Maurice-sur-Eygues, St-Pantaléon-les-Vignes, Suze-la-Rousse, Tulette (Costebelle), Tulette (Nouvelle), Vaison-la-Romaine and Vinsobres.

The average annual amount of wine handled by the Cellier is 297,000 hectolitres all of which comes from the ten member Co-opératives, which in turn represent 3,450 *vignerons* from the neighbouring countryside.

In 1974 the Cellier des Dauphins first mounted a large publicity campaign in leading French magazines and newspapers, and this then bold move greatly enhanced its image and renown. Its wines cannot be considered to be in the top rank, however; the reds often seem to lack character and style, and the rosé can be disappointingly harsh.

Le Cellier des Dauphins   26130 Tulette

DAVID ET FOILLARD

This *négociant-éleveur* company was founded in the Beaujolais in 1826 and now possesses a subsidiary that deals in all the wines of the southern Côtes du Rhône. These are headed in volume by the cheaper wines from the whole area—Côtes du Rhône, Côtes du Ventoux and Coteaux du Tricastin. A considerable quantity are exported, and the wines are generally of a quite reasonable standard.

David, T., et Foillard, L.   84700 Sorgues

A. OGIER ET FILS

Founded in 1824, this *négociant-éleveur* company is situated in the town of Sorgues, near Châteauneuf-du-Pape. It deals in all the *Appellation* wines of the Côtes du Rhône and buys them immediately after the harvest, in mid-October. The various wines are then left to mature in their modern cellars, for a duration of two or three years for the Hermitages and the Châteauneuf-du-Papes.

The quality of the wines is constant without being startling. The Côtes du Rhône is a sound wine, but it lacks the individuality of the best *domaines*. The house's Châteauneuf-du-Pape is probably its leading wine.

A. Ogier et Fils   84700 Sorgues

SOCIÉTÉ NOUVELLE DES VINS FINS SALAVERT

Founded at Bourg-St-Andéol in 1840, Salavert deals in all the main wines of the Côtes du Rhône and its neighbouring wine regions, such as the Côtes du Ventoux, Côtes du Vivarais and Côtes de Provence. The various wines are bought during the year following the harvest, and are aged and bottled in the company's underground cellars near the Rhône.

Although the company's reputation used to be based upon its fine Rhône wines, such as Hermitage and Châteauneuf-du-Pape, it has recently turned its attention more towards the cheaper wines of the Rhône Valley and Provence. These are generally very soundly made and represent good value for money. At the same time Salavert continues to produce worthy fine wines, its Châteauneuf-du-Pape being particularly notable.

Société Nouvelle des	
Vins Fins Salavert	07700 Bourg-St-Andéol

LA VIEILLE FERME

This branded wine is successfully produced by Jean-Pierre Perrin, whose family owns the Domaine de Beaucastel at Châteauneuf-du-Pape. Formerly made from grapes bought from Côtes du Rhône vineyards, it is now composed of grapes and wine bought in the Côtes du Ventoux area (q.v.). It is a good young drinking wine.

La Vieille Ferme	
J.-P. Perrin	84100 Orange

OTHER CÔTES DU RHÔNE NÉGOCIANTS

Abbaye de Bouchet	26130 Bouchet
Barbier, Léon et Fils	84230 Châteauneuf-du-Pape
Boissy et Delaygue	07130 Cornas
Brotte, Jean-Pierre	84230 Châteauneuf-du-Pape
Du Peloux et Cie	84350 Courthézon
Garnier, Camille	30200 Bagnols-sur-Cèze
Malbec, Eugène	84230 Châteauneuf-du-Pape
Meffre, Ets. G.	84190 Gigondas
Mouret, Michel	84340 Entrechaux
Paul-Etienne, Père et Fils	07130 St-Péray
Revol, Léon	26600 Tain l'Hermitage
Sirop, Pierre	84110 Vaison-la-Romaine

LEADING CÔTES DU RHÔNE CAVES CO-OPÉRATIVES

With sixty-six Caves Co-opératives spread out in the Ardèche, Drôme, Gard and Vaucluse *départements*, there is obviously an enormous selection of different Côtes du Rhône *génériques* from which to choose. By no means all these Co-opératives are bottling their wine, although the trend is in that direction. Since the 1970s less well-known Co-opératives have started to bottle a part of their production—generally that wine destined for ageing in the few casks owned by the Co-opérative—or they have formed themselves into a group with their neighbours for the centralized bottling of their best wine. The Union des Caves de l'Uzège, based at Uzès in the Gard, is an example: it has sixteen member Co-opératives.

Particularly recommended among this mass of producers are three Co-opératives, those of Puyméras and of Villedieu in the Vaucluse and of Vénéjan in the Gard. Puyméras makes an extremely sound Côtes du Rhône *rouge*, fully styled in an old-fashioned way and helped by six months' ageing in cask. Perhaps high altitude is the secret, for the neighbouring Co-opérative of Villedieu also draws its grapes from vineyards about 250 metres up and makes a very good job of vinifying them. Marginally less impressive than the wine of Puyméras, their Côtes du Rhône red is also traditional, with some ageing in cask, and although not an abundantly fruity wine, has an interesting complexity of spicy and tannic flavours. Their white wine is also very respectable; made mainly from the Bourboulenc and the Grenache Blanc with minor support from the Clairette, its fruitiness would have even more zest with just a little more acidity.

Vénéjan is about 4 kilometres north-east of Bagnols-sur-Cèze and is as pretty a Provençal village as one could wish to encounter: cobbled stone streets with wisteria tumbling down the outside of the soft stone houses in cascades of pale blue and a finely restored twelfth-century chapel on a small hillside. The Co-opérative bottles about 15,000 litres of red and rosé every year, and its red is of major interest. Pale, with touches of pink at the top, it displays a satisfying soft blackcurrant fruit, which has charm and balance enough to mould in well with the wine's acidity. It makes an attractive summer wine, one that should be drunk within its first two years.

There follows a list of the principal Caves Co-opératives making Côtes du Rhône red, white and rosé.

Co-opérative Vinicole 'Comtadine Dauphinoise'	84110 Puyméras
Cave Co-opérative de Vénéjan	30200 Vénéjan
Cave Co-opérative 'La Vigneronne'	84110 Villedieu
Cave Co-opérative des Vignerons	30200 Bagnols-sur-Cèze
Cave des Vignerons	30300 Cavillargues
Cave des Vignerons du Duché de Gadagne	84470 Châteauneuf-de-Gadagne
Cave Co-opérative des Coteaux	30210 Fournes
Cave Co-opérative Vinicole	84310 Morières
Cave Co-opérative Agricole du Nyonnais	26110 Nyons
Les Vignerons du Castelas	30650 Rochefort-du-Gard
Cave Co-opérative de St-Hilaire-d'Ozilhan	30210 St-Hilaire d'Ozilhan
Cave Co-opérative Vinicole 'Cécilia'	84290 Ste-Cécile-les-Vignes
Cave des Vignerons Reunis	84290 Ste-Cécile-les-Vignes
Co-opérative Vinicole Les Coteaux du Rhône	84100 Sérignan-du-Comtat
Cave Co-opérative Vinicole La Suzienne	26130 Suze-la-Rousse
Cave Co-opérative de Tresques	30330 Tresques
Cave Co-opérative Costebelle	26130 Tulette
Co-opérative Vinicole des Coteaux de Tulette	26130 Tulette
Cave Co-opérative des Vignerons	84110 Vaison-la-Romaine

17

Other Wines and Liqueurs

AIGUEBELLE

Aiguebelle liqueur comes from a Trappist abbey set in some remote hills 16 kilometres south-east of the nougat town of Montélimar. It is not one of France's best-known liqueurs, and its popularity has always been fairly localized around its region of production. Its similarity to the more celebrated, more widely marketed Green Chartreuse may have contributed to this, for both are made on a secret, herb-based formula, and both are green liqueurs.

In 1137 the abbey of Notre Dame d'Aiguebelle was founded by the monks of an expanding Trappist order whose seat was in the Champagne country. The Trappist philosophy of life is rigid; industry and dedication are all-important, and the monks' day is consequently divided into four strictly defined stages: prayer, work, reading or study, and reception. From the very beginning, opportunities for outside industry were limited at Aiguebelle since the surrounding countryside was particularly craggy and non-productive. Thus for many years, throughout the Middle Ages and beyond, the monks were able only to eke out the most primitive rural existence. The abbey was then abandoned at the time of the French Revolution, but shortly afterwards, in 1815, some enterprising Swiss Trappists arrived to restart the community with greater energy than ever before.

So successful were the Swiss monks that by the start of the twentieth century Aiguebelle found itself barely able to support the dependencies that had sprung up since 1815. Unfortunately, a steady source of income—and wine—had been forfeited during the Revolution, when the Abbey lost its land holdings at Gigondas

and Vacqueyras in the Vaucluse *département*. The spartan nature
of the country around continued to rule out any serious agricultural exploitation, so the brothers were compelled to find another
source of income, somehow or other.

The solution lay in the monastic archives, which contained old
'elixir' recipes dating from different times during the abbey's
existence. Father Aelred, a large benign monk who has been at
Aiguebelle since 1958, proceeded to explain how the Aiguebelle
Trappists had decided to use their recipe: 'In olden days, the
Fathers here would make up a very potent elixir that was at least
60° Gay Lussac. Local plants like sage, verbena and rosemary
were macerated and then distilled, and the fiery mixture would be
drunk in the main by the inhabitants of the Abbey. At that time
each monastery would have a specialist herbalist, who would be
charged with creating a magic recipe, the contents of which, of
course, remained a closely guarded secret. Early in the twentieth
century the Fathers decided to go back through our archives and
came up with an old elixir recipe. This formed the basis of a liqueur
that they resolved to produce commercially. In view of the fact
that they couldn't be agricultural, they became industrial instead!'

At first, the precise ingredients of the magic formula eluded the
Fathers. By 1930, however, a suitable composition had been
perfected: a mixture of thirty-five Provençal plants and roots were
to make up the Green Liqueur of Aiguebelle. Soon afterwards
twenty other liqueurs were devised, notably a Yellow Liqueur
that was, in fact, a sweeter cousin of the Green. All these were
made on quite a large scale, and the range of choice was broadened
by the subsequent production of '*eau-de-vie*' brandies, such as
framboise (raspberry) and *mirabelle* (plum). In 1960 the monks
started to make concentrated fruit syrups as well, and these have
now come to form nine-tenths of the business.

The Green and Yellow Liqueurs are the two most important of
the abbey's selection of liqueurs and brandies. They are composed
of root plants, cloves, herbs and flowers that come from as far
afield as the Equatorial regions. About eight of the sixty white-
robed monks occupy themselves with the distillery, and first
macerate the plants and flowers in neutral alcohol spirit. This
mixture is then distilled very slowly for twelve hours in copper
stills and is afterwards left to stabilize in glass-lined vats for

around eighteen months. Before bottling there is a small addition of sugar syrup to provide a little extra sweetness: the Yellow Liqueur receives a larger dose than the Green.

The Aiguebelle Green Liqueur is a sweet, quite smooth drink that seems to possess traces of mint in its flavour. A certain aromatic spiciness comes out in the aftertaste, and the liqueur is also believed by some supporters to have outstanding restorative qualities. The Yellow Liqueur, which is made from about twenty-five assorted plants, is sweeter still and carries less diversity of flavour. Among the other liqueurs, the apricot is outstanding.

Consumption of the liqueurs has fallen away since the Second World War, when a peak was attained through the presence in France of the combined American forces. Many southern French bars have a bottle on their shelves, but it is usually dust-covered and hidden behind rows of Aiguebelle fruit syrups. For the Trappist monks, however, the Green Liqueur carries a special importance and a special memory, since it was that which originally enabled them to increase their contacts and aid as far abroad as Hong Kong, the United States and Brazil.

Distillerie d'Aiguebelle   26230 Grignan

CHÂTILLON-EN-DIOIS

The wine-producing region of Châtillon-en-Diois is very restricted, with vineyards covering no more than 150 acres. It is centred on a dozen villages and hamlets to the south and east of Die, and all the wine—red, white and rosé—is made by the Cave Co-opérative of Die.

In 1974, Châtillon-en-Diois was promoted from VDQS (*Vin Délimité de Qualité Supérieure*) status to full *Appellation Contrôlée*. As a result the red and rosé wines have to be three-quarters composed of the Gamay Noir grape, with one-quarter coming from the Syrah and Pinot Noir grape varieties. The white wines also bear a Burgundian slant and must be made from the Aligoté and Chardonnay grapes, of which 14 acres have been planted.

The principal vine-growing communities are Châtillon-en-Diois, Menglon, St-Romain and Laval d'Aix. All are in the beautiful, wild, mountainous countryside that follows the River Drôme as it runs south of Die and on to the most southerly wine-producing village, Poyols, which is 19 kilometres from Die.

Every year a total of about 275,000 litres of wine is made. These undergo a brief vinification, with a rapid fermentation and bottling early in the new year. Unfortunately, the wines are all thoroughly nondescript, the red in particular failing to live up to its noble Gamay-Syrah-Pinot 'breeding'. Often very pale, weak and watery, it possesses little intrinsic charm or character; it merely remains a point of amazement that such a wine can have been considered worthy, on its own, of qualifying for the highest accolade in French viticulture—full *Appellation* status.

Cave Co-opérative de Die   26150 Die

CLAIRETTE DE DIE

About 65 kilometres south-east of Valence, the old town of Die nestles easily into the first Alpine mountain ranges. Beside it the River Drôme runs on a steady course towards the Rhône, and the green, poplar-lined Drôme Valley exactly traces the vineyards of Clairette de Die. These extend for 56 kilometres on either bank, all the way from Aouste, 3 kilometres east of Crest, up to Luc-en-Diois, 19 kilometres south-east of Die.

As the vineyards go east, the countryside becomes steadily more alpine. Little chalets that stand away from the sleepy villages are dwarfed by the high mountains looming over them; sudden patches of luscious, dark green grass are cropped by grazing goats, and at the foot of the hillsides tight little clumps of pine trees add extra colour to the vivid scene.

Wine has probably been made in the region of Die for almost 2,000 years, since there was a lengthy reference to a local wine in Chapter 9 of Pliny's *Natural History* (*c.* AD 77). Here Pliny criticized the thirteen known varieties of sweet wine then found in Greece and the Roman Empire, some of them, he said, being products of art and not of Nature, while others were guilty of being given mixtures devised to make them simulate honey. One, known as honey wine, even received salt and honey in its must, thereby producing a very rough flavour. The star wine, for Pliny, was the natural form of 'Aigleucos' or sweet wine then being made by the Voconces people. 'In order to make it,' Pliny wrote, 'they keep the grape hanging on the tree for a considerable time, taking care to twist the stalk.' When Pliny was writing the capital town of the Voconces was called Dea Augusta; today it is Die.

The wine Pliny referred to is sparkling today but is still made by natural methods, with no addition of any substance or liquid to give it its bubbles. It goes by the title of Clairette de Die *Tradition*, or *Demi-Sec*. Meanwhile another sparkling wine is now made, along formal Champagne lines, and this sells as Clairette de Die *Brut*. Unlike the *Tradition*, which is made from the Clairette and Muscat grapes, the *Brut* comes solely from the low-scented Clairette grape, and has less individual style about it. Finally, there is a little still dry white wine of quite reasonable quality, made generally from the Clairette. This was Die's main wine until 1926, when the first sparkling wine experiments took place.

Because the wine region is so long, the composition of the vineyards is very varied, and the *Tradition* wines from different ends of the *Appellation* can vary very widely in character. The most common soil elements are limestone and clay, while the rock soil base becomes progressively harder the nearer one is to Die and the high Alps. This seems to suit the Muscat more than the Clairette, but in recent years it has been the latter whose plantation has increased. This is because it is a hardier vine than the Muscat, and because the more neutral-tasting *Brut* wine is easier to sell than the *Tradition*. The Muscat used at Die is the *petits grains* variety, which is also found at Beaumes-de-Venise and which gives the *Tradition* its strong, flowery bouquet.

Growers differ over how much Muscat should be included in the *Tradition* wine, however. The Cave Co-opérative of Die makes about three-quarters of all Clairette de Die, and its *Tradition* is composed of half-Muscat and half-Clairette. By contrast, the next largest wine house, Buffardel Frères, prefer a combination of three-quarters Clairette and one-quarter Muscat. Smaller *vignerons* sometimes rely on three-quarters Muscat and only one-quarter Clairette. For the drinker there is one easy answer— personal taste. Those who like the strongly scented Muscat will choose the third type of wine.

The *vendanges* commence in October and continue into November, by when the grapes are usually very ripe and sugary. On arrival at the cellar, the harvest is crushed, pressed, and the juice is run off into isothermal vats that are cooled to a temperature of minus 3 °C. This is left to settle for forty-eight hours and is then put through a centrifuge machine in order to rid it of all loose particles. Finally, the juice is filtered lightly, which removes the largest yeast cells and delays the start of fermentation.

This is the broad technique used in making the *Tradition*, where the principal idea is to ferment the wine extremely slowly, even to the point of filtering it when fermentation seems to be going too fast. Thus by the time the wine is bottled in January, there is still some unfermented sugar left in it, and it is the subsequent fermentation of this sugar inside the bottle that makes the wine sparkling. By prolonging the alcoholic fermentation for such a long time, the growers are able to achieve their sparkling wine without having to add any yeasts or extra sugar.

Clearly, the small *vignerons* do not possess the Cave Coopérative's isothermal vats, so instead they filter their wine a little more often in order to spin out its fermentation. They too start bottling around the month of February; by law all Clairette de Die *Tradition* must thereafter spend at least four months in the bottle, to make sure that all fermentation is completely finished before the wine is released for sale. In reality most growers leave their *Tradition* for about six months, while the *Brut* must by law always spend nine months in bottle before being disgorged.

The final operation in the elaboration of the *Tradition* sparkling wine is the *dégorgement*, or removal of the deposits gathered in the bottle during the second stage of fermentation. The wine is filtered under carbon dioxide pressurization so that all its natural gas will be carefully preserved. It is then re-bottled, and left for a month or two to settle down; consequently, it is always something over 1 year old when first put out on sale.

This is the oldest sparkling wine at Die, for the *Brut* did not appear until the early 1960s. The latter is vinified just like Champagne, with the addition of sugar and yeasts in order to make it sparkling, and with a *remuage*, or turning of the bottles, in order to clear the wine of its deposits. Less distinctively flavoured than the *Tradition*, the *Brut* has proved an easier wine to market, and has quickly come to account for around 40 per cent of all Clairette de Die; its promotion has been notably supported by Buffardel Frères, a house which is run by two brothers born in the Champagne country.

The difference in style between the two sparkling wines is startling. The *Brut* is usually paler and much less scented and fully flavoured; because of this it is simpler to drink than the *Tradition*, and a well-chilled bottle can disappear very rapidly on a warm summer's afternoon. The *Tradition* is the more interesting wine, however. It is often called *Demi-Sec*, and this description gives some idea of its basic style. Slightly lime-yellow coloured, it is a wine of appealing richness and roundness, whose flavours resemble apples or gooseberries; a good bottle has a long, just very partly sweet aftertaste. It is not a 'quaffing' wine like the *Brut*, but a glass or two is ideal as the introduction to a good meal.

Production of Clairette de Die has increased steadily over the years to around 6 million bottles, and one of the main reasons for this is the impetus given to the region by its ambitious Cave Co-opérative. Founded in 1951, this now has a well organized international sales network, and farmers have therefore been persuaded to enlarge their vine holdings. For many years Clairette de Die was pretty well unknown beyond the south of France, and so there existed little incentive to plant vineyards on a more widespread scale.

Other leading producers include Buffardel Frères and the CUMA (Co-opérative for the Use of Agricultural Materials). Buffardel Frères is possibly the best house in Clairette de Die, and its wines are always thoroughly consistent and well balanced. In exceptional years they give their wine a vintage, as in Champagne, and this *tête de cuvée* represents Clairette de Die at its very best. Otherwise all the wine is sold without a vintage, so that the wine of different years can be blended together to form a uniform style.

CUMA is a looser organization than either the Co-opérative or Buffardel Frères and consists of about thirty small farmer-*vignerons* who broke away from the Co-opérative in 1967. Each man makes and sells his own wine individually but shares out all equipment, be it for vineyards, wheat, maize or the sunflower plantations that have been making a comeback recently; for the vines this includes caterpillar-track tractors that are used on the slopes and all vineyard spraying tools, as well as a mobile filtering machine. The standards of all the growers are generally very good, although some have taken to using plastic tops instead of corks to stopper their bottles. The effect on the wine is somewhat dubious, since the plastic 'breathes' less than a cork. Among these smaller growers, prominent producers include Pierre Salabelle, Georges Poulet, René Aubert, Jean-Claude Vincent, Henri Grangeron and

Archard-Vincent. All make wine of very good quality, although like most Clairette de Die it is not intended for long keeping, three years being an average lifespan.

Leading Clairette de Die Growers

Achard, Claude	26 Barsac par Die
Andrieux, Albert	26 Saillans
Archard-Vincent	26 Ste-Croix
Aubert, René	26 Aurel par Saillans
Banet, Georges	26 Saillans
Barnier, Maurice	26 Pontaix
Barnier, Yvon	26 Pontaix
Bec, Martial	26 Aurel par Saillans
Buffardel Frères	26150 Die
Carod, A.	26 Vercheny
Cave Co-opérative de Die	26150 Die
Decorse, Fernand	26 Barsac par Die
Girard Fils	26150 Die
Grangeron, Henri	26 Ste-Croix
Granon, Michel	26 Pontaix
Long, André	26 Barsac par Die
Marcel, Emile	26 Ponet-St Aubin par Die
Marcel, René	26 Pontaix
Poulet, Elie	26 Vercheny
Poulet, Georges	26 Pontaix
Poulet, Roger	26 Pontaix
Raspail, Georges	26 Aurel par Saillans
Salabelle, Pierre	26 Barsac par Die
Truchefaud, André	26 Barsac par Die
Vincent, Jean-Claude	26 Barsac par Die

COTEAUX DU TRICASTIN

The Coteaux du Tricastin is the wine region that has expanded most quickly near the Côtes du Rhône, and since the late 1950s its vineyards have increased from almost nothing to nearly 3,500 acres. They are set in parched countryside east of the Rhône between Montélimar and Bollène, with their centre at Les Granges-Gontardes, a hamlet near Donzère.

Tricastin's main areas of production are Les Granges-Gontardes, La Baume-de-Transit, Roussas, Malataverne, Allan, Valaurie, Donzère and Grignan. All are tiny, very quiet communities that in some cases had become almost derelict before the increase in vine-growing. Les Granges-Gontardes, for instance, was a village that had lost its school, its shop and almost all its inhabitants to the nearby factories until some enthusiastic wine-growers arrived in 1964. The three or four families that went there at that time had been French settlers in Algeria, forced to leave the country after the granting of independence. Receiving favourable terms from the public authorities and agricultural banks, they proceeded to reclaim much of the wooded countryside around Donzère and Les Granges-Gontardes.

This land was generally poor and mostly supported thick masses of small oaks, pine bushes and lavender plants. It was also a renowned centre for black truffles, which have a definite preference for the sturdy little oak trees of the Tricastin. Even the truffle industry was in sharp decline, however. Before 1900 the local yield had been around 2,000 tonnes a year; after the First World War, many young men never returned to continue the tradition, and now the average annual yield is no more than 100 tonnes.

In 1964 Coteaux du Tricastin was promoted to *VDQS* (*Vin Délimité de Qualité Supérieure*) status, and at the same time large-scale replantation commenced on ground that had not held vines since phylloxera. With almost scientific care and precision, the choice of vines was made; some of the vineyards were model examples, their vines being selected according to various climatic and soil factors that had been closely analysed.

The pattern that emerged copied the general format of Châteauneuf-du-Pape, particularly because many of the new vineyards had been created on similarly stony ground. In places no earth at all is visible among the vine stems, and the effect of such ground—to give the grapes extra heat—is just as at Châteauneuf-du-Pape. Accordingly, the vines chosen were the Grenache (50–60 per cent), the Cinsault (about 15 per cent), the Syrah (about 20 per cent), the Mourvèdre and the Carignan. The latter, a high producer, was to be planted as little as possible.

Around Tricastin the *mistral* wind reaches some of its fastest speeds—over 100 kph on occasions—and this directly influences the working of the vineyards. Thus the vines have to be trained against strong 1·2-metre stakes that need to be firmly hammered into the stone-covered ground. When snow is in the offing—and it is not uncommon—the *vigneron* can do very little to protect his vineyards: any straw put down among the vines is promptly blown away by the *mistral*.

The *vendanges* last from the end of September well into October, and the red wines are generally given only a brief vinification; after crushing and destalking, the grapes are fermented for four to six days, and most of the wine is then stored in concrete vats for several months before bottling. The wine sold off in bulk to *négociants* all over France will leave the cellars more quickly, however, normally within three or four months of the harvest.

The best-known *domaines* at Tricastin are two of the oldest: the Domaine de la Tour d'Elyssas, with its two *Crus* Le Devoy and Les Echirousses, and the Domaine de Grangeneuve at Roussas. The Domaine de la Tour d'Elyssas was started in 1966 by M. Pierre Labeye and became immediately memorable for its vast 15-metre-high circular tower that housed the fermenting vats in spectacular style next to the cellars. The locals had never seen anything like it, but, alas, M. Labeye's futurism has become undone by the world recession, and the 260-acre property was put into the hands of the Receiver in late 1981, though it is still making wine.

The *domaine* sells about 200,000 bottles a year, including the two *Crus* already mentioned, a pure Syrah wine and some rosé. Most interesting is the Syrah wine, since it has greater depth and length of finish than either of the light-styled *Crus*. Nevertheless, all are good drinking wines; they should not be kept for more than about three years.

The Domaine de Grangeneuve at Roussas and the Domaine des Lones at St-Paul-les-Trois-Châteaux are owned by Mme Odette Bour, a widow who is helped by her two attractive daughters in the running of the properties. The Bours planted their vineyards in 1965 and started bottling their wine in 1974; the Grangeneuve wine comes from about 240 acres of vines made up of 50 per cent Grenache, 30 per cent Syrah and 20 per cent mixed between Cinsault, Mourvèdre and Carignan, the last-named grape being used in the rather unimpressive rosé. Their red wine is the best at Tricastin, one that fully justifies the decision in 1974 to award full

Appellation status to this area. It carries a deeper red colour than the wine of Elyssas and greater profundity of flavour. Certainly the presence of more Syrah than usual is evident, for this is the most complex and best perfumed wine in the *Appellation*. It is fermented in stainless steel after the grapes have been crushed in the normal way and goes out for sale about a year after the harvest. Its tannin level is then still quite pronounced, and it is better to drink the wine when it is between 2 and 3 years old.

In style the Tricastin wines resemble some of the nearest Côtes du Rhône wines from Suze-la-Rousse and Rochegude, which are themselves soft and easy to drink. Only rarely are these wines aged in wood—some *cuvées* from the Domaine de la Tour d'Elyssas and the Cellier des Templiers Cave Co-opérative at Richerenches spend a few months in cask—and with more and more private *domaines* beginning to bottle their wine, a greater variety of approach will no doubt be noted in the coming years.

Barely 5 per cent of the annual production of around 40,000 hectolitres is rosé, and this is noticeably inferior to the red wine. A tiny amount of white wine is also made, based on the Grenache Blanc, Clairette, Picpoul, Bourboulenc and Ugni Blanc, but it is only of passing interest.

The years 1978, 1979 and 1981 were by and large good ones at Tricastin, while the 1980s were rather light. As a rule the wines of Tricastin are made to be drunk before they are 2 or 3 years old, although the best *cuvées*, aged in cask, can live up to four years.

Leading Growers in the Coteaux du Tricastin

Bour, Mme Odette
    Domaine de Grangeneuve   26 Roussas
Vergoby Frères   26290 Les Granges-Gontardes
Domaine de la Tour d'Elyssas   26290 Les Granges-Gontardes
Cave Co-opérative Le Cellier
    des Templiers   84 Richerenches
Almoric   26 Allan
Berthet-Rayne, Père et Fils   26290 Donzère
Berthet, Paul   84290 Cairanne
Boyer, Philip   26130 Suze-la-Rousse
Brachet, Jean et Fils
    Domaine du Serre Rouge   26230 Valaurie

Cornillon, Ludovic	26130 La Baume-de-Transit
Estève, Jean-Pierre	
Domaine du Bois Noir	26130 La Baume-de-Transit
Etienne, Gaston et Fils	
Domaine Ste-Agnes	26 Malataverne
Feschet, Robert	26 Bouchet
Jalifier, Jacques	
Domaine de Raspail	26130 La Baume-de-Transit
Pommier, Hubert	
Domaine La Curate	26 Malataverne
Roth-Morel	
Les Estubiers	26290 Les Granges-Gontardes
Roux, Mme Renée	26130 La Baume-de-Transit
Le Terroir St-Rémy	26130 La Baume-de-Transit
Truffaut, Pierre	26 Malataverne
Les Caves de Montbrison	26 Montbrison
Cave Co-opérative Vinicole de	
Rochegude	26130 Rochegude
Co-opérative Vinicole	
'La Suzienne'	26130 Suze-la-Rousse
Le Cellier des Dauphins	26130 Tulette

CÔTES DU VENTOUX

The extensive Côtes du Ventoux vineyards, numbering over 20,000 acres, are situated along the southern flank of the massive Mont Ventoux (1,770 metres), and are mostly spread out over several communities that run in two lines across the south of the mountain. The upper line, composed of Caromb, Bédoin and Flassan, is nearest the mountain and is separated from the other villages, Mazan, Mormoiron, and Villes St-Auzon, by a sweeping 8-kilometre-wide valley that contains row upon row of wine grapes, table grapes and cherry trees. North of these, near Malaucène, Beaumont-du-Ventoux also makes a little Côtes du Ventoux as do Pernes-les-Fontaines, St-Didier and Apt further south below Carpentras.

The Ventoux countryside possesses an unrestrained natural beauty, and its villages are some of the least changed of the

Vaucluse *département* that runs east of the Rhône. The area has a long-established tradition as a centre of table-grape growing, with the Muscat eating grape a speciality, but it has attracted greater attention through its red, rosé and white wines, which were promoted to full *Appellation Contrôlée* status in 1974.

The style of these wines is surprisingly out of keeping with those from the nearby Côtes du Rhône vineyards, for they are invariably much lighter in colour and flavour. The grapes used in the wines' making are much the same as usual—Grenache, Carignan (maximum 30 per cent), Cinsault, Syrah and Mourvèdre—but they are in places grown at altitudes of 400 metres or more. While these grapes will not ripen up as well as those growing down on the plain, they cannot be considered responsible for the wines' lightness. It may be more a question of the soil composition and/or the vinification. The soil varies sharply all over the *Appellation* area, ranging between gravel, sand, clay and chalk.

The vinification of the Ventoux wines is certainly somewhat contentious. The *vignerons* have always made their wine *en café* and see no good reason why they should change. Vinification *en café* consists of a speedy, forty-eight-hour fermentation, a brief rest period in the vat and an early release for sale. Wines made in this way live up to their title: they are very pale, barely darker than rosé, low in alcohol (the minimum degree is 11) and have no tannins or depth to make them anything other than good for swigging back on a shaded café terrace. 'Uncomplicated' is how some connoisseurs might describe them, but sadly this seems to miss the point. Wines of a similar nature are made in many parts of Languedoc and the Midi, so it is hard to see why the red wines of Côtes du Ventoux should have been considered worthy of their own *Appellation* as long ago as 1974.

There are only a few private growers in this Co-opérative-dominated area, and their wines are interesting, for as much as anything they show the differences in the mentality of the growers. The most thoughtful wine-maker in Ventoux is certainly Jean-Pierre Perrin, who, as the son of the late and very respected M. Jacques Perrin of Domaine de Beaucastel at Châteauneuf-du-Pape has had a first-class grounding in winemaking. Jean-Pierre sells a branded wine called La Vieille Ferme, and talked about its origins and current composition: 'The Vieille Ferme as a property does not exist; I am merely a *négociant* buying grapes and young wines that I blend together in my cellars near Jonquières in order to make one uniform wine. I used to buy grapes from the Côtes du Rhône in order to make a Vieille Ferme Côtes du Rhône but switched to the Côtes du Ventoux in 1976 when grape prices in the Rhône rose too steeply. Since then I have never been back to the Rhône.

'The Ventoux provides me with grapes that are ideal for making a fresh wine good for early drinking; the only problem, in fact, is that the grapes produce wines that seem to oxidize quite young. Strangely, it is the tannins that oxidize, unlike Côtes du Rhône, in which it is the alcohol that oxidizes first.'

M. Perrin started the Vieille Ferme in 1971, with the intention of making what he called an 'everyday wine', and so successful has his marketing technique been that he is now selling 800,000 bottles a year, of which almost half go abroad, mainly to the United States, Britain and West Germany. His Vieille Ferme red Ventoux is a wine that shows up well the inclusion of up to 30 per cent Syrah in it, since it carries an attractive bright colour and crisp, clean fruitiness that becomes soft and appealing by its third year. It is certainly one of the best wines in the *Appellation*, a long way ahead of some of the abominations produced by the indifferent Co-opératives.

Another man who makes better wine than most of the Co-opératives is an English exile, Malcolm Swan, who cultivates 20 acres of vines near Mormoiron. He renounced the world of advertising for his vineyard and took over the Domaine des Anges in 1973. His wine is made from the Grenache, Syrah, Carignan and Cinsault grapes, partly traditionally and partly by *macération carbonique*. He is not trying to make a long-keeping wine, since he feels the region to be ill-suited to one. His method is sound, however, and the colour and body of his wine is superior to anything found in the majority of the Co-opératives, which have an alarming tendency to harvest every single grape and quite a bit of their foliage too, even in mediocre years like 1980. The Domaines des Anges wine will never be one that should be closely analysed over a fine dinner, but it is one that can be drunk with pleasure during the eighteen months following the harvest.

One of the other private growers, M. Guy Rey of Aubignan, makes a wine similar in style to Mr Swan's, and it too is perfectly drinkable without being very exciting. A third grower, M. Paul

Coutelen of Flassan, has a different approach in that he ferments his wine for a week and then ages it in cask for about one year. This sounds very fine, but, as mentioned by Jean-Pierre Perrin, the red wine of Ventoux has a natural tendency to oxidize early and seems unable to resist such ageing. As a result, many of M. Coutelen's wines have a perceptible 'woody' taste that overruns all their fruit and flavour.

About a quarter of the wine is rosé, although in some vintages the colour of the reds is barely darker than that of the rosés. They are vinified with just a rapid stay on the skins to extract some colour and can prove quite satisfactory, the Co-opératives of Bédoin, Mormoiron and St-Didier producing some of the best—attractive feather-weight wines that should be drunk well chilled and go well with Chinese food. A very little white wine is made too, generally from the Clairette, Ugni Blanc and Bourboulenc grapes. It is not an interesting wine, although the Cave Co-opérative of Mazan makes a respectable *cuvée*.

Estate-bottled Côtes du Ventoux is not very easy to find, since several of the Co-opératives are unwilling to take on the extra burden of bottling and selling much of their own wine. Consequently, the wine is sold mainly to *négociants* inside and outside France and as a result may often reach its final destination with an unusually strong, attractive dark red colour. Until the Ventoux growers change their outlook a little, such blending will remain commonplace.

Leading Growers in the Côtes du Ventoux

Combe, Philippe	
Domaine de Tenon	84150 Violès
Coutelen, Paul	84 Flassan
GAEC Aymard	84200 Carpentras
Rey, Guy	
Domaine St-Sauveur	84190 Aubignan
Ribas, Augustin	84330 Caromb
Quiot, R.	
Château du Vieux-Lazaret	84230 Châteauneuf-du-Pape
Soulard, J.	
Domaine Ste-Croix	84220 Gordes

Swan, Malcolm

Domaine des Anges	84570 Mormoiron
Cave Co-opérative d'Apt	84400 Apt
Cave Co-opérative de Canteperdrix	84 Mazan
Cave Co-opérative des Coteaux du Mont Ventoux	84410 Bédoin
Cave Co-opérative de la Montagne Rouge	84 Villes-St-Auzon
Cave Co-opérative Les Roches Blanches	84570 Mormoiron
Cave Vinicole La Pernoise	84 Pernes-les-Fontaines
Cave Vinicole St-Marc	84330 Caromb
Co-opérative Intercommunale 'La Courtoise'	84 St-Didier
Co-opérative Vinicole de Beaumont-du-Ventoux	84 Beaumont-du-Ventoux
Co-opérative Vinicole du Lubéron	84 Maubec

CÔTES DU VIVARAIS

The Côtes du Vivarais wine area is set in the Ardèche *département*, on the west side of the Rhône. It is a wild, picturesque region, whose natural wonders have always been better known than its wine; the centrepiece is the giant canyon of the Ardèche—'les Gorges de l'Ardèche'—that runs in a jagged line south-east to join up with the Rhône near Pont St-Esprit. All around there are woods and little hamlets, interspersed by sudden-plunging caves and grottoes, some of the deepest in France. Beside them race fast-flowing streams and rivers full of delicious trout and pike.

The Ardèche's natural beauty and unchanged way of life have recently brought it wide popularity as a holiday region. As a result, its unpretentious country wines have become considerably better-known. The best of them is undoubtedly the Côtes du Vivarais, the only Ardèche wine to be allowed *VDQS* status.

The Côtes du Vivarais has no 'capital' town of its own and is made up of a collection of scattered villages that run in a broad circle around the Gorges de l'Ardèche: Viviers is the most northerly point, and Pont St-Esprit the most southerly. The principal vineyards lie around Orgnac, St-Remèze, St-Montan, Vinezac, Ruoms, Barjac and Gras. All possess their own Caves Co-opératives.

Most of the local wine here is sold as straightforward *vin de consommation courante*. It is made from a mixture of 'noble' and hybrid grapes, its production per acre is high (about 3,000 litres), and it is usually drunk a few months after the harvest, at a price dictated by its alcohol strength. Light and ordinary, it is the sort of wine found in the freezer of any French café.

The Vivarais wines are more regulated, according to both grape variety and volume of yield. They follow the general pattern of the Côtes du Rhône *générique* wines, however, and are made from a combination of grapes headed by the Grenache, Cinsault and Carignan. Sometimes a little Syrah and Gamay are included.

The red and rosé wines must contain at least 11° alcohol by volume, and their production is restricted to around 1,800 litres an acre. The Caves Co-opératives who make them have no false pretensions about their wines: they seek to make light, refreshing wines that are easy to drink and easy to understand. Consequently, fermentation is brief, for between four and eight days, and the red wine is normally bottled before the start of the summer. When well vinified, it is an agreeably fruity wine, one that should be drunk rather than sipped and which benefits from being served chilled. The rosés are less good as a rule, sometimes tasting hard and metallic, while the very little white wine made is also disappointing.

About 6,000 hectolitres of Côtes du Vivarais wines are made every year, and the best Co-opératives are at Orgnac l'Aven and Ruoms, while one of the best *négociants* for these simple country wines is Salavert at Bourg-St-Andéol.

Leading Growers in the Côtes du Vivarais

Cave Co-opérative d'Orgnac l'Aven	07 Orgnac
Union des Caves Co-opératives Vinicoles de l'Ardèche	07 Ruoms
Cave Co-opérative des Coteaux	07 Vinezac
Cave Co-opérative de Vallon Pont d'Arc	07 Vallon Pont d'Arc

Co-opérative Vinicole	07 St-Montan
Boulle, Hervé	07 St-Remèze
Brunel, Léon	
Domaine du Belvezet	07 St-Remèze
Marron, André	07 Vallon Pont
	d'Arc

Appendixes

1. THE 'APPELLATION CONTRÔLÉE' LAWS

Note: 1 hectolitre (HL) per hectare = approximately 54 bottles per acre.

In years of abundant harvest the *Appellations* are permitted to submit wine in excess of the maximum yield to a tasting panel, which decides whether the quality is sufficiently high for the extra wine to be allowed *Appellation Contrôlée* status. Thus, for instance, Côte-Rôtie is permitted to sell up to 15 per cent above its 40 hectolitres per hectare limit, Condrieu up to 10 per cent above. This is known as the *droit de dérogation*.

BEAUMES-DE-VENISE

Vin doux naturel, or sweet fortified wine allowed.
Maximum yield: 28 HL per hectare, or 1,512 bottles per acre.
Minimum degree: 15° of natural alcohol.

CHÂTEAU-GRILLET

White wine only allowed.
Maximum yield: 32 HL per hectare, or 1,727 bottles per acre.
Dérogation: 10 per cent.
Minimum degree: 11°.

CHÂTEAUNEUF-DU-PAPE

Red and white wines allowed.
Maximum yield: 35 HL per hectare, or 1,889 bottles per acre.
Minimum degree: 12·5°.

CONDRIEU

White wine only allowed.
Maximum yield: 30 HL per hectare, or 1,619 bottles per acre.
Dérogation: 10 per cent.
Minimum degree: 11°.

CORNAS

Red wine only allowed.
Maximum yield: 35 HL per hectare, or 1,889 bottles per acre.
Dérogation: 10 per cent.
Minimum degree: 10·5°.

CÔTE-RÔTIE

Red wine only allowed.
Maximum yield: 40 HL per hectare, or 2,159 bottles per acre.
Dérogation: 15 per cent.
Minimum degree: 10°.

CÔTES DU RHÔNE

Red, white and rosé wines allowed.
Maximum yield: 50 HL per hectare, or 2,699 bottles per acre.
Minimum degree: 11°.

CÔTES DU RHÔNE VILLAGES

Red, white and rosé wines allowed.
Maximum yield: 35 HL per hectare, or 1,889 bottles per acre.
Dérogation: 20 per cent.
Minimum degree: 12·5° for the red wines.
12° for the white and rosé wines.

CROZES-HERMITAGE

Red and white wines allowed.
Maximum yield: 40 HL per hectare, or 2,159 bottles per acre.
Dérogation: 15 per cent.
Minimum degree: 10°.

GIGONDAS

Red and rosé wines allowed.
Maximum yield: 35 HL per hectare, or 1,889 bottles per acre.
Minimum degree: 12·5°.

HERMITAGE

Red and white wines allowed.
Maximum yield: 40 HL per hectare, or 2,159 bottles per acre.
Dérogation: 15 per cent.
Minimum degree: 10°.

LIRAC

Red, rosé and white wines allowed.
Maximum yield: 35 HL per hectare, or 1,889 bottles per acre.
Dérogation: 20 per cent.
Minimum degree: 11·5°.

RASTEAU

Vin doux naturel, or sweet fortified wine allowed.
Maximum yield: 35 HL per hectare, or 1,889 bottles per acre.
Minimum degree: 15° of natural alcohol.

ST-JOSEPH

Red and white wines allowed.
Maximum yield: 40 HL per hectare, or 2,159 bottles per acre.
Dérogation: 15 per cent.
Minimum degree: 10°.

ST-PÉRAY

Sparkling and still white wines only allowed.
Maximum yield: 40 HL per hectare, or 2,159 bottles per acre.
Dérogation: 15 per cent.
Minimum degree: 10°.

TAVEL

Rosé wine only allowed.
Maximum yield: 42 HL per hectare, or 2,267 bottles per acre.
Dérogation: 15 per cent.
Minimum degree: 11°.

2. TABLE OF VINEYARD SURFACE AREAS

In acres, to the nearest acre

VINEYARD	1971	1973	1982
Côtes du Rhône (including Côtes du Rhône Villages)	74,654	82,941	90,250
Beaumes-de-Venise VDN	390	457	575
Château-Grillet	4·2	5·7 (1977)	7·4
Châteauneuf-du-Pape	7,286	7,608	7,600
Condrieu	30	30	35
Cornas	132	185	165
Côte-Rôtie	172	178	252
Crozes-Hermitage	1,121	1,358	2,230
Gigondas	2,366	2,445	2,850
Hermitage	304	304	304
Lirac	617	1,722	1,525
Rasteau VDN	333	333	c. 275
St-Joseph	240	301	605
St-Péray	138	138	118
Tavel	1,630	1,778	1,875

NOTE: 1 hectare = 2·47 acres.

3. DECLARATION OF THE CROP (RÉCOLTE) FOR ALL CÔTES DU RHÔNE 'APPELLATIONS' (hectolitres)

	1970	1971	1972	1973	1974
Beaumes-de-Venise	4,403	4,441	3,403	5,172	5,113
Château-Grillet	65	47	28	84	87
Châteauneuf-du-Pape	91,700	92,792	71,398	98,472	80,499
Condrieu	138	142	66	206	122
Cornas	1,787	1,022	1,145	2,029	1,586
Côte-Rôtie	2,355	1,562	1,428	2,927	1,831
Côtes du Rhône	1,167,216	1,047,947	1,154,487	1,363,784	1,260,761
Côtes du Rhône Villages	68,882	115,496	69,283	154,506	70,277
Crozes-Hermitage	19,542	13,203	19,768	27,997	21,044
Gigondas	31,250	26,850	26,634	30,601	26,753
Hermitage	5,576	3,128	3,356	4,108	3,859
Lirac	14,644	16,786	13,870	24,404	11,724
Rasteau VDN	3,718	3,096	2,723	2,803	2,335
St-Joseph	3,145	1,821	1,962	4,093	4,310
St-Péray	1,453	1,458	1,183	1,447	1,716
Tavel	24,734	26,983	21,841	28,055	28,722

1975	1976	1977	1978	1979	1980	1981
3,294	5,185	4,604	6,922	6,304	7,562	6,597
40	87	63	29	97	116	75
62,660	93,333	86,466	90,398	98,873	101,033	86,394
105	176	115	96	298	363	310
810	1,424	1,354	1,551	1,854	1,894	1,718
1,468	2,132	2,108	3,077	4,128	3,378	4,185
91,638	1,514,862	1,358,189	1,538,346	1,504,386	1,697,963	1,411,450
79,394	68,728	65,241	109,263	133,482	101,420	118,982
17,748	20,014	17,548	27,106	34,387	40,783	33,541
17,503	27,729	23,166	31,416	33,946	37,116	30,460
2,022	3,304	3,159	3,136	4,895	4,582	4,093
10,704	10,077	10,741	16,175	21,843	20,088	17,183
1,722	2,363	1,087	3,099	5,087	4,120	3,896
2,188	4,684	3,812	5,726	8,492	8,426	10,272
880	1,447	1,646	1,061	1,423	1,981	2,053
9,971	28,426	29,161	30,624	34,788	35,411	30,098

355

4. EXPORTS

A. Côtes du Rhône Exports

Year	Volume (hectolitres)	% increase in volume over previous year	Value (francs)	% increase in value over previous year
1965	122,278	27·01	34,094,000	11·65
1968	170,204	16·45	46,307,000	13·93
1969	185,380	8·90	55,256,000	19·32
1970	191,416	3·25	73,623,000	33·23
1971	231,029	20·70	89,415,000	21·45
1972	271,897	17·70	123,064,000	37·65
1973	352,256	29·55	169,569,000	37·80
1974	364,598	3·50	160,649,000	− 5·25
1975	418,025	14·65	171,485,000	6.75
1976	368,637	− 11·80	198,164,000	15·55
1977	374,907	1·70	254,756,000	28·55
1978	392,685	4·75	313,467,000	23·05
1979	451,804	15·10	354,042,000	13·00
1980	516,282	14·60	377,274,000	6·49
1981	602,182	16·64	462,039,000	22·47

B. French Appellation Wine Exports

Region	Volume in hectolitres		
	1976	1978	1980
Anjou (Loire)	211,658	190,283	188,397
Beaujolais	328,942	384,991	474,918
Burgundy	388,114	434,314	354,019
Côtes du Rhône	368,637	392,685	516,282
Alsace	129,351	172,086	166,207
Bordeaux	1,072,280	1,230,500	1,156,262
Others (AC except Champagne)	247,951	383,774	502,498

C. Leading Côtes du Rhône Export Countries (volume in hectolitres)

Country	1970	1973	1976	1977	1978	1979	1980	1981
Switzerland	73,003	121,219	137,974	134,641	142,560	141,786	136,911	177,300
Belgium and Luxembourg	22,117	54,486	49,685	54,138	55,119	77,965	92,036	104,347
West Germany	18,553	29,934	31,365	37,323	39,065	47,397	64,381	68,230
Netherlands	4,608	19,566	26,409	26,525	33,155	44,296	59,362	61,424
Britain	9,668	31,971	24,213	32,376	34,584	45,939	47,896	55,040
Denmark	10,922	16,921	22,748	16,822	17,120	27,522	35,719	36,777
USA	23,291	31,739	24,049	23,652	27,520	23,338	20,748	24,001
Canada	–	–	9,734	12,282	11,778	6,369	16,439	21,964
Sweden	5,058	8,808	17,187	11,800	6,345	12,209	14,409	20,190
Ireland	–	–	760	1,598	1,396	1,908	2,013	2,866
Japan	254	761	906	813	826	1,512	1,602	1,456

5. CALENDAR OF WINE FAIRS HELD IN THE REGION OF THE CÔTES DU RHÔNE

Around 20 January: Orange (Vaucluse)—tasting competition of young wines. Gold, silver and bronze medals are given, and the Foire acts as a guide to the quality of the new vintage.

Around 20 January: Ampuis (Rhône)—public fair of the wines of Côte-Rôtie, with some wines of Condrieu present as well.

Around 25 April: Châteauneuf-du-Pape (Vaucluse)—*fête* of St Marc (patron of the village).

Around end of April: Tavel (Gard)—*fête* of St Vincent (patron of *vignerons*).

Around end of May: Vacqueyras (Vaucluse)—*fête* of the Côtes du Rhône Villages.

Around end of May: Roquemaure (Gard)—public fair of the wines of the *Cru* of Lirac.

Around July/August: Orange (Vaucluse)—permanent exhibition in the grottoes of the Antique Theatre of the wines of the Côtes du Rhône.

Around end of July: Côtes du Rhône Villages fair. Held in a different village every year.

Around 20/25 September: Châteauneuf-du-Pape (Vaucluse)—*Ban des Vendanges*.

Around 3rd Sunday in September: fair and wine competition at Tain-l'Hermitage.

Around mid-November: Vaison-la-Romaine (Vaucluse)—tasting of Côtes du Rhône *Primeur* wines.

Around 7 December: Cornas (Ardèche)—public fair of the wines of the Syrah and Roussette.

6. TASTING STALLS AND CELLARS ALLOWING VISITS IN THE CÔTES DU RHÔNE

Tasting Stalls (Caveaux de Dégustation)
(theoretically open 7 days a week)

La Maison des Côtes du Rhône Le Pont St-Bénézet	84 Avignon
Caveau de Dégustation	84 Cairanne
Caveau du Château	30 Domazan
Caveau de Dégustation	84 Gigondas
Caveau de Dégustation de la Cave des Vignerons	84 Rasteau
Caveau de Dégustation des Vins de Lirac	30 Roquemaure
Caveau de Dégustation	84 Sablet
Le Pressoir	26 Tain-l'Hermitage
Le Pressoir	07 Tournon-sur-Rhône
Caveau des Dentelles de Montmirail	84 Vacqueyras
Château de Simiane	84 Valréas
Caveau de Dégustation	26 Vinsobres

Cellars

The Rhône is not an area where large-scale vineyard holdings are the order of the day, with someone always available to receive visitors at the domaine. Consequently, it is advisable to contact a grower in advance to confirm a suitable time for a meeting, and he will arrange his cellar or vineyard routine accordingly.

As a rule growers in *all* the northern Rhône *Appellations* should be given notice of an intended visit, if only to make sure of finding someone at home.

Some of the southern Rhône growers who would like prior notice are listed below; one thing to remember is that it is wholly impolitic to be at a grower's house between the magic lunching times of 12.00 and 14.00. Otherwise those growers who do not request a specific hour be set should be visited between roughly 09.00 and 12.00 and between 14.00 and 18.00.

GARD DÉPARTEMENT

Château d'Aquéria	Domaine du Devoy
Château de Ségriès	Domaine de la Genestière
Château de Trinquevedel	Domaine des Moulins
Domaine de l'Amandier	Domaine de la Réméjeanne
Domaine de Castel Oualou	Domaine des Riots
Domaine du Château St-Roch	Domaine de la Tour de Lirac

VAUCLUSE DÉPARTEMENT

Charavin, Robert	Domaine des Lambertins
Château La Courançonne	Domaine de la Mavette
Château Fortia	Domaine de l'Oratoire St-Martin
Château Rayas	Domaine de Raspail-Ay
Château des Roques	Domaine St-Claude
Clos des Papes	Domaine St-Gayan
Clos du Père Clément	Domaine St-Sauveur
Domaine de Beaucastel	Domaine Ste-Apollinaire
Domaine de Cabasse	Domaine de Verquière
Domaine de la Cantharide	Domaine du Vieux Télégraphe
Domaine Durban	Le Bosquet des Papes
Domaine Durieu	Le Val des Rois
Domaine La Fourmone	Nicolet-Leyraud
Domaine du Gros-Pata	Trintignant, Jean

7. OTHER LABELS ('SOUS MARQUES') USED BY LEADING CÔTES-DU-RHÔNE NÉGOCIANTS

M. Chapoutier: Delapine
Delas Frères: Forrestier
Paul Jaboulet Ainé: Jaboulet-Isnard and André Passat

8. THE WINES OF 1982

The year produced one of the largest crops ever known in France, with *Appellations* all over the country regularly surpassing their maximum permitted harvest per hectare. The Rhône was no exception; yields of over 50 hectolitres per hectare were recorded in places in the southern *générique* area.

Such a large amount of wine generally suffers in quality terms, but 1982 is a little different. The summer was very dry, and intense heat was recorded in the vineyards throughout the Rhône Valley in June, July and August—36 °C at Châteauneuf and 40 °C in the vineyards at Côte-Rôtie, for instance. There was only a little rainfall, and harvesting started soon after 10 September, in many places two weeks early.

Those who harvested before the grapes became too ripe—and their ripening accelerated sharply in September—managed to exercise more control over their vinification. Although all the vines are very high in degree, some are accompanied by ample flavours, with excellent harmony of fruit and tannin—Côte-Rôtie and Hermitage reds, notably. Cornas, Crozes-Hermitage and St-Joseph are also good, the first of these perhaps a little softer than usual. All are slightly low in acidity.

The story is much less uniform in the south, where many of the wines are highly alcoholic but lacking in substance and colour. Careful selection will be necessary in the Côtes du Rhone *générique* and Villages: none of the wines will be particularly long-lived.

The southern red Appellations of Châteauneuf-du-Pape, Gigondas and Lirac all produced wines high in alcohol and a little light in colour. The growers spoke of a difficult vinification, as the maturity of the grapes and the early autumn heat gave rise to the risk of high volatile acidity. It is to be hoped that the more conscientious *vignerons* will bottle only their best *cuvées*.

At Tavel and Lirac the rosés are paler than usual and lack depth despite higher than average alcohol.

The Rhône whites are most successful at Condrieu and at Château-Grillet, where both quality and quantity were good. A lack of acidity is apparent in the whites of Crozes-Hermitage, St-Péray and St-Joseph, while the white Châteauneufs are amply flavoured and suitable for early drinking.

The year will be most memorable for the northern Rhône reds. The rest of the Valley's wines will probably be quietly forgotten in the years to come.

Glossary

APPELLATION D'ORIGINE CONTRÔLÉE The certificate of authenticity of wines of a high quality; such wines must conform to certain strict rules in order to merit the status. The word *Appellation* by itself often refers to a specific vineyard area—e.g. Côte-Rôtie, Tavel, Gigondas, etc.

BAN DES VENDANGES Public proclamation of the start of the harvest.

BENEAU A grape harvest holder, made either of wood or plastic.

BIGOT A special hoe used in the northern Rhône vineyards.

BONBONNE A large glass jug, stoppered with a flat, wide cork, used for holding bulk drinking wine. An average capacity is 10–15 litres.

BOULES The steel balls that are used in the target game of *pétanque*; also the name of the game itself.

CAVISTE A cellar worker

CHALAIS Dried stone terrace.

CHAPEAU The top of fermenting grapes.

CLAIE A straw or cane mat.

CLIMAT A named section within a vineyard.

CÔTE Slope; when used to designate a wine, as in Côtes du Rhône or Côtes de Beaune, the word usually refers to the most basic quality of wine made in its region.

COTEAU Hillside; *demi-coteau* is a gentle incline, and is a term often used in the sweeping southern Côtes du Rhône wine area.

CRU Growth; in the Côtes du Rhône it commonly describes a grower's best wine.

CUVE A vat.

CUVÉE The wine of one particular vat. *Tête de cuvée* represents the very best wine which a grower makes in any one year.

DÉROGATION The right to sell under the full *Appellation Contrôlée* label wine that is in excess of the statutory quantity allowed.

EAU-DE-VIE Distilled alcohol spirit. *Eau-de-vie de marc* refers to the spirit taken from the distilled grape *marcs* (q.v.) left over after fermentation.

ÉGRAPPAGE The destalking of the grapes prior to fermentation.

FOUDRE A large cask used for maturing the wine.

FOULAGE The crushing of the grapes before fermentation.

GÉNÉRIQUE   Generic, or a wine of the most basic *Appellation Contrôlée* category, such as Côtes du Rhône.

GOÛT DE TERROIR   Literally, earthy taste. It really means a profound, very 'thick' flavour in a wine that is thought to be drawn from the soil composition of its vineyards.

GRAIN   A single grape.

LIEU-DIT   A place name within the vineyards of an *Appellation*, often derived from an historical anecdote or legend.

LIQUEUR DE TIRAGE   A blend of sugar and yeasts, which is added to wine at the moment it is bottled to encourage a further fermentation.

MAISON DU VIN   A wine house: it often indicates an owner of vineyards who doubles as a merchant in other wines.

MAÎTRE DE CHAI   A cellar master.

MARC   The crushed leftovers of the pulp after it has been pressed. It is composed mainly of skins, pips and stalks and is often distilled to produce a grape-flavoured spirit.

MÉTHODE CHAMPENOISE   Wine that is made sparkling through the application of the pure Champagne-making process.

MÉTIER   Profession or craft.

MUID   An old term for a Rhône Valley barrel of 675 litres' capacity. Also used in Burgundy.

MUTAGE   The addition of alcohol spirit to a wine. It is performed with such fortified wines as Rasteau and Beaumes-de-Venise.

NATURE   A still wine.

NÉGOCIANT   A wine merchant.

NÉGOCIANT-ÉLEVEUR   A merchant who buys grapes and/or wine. The wine is left in his cellars to mature until ready for sale.

OUILLAGE   The topping up of a cask following the evaporation of its wine.

PARCELLE   A plot of land within a vineyard—usually belonging to a small-holder.

PÉPIN   A grape pip.

PÉTANQUE   The very popular French game of bowls, played with small metal balls.

PICHET   A short wooden stump used for immersing the *châpeau* (q.v.) during fermentation.

PIÈCE   A barrel of 225 litres' capacity. It can be used for primary fermentation, but more commonly serves to age the wine.

PORTEUR   A carrier of the harvest.

POURRITURE   Rotting of the grapes.

PRIMEUR   A short-lived wine that is made by an abbreviated vinification process. It is released for sale in the middle of November, and also passes under the name of *vin nouveau*.

PROPRIÉTAIRE-NÉGOCIANT   A vineyard owner who supplements his wine-holding by buying other people's grapes or wine.

PROPRIÉTAIRE-RÉCOLTANT   A vineyard owner who makes nothing but his own wine.

PUPITRE   A wooden holder in which bottles of wine made by the *méthode champenoise* (q.v.) accumulate their deposit around the neck of the bottle.

QUARTIER   A section of a vineyard.

RAISIN ENTIER   A whole, uncrushed grape. A term used when the grapes are not crushed before fermentation.

RANCIO   A wine that shows 'age' on its taste.

RAPÉ   The discard, or rejected portion of the grape harvest. Such overripe or underripe grapes can be made into a wine of the same name.

REMONTAGE   The pumping of the bottom of a vat of wine over the top or *chapeau* during its fermentation. This helps to keep the *chapeau* cool and aids colour extraction.

REMUAGE   The 'turning' of bottles of sparkling wine made by the traditional Champagne method. It acts to lodge any deposits in the neck of the bottle.

ROBE   The general appearance of a wine; not only its colour but also its lustre or brilliance.

SOMMELIER (SOMMELIÈRE)   A wine waiter or waitress.

SYNDICAT DES VIGNERONS   A wine-growers' union.

TONNEAU   A wine barrel of no specific dimension.

TONNELIER   A cooper.

TRIAGE   A qualitative sorting of the grape harvest.

VENDANGE(S)   The grape harvest. The word is used in both the singular and plural form.

VENDANGEUR   A grape picker.

VIGNERON   A wine-grower.

VIN· DE GARDE   A long-lived wine, one suitable for laying down.

VIN DÉLIMITÉ DE QUALITÉ SUPÉRIEURE   Literally, a delimited wine of superior quality. This is the category below *Appellation Contrôlée*, and the wine-making rulings, although similar in form, are accordingly less demanding.

VIN DE MÉDECINE   A 'booster' wine that is used to fill out a weak wine.

VIN DE PAILLE   Literally, 'straw wine'. It is a white wine made from grapes that are left to dry out completely before fermentation.

VIN DE TABLE   Table wine—a wine that bears no particular name and, often, no particular quality.

VIN DE TOUS LES JOURS   An everyday drinking wine.

VIN DOUX NATUREL   Literally, a sweet fortified wine. The *naturel* is therefore a slight misnomer.

VIN MOUSSEUX   Sparkling wine.

VIN ORDINAIRE   Ordinary wine, like *vin de table* the most basic category of wine that exists in France.

VRAC   Goods that are transported in bulk. In the wine world the term refers to wines that have not been bottled before they are moved around.

Index

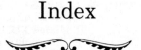

INDEX

374